Hidden Agendas

"Treachery and intrigue combine with blistering hot sensuality in this chapter of Leigh's SEAL saga. The title of this book is particularly apt, since many of the characters are not what they seem, and betrayal can have deadly consequences. Leigh's books can scorch the ink off the page."

—*Romantic Times*

"An evocative and captivating read."

—*Romance Junkies*

Dangerous Games

"A marvelous novel of suspense and raw passion."

—*Romance Junkies*

"Lora Leigh ignites the fire . . . with steamy heat added to a story that makes you cheer and even tear up."

—*Fallen Angel Reviews*

"Leigh writes . . . tempting, enchanting romance[s] that readers are certain to devour."

—*Romance Reviews Today*

Killer Secrets

Lora Leigh

St. Martin's Paperbacks

This is a work of fiction. All of the characters, organizations, and events portrayed in this novel are either products of the author's imagination or are used fictitiously.

KILLER SECRETS

Copyright © 2008 by Lora Leigh.
Excerpt from *Wicked Pleasure* copyright © 2008 by Lora Leigh.

For information address St. Martin's Press, 175 Fifth Avenue, New York, NY 10010.

ISBN: 0-312-93994-9
EAN: 978-0-312-93994-6

Printed in the United States of America

St. Martin's Paperbacks edition / March 2008

St. Martin's Paperbacks are published by St. Martin's Press, 175 Fifth Avenue, New York, NY 10010.

10 9 8 7 6

To all my co-conspirators,
I couldn't do it without you.

Prologue

Clipping into the icu unit of the private military hospital wasn't an easy task. It would be considered insane from most men's point of view. Even a SEAL's. But that was exactly what former Lieutenant Ian Richards of the Navy SEALs did.

Under the cover of night, he managed to slip into the hospital, make his way to the ICU, and wait until the guard at Nathan Malone's door dozed off before he slipped in, in the guise of an orderly.

His first sight of his friend nearly stole his breath.

Sweet Jesus. Nathan was in so many damned casts and wrapped in so many bandages he looked more like a mummy than a man. But it was a far sight easier on the eyes than the naked, ravaged SEAL they had dragged out of Fuentes's compound four months before.

Tortured, beaten, sliced and diced. His face had been so disfigured it was hard to tell he was human, let alone the friend Ian had known for the better part of his life.

How the hell Nathan had survived the nineteen months in Fuentes's care, Ian couldn't even imagine. Drugged constantly on the powerful date rape drug known as whore's dust, and encouraged repeatedly to rape the women brought to him, Nathan had lived in hell. The reports they had gathered indicated he had never taken one of the women locked in the cells with him, but the doctors and psychologists working with him said he might never recover from the amount of drugs pumped into his system.

Ian knew better. Nathan was strong. Too damned strong to let Fuentes win like this. But he had to be certain.

Even after the months Ian had been away, been considered a betrayer, a Judas to his friends, and marked as a deserter by the U.S. government, Ian had had to return to assure himself Nathan would survive.

Ian moved to the bed, sliding between it and the curtain that had been pushed back to allow the guards to see all but a very small section of the area. Right by Nathan's head. His covered, wrapped head.

"Damn, buddy, do you think they have you wrapped up tight enough?" he asked his friend, knowing Nathan couldn't hear him. Wishing he could.

Hell, somehow he had gotten used to being on the inside of a team, rather than fighting alone to survive. He had gotten used to the men he fought with, had grown to trust them, only to learn at the end of it, he was fighting alone once again.

Long ago, Nathan and his family had saved Ian and his mother's life. On a cold desert night, with only his screams of rage surrounding him, a boy and his father had found him, saved him and his dying mother, and given Ian a friendship he had never known before that.

And now, when his friend awoke, he would believe that friendship had been betrayed.

He grimaced at the thought of it, his jaw tightening in rage at the situation he had been forced into. Because of blood. Because sometimes, a man could do nothing about where he came from, he could only control where he went. And where Ian was heading, Nathan or Durango team couldn't go.

Ian could only go alone.

"We had a wild ride huh, bro," he whispered, his voice nearly silent, but the breath of the words easing a part of him.

Nathan was unconscious, comatose, but somehow, knowing the words were whispering past his lips eased Ian. Maybe, just maybe, his friend would hear a part of them, know, understand, that beneath the near silent whisper was the truth. It had been a wild ride, and now it was over.

He reached out, let his fingers touch his friend's shoulder as a grin tugged at his lips.

Nathan "Irish" Malone. All smiles and wild blue eyes, a man who as a boy had saved his life.

"Hell of a way to repay you," he breathed out softly. "But what's that old saying? Blood will tell?"

That was what Nathan used to say. When the chips were down, when everything was going from sugar to shit, he would flash that reckless smile, look at Ian, and laugh in his face. "Blood will tell, ole son." And they would go out fighting hell-for-leather because Ian's blood might be tainted with evil, but his heart was one hundred percent red-blooded American Navy Seal. That was Nathan's belief in him. What would he believe when he awoke? Ian wondered.

"Get strong, Irish," he said then. "You always were the wild card of the group, show 'em you're tougher, stronger than what put you here. Then look me up."

He tightened his fingers on his friend's shoulder, then slowly eased the grip, his head lifting as the hairs along the nape of his neck stood up in warning.

The sound was no more than a breath. Just enough. Not a shuffle, no more than cloth against flesh in the most subtle flexing of muscle.

His teeth flashed in a grin as his weapon dropped from the sleeve of his jacket to his palm. And it didn't whisper. There was no catch of metal over flesh. It was silent. Still.

There were some people that a man just had to give credit for trying. This was one of them. He knew where the body stood now, that subtle shift had been all he needed. He knew where and he knew who. Instinct and something more. A part of a man that knew a woman in a way that made no sense. An underlying certainty, as though a part of him knew a part of her no matter where they found each other. No matter the disguise she used.

Of course, it didn't help her cause that Ian had recognized something about her that no one else had. A delicate turn of pretty ears, a particular slant and curve of pretty earlobes. If a man wanted to take the time to memorize every shape and turn of her face as Ian had before that first mission where he met her, then he would have seen it.

Her picture had been given to them before a particular mission she was working. She wore one of many disguises; they had been warned to watch out for a woman who never looked the same. Ian had managed to identify the one thing that never changed though. Those pretty ears. That and a wicked, teasing glint in her eyes, no matter their color.

One of these days he was going to have to call her on that tease. He was going to have to fulfill the promise her eyes had made during the weeks they had put in together on a past mission.

He slid past the bathroom door, careful to let the sleeve of his jacket slide across the wall, to alert her to the fact that he was leaving the room.

He let the door open, stepped out, then grimaced and shook his head as the guard glanced toward him, as though he had forgotten something. He held up a finger with abashed embarrassment then stepped back inside. Silently.

The door swished closed. And he waited.

He was patient. She was smart.

He would have smiled, but so much as a twitch would be enough to warn her he was there. She was as smooth as fine whisky, as adept at her job as he was at his.

So he waited. And the patience paid off. The bathroom door edged open, and sure as hell, there she was. Like the sun edging over the mountain. Like a clear breeze easing through the stench he could sometimes feel gathering around him.

When he moved, he realized he was almost too slow. Or she was almost that fast. His hand went over her lips, his body braced, pushing hers against the wall face-first, his free hand pressing the barrel of his weapon against her neck warningly.

She didn't make a sound. Damn her. She didn't even fight him. She relaxed into his body instead. Her rounded buttocks cushioned his hips, her shoulders curved against the wall, and she bared the slender line of her neck as his lips pressed close.

Hair that should have been long and black was cut close and blond. Gray eyes were hazel, clear silky flesh had a coarse appearance. There was nothing of the woman he had seen on his last mission, or the mission he had found her on before that. The Chameleon was as ever-changing as a woman's emotions.

"I like the black hair better," he whispered at her ear. "And the gray eyes. Natural, weren't they, sugar?" He rubbed his nose against the ultrasoft lobe of her ear.

Her tongue flicked against his palm, almost surprising him, almost making him drop his guard. He chuckled softly at her ear instead and felt the smile against his hand.

"You shouldn't be here." He laid his forehead against her shoulder. "A man should be able to say goodbye to a buddy without an audience, don't you think?"

She looked back at him, hazel eyes cool. There was no fear there. No anger. No impatience. But beneath the calculating chill there was a hidden flame. One he never failed to respond to.

"Wrong time, wrong place." He stared back at her as she watched him over her shoulder. "Wrong life."

He let himself experience the feel of her for just a few seconds more, long enough to let the regret in his gaze telegraph to hers. Long enough to watch the flicker of indecision in her eyes. That second where he knew she was weighing her options and her escape.

"I'll miss you," he breathed against her ear. "I'll miss you more than you know, Kira."

A deft move of his hands, just the right pressure, and a

second later she slumped against him, thick lashes drifting over her eyes as darkness closed over her mind.

Ian swung her in his arms, lifted her from the floor, and stepped to the chair on the other side of the room. He placed her there, cushioning her head with a spare pillow against the back of the cushions and brushing the blond bangs back from her face with regret.

Wrong place, wrong time, wrong life. Because blood would tell. And this time, the hated blood that ran through his veins was telling in ways he had never imagined possible.

One

Six months later
Palm Beach, Aruba

HE WAS ROGUE.

Could there be any other explanation for the dark, avenging force that swept through the night?

The Chameleon scrambled through the warehouse, ducking behind crates and using the heavy support posts of the building to deflect the bullets raining around her.

The small team of highly trained Fuentes soldiers tore into the warehouse where the small cell of terrorists were waiting for the go-ahead that Ian was arriving for a scheduled weapons buy. They were there to kill him. But it was Ian who was killing instead.

She hadn't managed to learn how they had received that information, or from where the leak had originated. Her work within the cell had gleaned her nothing but a certainty that the determination to assassinate Ian Fuentes was escalating.

The assassins had been on the island less than twenty-four hours. The final two had arrived just hours before with the details of the strike they were to make against the heir to the Fuentes cartel.

None of them had known for certain that they were

striking against Ian until some hours before. Even the Chameleon hadn't been certain of the plan until the French assasins in charge had arrived, their eyes cold, hard, and outlined the operation.

They had no sooner given the final order than death had swept through the night.

She flinched as a bullet tore across the beam several inches above her crouched form. Ducking and rolling, her weapon ready, she pushed herself deeper into the shadows as she lifted her weapon and aimed at one of the few remaining lights shining overhead.

The bulb shattered, sparks raining down on the assembled crates and packages prepared for shipping the next day.

She moved, sprinting from her hiding place, as bullets tore into the crates around her. Her gaze swept around the room and she grimaced as she saw the black-clad Fuentes soldiers moving through the shadows with stealthy certainty.

They were trained, disciplined. These weren't the drug soldiers they had been when Ian Fuentes first arrived a year ago. This was a highly trained, effective fighting force. A team of dark, dangerous, SEAL-trained weapons.

Damn. The director of the Department of Homeland Security was going to have a cow when she sent in the report on this one. The rumors that Ian was taking out drug and terrorist forces alike hadn't been substantiated. Everyone who could talk somehow ended up dead.

She was going to have to make certain she didn't end up as dead as the rest of them.

Dammit, she had worked hard to get herself into position within the small terrorist cell working out of Aruba. A year of busting her ass and eating dirt with worms to get in place here, and now the team the terrorists had put together was just dead.

Moving quickly, quietly, she skirted the edges of the crudely built warehouse, working her way to the far wall where the loose boards there would allow her an easy exit. She didn't dare attempt to use the door.

"Not so fast."

The Chameleon froze as the barrel of the weapon was laid, almost casually, at the back of her neck.

She knew that voice. She knew the feel of that heated body behind her own.

She held her hands out carefully, allowing the Glock to fall from her gloved fingers to the dusty floor as she restrained the impulse to release the lever holding the knife beneath the sleeve of her light jacket.

Her backup was at her ankle; but it was dark, he might not see it.

Before she could do anything she was jerked upright and slammed into the wall hard enough to knock her teeth together. If she hadn't been anticipating it.

Eyes narrowed, her arms kept carefully at her sides, her head jerked up as powerful fingers locked around her throat and held her in place.

Icy brandy-colored eyes locked on hers in surprise.

He hadn't known she was here.

The Chameleon smiled and, while surprise held him immobile, she moved.

Her leg kicked up, almost slamming into his balls but barely glancing them instead. He went back, his fingers slackening on her throat as she tore out of his grip.

His hand gripped her wrist as she turned into the hold, her ankle twisting around his, almost taking him down. Once again, she managed to do no more than loosen his hold on her.

A graceful twist and she had an arm's distance between them as she crouched and stared back at him, eyes narrowed, her breathing heavy now.

Adrenaline coursed through her veins, her heart raced but not from fear.

"Let it go," she hissed back at him. "I'm no threat to you."

She would never be a threat to him. Not unless she had to be. She was here for him, and her heart ached because this wasn't the man she knew, the man she had fallen in love with in Atlanta.

She watched him, pushing back her anger and her fears of what he had become as his eyes narrowed further. His weapon was tucked into the front of his black mission pants, easily accessible. God only knew where hers was. He could take her out so easily, they both knew it. Just as they both knew he wouldn't. She hoped she knew that.

"Why?" The snarled question was soft, filled with banked fury. "Why are you here?"

Of course he knew who she was. He had always known who she was, no matter where he saw her, no matter her disguise.

"For you."

"To kill me?" He sneered. "DHS decide they couldn't handle the shame of having one of their own defeat them?"

She shook her head. "I'm leaving now."

"The hell you are." His lips lifted in a warning growl, his savagely honed features reflecting his fury now.

"The hell I am." She smiled back as his hand gripped the butt of his gun. "Will you shoot me, Ian?"

She backed away from him. Her exit was only a few feet away, the boards loosened just in case of such an emergency, prepared for her esape.

She closed the distance as she watched his face, his eyes. A second later it was her only warning. The gun was jerked from the band of his pants, he aimed for her and fired.

Kira threw herself back, knowing, certain, she was staring death in the face until she stumbled over the body behind her.

Whirling, she had only a moment to glimpse the fallen terrorist before she shoved the loosened board aside and slipped from the warehouse to the inky darkness beyond.

Just that easily he had killed one of his own men. For her.

She ran through the night, careful to stay down, to keep as many obstacles as possible between her and any bullets that might come her way.

The Chameleon had been bested by a Navy SEAL gone rogue. Or had she been rescued by a deep-cover agent now so immersed in the mission that he was no longer the man he had been a year before?

Something inside her ached at the thought of either answer. Over the years, Ian Richards had managed to see through every disguise she had used in the various operations where they had met up. She had been on the inside, he had always been part of the force sweeping in to clean up the mess her information had helped locate. Once again, he had seen through another disguise, but this time, they might not be on the same side. And the very scary part of that was the fact that she knew she wouldn't let it stop her. She had come to Aruba to claim what was hers before his father, Diego Fuentes, could steal his soul.

But she was there for another reason as well. If he hadn't gone rogue, then she was there to make certain that the SEAL didn't murder either the terrorist Sorrell that he had vowed to identify and capture for his father, or his father, the drug lord Diego Fuentes.

The Chameleon had no answers to the questions she had confronted the director of Homeland Security with. Was Ian operating under mission parameters of DHS? She had asked that question twice. Each time the same answer: DHS doesn't contract rogue SEAL operatives.

There were no straight answers, there was only supposition and her orders. Reestablish a relationship with Ian and ensure Homeland Security acquired Sorrell should Ian identify him, as they suspected he would. And keep Diego Fuentes alive.

Diego Fuentes was an asset. He was a DHS-contracted informant. And Ian had no idea the lengths the Department of Homeland Security was willing to go to keep him alive.

IAN SWEPT HIS GAZE ACROSS the floor of the warehouse as the team of trained soldiers moved in slowly, dragging the bodies of the assassins to the cleared center of the warehouse.

There were a dozen. Their faces were known to him, several had a price on their heads. Too bad he couldn't collect.

"There's one missing." One of his elite bodyguards spoke at his side. "The blonde. We haven't found her body."

And they wouldn't either.

Ian glanced to his head bodyguard, Deke. Deep cover, a ten-year veteran of the Fuentes cartel, his dark eyes reflected the same chill Ian knew his own did.

This world did that to a man. Planted in ice where a heart should be and diluted the guilt over the bloodshed. The bastards now lying in the center of the warehouse were murderers, kidnappers, rapists. They were terrorists who didn't care who lived or died as long as their fanatical agenda was observed.

He kicked at one lying on its side, knocking the body over until the dead eyes stared up at the heavily beamed ceiling.

"The girl that got away is Algeria Winters," Deke reported. "There's no sign of her, boss."

She didn't get away. He'd let her go.

Ian stared at the terrorist's body. He remembered this one from a mission in Russia several years before. Algeria Winters had been there as well. A Russian-born informant who often worked with Antoni Ruissard, the dead terrorist at his feet.

Anger tightened his jaw as his fingers clenched on the Glock he held carefully by his side.

"We have a team in place in Oranjestad as well as Palm Beach," Trevor stated. "We can get her description out, have her picked up."

Ian nodded slowly. "Go ahead."

They wouldn't find her. The persona Algeria Winters would be discarded before anyone else had a chance to see her. The higher cheekbones would be altered, that sharp chin would disappear, hazel eyes would change, and blond hair would become another color. Her next disguise would be as natural, as smooth as birth, and no one would ever know she was Kira Porter, except him.

He stared down at the dead assassin Antoni, the dark blond hair matted with blood, the head shot having taken off half his face. He wasn't nearly as handsome, as debonair, as he had been when Ian's men had raided the warehouse.

"Have the Misserns arrived yet?"

Josef and Martin Missern were the weapons dealers Ian was to have met at this warehouse. In less than ten minutes.

"Their limo just pulled in minutes ago," Deke reported. "They're being held outside."

Ian's jaw clenched. Would the twins, certain Sorrell contacts, have arrived if they had known about this strike?

Of course they would have, he thought cynically as he stared at the bullet-ridden bodies laid out before him.

"Secure the perimeter. Half of you take up sniper position, the other half are with me."

He had a dozen men. He had come prepared. Survival instinct, knowledge of his enemies, or just plain paranoia had precipitated the cautionary attack on the warehouse.

It wasn't the first time Sorrell had tried to take him out in the past year. Ian had learned to be on guard.

Of course, that was the price of walking away from a life of truth, justice, and the American way to take over the reins of a drug cartel. That cynical thought had something dark and bitter brewing in his gut.

As he turned and strode away from the dead bodies he knew none of the regret at the loss of life that he had often known during his years as a SEAL. The knowledge that he'd had no choice, that he was preserving the laws of his nation, didn't comfort him.

Because he didn't need comfort.

"What the hell happened in there?" Deke asked, his voice low, as the others moved out to secure the perimeter and to surround the heir of the Fuentes cartel. They left Ian and Deke in the center as they moved from the warehouse.

"Did you see Algeria?" Ian asked him carefully.

"Who could miss her," Deke breathed out roughly.

"Those Russian cheekbones and cool hazel eyes would be a dead giveaway a mile away. Knock-dead gorgeous and dangerous as hell. Have you ever seen such a pretty package housing such a black heart?"

Ian holstered his weapon as he stared at Josef and Martin Missern across the warehouse lot, although his attention was focused on Deke.

"You're sure it was her?" Couldn't anyone else see beneath the package, the disguise?

"Man, no one could imitate Algeria." Deke snorted, but his look as he stared back at Ian shifted. "Could they?"

Ian shook his head. "It looked like Algeria; I just didn't expect to see her here."

"Antoni was here," Deke pointed out. "They're known associates."

"She doesn't usually work assassination squads," Ian reminded him.

It was clear Deke didn't have a clue who Algeria actually was.

Ian rubbed at his jaw, pausing before stepping closer to the Missern limo and staring around the warehouse lot. The neat wood and metal buildings were grouped close together, their contents awaiting shipping or delivery. It was the perfect place for an ambush. So why hadn't the Chameleon warned him of it?

She had been the Chameleon tonight, partially. The disguise had been perfect, as it always was. The feature-altering latex appeared as natural as true flesh. The contacts in her eyes hadn't given a hint of their true color, and the wig, if it had been a wig, looked as natural as real hair.

It better be a wig. God help her if she had cut that length of silky black hair that had graced her head in Atlanta.

She looked like a witch in her natural form. Gorgeous. Wicked. Seductive. The persona of Algeria Winters was as dangerous, as lethal, as any disguise the Chameleon had ever taken though.

"We have another problem," Deke warned him then.

Ian glanced at him from the corner of his eye. "Just one?"

Deke grimaced. "Word came in as we were suiting up to attack the warehouse. Kira Porter sent a message to the villa saying hello."

Ian froze. Son of a bitch. Son of a bitch. She had called the villa? Which meant Diego knew, and that scheming, matchmaking bastard would be all over that one like white on rice. Nothing would please Diego more than to believe Ian had managed to catch the interest of a society princess such as Kira Porter—her real life persona. But it had also been the warning he wondered why he hadn't recieved.

He was going to wring her slender, graceful little neck.

"Ian, what the hell is going on here?" Josef Missern snapped, as he and his brother and chauffer stood with hands flat against the hood of the limo.

Black-clad Fuentes soldiers pointed lethal M-16s at their backs, their eyes behind the black masks filled with the anticipation of death.

He pushed Kira to the back of his mind. He would deal with her later. But he would deal with her. And when he did, he promised himself, she wouldn't enjoy it nearly as much as she believed she was going to.

"Treachery, Josef." Ian strode across the distance with lazy ease as he watched the weapons dealers with a cold smile. "Treachery and death. Would you like to join in? I can arrange it for you."

The Frenchman paled as his brother stared back at him in horror.

Oh yeah, they had known what was going to happen here, and they were the perfect messengers to inform Sorrell that his highly paid assassins had failed.

As for the missing Algeria Winters, aka the Chameleon, aka one satin-fleshed, gray-eyed, black-haired Kira Porter? Well, he would take care of her on his own. And whatever her agenda, she could fly right back to Washington and let her handler know she had failed.

Ian had warned them when he left to stay the hell out of his way. He would kill and ask questions later before he would risk his own life, and his own plans. He was here for vengeance, and by God, vengeance would be his.

Two

"SO WHERE THE HELL IS Kira Porter?" Ian slammed the door to his office the next night and faced the bodyguard who had stepped inside with him.

His orders to Deke that morning had been simple: Find Kira Porter.

Deke looked as damned tired as Ian felt. Waylaying assassins and buying arms from gun smugglers at midnight, trying to justify letting the scum of the earth live another day, and doing it with only a few hours' sleep in the past two days hadn't helped his mood.

Nearly being knocked on his ass by a pint-sized black-haired witch with more guts than common sense wasn't helping either. It didn't matter to Ian that she was one of the most experienced and competent contract agents that he knew. It sure as hell didn't help that she likely knew exactly what she was doing. The fact that she was there had the blood boiling in his veins. Unfortunately, it wasn't all anger that was causing it.

"Miss Porter checked into one of the hotels on the beach," Deke reported as he frowned down at the pocket PC he was tapping quickly into. "We tracked her down pretty fast. We lost Algeria Winters though. She was on a private flight off the island within hours of the hit the other night. She's slick."

Ian grunted.

Deke was able, a master at strategy and a hell of a gutter fighter.

"And we're just now finding out Kira's here?" he gritted out, stalking to his desk and planting his hands flat on the deep, glistening wood as he stared back at Deke. "Where the hell are these informants I'm paying good money for? Wasn't her name on the fucking list?"

It was all he could do to keep his voice level, to rein in the need to pull at every hair in his head. Kira Porter had a habit of doing that to a man. She raised a man's frustration level just by being in the same room with him.

For a moment, one flashing second, he remembered more than frustration though. He remembered slipping into her Atlanta condo, trapping her in her bed, and demanding to know just exactly what she was doing there living next door to a senator's daughter who had been kidnapped two years before by Diego Fuentes.

He remembered waiting for an answer as his cock swelled beneath his jeans and visions of fucking her until she screamed his name had danced in his head. Those dreams still danced in his head. He was just smart enough to keep them under control. For now.

Damn it to hell. He didn't need her here.

"I'm not hearing any answers," he snarled. "Did I or did I not put her name on the list of those that I wanted to be notified if they arrived on the island?"

"You did." Deke nodded. "Someone must have been sleeping on the job. She's been here a week now, her and her bodyguard. Evidently her uncle owns some interest in a few of the hotels on the island and she's here checking those out. I got the information on our way back from the buy. I don't know why her name slipped past our informants."

"Then maybe you should wake someone's ass up," he

snapped, glaring at the other man furiously. "It's your job to get this information and to make certain those well-paid little snitches stay on the ball."

He dropped into the chair behind him, pushed his fingers wearily through his long dark blond hair, and glowered back at the other man.

Hell, this was just what he needed. He had a hard-on stiff enough to hammer nails.

He rubbed his hand over his cheek, grimacing at the rough day's growth of beard and wondered why the hell he hadn't just killed those damned Missern brothers rather than letting them go. Son of a bitch, he had known those two were going to betray him the minute the runner had arrived that afternoon changing the location of the buy. Not that either of the Missern twins had actually been there. Hell no. A highly trained team of assassins had been there instead, and one luscious little spy.

He should have put a bullet in both their heads and left them lying there after he wiped out that warehouse. He knew they had betrayed that buy to Sorrell, knew they were behind the information suddenly leaking to the French terrorist intent on taking over the cartel that Diego Fuentes had built.

If it were anyone else but a terrorist, he would have handed it to them on a silver platter rather than using what he was learning was considerable skill in deceit, treachery, and running drugs to keep the cartel growing in blood money.

But he was running out of time as well. If he didn't have Sorrell's identity soon, then there would be no way to counter the terrorist strike Ian and DHS knew Sorrell had planned against a major U.S. installation. Which one, they didn't know. When and where, no one was certain. All Ian knew was that he had until the next month, because after that, it could happen any day.

He shook his head wearily. "Get out of here," he ordered. "Catch a few hours' sleep. We'll be heading out tonight and

we'll need to be on our toes to deal with that one. She's hell
on wheels and damned hard to pin down."

"She's been hitting the clubs since she arrived as well,
pretty much nightly, several a night and never the same one
twice. Our guys at the clubs claim she watches the door for
a few hours, sips at a drink, then leaves quietly. She's been
watching for you," Deke reported.

Tonight she was going to find him.

He nodded abruptly at the information and waved toward
the door, almost groaning at the need for sleep as Deke
closed it behind him.

He felt like a man with a hangover and he knew he
hadn't had that particular pleasure for too many months
now. And it was too early this morning to start drinking.

He stared around the room instead. The wide windows
that caught the sun, shades partially drawn across them and
spilling slanting rays of light onto the wood floors. The
cream-colored walls, the heavy wood furniture. It was a
masculine room. Two heavy, dark leather chairs sat in front
of his desk; along the side of the room an overstuffed couch
and two chairs were grouped around a coffee table. A bar at
the far end and a plasma television on the wall close to his
desk.

It wasn't his office. The villa was leased, the grounds
heavily patrolled, and the small island a haven from the estate in Colombia that had seemed to grate on his nerves
worse by the day when he had been there.

Hell, he didn't need this.

He ran his hands over his face once again and restrained
another curse. Kira was a complication that he knew he
should have anticipated. He had known a year ago that she
could fuck his plans up royally.

Because he wanted her. He wanted her until the want
burned in his guts. Until the hunger for her interfered with
his ability to even take another woman.

He hadn't had a woman since meeting up with Kira in
Atlanta last year. Since he lay over her in the monstrous bed

in her condo, felt her body conform to his, and her kiss burn into his soul.

He had been insane to kiss her at that point and he had known it. If it had stayed at a kiss, maybe he could have retained a measure of control. But now, he had to touch, taste sumptuous flesh and push to the edge before he pulled back in the gathering realization of where it was going.

If he had taken her that night, he never could have never walked away from her.

He shook the memory away at the sound of a brief knock, his head lifting as Deke stepped back into the office.

"I told you to get some rest, Deke," he sighed.

They had existed on catnaps for most of the week, working to get the arms shipment in place on this tiny island and make certain that parts of it headed to Colombia in a timely fashion. The processing warehouses for the cocaine the Fuentes cartel dealt in was in too much danger from the forces looking to take over the business.

He had to hold on, just a little bit longer, then he could blow those fucking warehouses to hell and back himself.

"I'm heading that way soon, boss." Deke stepped into the room and closed the door behind him. "I was checking a few things. I don't like it when people slip in that we don't know about. These came in after I made contact with some other informants."

Deke handed him the reports as well as several grainy color photographs. He laid the report aside and looked at the photos first.

Two known Sorrell agents had come in by way of New York. Ian recognized the French nationals with a little sneer of his lips. The other was the assassin they had taken out in the warehouse the night before. The assassin's dossier was thick, his kill rate nearly one hundred percent.

"They paid good money for him," Ian murmured. "Sorrell isn't going to be happy that he failed."

"We got lucky last night, boss," Deke said. "I can't see the Missern brothers fucking up like that, even if they are in bed with Sorrell. It's all about the profit to them. I'm suspecting a leak in-house."

Ian suspected that as well. It wasn't the first time Sorrell's men had been where they shouldn't have.

"Look into it." Ian flipped the pictures to the desk and ran his hands over his face before leaning back in the chair and staring back at Deke thoughtfully.

He waved at the bodyguard to take a seat, his eyes narrowed as Deke stared back at him expectantly.

"Sorrell's gearing up," he murmured. "He wants the cartel bad enough to try to take me out now. What would his next move be?" He knew what he suspected, but he needed confirmation of it.

"He'll keep trying. Odds are, he'll get lucky," Deke told him. "Until we find a way to neutralize it. We need a position of strength, Ian. Something that will make him crawl out from his hole."

"What about this rumor of a daughter that we keep hearing about? Have you managed to learn anything there?"

Deke shook his head. "Nothing substantial. Just that she exists and Sorrell is searching for her. We know he has a son, but only because he's slowly shifting some of the smaller responsibilities to that son's shoulders. He goes by the name Raven."

Ian rubbed at his chin thoughtfully. "Pull in a few of our contacts in France and see if you can't learn more. If we get to her first, we could use her."

His gut clenched at the thought of that. If Sorrell had a missing daughter as they had heard for years, then no doubt she was better off staying anonymous. Unfortunately, if she did exist, he couldn't allow that anonymity. He needed her too damned bad.

A second, a moment's thought went to the fact that he was willing to use such an innocent before he hardened his resolve. There was no time to worry about the innocence of Sorrell's daughter. The game he was playing here was too deadly, too imperative.

"There was a call that came in this morning as well." Deke nodded to the report. "Joseph Fitzhugh and his son. Some kind of English aristocrats that say they know you. They wanted to meet and talk."

Ian grimaced at the names and shook his head. Fitzhugh and his son had flown to Colombia when Ian first left the SEALs and arrived at Diego's estate. He had met the diplomat in the line of duty years before, and Fitzhugh felt it was his place to try to convince Ian of the error of his ways. He wasn't the first, he wouldn't be the last.

He shook his head. "No meet."

"I assumed you would say that." Deke nodded somberly. "Must be hard as hell, boss, having all these so-called friends coming out of the woodwork. I haven't seen Durango team yet though."

"You won't see Durango team," he said. "But they're on the island. I can feel Macey's sniper scope like you feel a mosquito biting into your flesh."

He'd been feeling it for more than a week now. That itch at the back of his neck, the curl of anger in his gut. For some reason, he had expected them to know better, despite how well he had laid in the evidence that he was indeed a traitor. It was contradictory and illogical, but feeling that scope's bull's-eye on his head was pissing him off.

Deke frowned at Ian's admission. "We can't afford to have you taken out, Ian. Not at this stage of the game. They have to be pulled back."

Ian shook his head.

"We continue on," he told him. "He hasn't taken the shot yet, he's not going to. He's waiting. He knows I'm aware of him. Let's see what plays out."

Deke breathed out roughly at the order. "I don't like this. They shouldn't be here."

Ian shrugged. "Kira is the bigger worry," he told the bodyguard. "She's unpredictable and she's trouble. I don't want her involved in this, and I know her. She's here because of me, not because of her uncle's business."

Deke's eyes sharpened at that information. "Enemy or friendly?"

Ian snorted. "What's her present mood? Your guess is as good as mine. One thing is for damned sure, it's not going to be anything you expect. Count on that and wear a protective cup in the process. Because that woman will end up busting all our balls if we give her so much as half a chance."

Deke had no idea the trouble Kira Porter could cause. But Ian did; he knew and he didn't like the anticipation throbbing in his cock at the thought of it.

"So where do you go with her from here?" Deke asked.

Ian shook his head. "I'll catch up with her tomorrow night. Let her play for now. Let her think she's safe."

His jaw clenched at the suspicious look Deke shot him. He knew the other man wondered just how deeply Ian was letting this life affect him. And Ian admitted, it was damned deep. Sometimes, he didn't recognize himself or what he had become.

"Your mother called again," Deke finally told him. "You have several messages on your personal machine."

Ian stilled. Marika Richards had no idea of the game her son was playing, and the pain he knew she was feeling cut at his soul.

She had nearly given up her life for him countless times when he was a child, fighting to keep him away from Carmelita Fuentes's murderous hands. Diego's now deceased wife had hunted them like animals for ten years, before Ian's stepfather, John Richards, had found them.

For a moment, just a moment, he let himself remember his mother's smile. No matter how frightened he knew she had been, she had always found a way to smile at him, to promise him that all things pass: anger, pain, danger.

Be the best you can be, Ian. Be strong and brave, and know you're being just. That's all that matters. Know you're being just.

Those words whispered through his mind and sliced at

his heart. He knew she wouldn't see what he was doing as just. She would never condone him killing the father who had nearly destroyed both of them so many years ago.

Sometimes, though, a man had to do what was necessary to protect the just, the innocent. Too many lives were held in the balance now. Sorrell and Diego Fuentes both would have to die.

But first, he had to find Kira Porter and make damned certain she left Aruba. How the hell was a man supposed to destroy the monsters of the world when he knew a delicate bit of satin and lace was going to stand in his way? And she was there to stand in his way. He knew it. He could feel it. And he would be damned if he was going to allow it.

Three

HE WAS THERE. SHE KNEW he was.

The moment Kira stepped out of the elevator of her hotel that evening she knew Ian was waiting in her room. Her breasts hardened, her nipples peaked against the thin leather bustier covering them, and her body came alive with instant, blazing heat.

It wasn't any particular premonition. She would have liked to say she could just feel him. The truth was it was the presence of the bodyguard leaning casually against the wall several feet from her door that clued her in.

Deke Santiago. Age thirty-six, married once, widower. A dishonorably discharged Ranger. Dishonorable because he had nearly killed his commanding officer for screwing his then wife.

The court-martial had earned him a year in Leavenworth because he couldn't prove the adultery. There, he had met up with one of Diego Fuentes's lieutenants; four years later he had flown into Colombia and begun his life of apparent crime.

She paused as the elevator doors closed behind her, flicked a long swath of black hair over her shoulder, and sighed with an edge of irritation, aware of the security cameras trained on her. She had an appearance to maintain.

That of bored socialite and thrill seeker. Anyone searching for information would check security cameras. She knew, because it was something she did.

She moved along the hall, ignoring him. That's what she did with bodyguards, she pretended to ignore them. Her own, Daniel Calloway, was proof of that.

"I won't need you to check the room tonight, Daniel," she informed him as they neared his connecting room. "You can go on to bed."

"Are you sure, Ms. Porter?" His voice was colored with suspicion as he held to his role and Deke's lips quirked mockingly at the challenge in Daniel's voice.

"I'm positive. I'm certain the room is secure."

Daniel wasn't a stupid man, he knew Ian was there as well as she did. He entered his own room and closed the door behind him as Kira pulled her key card from the lining on the inside of her sinfully high-heeled boot.

She had hit the clubs early that evening, hoping to catch a glimpse of Ian before he found her. It seemed it had been a wasted effort. How long had he been waiting in her room instead?

She was nervous. She hadn't been nervous over a man since the last time she had seen Ian. Before that, she had never known a moment's nerves with a potential lover.

She could feel the blood rushing through her veins, need pooling between her thighs, and a haunting ache tightening her chest. An ache that had little to do with the arousal, but much to do with the emotions he inspired in her. Emotions as alien as the nerves.

"Is he upset?" She twirled the card in her fingers as she stared back at Deke, allowing a small grin to curl the edges of her lips.

Deke glanced at her door, a grin quirking his sensual lips. "Ask him yourself and see."

As she turned back to the door it swung open. A hard hand gripped her wrist and jerked her inside before the door slammed closed behind her.

She was pushed against it, her breath whooshing from her lips as her hands were gripped in one of his, held high above her head, and every inch of her body was molded to the hard length of his.

Her juices pooled between the lips of her sex then eased into the silk of the thong she wore beneath her leather pants. Her nipples spiked impossibly harder, and she swore she could feel a bead of sweat tickling between her breasts.

No one had ever felt like Ian. Hard, in control, commanding. Every touch, every action, gauged for maximum pleasure.

The hand holding her wrists tightened as the fingers of the other threaded through her hair and pulled her head back to stare into the blazing heat of his deep brown eyes. Eyes almost as rich as brandy, fired with dark little hints of red and filled with fury.

Dark blond hair fell over his forehead; the rich mix of colors, sun lightened and thick, lying long along his nape and falling over his brow made her long to bury her fingers in it again.

He turned her on in ways she had never been turned on before. She dreamed about sex with Ian. Lusted for it. Ached for it. She had agreed to deceive him for the slightest chance to be touched by those hard hands again.

"What the fucking hell are you doing here?" he snarled down at her as his head lowered.

His lips buried in her shoulder, opening to allow his teeth to grip the flesh there, his tongue to lap over it with quick heated strokes as she jerked against him.

"Business." Her head lowered as well.

The strong column of his neck was there for her enjoyment. Her teeth raked it. She licked slowly and the taste of male lust exploded against her taste buds.

God, he tasted good. She sucked at the flesh, a little moan escaping her throat as he picked her up, turned her, and in the next second bore her to the bed.

"Ian." She gasped his name, feeling the hard length of

his body covering hers, his thighs spreading hers, his cock pressing hard and demandingly into the butter-soft leather covering her sex.

Her hands were still stretched above her head, her breasts perilously close to spilling from the cups of the leather bustier she wore.

She felt bound. Helpless. She had never felt that way with a man before. She had never wanted to feel that way until Ian had shown her the pleasure to be found there. Now she craved it. Craved him with a hunger that refused to be quelled.

"You have no business here." His lips drew back from his teeth as his free hand tugged at the ties that secured the front of the bustier. "No business here. No business close to here."

The top loosened, spread apart, and with a flick of his fingers the cups covering her breasts were released. Her breasts spilled free, nipples hard and pointed, flushed red and aching for his touch.

"You're here." It was a statement and a moan as his head lowered and his lips covered a tight, sensitive nipple.

He wasn't easy on her, and she didn't want easy. His teeth gripped and tugged, his tongue lashed with wicked wet heat. Her eyeballs were going to roll back in her head it was so damned good. He sucked on her like a starving man.

Long moments later his head lifted, thick dark blond lashes fanning his cheeks as he stared down at his handiwork.

Her nipple was tighter, if that was possible, gleaming wet and ruby red.

"You wore too many clothes," he growled, his voice, which was rough on a good day, grating now.

"I didn't want to appear too easy," she gasped as his lips moved to the opposite breast and began their less than tender ministrations.

God, this was what she had loved about the first and only time he had touched her. He didn't treat her like spun glass.

He didn't touch her like she would break. He touched her like a woman well able to satisfy the dark, hungry sex drive she knew he possessed. That he possessed and she craved to experience.

"Not easy enough." He nipped the side of her breast, his free hand moving to her hip, tugging at the laces on her pants now as his lips moved back to hers.

Oh God, the taste of his kiss. It was incredible. It was enough to steam her eyeballs, not to mention what it was probably doing to the glass balcony doors across the room.

She stretched beneath him, arched closer, rubbed against the erection seated firmly against her pussy and wished she could purr. It felt that damned good. So good, she wondered if she could come from his kiss alone.

Hell, she had never done that, but this was close. This was edging closer. His tongue curled along hers, stroked it, then teased her by licking at her lips. Then he bit her.

Kira jerked her head back, glaring at him before she returned the favor by nipping at his lower lip. His hand tightened in her hair, jerked her back, and his lips slammed over hers.

He released her wrists, wrapped his arms around her, and began thrusting between her thighs, stroking the silk of her panties and the leather of her pants against her, rubbing against her clit and causing little snarls to echo in her throat.

Damn him, he was burning her alive.

Her hands buried themselves in his hair, pulled at it. Her knees lifted and bent, clasping his hips as she dug the sharp heels of her boots into the bed and tried to defy the layers of material between them.

She wanted him, bad. She wanted his cock pounding into her. Wanted him fucking her, filling her, stealing her senses and her much lauded control with the lusts that blazed between them.

This was no place for those lusts. The middle of an investigation, in the eye of a storm that threatened to close in on Ian like the narrowing spout of a cyclone. And yet, just as before, the wild hunger flared through her, rocked her, seared her senses. Opened something inside herself that she didn't recognize. A core of femininity. A certainty that the rabbit hole the woman hid within had been discovered. The agent she had become could no longer hide the woman desperate to reveal herself.

She was immersed in thick, white-hot sensation and flowing with damp, desperate need. And when his hand slid into the loosened edge of her pants, his hips pulled back, and his fingers found the bare flesh of her saturated sex, Kira knew she was doomed.

She froze, but Ian didn't have any such inclinations. His fingers found the narrow, sensitized slit, slid through it, and two fingers speared into the snug, slick entrance of her vagina.

"Oh God!" She tore her lips from his, the words bursting from her lips as she felt the muscles surrounding his fingers spasm, felt her juices spurt around them.

"Damn you, you're hot!" He bit her neck, just like a damned freaking vampire. Just bit right into it and sent her eyes rolling back in her head again as a shudder tore through her.

Her hips jerked, working her sex on his fingers as she felt the explosion just a breath away. Just a frickin' breath. It was so close she could feel it, taste it, smell it.

"Oh, it's not that easy," he snarled, his fingers stilling inside her, just filling her, holding her on the edge of a precipice that was painful.

"Would be," she panted. "If you wouldn't be such a *jack-ass*!" She just wanted to come. It wasn't like she wanted national secrets or something. Hell, she already had those.

His smile was tight, hard. His hair, mussed from her fingers, fell around his dark tanned face, his lips swollen from her kisses.

He looked like the dominant male he was. A sexually dominant, fierce and forceful, take-all-control kinda guy. He wasn't going to let a lover control her sexuality or his. That was his prerogative, and by God if he didn't know how to do it. Not exactly her normal taste, but he had become a craving.

"What are you doing here, Kira?" He stroked her, inside, just the sweetest, most delicious rubbing of her internal muscles with the tips of his fingers.

Shiverlicious. She shivered and gasped and grew wetter, it was just that damned good.

"Business. Working." She tried to breathe. Hell, breathing was overrated anyway. If she held her breath, just held it, she could almost fall off the edge from those rasping little strokes inside her pussy.

"Working huh?" He bent and ran his tongue over a stiff nipple. "You do remember how I punish liars, don't you?"

Was that really her moaning like she wanted to be punished? Oh hell no, couldn't be. She didn't play those games, and she wasn't into any kind of submission. Until it came to Ian. Her butt clenched, she couldn't help it. And she knew he felt it. She knew she felt his knowing chuckle against her nipple.

"Bite me," she groaned. She didn't order or snap. Nope, she groaned, like a helpless whimpering little submissive begging for her master's touch.

"Where?" His teeth rasped over her nipple.

"That works."

He bit her. Not too hard. Just enough. He closed his teeth on her nipple just enough for her to feel the pleasure/pain.

Sweet Holy Mother . . . She arched, bearing down on the fingers filling her, and thought for certain she would go off like fireworks from that alone.

God help her, she needed to orgasm.

"Might as well answer me." He blew another breath over the tight, tormented peak. "What are you up to, Trouble?"

"Trouble," she agreed, a moan filling the word as his fingers shifted inside her, reached higher and found the most amazing little bunch of nerve endings. Hell, where had those come from? That wasn't the G-spot, it might even be better than the G-spot.

The I-spot. The Ian spot.

"Oh God, just let me come," she panted, her hands tightening in his hair as her breathing became harder, rougher.

"Tell me," he whispered, but despite his seeming determination, he wasn't unaffected.

Kira stared into his eyes and saw the near black irises, the burgundy glow of lust, and the flush mantling his cheekbones. Heavy sensuality shaped his lips and gave his gaze a drowsy, wicked appearance.

"I swear on my uncle's bank account. Business. Just business. Now get me off, dammit." She tried to writhe beneath him, tried to go that last little sensation into orgasm without his help.

"Goddamn you!"

Before Kira could react his fingers had slid from her body, jerked from beneath her pants, and he was jackknifing from the bed to glare at her as he stood over her.

And there she lay, panting, her nipples standing as straight and tall as the imperial guard and her vagina still gushing with need.

"Tease!" She rolled to the other side of the bed, sat on the edge, and jerked her boots off first, then tugged her pants from her legs.

Clad in nothing but a white silk thong, she jerked the bronze silk robe from the chair by the bed and shrugged it on as she turned to face him.

"You know, Ian, this habit you have of leaving me a second before I get off is becoming annoying."

"Your habit of poking your nose into my business could become dangerous," he snapped, fury contorting his expression. But lust gleamed thick and bright in his eyes.

Kira pushed her fingers through her tangled hair, shook it out, and cast him a mocking look from beneath her lashes.

"Oh really, Ian," she drawled then. "You brought your business to me, remember? The night you slipped into my condo and crawled that tight ass of yours into my bed during that op in Atlanta. Don't start crying foul now. You're just pissed off because you finally met a woman unwilling to play the ready-and-willing submissive. Speaking of those, didn't you ever get bored?"

His lips thinned and she swore that muscle jumping in his jaw was going to tear right out of the tightly stretched flesh of his cheek.

Damn, he was a tad upset.

Poor baby.

"What kind of deal is Homeland Security running here, Kira? Don't fuck with me. Not now. Mess in my business here and I might have to kill you."

And damn if he didn't sound as though he meant it. He was almost believable. Maybe. If she were on mind-altering drugs, she thought with a sniff.

"The big bad cartel leader now, are you?" She tossed her head back and let a low, seductive laugh whisper from her throat. "Come on, Ian, you enjoy the game too much to kill me. Besides." She moved closer to him, ran a finger down his heaving chest, and whispered the words that she knew had the potential to rock his little world. "Why would they run an op against their favorite bad boy spy?"

It was a guess, nothing more. A supposition. A hope, but the reaction was far more than she anticipated.

The change was frightening. The lust in his eyes was instantly replaced with icy fury. His expression tightened further, the harsh planes and angles of his face cast into savage relief a second before he grabbed her.

Between one breath and the next Kira found herself, arms locked behind her back, her back to his chest, and his powerful arm braced around her neck as his lips lowered to her ear.

"Get out of Aruba, and take your accusations with you. Get as far away from me as possible or I'll fuck you until you're dying from the orgasms. And once I've had my fill of you, I'll break your pretty neck."

His arm tightened around her neck for emphasis as his hard, corded body vibrated with tension against her. She should have felt at least a frisson of fear. She assumed that was the point behind the hold on her. It wasn't painful, but it reminded her to the very core of her being that he was broader, stronger, and a hell of a lot more experienced in violence than she was.

She didn't try to break loose. She knew better. For every move she had, Ian had one to counter it. Instead, she relaxed into the embrace, became soft and pliant, aware that he only tensed further behind her.

"Go ahead, Ian," she said softly. "Kill me. If you can."

HE COULDN'T.
      Ian stared down at her face, felt her body relax into him, and felt like a drowning man. Only it was soft, willing woman he was drowning in. The scent and feel of the one woman he had learned was a weakness he could ill afford.

"You're playing a very dangerous game," he whispered against the soft silk of her hair as he felt her ass flex against the hard length of his cock.

Her unique, pretty little ears were at his lips, the little slant and soft curve of the lobe tempting his lips.

His dick was throbbing, aching. Just the thought of her could do this to him, make him crazy to fuck her, to hold her to him and bury himself inside her.

Luck had been on his side in Atlanta eight months before. There hadn't been the time or the opportunity to take her, and each time he'd managed to get his hands on her there had been an interruption.

There would be no interruptions now, the wild side of his brain reminded him with frantic lust. He could push her against the wall, bury himself inside the hot grip of her pussy, and find the relief he needed with teeth-clenching desperation.

"And you're not?" she asked him as he slowly released her hands.

Hands that slid down and curled over the hard ridge of his erection, stealing his breath.

"Do you think you really managed to slip into that naval clinic unseen, Ian?" she whispered then. "You're good, big boy, but you're not that good. Don't you know that entry point you found unsecured was unsecured for a reason? That the guard was napping, for a reason. That Nathan's bathroom door was closed. For a reason. I knew you would be there. I knew, all I had to do was wait, because I knew the signs that a path had been made for you. You're working an op here and we both know it."

He released her slowly, his hands curling over her shoulders as he pushed her away from his body, despite every cell in his cock screaming no.

She turned slowly to face him, wearing nothing but the bronze silk robe and panties so tiny he wondered why she bothered. Witchy gray eyes stared up at him, the cloudy color ringed with a thin circle of gray-blue that had always fascinated him.

The dangerous statement had cleared the mind-numbing lust from his brain and left him chilled to the bone. His contact at DHS had arranged the visit, he knew that. *But how had Kira known it?*

"There's no op in progress."

He breathed in through his nose before he moved away from her, pacing to the chair where his expensive silk jacket had been laid. Shrugging it on, he turned back to her, remembering the job, the dangers, and the price of failure.

"He saved my life when I was a kid," he stated, hearing his own raspy voice and recalling that his screams at that time had nearly broken it. Nathan's was worse. His voice was so ruined that the sound of it would always remind the other man of the hell he had endured.

Kira nodded. "He told me about that."

Ian clenched his teeth. "I needed to say goodbye. That was all."

Her lips pursed. "Just saying goodbye? All security measures were allowed to lapse so a drug lord could say goodbye? Give me a break, Ian."

"Money in the right hands works wonders," he assured her, staring back at her with the same icy expression he had perfected over the past several years. "I'm here by choice, Ms. Porter, don't make the mistake of thinking otherwise. And trust me when I say, I don't intend to leave."

Her gaze flickered then, whether with indecision or belief, he couldn't be sure. Reading Kira was like trying to navigate through lake fog. Damned near impossible.

Finally, another of those irritating, knowing smiles shaped her lips and she shrugged with a graceful shift of her slender shoulders.

That smile was designed to make men crazy. To make them dream of wiping it off her face with passion, or with their dick filling that hot little mouth. Ian had quite a few fantasies concerning the latter.

"Whatever," she finally answered smoothly. "Uncle Jason is considering buying a villa here, did I mention that? He's flying in tomorrow to check out a few possibilities that I found today. You go ahead and play your little games, Ian, I'm sure I can find a way to occupy myself."

"Get the hell out of Aruba, Kira," he ordered her harshly. "Don't turn this into a pissing match, because you'll lose. The hard way."

She clicked her tongue then. "Really, Ian, you're losing your perspective. Drug cartel leaders don't give warnings, they act. I guess you'll just have to try the cement slippers next." Her eyes widened. "Or are they using something else here in the Caribbean? Sometimes it's just so hard to keep up."

He'd had enough. He'd warned her. She was an experienced agent, she knew the game, the rules and the dangers. If she got her ass killed, then it was out of his hands. He'd warned her.

"Good night, Ms. Porter." He moved across the room and headed for the door. "I trust you'll take ample care of yourself while you're here."

"I always do, lover."

He jerked the door open then slammed it behind him as he stepped into the hall. Deke straightened from the wall, his gaze narrowing, his eyes flickering with interest as he glanced at the suite door.

"Let's move." Ian stalked down the hallway without explanations. He'd be damned if there was any way to explain Kira, even if Deke was aware of exactly who and what she was.

Oh yeah, she was the niece to Jason Maclane all right. And one of the most clever damned contract agents Homeland Security had on its payroll.

The Chameleon, that was her code name. And why was that her code name? Because she was as changeable in her appearance as she was in her moods. Because her job wasn't to confront a damned thing, it was to watch and listen and flit around the elite little parties that catered to the rich and notorious, and the dirty little deal makers. To shift and change according to her location, to become seductive or dangerous, to fit in with the diseased, disgusting parasites of the world.

And he should remember that one, he told himself as he followed Deke into the elevator. Kira knew the rules of the game. She didn't need him to protect her.

Four

IAN'S MOOD THE NEXT MORNING was less than cheerful. He always awoke quickly, but opened his eyes slowly. He felt his surroundings out, let his senses hone in to detect any shifts or dangers before he allowed himself to move from the bed.

This morning, he awoke in a mood designed to piss even himself off. His skin felt stretched, irritation tightened his guts, and damn if he didn't still have the hard-on from hell throbbing between his thighs.

He took care of the hard-on in the shower, masturbating as he closed his eyes and imagined Kira, on her knees, her lips surrounding him, her tongue licking and stroking as she sucked him to her throat and made his teeth clench with the need to hold back.

Not that his hand came anywhere close to the imagined feel of her mouth, but the thought succeeded in spilling his semen to the shower floor and taking the bitter edge off his lust.

Hell, he could have gone to Astra's room and awakened her last night. He could have fucked her all night long, and rather than giving him grief, she would have smiled and licked her lips in anticipation.

She was one of many women that Diego seemed to delight in filling the villa with. He liked pretty women, and he liked having them near. Women who liked rough sex. Hell, they went beyond a little rough sex. They were women who enjoyed the pain Diego could mete out.

Ian grimaced at the thought of that. He had seen one of the maids, Eleanor's, back beaded with blood from the stroke of Diego's whip, and still she had begged for more. Not more sex. Not more fucking or a deeper penetration, because Diego rarely fucked one of his toys. No, it was the pain that got both of them off. Diego got off giving it, and Eleanor could climax from it. Ecstasy would wash over her face and her body would tremble with it.

It was enough to make a jaded man wonder what the hell had gone wrong with the world. For all his cynicism and experience, he still couldn't understand that one. But it wasn't Astra he wanted, it was Kira.

Stalking into the breakfast room nearly an hour later, he found Diego at the breakfast table. Just what he needed that morning, a healthy dose of dear old pop.

"Ah, good morning, Ian." A smile creased Diego's swarthy face as he laid his forearms on the table and regarded him with something resembling pride. "I trust you slept well?"

Could his morning get any worse?

"Morning, pop." It was the most disrespectful title Ian could come up with. It was the one thing that had earned him his stepfather's ire when he used it.

John Richards wasn't a man to stand on ceremony, but he did demand respect, and he earned it. Ian could call him John or Dad, his choice, John had informed him. But call him pop again and he would show Ian a pop he wouldn't forget. Ian almost smiled at the memory.

Diego frowned. He didn't like the title any more than John Richards had.

"'Father' would be a much better greeting," Diego informed him, not for the first time.

"Too stiff." Ian moved to the sideboard, piled his plate high with fluffy scrambled eggs, sausage, bacon, and toast. For all his faults, Diego had an excellent cook, and she seemed to have grown fond of Ian. " 'Father' sounds like something from the fifties," he continued, passing over the fruit and various sweets the cook had laid out as he turned and moved to the glass-topped breakfast table.

Sunlight spilled through the open doors and tall windows that surrounded the room as Ian took his seat and let the little dark-haired maid pour his coffee.

"Thanks, Liss." He smiled as she moved back.

"You are welcome, Mr. Fuentes." Her lilting English was a little shy, but Ian had learned early just where this little cat's loyalties lay. And they weren't with him.

"Set the coffee on the table, Liss," he directed her. "And then you can leave."

She looked to Diego. The obvious cut was irritating.

"Liss, he didn't give you the order, I did," he told her softly, meeting her dark eyes with the promise of retaliation in his own gaze if she didn't do as ordered.

"Of course, Mr. Fuentes." She set the silver pot in the center of the table, between him and Diego, and then headed for the wide double doors, the short skirt of her uniform swishing.

"Close the doors behind you," he ordered, before nodding to Mendez to follow her out. The other man would stand guard at the doors. Deke and another bodyguard stood guard at the patio and the fourth had positioned himself at the door leading to the kitchen.

Only Deke knew his true purpose there, but the other three were slowly proving their loyalty to Ian rather than the cartel.

"I do not like how you require that I serve myself," Diego snapped as he reach for the coffeepot and refilled his cup. "I have the servants for a reason."

"And I'm always amazed that they survive it." Ian grunted at the thought of the perversions the maids shared with Diego. "But I see no reason to have to kill one of them because they overheard the wrong thing."

"You should not discuss business with breakfast," Diego instructed him. "It is bad for the digestion."

"Right now, business is bad for health, period." Ian sipped at his coffee as he stared back at Diego. "I'm canceling our relationship with the Radacchio consortium. My men were hijacked on the way to the delivery point and I lost two of them. We nearly lost the shipment."

The report of the lost coca shipment hadn't been as bad as learning that the two men he had lost were handpicked agents he had put in place. That pissed him off.

"Sorrell?" Diego narrowed his eyes thoughtfully as he watched Ian.

Sorrell was the reason Ian was there. The elusive terrorist, as yet unidentified, had managed to slip through every net that several countries and more than a dozen law enforcement agencies had attempted to use to catch him.

"That's what I suspect." Ian shrugged as he dug into his breakfast. "Valence Radacchio claims otherwise, but the strike was well prepared and centered where security should have been the tightest. They dropped the ball, and rather than getting embroiled in a blood feud with them, I'd rather sever ties instead."

"Valence has worked with me for many years," Diego mused. "He has always moved our product through Colombia and onto the ships. If we sever this relationship, we will be forced to forge a new one."

Ian shook his head. "We move our own product. Why use a middleman when we have the necessary manpower and the network to do it efficiently? It saves time, money, and risks."

The product, of course, was drugs. Radacchio collected the bales of cocaine from the processing warehouses and transported it across the mountains to waiting ships. From there, he delivered it to various points to another drop-off where others then collected it, broke it down, and shipped it to other points.

Until Sorrell had begun hitting the processing warehouses. The first thing Ian had done when he took over the Fuentes business was to relocate the warehouses and have his men deliver the goods to Radacchio instead.

"Is Valence aligned with Sorrell, do you think? Or has the bastard merely managed to obtain information about our supply lines?"

Ian shook his head. "I don't know and I don't care. But Radacchio knew the location of the former warehouses. We changed our locations and began delivering to them rather than having them pick up the bales from us and the hijackings stopped. Now this strike? I'm inclined to once again cut them out of the loop. We'll see what happens then."

"He will not be pleased over this," Diego warned him. "We pay him well for his consortium's work."

"Then he can find another client, one with a bit less paranoia than it seems I possess." Ian's smile was tight. "I don't have time for a drug war, Diego. We'll do it my way first."

Diego's black eyes gleamed with excitement.

"The wars spice up life, Ian." Diego grinned with all apparent anticipation. "They keep you on your toes."

"I'd been a ballet dancer if I wanted to dance on my toes, pop," he said.

Diego sighed in regret. "Radacchio will demand a meeting to discuss this."

"Then tell him he can talk to me. And that's another thing; either I run this shit or I don't. Stay out of it. Don't try to negotiate with Radacchio like you did the Misserns last month. I won't be happy."

The announcement had an angry frown creasing Diego's face. "What do you mean by this?" he burst out. "Stay out of what business? Fuentes business? I remind you, I am the Fuentes. It is my business."

Ian lifted his head and stared back at Diego silently.

Diego flinched as Ian stared back at him unblinkingly.

"I do not like this," he muttered. "I am not so old that I cannot be a part of my own business any longer."

"You have your job."

"Bah. My job. It is no job to oversee the farms and production of the coca. A child could do this."

"We have a deal," Ian reminded him, his voice hard. "Don't fuck me over on it, old man, or I'll be gone even faster than I made it here."

It wasn't an idle threat. If he couldn't control the cartel, then Ian didn't have a hope in hell of drawing Sorrell in. He knew it, and Diego knew it. To safeguard the business from being forcibly taken by the terrorist, Diego needed Ian. Ian needed control.

"You are hard, Ian." Diego sighed. "Harder than even I believed. More so than my investigations into you revealed."

"I'm a product of my childhood, pop," he bit out. "Remember?"

Diego grimaced. His black eyes were, for the barest moment, bleak with sorrow. It was a sorrow Ian refused to acknowledge, even to himself. He didn't care about Diego's past regrets, his hopes or his dreams, no matter the illusion Ian allowed him that he did. All he cared about was catching Sorrell and delivering him and Diego Fuentes into the hands of justice. Or, their heads on a platter. The latter if he could get away with it.

"If I could go back, I would give my life to have spared you that pain," Diego said softly, with apparent sincerity.

"There's no going back." Ian shrugged. "Just think, it made me hard enough to straighten your little world out, pop. We haven't had a successful hijacking or a missed load since I arrived."

"For a man who does not enjoy war, you shed enough blood," Diego griped. "And refuse to allow me in on the fun. I was pleased though. The agents of the U.S. that you uncovered last month will steal no more information from us, yes?"

The men he had killed had been perverted monsters posing as American agents. They had worked for the DEA, drawn their pay, and given just enough information to make them viable. Until they tried to kill Ian in the name of that bastard Sorrell.

Killing agents was something Ian preferred not to do, but when a man had the barrel of a gun aiming in his direction, he did what he had to.

"I have to head back to town this morning." Ian glanced at his watch and grimaced. "I'm meeting one of our lawyers at the casino. One of our Miami clubs seems to be losing a tidy little profit. I want to know why."

"Why did you not have him come here?" Diego stared back at him in angry confusion. "You do not go running like a hound to the underlings, Ian. They come to you."

"Good idea, pop." He sneered. "Let's just throw a party for all of them so they can scope out our security and hit the house in the dead of night. Why the hell do you think so many of your friends end up dying in their beds from an enemy bullet?"

Diego's expression flickered with anger. "I am aware of the risks to this life. I have lived many years and survived many attempts against mine. We are Fuentes. We do not hide and we do not scrape to those beneath us by observing their rules. They come to us."

"And Sorrell has managed to turn some of your most loyal associates his way simply because of your arrogance," Ian snapped. "Let's not make this harder than it already is. I'll be back in a few hours. Until then, try to stay out of trouble."

Diego hated nothing more than being talked to as though he were a child, and though Ian tempered it, there was nothing he delighted in more. He was afforded very few pleasures in this little game he was playing and he took them where he could.

"Should I consider myself under house arrest while we are at it?" Diego burst out angrily as Ian made to leave the room. "You will not tell me who I may or may not invite into my house."

Ian shrugged. "Invite them all for all I care. I don't sleep deep enough for anyone to slip into my room unawares. You do, though. I'd remember that."

He opened the doors and stepped into the foyer before Diego could say more.

"Mendez, have Deke and the others join us outside," he ordered the waiting bodyguard. "We have a lawyer to meet."

Ian strode through the marbled foyer to the front door, almost grinning as the houseman rushed to open the wide doors ahead of him.

He stepped onto the sunlit portico, gazing at the ferns, palms, and swaying greenery that surrounded the large circular driveway and sheltered the paved road that led from the gated entrance. The entire property was enclosed by a ten-foot stone wall that Ian had had wired for security. Guards were posted around the property, and the additional training Ian had insisted on had paid off several times when attempts were made to slip into the estate.

He was vulnerable and he knew it. Shoring up his defenses and inspiring loyalty throughout the Fuentes networks was imperative now. He needed men who were loyal to the heir of the cartel rather than the cartel leader himself. Soon, Ian would know every dirty little player, every scumbag assassin and petty drug dealer Diego possessed.

He would know the whores, the pimps, clubs, and owners and which location yielded the highest sales. He was gathering the names of political buyers and sellers as well as those within the law enforcement community that not just Diego, but a dozen other drug kingpins, were blackmailing.

By the time he brought Sorrel and Diego down, there wouldn't be a secret of Diego's that Ian didn't know. And that brought satisfaction. If he lived to achieve his objective, then two fewer drug-dealing terror-selling sons of bitches would cease to breathe air.

He should feel a measure of guilt, he was sure. Diego

was after all his father. The same father whose wife had
nearly killed Ian's mother, as well as Ian. Who had been responsible for the most terrifying night of a ten-year-old
boy's life. The night his mother had lain bleeding to death
in his arms.

Because of Carmelita Fuentes. Because Diego was a
drug-dealing slime pit with more enemies than friends and
hands so bloodstained Ian could smell the stench of them
anytime he was around the other man.

And soon, his own hands would carry the same stench,
Ian thought with a sigh, as Deke pulled a white Range
Rover to a stop in front of the villa.

Rather than driving this time, Ian stepped into the back
seat, accepted a briefcase from Mendez, and opened it as
the doors closed and the vehicle drove way.

The fourth bodyguard was in another Rover behind
them, providing backup and an additional vehicle in case
this one encountered any unforeseen accidents. In this business, Ian had learned to expect the unforeseen.

DIEGO WATCHED AS THE ROVERS left the estate, a frown
on his face, his jaw clenched with worry and concern as
Ian left the protection of the estate. He worried, a sign of
old age perhaps. Each time Ian left, Diego feared it would
be the last time he saw him.

"El Patrón." Saul entered the breakfast room, closing the
doors behind him and facing Diego with an inquisitive expression. "You sent for me?"

Saul was old. His shoulders were stooped, his dark eyes
a bit dull, his face creased with age. He had been Diego's
father's most trusted advisor. At Carmelita's death he had
returned to Diego's side.

Diego nodded slowly. "Have you learned anything from
our sources?"

Ian had eliminated the spy in the U.S. government that
Diego had drawn closest to him, Jansen Clay, but there were

others, much more important contacts, who relied upon
Diego as much as he relied upon them.

"No teams are being sent for him, as you requested."
Saul stepped to the sideboard and prepared himself a plate
of fruits and sweets. "There are reports that Durango team,
the friends he fought with, have protested this action vocif-
erously, especially the one known as Macey, but they are
being contained. Orders have gone out to watch his actions
only, and to learn what he has planned. It seems the Americans are more concerned with your promise that Ian will
eliminate Sorrell than they are with capturing a traitor." Satisfaction echoed in Saul's voice, as it did in Diego's heart.

"The boy, he takes too many risks." Diego sighed. "He
goes now to meet with lawyers rather than having them
come to him. As though he dares Sorrell or the other cartels
to strike at him."

"The other cartel leaders are learning to stay out of his
way, Diego. As with yourself and the Americans, they
merely watch him."

"And your report on his activities?" Diego asked.

As much as he loved the boy, and he did, loved him more
than he had loved his youngest son or that viper Carmelita,
he couldn't forget that betrayal could come from within.

"He has met with no agents that he hasn't killed." Saul
chuckled. "Of course, they attempted to draw blood first.
He does not party, nor does he partake of our product. He
does not surround himself with the whores and drug
groupies that vie for his attention other than necessary. And
those who cling to his arm at those times are well known to
us, and not associated with any government's law enforcement agencies. For all appearances, my friend, he has up-
held his word. His loyalty is to you."

Diego nodded slowly. "And your own impressions of
him?"

Saul sighed then.

Diego turned and watched him with an edge of sorrow.
Saul's impressions were as reliable as other men's reports.

"I must know this, my friend," he said softly. "What do you believe goes on in my son's mind, in his heart?"

"There is still much anger," Saul stated as he laid his arms on the table and regarded Diego. "He has softened toward you marginally. He does not refuse to hear the stories I would tell him now of your youth and your dreams. He listens. But I can see the rage in his eyes. The events of his childhood and Carmelita's torments are not forgotten."

Diego clenched his fingers into fists before forcing himself to relax them.

"He blames me." Diego moved back to the table, taking his seat with a heavy breath of regret and staring across the table at Saul. "As well he should. I should have known Marika had not been killed as my father reported. I should have known that his fascination with her would result in a betrayal."

"He was an old man, Diego." Saul shook his gray head sadly. "The little blond nurse you brought to him was seen as an angel. An angel that should not be mired in the blood and treachery of the cartels. He sought to save her. It was only by chance that Carmelita learned of her and of the child."

Diego stared at the table, his finger smoothing over the lace cloth that covered it as he remembered Marika Desmond. An unusual name, for an unusual woman. She had been named after her Slavic grandmother, and she wore her name with pride.

So blond her hair had glistened white beneath the Colombian sun. Her smile had been filled with dreams and with purpose as she came to the villages as a nurse, healing the sick and touching all with her kindness. She had been unaware of who Diego was, and she had taken him into her bed with a love that had touched his soul.

He had known her such a short time. Only months. And he had never forgotten her. To learn she had spent the years of his marriage to Carmelita living in fear, that Ian had nearly died more than once, still filled him with rage.

Diego's father had arranged it so it appeared Marika had died. Carmelita had attempted to arrange her death in truth.

"We made a strong son," Diego whispered, wishing he could call Marika, wishing he could thank her for Ian's life, but his son forbade it so violently that Diego feared his wrath if he attempted it.

"You did," Saul agreed.

"Has she attempted to contact him?" Diego lifted his gaze to Saul once more. "Have you heard her voice?"

"He refuses to speak with her," Saul said heavily. "He has broken all ties, Diego, even those with his mother. I questioned him just this past week about her. He said he does not speak to her in an effort to not add to her pain. She would only plead for his return, and he has sworn he will not leave the cartel."

Diego wrapped his hand around his coffee cup and stared into the cooling liquid. Memories of Marika washed over him, staining his soul with his own regrets.

"She is well?"

"She is well and happy with her American husband. And protected, Diego. Ian and John Richards see to this, though Richards is unaware of the two men Ian has ordered to watch her."

"And my son is loyal?" He lifted his eyes to Saul again, needing the confirmation.

"In my estimation, he is loyal. And within a few years, my friend, perhaps he will even call you father."

Diego breathed in roughly. He needed to be called father, perhaps even one day, grandfather. Recalling the information he had received last night, he thought that maybe with a little push, his son would take the American heiress to the Maclane fortune. If nothing else, as a lover. Diego did not care if his grandchildren were legitimate or not. It was blood that mattered. Now, he understood his father's beliefs in family, no matter the betrayal. Blood mattered.

Five

SHE WAS A FOOL, AND Kira admitted it as she allowed the waiter to lead her to the small table of the restaurant where she had arranged to meet her uncle that afternoon. The same restaurant where she knew Ian would be having lunch. Money in the right hands, and before the morning was over she had known where to find him.

She was pushing him, pushing herself, and she knew it. Ian was playing with fire, and she didn't just mean the operation he was working against Fuentes and Sorrell.

She was terribly afraid he meant to kill Diego Fuentes, a monster, a brutal, merciless bastard who preyed on the weak. But he was still Ian's biological father. A son should never have to kill his sire. The repercussions would be horrifying.

She had no proof of it, no verification. All she had was her own intuition, which she admitted was colored by her desire for him. And something much more.

There was a part of her that refused to let go of Ian. A part she had never known existed until last year. As though beneath the darkness that had been her life for the past ten years, a shadow of light had begun moving, weakening her, reminding her that she was a woman.

"Kira, is that you?"

Her head lifted, a smile of pleasure pulling at her lips at the sight of the small redhead who was coming to her table. Tehya Talamosi, with her shadowed eyes and somber face, and Kira's suspicions that she was as much an agent as the Chameleon was.

"Tehya, what are you doing here?" Over the years Kira had met the other woman in several different countries, where she was usually involved with relief efforts of some sort.

"Vacation." Tehya shrugged, her gaze flickering around the room. "I just wanted to stop and say hi." She ducked her head almost shyly, allowing her long hair to shield her face.

"It's good to see you again." Kira watched her closely. She couldn't be old enough to be an agent, yet Kira had the same feeling, the same internal defenses jumping to life, with the girl as she did with any other agent. Or enemy.

Tehya smiled back at her, her gaze flickering toward Ian and a few other scattered tables before she nodded and turned to walk through the restaurant.

In a glance Kira once again took in the way her denim-clad legs moved. There was a stiffness that hadn't been there the last time she saw her, a few years before. Her shoulders were straighter beneath the light cotton T-shirt she wore. And as always, Kira felt the need to protect the other girl.

She shook the feeling off. If Tehya needed her protection she had ample opportunity to ask for it. Kira made a mental note to have Daniel run her name through DHS tonight, see what he could dig up on her. This mission was too important and the realization that an unknown could be on the perimeters of it worried her.

Hiding behind her menu, she lowered her head and closed her eyes at the sound of Ian's voice as she pushed Tehya to the back of her mind. So dark and rough. He was angry, she could tell. His voice roughened to a gravelly sound when he was angry. When he was aroused it was guttural. And once she had heard him chuckle, the sound like a coming storm at midnight. Rich and laced with sensuality.

Last night, his voice had been gravelly fury as he held her beneath him. Fury and arousal. The sensuality had been there, in his voice, in his dark eyes, in the brooding expression on his face. And the sound of it had struck her womb like an explosion of heat and light.

She let a little smile touch her lips at the thought of Ian's reaction to her arrival. In hindsight, she could look at it with amusement, though the night before, her sexual frustration had been less than amusing.

"That smile makes grown men's knees tremble in fear."

Kira's gaze jerked from the menu to Ian as he stood looking down at her. She tried to pretend surprise. She had felt him, had known he would end up speaking to her.

"Ian, what a surprise," she said softly, laying the menu on the table as she crossed her legs, braced her elbow on the table, rested her chin in her bent wrist and gave him a mischievous, flirty look.

"A surprise, huh?" He tucked his hands into the pockets of his slacks, causing the finely woven white cotton shirt he wore to ripple over his abs.

The shirt was a little loose, subtly shaping his broad shoulders and tight, leanly muscled body. His overly long dark blond hair was pulled to the nape of his neck, casting the harsh angles of his face into aching relief.

"Of course it's a surprise." She rounded her eyes and stared back at him as though his tone shocked her. "Do you think I'd stalk you?"

"Only if I gave you the chance." He didn't smile but he stared at her with hunger. A somber, dark hunger that had her stomach clenching in answering need.

"Would you like to join me?" She waved her hand to the three empty chairs. "My uncle should be here momentarily. I've chosen the most gorgeous little villa outside of town. A lovely white and red stucco with an outdoor pool and wraparound balcony. One side of the property is even bordered with a ten-foot handplaced stone fence."

His eyes narrowed on her. Of course she had picked the

villa next to Diego Fuentes's, and Ian's. Did he believe she
was going to make this easy for him?

His lips thinned as she smiled back with subtle satisfaction.

"No. But you can join me." He gripped her arm with the
pretense of helping her from her chair before pulling her
along with him into the reception room of the restaurant.
From there, he led her to a hallway at the far end of the
room and then to an unmarked door that he unlocked,
opened. He pushed her into the darkened room.

Kira found herself flat against the wall, the door slamming closed behind them, even as Ian's lips captured hers in
a kiss that curled her toenails.

This was what she needed.

Her arms wrapped around his broad shoulders as he
lifted her to him. Her breasts pressed against his chest, became swollen and sensitive, desperate for his touch.

When had she become so addicted to him? When had
his touch become the focal point of all her fantasies and
hungers?

Surely it had happened before Atlanta? One stolen night
of sexual frustration couldn't have developed over nearly a
year to this burning hunger? Or had it? Perhaps it was a
product of years of meeting him in the heart of danger, their
eyes connecting, knowing he knew who she was each time,
seeing the recognition in his gaze, in the slight tilt of his
head in acknowledgment. So many years of it. Meetings in
the dead of night, bullets blazing, nothing mattering but the
success of the mission and the lives at risk.

And each time, her fascination for him had grown.
Grown until she had researched him, tracked him, accepted
assignments that were almost guaranteed to be supported
by the team he fought with. Because he fascinated her. Because he had known her in all her disguises when no one
else had.

What else did he know about her?

He knew how to stroke his tongue against hers and fracture

her thoughts. How to grip her hips and pin them against the hard ridge of his cock, and how to make her long to ride it.

"What the hell are you still doing here?" he groaned as his lips slid from hers to nip at her jaw, then her collarbone. "I told you to get out of Aruba."

"Go with me," she panted, arching closer, holding him to her. "We could find a beach. Lots of sun and sand. Make love all day."

He stilled and she felt her breath hitch in agony. He was going to let her go again. She knew he was.

"Kira, you're killing me." He sighed against her shoulder a second before he tasted her skin with his tongue. "You're playing with fire, baby, and you know it. This is no place for you."

"I can help you." She didn't have a choice. If she hadn't taken the assignment, then it would have been given to someone else. Someone who couldn't have understood the rage he was going to feel when he learned Diego would walk free. She understood. She ached because of it, hated it, and something inside her refused to let him face that alone. She knew, *knew* what he was doing. And she knew why. She understood why. And she couldn't let him face the realizations and the betrayals alone. His head rolled against her shoulder. His lips pressed tightly to her neck. "You'll distract me. You'll get us both killed. I can't concentrate like this. Sorrell will pick me off like a duck in water. Is that what you want? God!"

He jerked away from her, the lights flipping on, blinding her for precious seconds as he moved away from her. To check the room.

She leaned against the wall and watched as he moved around the office, checked the closet, then dragged his fingers through his hair and faced off with her from the distance of the room.

His brows were lowered, his expression tormented.

"You're not leaving, are you?"

She lifted her shoulders, suddenly uncertain, wondering

if the attraction between them wasn't as strong for him as it was for her. She had counted on that. Counted on the fact that he ached for her just as much as she ached for him.

She was as fully trained as he was. If he could get under her skin so easily, surely she was under his as well.

"I won't leave."

"Why?" he bit out. "Why stay where you aren't wanted, Kira?"

Oh, that hurt. A lot. She crossed her arms over her breasts and narrowed her gaze at him, allowing it to flicker to his obvious erection. Her lips curved in a smug smile before her eyes lifted to his.

"I'm not wanted in any way, Ian?"

She hated pushing him. Hated being forced to hide the truth from him. But God help her, Diego Fuentes, and Ian if Diego learned the truth of why Ian was there now.

"How you're wanted doesn't matter," he informed her, his expression turning stony. "What you think you're doing does. You're poking your nose into something you have no business being involved with. Get out while you can."

It was too late to consider walking away. It had been too late the day she realized what Ian's mission was.

"I'm staying."

He breathed out almost wearily, frustration flickering across his expression as he stared back at her.

"Don't get in my way. Hurting you isn't something I want to do or to see happen. But mess with what I'm doing here, and you'll regret it."

He moved toward her, but not to touch her, only to jerk the door open and escort her from the room.

His bodyguards were waiting outside, and behind them stood her bodyguard, Daniel. The sight of them had a grin tugging at her lips. Five men, each wearing expressions of varying degrees of disapproval.

"Goodbye, Kira." Ian nodded to her as he closed the door behind them and moved toward his bodyguards. "I hope your visit in Aruba goes smoothly."

"I'm sure it will," she murmured, a smile touching her lips as she watched him walk away, his men surrounding him, protecting him.

"He's a hard man," Daniel reminded her as he drew close to her and they moved back to the dining area.

"Yes. He is," she agreed, smiling gracefully at a few of the diners she recognized and the waiter who hovered close in case he was needed.

She stopped momentarily to talk to Joseph Fitzhugh and his son Kenneth. The English-born industrialist and his son dabbled in politics occasionally and contributed heavily to several of the charities Kira was involved in.

Thankfully, she had never had to fend off Kenneth's advances, though he was always charming, almost sociable.

She returned to her chair, aware of Daniel taking his place once again at a table behind her and watching her as her uncle, Jason McClane, entered the dining room.

"Kira, sweetheart, the plane finally landed."

Jason stopped in front of the table, accepting the chair the waiter pulled out for him and lowering his massive body into it.

Six and a half feet of pure, powerful muscle and Kira imagined she heard the chair groaning under the burden.

Jason McClane wasn't a small man. He wasn't a subtle man. The Texas native and multinational business owner did everything on a very large scale. Except his work for the Department of Homeland Security.

He was her handler and, in turn, he had his own handler. The Chameleon was actually two people, herself and her uncle. Neither was officially listed with any law enforcement agency, but the information they brought in was invaluable.

"I hear you've chosen a place to play," he teased her, his gray-blue eyes sharp and knowing.

"The Villa de Angelic." She leaned forward as though overly excited over the purchase and the property. She was still trying to regain her equilibrium after being in Ian's

arms. "And you're going to love it, Uncle Jason. It's so me."
And so very close to Ian.

He chuckled at that. "I've learned to trust your taste,
sweetheart," he announced. "So have you ordered yet?"

"I was waiting for you." Her affection for him wasn't
feigned.

"And now I'm here. We'll enjoy our lunch and then
check out your Angelic Villa."

That evening, well after the sun had made its stunning
exit from the sky in a multihued splendor of brilliance, she
and her uncle smuggled her weapons into the newly leased
villa and stored them in the false bottom of the locking
cedar chest at the foot of the filmy-curtained king-sized
bed. But first they had made a complete sweep of the house
for electronic bugs.

Kira sighed wearily as she straightened, glanced at the
clock on the bedside table, and calculated her chances of
catching up with Ian that night at one of the clubs. Considering the amount of time it would take to get ready, they
weren't good.

"Daniel will be staying down the hall," Jason told her as
he stored the little electronic black wand used to detect the
listening devices into a secure section of the overnight bag
she kept by her bed.

"Will you be staying in Aruba?" Kira kept her voice soft
as she moved to the curtained balcony doors and looked out
toward the stone fence that surrounded the Fuentes estate.
She could see the upper floor of the villa, and if her source
was right, she was staring directly at the window to Ian's
bedroom. It was the single most important reason for the
acquisition of this particular property.

"I have to fly out day after tomorrow," he told her softly.
"I'll take one of the guest rooms and set up the security
while you go let yourself be seen tomorrow. I'd be interested to know which players we have gathering here."

"Too many if those I saw in the clubs last night were any
indication." She sighed, watching as the bedroom light in the

other villa flipped on then seconds later was dark again. "Ian has a bull's-eye on his back, Jase, and if I'm not mistaken several of the players based here believe America would give them a quiet nod of approval if they took him out."

"Ian made the decision himself," Jason pointed out, apparently satisfied that there was nothing compromising in the room, then moved to where she stood by the balcony doors.

"You're fascinated with him," he stated, stopping behind her to grip her shoulders and pull her back against him. She felt his lips at the top of her head and his steady affection surrounding her.

They were each other's rocks, and had been for twenty years now. Their shared past had shaped their shared present and all the choices that had brought him there.

"What would Daddy have thought of him?" she suddenly asked. She hadn't wondered in years what her parents would have thought of anything.

"He would have respected his strength," Jason answered simply. "But he would have worried about it as well. Your man isn't known for his tender ways where women are concerned, sweetie."

No, Ian was known for tying them down, torturing them with demanding caresses and warm spankings. He was known for his sexual demands and his determined lusts. He wasn't known for roses and champagne or poet's verses.

"I'm not exactly known for my tender ways where men are concerned either," she pointed out teasingly.

"No. You're not." There was an edge of sorrow in his voice. "Your father would have gutted me for drawing you into this life and your mother would have never forgiven me."

Kira leaned her head back against his chest and clasped his hands at her shoulders.

"Momma told me once that you were destined to do great things," she told him, remembering how much her tiny mother had adored her overgrown brother. "She loved you as fiercely as she loved me."

And her momma had been taken away from them both. Her momma, her daddy, and the woman her uncle had been engaged to. A terrorist's bomb had killed them while they were on vacation in Greece, though it had been speculated that the bomb had been meant for them. Her father had been as immersed in the covert life as she and Jason were.

"She would have been proud of us," she finally whispered, surprising herself with her introspection.

She had been doing that a lot these past months. Reflecting, thinking, considering the choices she had made, and her life in general.

She was thirty years old. She had a failed marriage behind her and no children. Her marriage to Kane Austin had been the first casualty of her secret life and covert activities.

She had no family but Jason, and so few true friends that at times the loneliness bore down on her.

And lovers? They didn't last long even when she did find time to get involved with a man. She was too intent on partying and playing. They didn't really know her, so they had no idea why the parties, the trips, and the shopping were so damned important.

No one really knew her. Except Jason. And Ian. That part of her that she hadn't even known herself, had only begun learning in the past year, ached with loneliness. Ached for the man who held himself just out of reach.

Ian knew her. Ian had done what no one else had, he had made it a point to learn about her. He knew about her parents, about Jason, but more importantly, he knew who and what she was. He had informed her, his voice filled with amusement the night he slipped into her condo, that he knew her as no one else ever would. And he was right. He knew how to touch her, how to make her heart and her body come alive. And he knew the woman she hid from the world.

Which could be a liability if she thought there were so much as a chance of his turning against the friend who lay so helpless in that damned clinic.

"Where do you go from here?" Jason kissed the top of her head before moving slowly away.

"For now, I wait a bit." She shrugged, turning back to him. "He'll show up."

"You seem certain." His gaze was piercing in the dark.

Kira hid her smile. "I am certain." He was growing as desperate for her as she was for him. She dreamed of nothing else, and sometimes, she thought of nothing else.

"I have a few contacts here," he told her. "Let me know if you need invitations."

"Dozens have already poured into the hotel," she reported. "The flies are converging like a plague."

Jason grimaced. "I was hoping to eat dinner tonight."

Kira widened her eyes innocently. "What did I say?"

"Trouble," he muttered. "That's all you are."

Kira rolled her eyes. She was growing tired of that accusation.

Six

IAN STOOD AT HIS BEDROOM window, the technologically advanced night-vision goggles sitting securely over his eyes as he stared at the bedroom window in the villa across from him.

He should have been ashamed of himself. Hell, he was using a set of military hardware that even soldiers in the field didn't have yet, to spy on a woman. He watched as Kira leaned her head back against Jason McClane's chest and lifted her hands to clasp the ones at her shoulders. The pose was entirely too intimate, too close. He felt anger twitch the muscle in his cheek as McClane kissed the top of her head and rubbed his cheek against her hair. He knew he wasn't the least impartial when it came to Kira, and possessive instincts he didn't know lived within him were now tightening at his gut.

He wanted to kill McClane for touching her, and that was a bad thing. As the two moved back from the balcony doors, Ian pulled the goggles free of his face and tucked them once again into the wall safe.

The villa the Eventeses had leased for the season had every amenity, right down to personal safes in each bedroom.

Pushing his fingers through his hair, he paced his darkened bedroom, feeling lust edging into desperation as he thought of her, possibly allowing another man to touch her.

He shook his head. He'd watched Kira and her uncle together before, and though there was a surfeit of affection, there seemed to be no sexual tension. But that assurance wasn't easing the tightening in his gut, or in his cock. He knew it wasn't even possible that she would do something like sleep with the bastard. He *knew* that in his head, but logic could never apply to how he reacted over Kira, especially when another man was around, no matter who that man might be. He wanted to be the only one who touched her.

He didn't even bother to jack off again. Masturbation wasn't helping. He knew this mood, or at least a weak facsimile of it. The tension invading him wouldn't ease until he fucked her. Until he fucked her until neither of them could breathe for the pleasure tearing through them.

So why was he waiting? She was over there, accessible to him, and it was more than apparent that she wasn't going anywhere.

But she was a woman.

Ian snorted at that thought. Oh yeah, she was a woman. She was all woman. And Ian couldn't push back the thought that it was his responsibility to protect her, to shelter her. He didn't want her involved in this mess, and yet she seemed determined to immerse herself in it.

So determined that no more than a few months after her own brush with death during that Atlanta assignment, she had been in Nathan's hospital bathroom, lying in wait, eavesdropping on their conversation.

A mocking grin shaped his lips. She had known his visit to Nathan had been arranged. She had said as much. She had guessed all along that this was an operation. But how much of that operation had she guessed?

And now, here she was, poking her nose into the most dangerous assignment he had ever undertaken, for whatever reason.

He needed to know that reason, he realized. He needed to know why she was here and what she wanted. And he needed one more taste of her. Just to see if she was as hot, as sweet, as mind-numbing as he remembered.

He needed his head examined was what he needed.

Ian grimaced as he threw himself into the cushioned chair in the sitting area of his room and stared broodingly at the window that looked out over her villa.

Propping his hand on the arm of the chair, he rubbed at his lips with his finger and glared at the window. That damned woman was nothing but trouble. She was going to make him crazy.

Going to? Hell, she already had made him crazy. He should be in his study going over the supply routes the cartel soldiers used to transport the drugs from the warehouses to the transport ships and cargo planes flying them out.

He had a million different details to see to. If Diego Fuentes had been decent enough to apply his genius to a legitimate business then he could have enjoyed a far healthier lifestyle. And perhaps Ian could have respected the man whose blood he shared.

And though he hated admitting it, Ian knew they were possibly too much alike. They were just on wrong sides of a war and the fine line between decency and immorality.

He had to deal with Fuentes and Sorrell, Ian told himself, he couldn't afford to worry about Kira in the mix. Pushing himself out of the chair, he stalked to the door of his bedroom suite and jerked it open, intent on doing the job he had set for himself that night.

The supply lines had to be changed and the product insured. Until he caught Sorrell, he had to show the bastard that the Fuentes cartel had the best supply lines, the best underground network, and most efficient men in the business. That was the reason Sorrell had pinpointed Fuentes to begin with. Because the cartel moved its drugs with the least amount of difficulty or interference.

Ian had caught on quickly after entering the business to how Diego and his father before him had set up the cartel's vast network. They didn't just have drugs going into every nation of the world, but they transported weapons, information, and a vast array of other illegal products. Pirated software and music, clothing and accessories. Even, at odd times, criminal figures looking for escape.

The cartel had it all, except terrorism. Diego Fuentes had never allowed himself to be infected with the fanatical beliefs that drove such men. He'd supply them with arms; after all, according to Diego, that was business. But he would not allow the network he had worked a lifetime to build to be threatened by the infiltration of terrorism.

At least he had a line in the sand, Ian thought mockingly. He could infect babies with drugs, murder his own people, make whores out of runaways, and kidnap helpless young women, but he wasn't a terrorist.

Breathing out roughly at the thought, he flicked his fingers at his bodyguards—Deke, Mendez, Cristo, and Trevor—and headed to the study.

The four men had been working on suggestions for the new supply routes as well as security for the warehouses and transportation.

He stood in the middle of the study as the others entered. Cristo, shorter than the others but no less dangerous, closed the heavy door as Trevor Mandrake moved to the safe in the wall, coded in the combination, and pulled free a hand-sized electronic box and flipped it on.

Trevor moved around the room, watching the digital and analog displays before giving Ian a short nod that everything was okay.

The first three months he had been with Diego, he'd had to sweep his study as well as his bedroom each time he entered it. The son of a bitch had been determined to spy on him. They would fight over it, agree that Diego wouldn't spy on him, then Ian would find more bugs. Diego had finally begun realizing the futility of it in the last few months.

"We haven't found a bug in a while," Deke said. "The old man giving up?"

Ian shot him a chiding look. Diego Fuentes didn't give up, he just waited until a person was suitably comfortable.

"The villa next door was leased today," Trevor announced, moving to the desk as Ian sat down in the sinfully soft leather and stared across the gleaming cherry top. "Kira Porter and her uncle Jason McClane moved in this evening. I did some preliminary background checks. They're coming up clean."

Trevor powered up his laptop, coded in the security passes, and brought up the file he had pulled together on Kira Porter. It was amazingly in-depth.

Ian leaned back in his chair and stared at the file Trevor was currently scrolling through. There was nothing about her work as an unofficial agent for the DHS, and nothing in there concerning her code name, Chameleon.

"This woman is no one to fuck with," Trevor said, his voice unaccountably serious. "She has a black belt in Tae Kwon Do, training in heavy weapons and hand-to-hand combat. Her cousin managed to buy her a six-month training session with a team of off-duty SEALs ten years ago. She goes back for four weeks once a year to renew that training. Her bodyguard, Daniel Calloway, is one of the original SEAL team members that trained her. They train almost daily from what I understand. And the few times anyone attempted to kidnap McClane's darling niece, they turned up dead within weeks. He doesn't take prisoners, he makes examples."

"Makes sense to train her," Deke mused. "McClane is protective of her. She's the only family he has left."

"Enough about Ms. Porter." Ian leaned forward and hit the command key, closing the file Trevor had been scrolling through. "She's an interesting event in our otherwise dull lives, I realize, but we have our own business to conduct." He flicked his fingers from the laptop to Trevor, an indication to use the equipment for the reasons they were there

rather than going over information that, as far as they were
concerned, had nothing to do with the business at hand.

"Okay, delivery routes and points of transport." Trevor
pulled up the satellite map on the laptop. "Here's the current routes." He highlighted the mountain passes and broken roads that led to several makeshift airfields and
shipping ports. "We've had reports that Sorrell has men
watching two of those routes, here and here." Trevor
pointed out the routes into the U.S. "This could be the line
he's wanting to use to transport the explosives and men for
the strike rumored to be in progress against America."

"He's escalating against us to grab those lines," Cristo
Mendez pointed out. "Not that I give a damn what happens to a few hundred U.S. soldier boys, but if they grab
those lines then that mess is gonna slap back on us," he
growled.

"Let's move the lines for now," Ian suggested. "See what
he goes after when we switch. The lines as they are lead
into California and then Nevada, and the second one has a
lead into Annapolis. Let's see how we can reroute them
while still making it appear we're unaware of his spies. I
want to know what this bastard intends to use the Fuentes
lines for."

Ian listened to the others' suggestions, watching the
computer screen as Trevor and then Deke laid out the new
supply routes and calculated the risk factors.

There were no hidden roads anymore, satellite recon had
canceled those out. Now, the major job was to keep the
product en route, get it to its location and do so with the
least amount of bloodshed. Because the various agencies
weren't going to make it easy on him. As far as they were
concerned, he was a traitor now. A SEAL gone bad, and
they were out to fuck him. They had no idea of the danger
America was facing if Sorrell managed to grab the Fuentes
power hold.

But Kira knew the truth, and Ian needed to know exactly
what she intended to do with that truth.

Seven

KIRA KNEW IAN WOULD COME to her. How she knew, she wasn't even going to guess; when it came to the things she knew about Ian, her perception worried her. The things they seemed to sense about each other was almost terrifying.

Kira hadn't even known the woman that resided within herself. She had been the Chameleon for so long, that when Ian awoke that emotional, sexual part of her last year, she hadn't known what to do with herself, or how to handle it.

She was learning though, and if she had to learn, then he could learn with her. He couldn't convince her he wasn't working an operation here. She knew better. As he knew her in all her guises, she knew him as well. And she was waiting on him.

The security her bodyguard Daniel and her uncle Jason had laid along the perimeter hadn't included the stone fence between the two villas. She wanted that clear. She wanted a straight, easy path for her bad boy SEAL to get to her.

Traitor, he was called. The order that had gone out from the law enforcement agencies worldwide was capture only. They wanted information; they wanted to crucify him in public for his defection to the other side. They wanted to make an example of him.

He had excellent security; she had to give him that. The four men he had gathered around him were considered the best killers in the Fuentes cartel. Or in the world. They were hard, jaded, cynical, and paranoid. And they knew no fear. They were also die-hard Fuentes soldiers and completely loyal to Diego.

There were already three confirmed attempts to kidnap the reigning Fuentes heir. And two attempted assassinations. Ian had already lost a previous team of security personnel that Diego Fuentes had placed around him.

As she lay back, propped up on her pillows in her huge bed, holding one of the steamy romance novels she invariably got off on, she watched the figure that stepped through the open balcony doors.

His dark blond hair was loose, framing his quiet expression. The tobacco-brown eyes were lit with an inner fire that burned inside her as well.

He was restraining himself. She could see it in the tension of his shoulders, the determination in his expression.

She laid the book on the bedside table, though she did nothing to cover the black boxer-type panties and matching tank she wore.

She hadn't dressed to seduce. She'd be damned if she would allow him the excuse that she had enticed his hard-won control. Besides, seduction wasn't on her agenda. There were no lies between them, they both knew why he was there, they both knew the hunger rising between them wouldn't be denied for long.

"You're not leaving, are you?" He was a straightforward kind of guy. She liked that. And his voice assured her that he wasn't accepting excuses this time.

Ian stood at the foot of the bed, one hand gripping the heavy post beside him as he stared at her with banked fury.

"No."

The curse that sizzled from his lips told her that wasn't an answer he wanted to hear.

He stared around the room then, before pulling a small

electronic box from the pocket of his slacks and flipping a switch on it.

Kira came to her knees in the middle of the bed, excitement lancing through her body.

"It's the new model?" She knew the wand Jason had used, for all its technological advancements, was nothing compared to what he held in his hand.

He flicked her a dubious glare. "Down, girl. You're not getting it."

Kira pouted as she placed her hands on her hips and watched him impatiently.

"You could at least let me look at it."

"Not on your life. I'd never get it back." He left the device on as he set it on the dresser across from the bed.

Kira stared at it, fascinated by the little blinking lights on the monitor, dying to get her hands on it. She was a freak for security electronics, and the so-far rumor-only Type X electronic detector made her salivate. It detected not just analog or digital listening devices, but also hyperbolic equipment trained in the vicinity as well as GPS technology.

She dragged her gaze from the fascinating little toy and back to the mesmerizing man.

"I don't need your help." He stood at the foot of the bed once again, tension humming through his body.

"There's a price on your head," she informed him. "It might be for capture only, but that doesn't make you safe."

"I'm aware of the price and the fact that it's rising daily," he told her softly. "I want you to leave, Kira. When this is over, I'll find you . . ."

"If you're still alive to do so?" She moved from the bed, pacing to the small table across from her and the bottle of wine and glasses set out there. "I'm not willing to wait."

"I can have you pulled off this," he told her then.

She had known he would play that little ace he thought he had.

She poured two glasses of wine before turning and moving to him. He accepted the glass, still frowning at her, his brows lowered broodingly.

"I have carte blanche, being a contract agent and all." Kira kept her voice to a mere breath. "You can't pull me off anything, Ian."

Frustration gleamed in his eyes. Kira sipped her wine, returned to the bed to stretch out on it and lean back into the mound of pillows.

He still held his wine loosely, close to his thigh, staring at her, working through this new complication, as well as the obvious arousal straining his slacks.

The white cotton shirt he wore outside his pants hung nearly to his thighs, the ultrasoft material giving him a relaxed though sophisticated appearance.

"Would you like to discuss it?" she finally asked, bringing her glass back to her lips.

"Your security is slipping," he informed her then. "We have the information on your training and your SEAL instructors."

"Of course you do. So do all the bad guys." Amusement curled through her. "A knowledge of strength is the best deterrent when it comes to those believing they can slip in on me. If you checked my past out at all, you'd know I'm heavily into deterring problems."

And being prepared.

He brought the wine to his lips, sipped, then turned and walked back to the sideboard where he placed the delicate glass beside the bottle. When he turned back to her, Kira glimpsed the barely restrained dominance eating at him. His control was shaky, as shaky as her own. Especially when his gaze slid to her breasts where her tight, hard nipples pressed into the thin tank top.

"Do you get off on fucking traitors?" he asked her then. "I wonder if your boss knows about that?"

Kira rolled her eyes. "You're not a traitor, Ian."

"You can't know that for sure, can you, Kira?"

She let a knowing smile shape her lips. "If that were true,

you would have already attempted to kill me, not protect me. Forget the protection stuff, okay, lover? It doesn't work with me."

She tightened her thighs, an instinctive attempt to hold back the moisture collecting there. She was so wet, so hot, that she knew if he touched her that an orgasm would be imminent. And if she didn't get off this time, then she was going to shoot him herself.

"What does work with you?" His gaze flicked over her body again. He knew she was aroused, knew she was aching.

"It's according to what you want."

"You. Out of Aruba," he snapped.

Kira sighed with amused indulgence and almost laughed at the male frustration that flashed in his eyes. "It's not going to happen. Do you have any other desires that you'd like to pass by me?" Her gaze flicked to his thighs then back again as her brow arched in mocking curiosity.

It wasn't a subtle hint, but she and Ian had passed subtle the first time he had slipped into her condo in Atlanta nearly a year before.

"This is fucking insane." His voice changed, became harsher, more grating as his fingers went to the buttons of his shirt.

Kira tensed. Sudden, almost violent arousal poured through her body, speeding her heart to the point that it nearly strangled her as she fought for breath.

The buttons were loosened slowly with the fingers of one hand, revealing a wide, muscular chest covered with a mat of short, silky-looking black hair. Not too thick, but not thin, just enough to rasp a woman's nipples, cushion or warm them. Her nipples throbbed at the thought.

"Then why are you here?" She could feel the perspiration building between her breasts, moisture gathering more thickly between her thighs.

Rising, she came to her knees once again, watching, mouth watering, as he shed the shirt, shrugging it from his broad, well-sculpted shoulders with a ripple of power that echoed in her womb.

"I'm here because I'm crazy," he murmured, his legs shifting as he pushed the shoes from his feet while loosening the slender leather belt and the catch of the cool cotton slacks he wore. The zipper eased down.

Kira's lips parted, her breasts rising and falling furiously as she fought for oxygen. The air was indolent with lust now, thick, heavy, nearly impossible to breathe.

"Are you just playing again?" she whispered, suddenly desperate to know. "Please, Ian, don't play with me. Not this time."

"No games tonight, Kira. Not from either of us," he growled. "And so help me, I better get the woman rather than the agent, or you'll pay hell for it."

The slacks cleared his thighs, revealing the thick, heavy length of his erection. It was furiously engorged, the mushroomed crest flushed dark and throbbing, a glimmer of pre-cum glistening erotically.

"You always get the woman, Ian."

She licked her lips, easing closer, on hands and knees now, starving for a taste, just a taste of the rich male essence tempting her.

"You're as fucking crazy as I am," he snarled, reaching out, gripping the thick strands of her hair and pulling her back to her knees.

Dominant, powerful. It was there in his face, it raged in his eyes.

"I want to taste," she moaned, drugged now on the power, the hunger radiating in his gaze, and the arousal-based adrenaline pumping through her veins.

There were erogenous zones where she didn't know there were erogenous zones. Hell, every damned cell in her body was erogenous at the moment.

"Me first." The other warm arm wrapped around her hips, jerking her to him as his wants, by right of might, became uppermost.

As his head lowered, hers snapped forward, her teeth nipping at his lower lip before his fingers pulled her back. The sharp little burn of pulling hair had a shaky groan whimpering from her throat. She loved it. Needed it. She wasn't submitting. Fuck submission. He might be an alpha male, but by God, she was his match.

Her hands lifted, her nails raking over his chest as his gaze pinned hers. Her lips parted, teeth clenching, as she drew in a ragged breath.

He didn't flinch from her nails. Instead, his lips curled into a sexual, sensual smile of acknowledgment as the reddish-brown lights in his eyes fired to a darker, burning hue.

She loved it. There was no male irritation because she wasn't simpering at his feet. And there was no submission in his gaze either. Just pure, blazing hot, male hunger and challenge.

"I don't give in," he told her, that raspy tone sending shivers down her spine.

"Neither do I." She let her fingers play in the silky hairs that grew low on his abdomen.

"I'm stronger," he promised her.

She smoothed her palms up his stomach, his chest.

"I sure hope so," she crooned as she captured a hard male nipple against her thumb, and pressed, just enough. "Oh Ian, I definitely hope so."

His lips slammed over hers as his hands gripped the hem of her top and jerked it over her breasts. He released her lips, just long enough to wrestle her out of the material as she tried to capture his kiss again. She needed the taste and heat of it. The incredible feel of his lips moving over hers, dominating hers despite the sensual struggle she put up.

She wanted to control the kiss, and that was what she fought for. He was determined to control the kiss, and the right of might definitely held sway here. Especially when his arms surrounded her, his head bending, forcing hers against his powerful bicep as he licked and sucked and drove his tongue against hers until she was quivering. Hell, she never quivered for sex. But she was quivering for Ian. Shaking and trembling, her pussy clenching, her breasts throbbing, and imperative, desperate little mewls of pleasure tearing from her throat.

She spread her fingers through his hair and arched closer, rasping her nipples over the luscious mat of hair that covered his chest as his cock slid between her thighs, pressing into the material of her panties, driving her crazy with the need for more.

He pulled her head back, pulling at her hair as the fiery sensation streaked from her head to her nipples, then to her clit. She had never liked having her hair pulled until Ian. Until he showed her the pleasure and the pain, the agony and the ecstasy of being in his arms.

"Just this time," he groaned, his lips moving down her neck. "I'm going to fuck you until you're out of my system. Gone. Out of my head." His tongue licked over her collarbone. "Over."

"In your dreams." Her head tipped back as pleasure suffused her. "Oh God, Ian. In your dreams."

Pleasure like this didn't just go away. It tortured and tormented after the act, she could feel it, knew it, even though the pleasure itself was so new even to her. The jaded Domme, the feminine sexual dominant that demanded submission from her males. She was no novice to sex play, or to sexual games. But she was a novice to this pleasure, to the sensations rippling through her and holding her spellbound in Ian's arms.

As his lips surrounded the hard peak of a nipple, her lips went to his neck. Teeth raking, tongue licking, her hands stroking over as much of his flesh as she could reach.

Hard muscle rippled beneath her touch as the heat and suckling pleasure of his mouth threatened to dissolve her. He held her close to him, arms surrounding her, as though he would never let her go. And she didn't want him to let her go. She wanted him to hold her forever.

"Not enough," he growled, moving, flipping her back on

the bed before she could do more than gasp, and jerking the boxer-type panties from her thighs and over her feet before she could fight.

She moved to twist away from him, to attack him with her own passion, her own needs. Before she could roll from him, his hands pulled her thighs apart, his wide shoulders wedging between them and his lips descending to the bare, saturated folds of her pussy.

Kira froze. She couldn't help it. Hell, it wasn't like a man had never gone down on her before; they had. She wasn't a virgin. She was experienced. Until Ian got his lips in the slick, bare flesh between her thighs. Suddenly, she didn't know what the hell to do.

Because he didn't touch her like an unfamiliar lover. He touched her like he knew her. Knew what she wanted. Knew what she needed. Knew that the sudden hard thrust of his tongue into her pussy would freeze her with delirious pleasure.

"Ian?" She stared down her body, watching as his lashes lifted and he stared back at her with slumberous, hungry eyes.

He licked. A long, slow swipe of his tongue that sent a ripple of white-hot sensation racing across her flesh. Especially when he reached her clit, flickered over it, then bestowed a firm, heated kiss to it.

"You don't like it?" He lifted his head enough to whisper the words, blowing a soft breath over the too-sensitive nub of nerve endings.

She stared into the heavy, brooding gaze. What was she supposed to say? Was she supposed to answer him?

"Stop talking and keep licking," she gasped, her hand pressing his head lower, his lips back to her waiting flesh.

He chuckled, but he licked. Oh God, how he licked. And sipped, and scraped his teeth over the swollen folds until she was writhing. Writhing and desperate because it wasn't enough.

She tried to twist, to throw her leg over his head and rise

to her knees, to sit on that handsome face, that thrusting tongue. So she could get his cock in her mouth. She was dying to taste that wicked hard flesh, to tongue the precum from the tiny slit at the top.

"Stay still." His hand landed on her butt as she arched again.

"You didn't!" she gasped. He had smacked her?

Okay, so it didn't hurt, it was actually kind of sexy. But only submissives got spanked. She was not a submissive.

"Stay still or I'm tying you to the bed."

"Like hell." Her heels dug into the bed as she struggled from beneath him.

She assured herself that she couldn't have expected what came next. The way he used her momentum against her, flipped her to her stomach, then tied one hand with the long, thin gauze that fell down the post of the headboard.

Tied her wrist, quick as you please, as he straddled her back and held her into place. In the next second, her other wrist was similarly bound with the filmy curtain on the other post.

"Ian, you bastard!" she cried out hoarsely, almost laughing, unable to believe how quickly he had managed to restrain her. And he had restrained her effectively, wrapping the material around the posts close to the mattress so she couldn't pull herself up.

"Now, let's see if you can't be a good girl and let me have my treat," he growled at her ear. "Be very thankful, Kira, that this night is all that matters. Otherwise, I'd show you exactly how I would control that hot little body of yours."

Within a second he was pushing her knees into the bed, raising her hips and stretching out on his back. Sort of the position she wanted, except it was the wrong way.

"This is so wrong," she said, panting as she felt his broad hands cup and palm the cheeks of her ass.

Then he spanked her again. Light little taps, sharp ones, heated heavy caresses as his tongue plunged into her pussy and had her writhing into the caress.

"Untie me." Her voice was strangled, the imperative need for orgasm rising hard and fast inside her. "I want to touch you too. Taste you."

"Not on your life." He nipped at the swollen curve of one labial fold. A soft, gentle little bite that had her jerking in painful pleasure. Damn him, that shouldn't feel so good. It shouldn't feel exquisite. She shouldn't be enjoying weakness, she should be fighting for strength. For control.

But oh, it was so good. Her hips pressed down, driving his tongue deeper, feeling him *lick*. Sweet mercy, his tongue was curling inside her, dragging over the so-sensitive nerves there, and making her pant, making her beg for release.

"Ian, I swear, I'm going to make you pay," she cried, feeling perspiration coat her body as he shifted, his tongue retreated, only to curl around her clit.

He played there. Sucking the little button into his mouth, rolling it over his tongue, kissing it deep and hot. He blew against it, he moaned against it, and then he licked around it, next to it, close to it, but never enough. Never enough.

"Please . . . oh please, Ian, don't let me lose it." She was so close. So close she knew she was going to lose it. That she was going to be pushed to the point that it fizzled and left her with a violent ache that couldn't be satisfied.

Not again. Oh God, she couldn't bear it if Ian did that to her. If he brought her so close, only to push her past the point where she could come at all.

Her body was weird. Her sexuality was weird. It would kill her. She couldn't handle it.

"Ian, it's been years." She twisted in her bonds. "Oh God, it's been so long. Please. Don't let me lose this. I have to come. Please, Ian."

She was desperate. He kept licking around it, building it higher. She could only go so high, then, *phfft*, it was just over. A violent ache that lasted for days and no relief. She would kill. She swore she'd shoot him with his own gun.

Then two fingers slid into her pussy. Not just slid in,

thrust in, filled her, fucked into her with deep, hard strokes as his mouth covered her clit, sucking and licking, *right there.*

She screamed into the pillow. She bucked and jerked, twisted and exploded with such force she swore she felt her mind dissolve. It was exploding, melting, heat was lashing at it and disintegrating it, as the most deliriously violent orgasm of her life ripped through her.

She was dying. She had never known why the French called it the "little death" until now. She was dying. Done in by the most exquisite orgasm in her sexual history, or so she thought.

Before she managed to come down, before the first agonizing shudders had finished with her, Ian, diabolical lover that he was, pushed her higher.

He slid from beneath her, his fingers retreating. A second later the iron-hard length of his cock was tunneling inside the gripping, spasming muscles of her pussy with hard, heavy thrusts.

Gripping the material of the curtains that bound her hands, Kira pulled herself up, her muscles tightening through her body as she tried to breathe. Just one good breath as the first orgasm continued to tremble through her body even as he lengthened it and built the next.

The feel of his thick erection working inside her as his hands gripped her hips, held her in place with dominant force, was her undoing. She had never been a submissive, either sexually or in life, but oh God, she could definitely see the benefits at this moment.

"Ian . . ."

"I'm here, Kira." His voice was so rough, guttural as he moved heavily behind her. "I have you, darlin'. I won't let go."

One hand cupped a breast, his fingers working her nipple as the other moved between her thighs, playing her clit with just the right amount of pressure.

It was violently sensitive, but he knew how to touch, how

to stroke. Just as he knew how to fuck her. He didn't go easy on her. He made pleasure and pain combine, thrusting hard and deep inside her, flesh slapping together, their moans mingling.

She couldn't bear this. Kira wasn't certain when she realized the line she had just crossed, when she realized that pleasure and emotion were comingling. She knew she couldn't bear it. She knew it was too much, too soon. She wasn't ready for this.

She tightened in his arms, fighting to pull back, to hold on to that measure of control. She shifted, mind and body, pulled on her training, on what she had become. She would give him the illusion she gave everyone else.

"Oh, no you don't." He bit her shoulder. Bit her. Again. "Do you think it's that easy? That I'll let you draw back now? By God, I won't take the Chameleon. I'll have the woman."

"Please." She shook her head, her upper body falling back to the bed, leaving her rear up, her pussy open to him as he pounded inside her. "Ian. I'm . . ." She was what? Scared? Lost? "Please . . ."

"I have you, Kira." He came over her, his voice thick now as the sensations began to build to cataclysmic levels. She heard the restraint in him though, and ached for it. Heard the regret that shadowed the dominance she knew he was capable of displaying. "I'm right here. Just come for me, baby. Give it to me. Give it all to me."

She was helpless. Bound, both physically and mentally, and she knew it. She was lost.

When the second orgasm came, she didn't bother fighting it. She screamed, crashed, jerked in his arms, and felt the muscles of her pussy clench violently on the suddenly throbbing length of his cock.

He had thought to use a condom? At least he had a brain. She could hear his release in his shattered groan, in the jerky thrusts, the throb of his erection, but she didn't feel the wetness of his semen.

For a wild moment, she regretted that. Wanted it. For one impossible, insane moment, Kira wanted things she knew she should have never considered. Had never considered before in her life. She wanted more than just the sex. And she wanted more than the restraint that tightened his body despite his release.

She wanted all of him. She wanted to defy that hard-won control that held him back, that kept a tight rein on the obvious hungers he was denying himself. She wanted to challenge him and feel him meeting her head-on.

She wasn't a submissive, but a part of her was dying to submit. To meet his dominance head-on, to push at the boundaries he had set, and to weave herself as firmly around his soul as she knew he was weaving around hers.

Eight

IAN RELEASED KIRA SLOWLY FROM the filmy lengths of material that hung along the side of the bed. The thin panel he had used bound her wrists, holding her body in place for him, something he doubted Kira had tried often.

He ran his hand along her back, clenched his teeth and merely caressed the rounded globes of her rear rather than watching them blush, hearing her scream as she found more pleasure in an erotic spanking than she could imagine, and feeling her come apart as she found the threshold between that pleasure and pain.

There were so many ways he wanted to touch her, fuck her. So many things he could do to her body that would leave her shaking, gasping his name, immersed in a pleasure he knew she had never reached before.

She was a strong woman, there was no doubt. But he knew her strength and he knew the hungers that even she didn't understand herself. And he knew that sexual, independent creature inside her was dying to defy the dominance he kept tightly leashed.

She was collapsed beneath him now, on her stomach, her head buried in the pillow as she fought for breath.

Ian straightened the filmy panels then rose and discarded

the condom he wore before stretching out beside her in the bed.

A dumb move, he told himself as he pulled her into his arms and held her against his chest. A really dumb move, because she felt so right. She felt as though she belonged against his chest and in his arms. She fit him, and damn if that knowledge didn't rock his soul all over again.

"We have reports that Sorrell is becoming irritated with your defiance of him," she said as one hand smoothed over his chest. "You're encouraging the smaller cartels to defy him as well. He'll strike against you soon."

"I'm not discussing Sorrell with you, Kira." Ian stared at the ceiling through the diaphanous material that stretched across the canopy frame above. "I'm not discussing any of this with you."

"I'm here to help you, Ian." Irritation colored her voice as she lifted her head to stare back at him. "I have my own sources I can work. You're fighting a very dangerous man. Don't throw away an opportunity to gain any advantage you can."

"You being the advantage?" He let his hand smooth over the fall of hair that caressed his chest now. Her hair was softer than silk and warm enough to comfort a man on a cold winter night.

"I'm a hell of an asset." There was no ego there, it was simply the truth and Ian knew it. She was a hell of an asset.

"This is my fight." And he didn't want her anywhere close to the danger he knew was coming. "I'll take care of Sorrell."

He would identify him, and if he couldn't kill him then he would walk away and allow others to do it. Either way, when the game was up, he didn't want Kira anywhere close to the violence that would ensue.

"I want you on a plane out of here, this week," he told her then, meeting her gaze as he allowed the tips of his fingers to caress the gentle curve of her cheek. "Go back to the States and forget about this."

Her smile was a soft curve of sorrow. "Do you really think I'm going to do that? I've found in the last months that I would do a lot for you, Ian. But I won't do that."

"That isn't your fight."

"I've made it my fight."

Where in the hell had she developed all this stubbornness? She was the most intractable woman he had ever met. She didn't argue, she didn't scream or yell. She stated intentions and then followed through. He knew that. Besides what he had learned of her in Atlanta, his investigation into her had yielded the proof of it.

"I won't come back here," he told her then. "Tonight won't exist after dawn arrives, and it won't happen again."

She shook her head, causing her hair to ripple over the muscles of his chest and his taut abdomen.

"It may not. I hear you're a man of your word. But I'm not leaving Aruba until I finish what I came to do."

"Which is?" Frustration colored his voice. "What the hell do you think you can accomplish here?"

"I can watch your back and gather the information you need from the sources you can't access as the Fuentes heir. That's my mission and I won't leave until this is over. You can make my job easy, or you can make it hard. It's your choice." She lowered her head as she spoke, allowing her lips to caress his shoulder, her fingers to knead the bunched muscles of his biceps.

Ian continued to stare at the ceiling, frowning, trying to distance himself from emotion and to use the only weapons he had on hand for the perilous operation he was conducting. He had the smallest team they could put together; hell, it was so small he didn't have a hope if the Fuentes soldiers didn't follow him against Sorrell. That was his strength, the loyalty the cartel possessed. It went beyond money, to familial affiliations. Diego was related to the better part of his generals. His generals were related to their lieutenants and their lieutenants were related to the soldiers. It was a circle that continued on and on.

There might be a few spies, a few speaking from both sides of their mouths, but they all agreed. Terrorism made it hard on the drug trade. Terrorist fanatics made it even harder to sell drugs. Ergo, don't let the French terrorist in on the business.

Some of the smaller cartels were too weak to fight the pressure Sorrell brought to bear, but the larger cartels opposing him were now doing what Ian had begun eight months ago. Absorbing those smaller operations with the promise of protection.

This wasn't a game, and there was a hell of a lot more to it than drawing in information. If Kira aligned herself with him, then for the first time in her own career, she would no longer be giving the appearance of a neutral party. She would be compromising herself. And that begged the question, why?

For ten years she had worked as an undercover independent operative for various agencies. First the Federal Bureau of Investigation, and then the Department of Homeland Security. Why risk herself and her supposed neutrality now?

As Jason McClane's niece, and a stockholder in the various companies and properties he owned around the world, Kira was known as his "source." One of the few people he relied upon when it came to investing in certain businesses. He was well known for working in the hot spots of the world, for turning a profit out of humanitarian aid by building contacts. And Kira was well known in those hot spots. It was one of the ways she gathered her information on insurgencies, the movers and shakers involved in those conflicts, and where they might be going. And in certain instances, disguised and dangerous, she was known as the Chameleon. Able to blend into her surroundings to gather information that had nothing to do with McClane or his various businesses.

He'd seen her as a blonde, a redhead, and a brunette over the years. She could use makeup like a weapon, changing her features so drastically that the true persona of Kira Porter wasn't even recognizable. Unless you followed body movements rather than faces, which few people did. The shift of a hip, a particular gleam in the eye that had nothing to do with color, the soft curve of an ear unique to one woman, or perhaps just an underlying scent. Or maybe it was just one woman's effect on a particular man and his ability to recognize it. Because in each instance he had become harder than iron and so damned aroused he was nearly panting when he saw her. No matter her persona.

Durango team, the unit he had fought with for the past five years, had run several ops based on information provided by the Chameleon. In each instance she had been on the inside of the op and present when it went down. And each time, Ian had recognized her, though the team had never been given her identity. Hell, he'd even taken her prisoner once when the team had been sent in to rescue an American diplomat being held in South America.

She poked her nose into places too damned dangerous for his peace of mind, he was beginning to realize.

"I'm certain my ceiling is perfectly interesting," she said sarcastically. "I was attempting a discussion here."

Ian looked down to where she rested on his chest. The irritation in her gray eyes brought a smile to his face. Damn, he should be running as fast as possible from her.

"I don't need your help, Kira. You'd help me more by leaving."

There was no doubt he was going to have to stay away from her.

"I think you're well aware that's not going to happen," she gritted out. "Do you think you're the only one who has a stake in identifying and capturing that bastard? Sorry, Ian, no-go. It's just as important to me."

Of course it was. One of Sorrell's militant groups had claimed responsibility for the blast that killed her family and Jason McClane's fiancée twenty years before.

"You can't let this get personal, Kira," he told her

somberly, aware of the irony behind his statement. "And this is no place to try to fight what's between us, as well as the job at hand. It risks both our lives."

"I don't believe that. What we have between us makes success that much more important. It will make working together easier."

"For you maybe." He brushed her hair back from her face, wondering at the almost innocent quality in her face. She had an air of purity, of life, that never failed to amaze him. Or to challenge him. She had no idea what she was asking for when she asked to share his bed.

"For you as well." A frown tugged at her brow as her gray eyes darkened.

Ian shook his head. "I'd be too concerned with protecting you, watching out for you, than I would be on the danger. I can't afford that distraction. I can't afford the cost to my soul if you were killed here." He was a chauvinist. He had never pretended to be otherwise. When a woman was anywhere in the vicinity working an op, a part of him was always looking out for her. Women were strong, no doubt. Resourceful and intelligent. But the primal male inside him still insisted that they were to be protected.

"It's my risk to take," she informed him. There was no anger in her tone, only strength, purpose. She was a force to be reckoned with, his head knew that. She was an experienced operative. But his heart, right there below his head, clenched in fear at the danger she could be in.

She was his to protect. The only way to protect her was to get her out of the game.

"We're not going to agree on this, Kira," he finally said. "Let's enjoy what we have of the night, because you are not a part of this mission."

Before she could protest further he pulled her lips to his, catching them in a kiss as soft as sunrise and as hot as lava. That was what she was. Sunlight and heat, and for just a few more hours, he needed that heat. He needed Kira in ways even he didn't understand. And that scared the hell out of him. She softened a part of him that he had never believed would soften. His determination to always remain detached was like ashes in the wind with her.

But she came to him, like a pure fresh breeze pushing out the stench of evil he lived with. Her lips moved on his, heated silk, her hands flowing over him like pure passion.

This time, he let her have her way. He lay back and watched and let her touch and her passion flow into him. Let himself enjoy the sheer rapture of her touch.

This wasn't the time to assert his own control. His own dominance. He wanted her to carry away the knowledge that he could be gentle, that he could touch her with tenderness. Because once the sun rose, he would once again be a product of the world he lived within.

What was it about her? As her lips moved over his, her tongue tempting him, teasing him, as he let his hands coast over her back, that thought slid through his brain.

What was it about Kira that made her touch so special? Her sighs worth so much more than any others he had ever caused? And it only made him ache more for the screams of pleasure he knew he could draw from her.

He didn't know why, and as her sharp little teeth nipped at his lower lip, at that moment, he didn't care. His hands bunched in her hair, rubbing the strands against his palms as she kissed her way down his body and his cock rose to full strength in welcome.

Hot lips moved over his chest. Her tongue licked and played with the hard flat nipples there, the sigh of her breath over them causing him to stretch beneath her in pleasure.

Sharp nails scraped down his abdomen, sending pinpoints of wicked sensation to attack his balls. And he touched her. Caressed her back, her shoulders, cupped her head in his hands and groaned in hunger as her lips reached his abdomen.

Sex had always been one of his greatest pleasures. Sex with Kira could become addictive though.

"I've been dying to taste you," she whispered as she

moved between his thighs, her hands wrapping around the length of his shaft firmly, enclosing him in soft heat as he felt his heart racing.

"It's all yours," he murmured, the sound of his own voice surprising him. It was gravelly at the best of times, but the roughness to it now went beyond that.

Emotion always made it deeper. He didn't want to look into the emotions she raised inside him. He couldn't do that, not yet.

But he could let the pleasure wash over him, and when her damp, wicked mouth surrounded the head of his dick he didn't have a choice.

"Damn. That's good, Kira. So good." It was like liquid hot ecstasy. Her mouth surrounding his flesh, hot and wet, without a condom, each sensation raking over sensitive nerve endings and cording his muscles with tension.

The sight of her consuming his cock was enough to blow his mind, assuming he had any mind left after that earlier orgasm.

Which he didn't. Because when her mouth tightened on the head of his cock and her tongue flicked over it, he latched his fingers in her hair and held her there. Right there. Where her tongue flicked over the sensitive under-crest and sent shards of sharp sensation racing through his shaft straight to his tightened balls.

"Your mouth should be licensed," he groaned. "It's damned wicked."

The fingers of one hand stroked the shaft as the other moved to the tight sac of his scrotum. There, her nails scraped and played and had his teeth clenching at the lust overwhelming him.

Ian let her have him. All of him. He pushed the danger to the back of his mind, the operation and the evil he faced on a daily basis, to relish her touch.

"So good," he whispered as she sucked at the head of his cock, forcing him to tighten, to hold back. "I love your mouth. Your touch."

A moan rippled over the tight flesh.

His lashes lifted to stare down his body at her.

Her face was flushed with passion, her eyes darkening, swirls of gray and blue-gray color intermingling in a storm that mesmerized him.

She pulled back, let him watch her tongue curl around one side of the wide crest and watched a small drop of precum form on the head of his cock. Kira smiled a sultry smile, and when her tongue raked over it, drawing the little drops inside her mouth, he ground his head into the mattress to keep from releasing then and there.

"Come here." His hands slid to her shoulders, urging her to him. "Ride me. Let me feel that sweet, hot little pussy taking me again. Just one more time."

He reached to the bedside table, fumbling for one of the condoms that he had left there.

Kira took care of that quickly. Within seconds she had the hard length of his erection sheathed and was throwing one leg over his hips, coming down to him, letting him watch.

Damn her. She moved slowly, letting him watch as the engorged crest parted bare, slick folds and began to disappear inside the hot depths of her pussy. An inch at a time, rising and lowering to take more, until with a groan, he was seated fully inside her.

He stared up at her, his hands moving to cup her breasts, flick her nipples before they moved to her back and drew her down. He wanted as much of her as he could get. Every touch, every taste, every sigh.

He watched her breath hitch as he fought just to breathe himself, feeling the snug grip of her sex stroking him, milking with exquisite tendrils of pleasure. Taking him places he swore he had never been before with a woman. And when her lips touched his, the last fragile bonds to control were erased. One hand clasped her hip, the other the back of her head, holding her to him as he began to thrust, meeting each downward stroke of her pussy with a powerful lunge.

He snarled against her lips, because it was too damned good. Because walking away from this was going to fucking kill him.

He rolled with her, trapping her beneath his plunging hips, and felt her legs wrap around his back. Her hands were in his hair, on his back, scratching, holding to him as he fought to hold back, to force her to hold back.

He wanted to talk. Wanted to tell her how perfect she was, how hot, how exquisite. But he couldn't. Not yet. Because electricity was sizzling from his balls, up his spine, and centering in his brain. Lust was tearing through him, adrenaline spiking, and they were both coming.

He buried his head in shoulder, shaking from the hard, fierce jets of release that felt more like glowing bursts of rapture.

He wrapped his arms around her, desperate to hold on to her. Just for a little while longer. Then he would let her go. Just a little while longer . . .

Nine

As dawn neared, and the darkness outside began to lighten, Ian slipped from Kira's bed and found the clothing he had discarded earlier that night.

He finished dressing, slipped back onto the balcony, and dropped over the side of the rail to the ground below. Crouched by the wayaca tree that had given him the boost to the balcony that he had needed the night before, Ian narrowed his gaze, staring around the garden that separated him from the stone fence on the other side.

Confident he wasn't being observed, he made his way quickly through the flowering shrubs, bougainvilleas, and various trees until he reached the ten-foot stone fence. Once again using one of the many wayaca trees spread around the property, he made his way to the top to the divider and dropped into the Fuentes grounds once again.

From there, it was only a short distance to the villa. Diego's night guards didn't notice his passing, and the dogs the guards used never flinched at his scent. He was a part of the grounds, nothing to get excited about, so they did nothing to warn the guards of his presence as he climbed to the balcony outside his bedroom and let himself back inside.

As he closed the glass doors behind him, Deke rose from

his reclining position on the couch in the sitting area of the room and stretched stiffly.

"You said an hour." The other man reminded him irritably of the amount of time he had been gone.

Ian let his lips quirk at the querulous tone. "I had the cell phone on me, you could have called if you needed me."

Deke snorted at that one, his eyes narrowing on Ian then. "Man, you look like you been rode hard." There was a note of envy in the bodyguard's voice. "Bastard. Hope you enjoyed it enough for the both of us."

Ian almost chuckled. Deke's lover, an American law graduate, was waiting patiently at home while he played in the criminal element, both of them surviving on the impromptu, secretive visits the other man managed to make every few months. Sometimes, only a few times a year.

Yeah, he had enjoyed the night enough for four men, and still he was far from satisfied.

"You gonna try for a few hours' shut-eye before the day begins? I can take up watch in the main room."

Ian shook his head. "Did you manage some sleep?"

"A few hours." Deke nodded.

"Go catch a few more," Ian instructed him. "I'm going to shower and take care of a few things before we meet later. We have that meeting with Radacchio and his three sons later this afternoon. I'll catch a nap on the way there and then on the return."

"Yeah, good ole Radacchio called daddy dearest just after you left. That meeting might not be so important, because Diego informed him in rather bloody terms of the fact that the Fuentes cartel will no longer require their services."

Ian grimaced and shook his head. He should have known Diego wouldn't leave it alone. Hell, a part of him had known. Diego had ruled with a bloody hand, and he saw no reason to do things differently now that Ian was stepping into the cartel. For some reason, he thought he could make Ian enjoy the killing, the drug wars, and the blood lust that fueled them.

"I'll take care of Diego before we leave." He sighed. "Be ready to roll by nine. I want to be in place and I want the meeting site secured before we enter. I don't put betrayal past Valence Radacchio any more than I put it past any of Diego's other business associates but I want to hear what he has to say about that last attempted hijacking."

Deke touched his fingers to his forehead in agreement and farewell before slipping from the bedroom, then the adjoining sitting room. Left in the dark alone, Ian stared around the bedroom, his eyes narrowed, as he considered the spy Sorrell had on the estate now.

He'd received proof of the transfer of information before leaving the night before. Not that she had been able to take much to her contact. Ian didn't keep Diego in the loop for the most part, knowing his habit of discussing everything that passed by him with Saul. Diego was careful, he was smart, but one of Sorrell's spies had slipped by him.

Shaking his head, Ian headed for the shower. He needed to clear the scent of Kira from his head so he could think and move on with his own plans. No doubt, he was going to have to find a way to get rid of her now. The past night had proved his weakness to her. He would never be able to stay out of her bed knowing she was so close.

And it wouldn't take long for someone to catch on to the affair and to betray it to Sorrell or one of the other cartel enemies. Hell, even to Diego, which would be just as bad. He knew his dear old pop. The minute he learned Ian had a lover, a woman who meant more than a one-night stand, then he would start plotting, conspiring. Because nothing mattered more to Diego than learning a weakness; he had a need to exploit. And Ian was smart enough to know just how easily he could be manipulated if Kira were in danger.

He had realized that somewhere around the time he had looked down and seen his cock spearing between her lips, seen the hunger in her eyes, and the need glowing in her face. Or maybe about the time she had stopped fighting him, stopped fighting the control he stole from her and let him enforce his own.

TWO HOURS LATER, IAN STALKED into the servants' quarters on the first floor of the villa, his foot landing squarely on the locked door of Liss Dannear's bedroom door and splintering it from the hinges.

With Deke behind him, he moved slowly into the room, his eyes narrowed on the two women now cowering on the bed.

"Surprise, surprise." His smile was tight, hard, as he looked from Liss to Eleanor. "My, my, ladies, been up to fun and games, have you?" It seemed the known and the suspected information leaks were keeping more intimate company than Ian had guessed.

Eleanor's kittenish features were twisted into shock and dismay, while Liss lowered her eyes quickly, but not before Ian glimpsed the anger that filled them.

He stared at them coldly, aware of Deke and the others spreading out around him, the automatic rifles they carried held confidently in their arms.

"El Patrón, it . . . it is not as it seems," Eleanor gasped, her dark brown eyes widened in distress as Liss cowered against her naked body.

Their bodies quivered, breasts bare, as the women made no attempt to cover themselves. The obvious signs of recent sex lingered on their thighs, on the reddened discoloration of their nipples, and the dampness of the sheets beneath them.

"Oh, I think it's very much as it seems." He jerked a wooden chair forward, straddled it, and braced his forearms on the back. And then he smiled at them. A triumphant, knowing smile.

Eleanor pulled the sheet toward them.

"Leave the sheet alone." His hardened voice rasped through the silence that had been broken only by Eleanor's gasping breaths.

"El Patrón Fuentes does not mind how we find our pleasure." Liss suddenly had the temerity to speak up. She tried to simulate fear, but there was too much triumph, too much anger in her for her to carry it off.

"Liss, you forget who rules the roost here. That rooster has done cocked his last crow, so to speak, as far as decisions in this house are concerned, are we clear?"

She licked her full, wide lips as she flicked a glance around the room, obviously judging the threat. And coming up with death.

"Ian, it is so small a transgression," Eleanor whispered then, her limpid gaze imploring. "It was just a bit of consolation."

"Your sex games or preferences don't concern me, Eleanor," he assured her with an easy smile. It was a smile she didn't seem to find much comfort in. "Your association with Liss and, shall we say, cartel enemies does concern me."

He was watching Eleanor directly, though he caught the flash of fear in Liss's gaze with his peripheral vision. Poor Eleanor, she wasn't the liar she wanted to believe she was. Guilt marked her chocolate-brown gaze as surely as the forceful touch of Liss's lips on her breast had marked the taut mound.

"I do not know."

"Don't lie to me, Eleanor." He reached his hand out to Deke. Four pictures were placed in it, prints taken from the digital camera that had marked Eleanor and Liss's trip to the market the day before.

The two women were photographed speaking with a known Sorrell contact, Ernesto Cruz, then accepting two less than thin plain envelopes. Liss, greedy little bitch, had opened hers and fanned through the bills there.

He tossed the pictures to the bed where the women stared at them in rapt horror.

"I'm going to assume you gave them the only piece of information you could have acquired. The meeting with Radacchio that you believed was taking place late last night?" Liss stared back at him furiously, not bothering to hold her rage in, as Ian continued. "Ernesto's friends didn't find Radacchio at that meeting. They found a small army instead. His friends were returned to Ernesto in pieces this morning." The women paled, terror rounding their eyes even as Ian felt rage scour his soul.

Sorrell had sent the best he could acquire on short notice. Two of Ian's men had died, but Sorrell's men hadn't lived to take another breath.

It didn't matter that they were all criminals of varying degrees, murderers dozens of times over, each and every one of them, all in the name of the mighty coca and the almighty dollar.

"I lost two men last night, Eleanor," he said softly. "Two of my best. I'm not happy over that."

Her lips trembled as she quivered, fear paling her dark face and dampening her eyes.

"Ian, there was supposed to be no one hurt." Her breath hitched with panic. "They promised—"

"Are you a fool, Eleanor?" he snapped. "Look at Liss. Look at her." Eleanor's gaze shot to Liss's defiant face. "She thought Sorrell would triumph. That I'd die in the bloodbath her boss arranged."

"No, Ian," she cried.

He whipped the Glock from the inside of his jacket, the barrel aimed at Liss's head. For a moment, he had the satisfaction of her fear, but just for a moment.

"You won't kill us," she said quietly, confidently. "You do not kill women, do you, Señor Fuentes? You are not El Patrón. Only El Patrón understands this world. You are but a braying little burro—"

A weapon exploded, tearing into her skull, splattering the back of her head onto Eleanor and the wall behind her as she was flung backward.

The weapon had no sooner discharged than Ian was ducking and rolling, coming up, the gun braced in his hand and centered on the chest of the man who stood in the doorway.

Diego Fuentes. Ian's finger clenched, the need to tighten, to fire, nearly overwhelming his control. He could get away with it. He could kill the bastard and swear it was an accident. His superiors wouldn't question it, and he could still go after Sorrell. It would be so easy.

Diego's black eyes met his, knowledge in the curve of his lips as he lowered the gun. His pristine white silk shirt contrasted with his swarthy skin, the stiffly pressed black trousers and obscenely expensive loafers untouched by the blood he had just spilled.

"They are not women, they are traitors. Traitors die," he spat.

"So what does that make me, old man?" Ian suddenly snarled, coming to his feet as fury coursed through him. "I betrayed my country for you. What makes you think I won't betray you as well?"

"Blood is stronger than country," Diego said. "My blood in your veins. My heart pumping inside you, a part of me forever bonded with you because you are my son. Dispose of those whores and wipe them from your mind. No one betrays what is mine, and by all that is holy you are my son."

Eleanor was sobbing now, her body protected by his own as he stood between her and Diego.

"We agreed this operation would be handled my way!" Ian bit out, coldly furious. "You don't kill without my permission."

"As though I would ever receive it," Diego spat back. "You will throw her carcass into the streets and that whore she slept with will take back to her diseased owner my answer to his quest. 'Get fucked, Sorrell.'"

Good God, have mercy. Ian wanted to put his fist in the man's stupid mouth and shut him the hell up. Or a bullet in his black heart and stop this charade for good.

"Get the fuck out of here," he snarled. "Now."

"So you can bargain with her?" Diego sneered. "You

bargain with your enemies as though they were business associates whose word you can trust. You are the fool."

"And you're as dead as she is if you don't get the fuck out of here!" Ian's voice lowered dangerously as the need to silence the bastard raged inside him. "I'll deal with you later."

Diego smiled mockingly. "But you will not kill me, and still Liss is dead. My answer to the bastard that would strike my son. Eleanor can give it to him herself." Then he turned and strode from the room.

Ian turned to look at Eleanor. She had stopped sobbing and now stared at Liss's cooling body in horror.

"Ernesto will have me killed," she whispered, pulling her gaze to Ian. "I only helped Liss, as she asked me to do. So we would have the money to leave Aruba and to return home to Colombia. Enough money to help feed our families . . ." Her voice trailed away as she reached out a trembling hand to touch Liss's slack face.

The scent of blood and death filled the room now, wiping away the sweet scent of sex and fear.

"Deke, get her on a plane," Ian told him quietly. "I want her safe." He wiped his hand over his face, suddenly aching as he stared at the mess Diego had made of Liss.

Ian had had no intention of hurting her. Frightening her, yes, convincing her to give him information, definitely. But God help him, he would never have hurt her.

"Should we have her interrogated?" Deke's voice was just as quiet.

"On the plane." Ian nodded. "I want her flying out of here to a safe house within the hour."

The Cessna waited on a private airfield outside Palm Beach, just in case it was needed, the pilot on twenty-four-hour call.

"Come on, Eleanor." Deke wrapped his arms around her and helped her from the bed. "Let's get you dressed. Get you out of here."

She stared at Ian, shell-shocked, desperate. "Don't kill me, Ian, please." Tears fell down her cheeks as her reddened lips trembled. "I am so sorry." She held on to Deke's arms as though terrified Ian would jerk her from the suddenly gentle embrace.

"I'm not going to kill you, Eleanor. Go with Deke. Let him take care of you." Ian's gaze moved back to Liss. "Have Liss buried. Quietly. Get this taken care of." He turned and stared at Liss's blank expression. "Son of a bitch, some days it doesn't pay me to wake up in the morning."

"You'd have to sleep first, boss," Deke murmured as he helped Eleanor dress.

"Shut the fuck up, Deke," Ian snarled.

He left the room, his gun still clasped in his hand, and headed through the villa to the one place where he knew he could find Diego at this time of the day. Nothing turned that bastard off his food. The son of a bitch could murder a woman and sit down to breakfast as though he were royalty five minutes later. And that was exactly where he was. At the breakfast table, a cup of coffee and a plate of fruits and sweets in front of him, his assistant Saul sitting across from him.

Before Ian realized his intentions, his hands were on the older man's silk shirt, clenching the fabric in his hands as he jerked Diego from his chair and threw him against the wall.

Shocked, wide black eyes met Ian's, then narrowed in fury. But no anger Diego could have been feeling could possibly come close to the rage building in Ian's gut now. The remembered sight of Liss, slumped back, her brains splattered on the wall behind her, sickening him.

"Ever. Ever. Fuck me over that way again, and I walk. Do you understand me?" He was in Diego's face, nose to nose, a killing rage pumping through him.

"She betrayed me," Diego snarled.

"You stupid fucking bastard, she had information," Ian rasped, murderous fury burning in his gut. "Information I needed. Do you understand me?" He threw his father away from him, his fists clenching, the need to do something, anything, raging through him. Damn Diego. Liss had been a fucking child. An easy-to-use, impressionable, filled-with-anger young woman who didn't know shit about this world. And Diego had just killed her. Without a second thought. Without questions.

"Fuck it," he muttered. "I'm out of here."

"You would leave Sorrell to destroy us all?" Diego moved to place himself in front of Ian, his expression knowing, cold. "What of all your justice and belief in freedom," he sneered. "I move to defend you and you whine over blood spilled. What will you do when Sorrell achieves his objective to strike at your precious country?"

Ice was forming in Ian's soul now. This man, this fucking monster, was his father. A man who had just killed a fucking nineteen-year-old girl as though she were a diseased animal rather than a beautiful, vibrant young woman.

And he couldn't walk away. No matter how much he wanted to, no matter how badly he wanted away from the blood and death, he couldn't walk away. Not yet.

Ian clenched his teeth. His fingers tightened on the grip of the gun as a grimace contorted his features. "Stay the fuck out of this, Diego. Stay out. Or I walk."

He moved away from Diego, stalking out of the breakfast room.

Deke moved into the foyer, his expression somber as he gave Ian a short nod. Ian breathed in a heavy breath. Eleanor was in safe hands and being escorted to the plane by the same hands that would bury Liss's body. The only other agent Ian had been able to get into the Fuentes home would take care of her.

Stepping into the bright sunlight, Ian drew in a deep, cleansing breath, and swung his gaze to Kira's villa. God, he wished he had stayed in the bed with her. Wished he were wrapped around her lithe, softly scented body, holding her warmth close to him. And it was the worst thing he could wish for. He was the most dangerous thing she could have right now. And she was the one thing he couldn't allow himself.

DIEGO BREATHED A SIGH OF relief as the doors slammed behind Ian, leaving him and Saul alone in the breakfast room, the ramifications of his actions slamming into his brain.

He turned to Saul, his fists clenching, his muscles trembling, from the fear and fury inside his soul.

"A mistake," he whispered. "That was a horrible mistake I made."

"You must think first, Diego." Saul's face was pale as well. "You walk a very fine line with your son. Our rules that we see as so simple are not so simple to him."

Diego wiped his hand over his face and slumped in his chair once more, the food before him suddenly unappetizing.

"He would not have done it," he whispered. "My son, he would not have eliminated that threat."

"And had we heeded his warnings about the servants, then it would not have been necessary," Saul reminded him gently.

"I will make it up to him." He pushed his fingers through his hair, his chest aching, his heart heavy as he remembered the pure, unadulterated hatred that had glowed in his son's eyes. "How can I make this up to him, Saul?"

"Follow his wishes." Saul was shaken as well. "We will do as he says, yes, Diego?"

Diego stared back at him, agonized when a sad smile suddenly shaped his lips.

"Do you know, Diego, who your boy reminds me of?"

He shook his head, uncertain about the flash of affection in Saul's eyes. That old man cared for few people.

"Your father," he said gently. "A young, proud, hot-blooded Aquiles Fuentes. This is who he reminds me of."

Diego blinked at his father's old friend and tilted his head thoughtfully. Yes, he thought, a smile of remembrance creasing his face. Like his father, Aquiles. This was who Ian reminded him of as well. A strong, proud man. A warrior, an innovator. That was his son. Yes, perhaps Saul was right; for now at least, they would follow Ian's directions.

Ten

SHE NEEDED HIM.

A week later Kira admitted to the real reason why she had followed Ian to Aruba, why she had decided to stick her admittedly curious nose into his business, and it was why she was ignoring his piercing gaze seven days later as she sat in one of the open lounge sections of the Fuentes club, Coronado's.

The club was one of the most popular on the island, filled with tourists and regulars, hard-driving music, and undercurrents of the shadowy world that existed within the center of the popular gathering spot. It was a hotbed of illegal practices and shady deals and Kira was sitting smack in the middle of Sorrell symathizers posing as Fuentes contacts.

Being here had nothing to do with protecting the DHS interests in keeping Diego Fuentes alive and upholding their agreement to allow him to escape capture and prosecution. She was here because of Ian. Because of what he made her feel, made her hunger for.

She flicked a look beneath her lashes in Ian's direction. She could feel his fury even across the distance of the booths separating them.

Of course, the fact that she was sitting with two of his

own suppliers couldn't be comfortable for him. Or the fact that for the last few days, several of Sorrell's contacts had made a point to inform her that they knew of her association with the Fuentes cartel heir.

Sorrell knew she was aligned with Ian, and it appeared he believed the McClane heir could become an asset he could use.

"Kira, it was a surprise to see you here after your accident last year." Martin Missern, the beach boy weapons broker, smiled his most charming smile as icy blue eyes flicked over her bare legs revealed by the bronze stretch silk dress she wore. His gaze then lifted to the now barely noticeable scar close to her shoulder which was revealed by the thin strap that held her dress over her breasts. He and his brother had joined her without invitation based on an introduction made more than a year before.

The bullet she had taken in Atlanta last year in her role as the friend of a senator's daughter had nearly taken her life. Thankfully, Ian's and her uncle Jason's quick responses had saved her. A premier plastic surgeon had removed the unsightful scarring later.

"I was rather surprised myself to be moving so freely," Kira admitted with a smile. "But Jason has several business interests here that required my presence. And Daniel looks after me."

Daniel was presently hovering over her like a warning specter from behind her seat. He took his duties as body-guard very seriously.

"I saw you conversing with Ian Fuentes last week." Martin finally broached the subject Kira had felt coming for the past half hour. "You are good friends, yes?" His smooth French accent did nothing to fool her. Charming he might well be, rather like a cobra, just waiting for the right moment to strike.

"We're acquaintances," she admitted. "We met in Atlanta last year."

"Ah yes, you are dear friends with Senator Stanton's

daughter." Martin nodded as though that point of information were important. "He was a SEAL at that time, was he not?"

"I believe he may have been." She arched a brow inquisitively. "Though it appears he isn't one any longer."

A smile shaped the weapons broker's full, sensual lips.

"This is true." He nodded. "He has shaped up his father's cartel excellently in the past months. He's giving many of the other cartels a run for their money, quite literally."

Kira let a sneer shape her lips. "The advantages of knowing how the enemy works, perhaps?" she pointed out, referring to the fact that it was widely known that Ian had worked several missions involving drug and weapons trafficking.

"Ah yes." Martin smiled. "This was an excellent advantage. Would it be safe then to say that you are not friends? Perhaps friendly enemies?"

"Perhaps." The smile that shaped her lips was deliberately mysterious. "Why do you care, Martin? The last I heard your import-export business had nothing to do with the cartels. The Fuentes cartel shouldn't concern you." The Misserns' very legal, very profitable business was no more than a front for their weapons cargos.

"Ah, but the Fuentes cartel affects many of us," Martin's twin, Josef, pointed out from beside his brother. "It is a well-known fact that Ian Fuentes is shifting his home base from Colombia to Aruba, or perhaps even one of the smaller islands. He wishes to avoid the American and Colombian authorities, yes?"

"Well, he is a deserter. And a drug lord," she pointed out. "I would guess he'd have to be rather careful. SEALs tend to get a little irked when one of their own turn dirty."

She was talking the talk, walking the walk, but something inside her felt as though it were splintering. She knew better. Ian was dodging former friends as well as the criminals salivating to see him taken down. He was treading water so deadly, so dangerous, that she wondered how he would escape the consequences. Or even if he could.

He was going it alone, on his own, attempting to identify

and eliminate a terrorist that no one had been able to identify in nearly twenty years of investigations and missions to do just that.

But Ian was in a position no one had ever been in. He owned the cartel Sorrell needed to gain access into the United States. The Fuentes operation had, over the years, managed to create a secure underground operation to move its drugs and people through the United States, into Canada and Mexico.

Two generations of master chess players. Diego Fuentes and his father had begun what Ian was now strengthening. Even the drug enforcement agencies were scratching their heads over how he was managing to bypass their security, their snitches, and their determination to catch him.

Martin Missern glanced past her then, his smile turning smug before he moved the hand resting on the back of the leather booth and brushed a long lock of her black hair over her shoulder, once again revealing the cleavage that the deep cut of her dress left bare.

Kira's gaze flicked to his hand, then back to his eyes.

"Touch me again, Martin, and you might have a stub where that hand used to be," she warned as Daniel's shadow fell over him, causing Martin's bodyguards to tense as well.

Martin flicked his hand at the goons posing as security and flashed her a rare smile of amusement.

"Fuentes is watching you very carefully, little one," he said. "Are you certain there is not more than mere friendship that binds you? I have not seen our friend over there so upset over a woman in all the years I have known him."

And there were a lot of years to back that up. Ian and Martin had clashed more than once, and several times the drug runner had come against the SEAL team Ian had worked with.

"Perhaps it's indigestion." She shrugged, refusing to glance back at Ian again. "I'm not here to discuss Ian's problems, I'm here to enjoy a few drinks. You're interfering in that."

A small frown flitted around his brow. "So inhospitable?" he asked. "You confuse me, *ma petite*. The niece of one of the world's richest men, and you resort to lowering yourself to a traitor and drug cartel owner? How can this be? Surely your tastes are more refined?"

Kira folded her hands in her lap and watched him silently, archly, for long moments.

"Daniel, could you have the valet bring our car around now." She directed her response to her bodyguard. "Mr. Missern is beginning to bore me." She moved to slide from the booth.

"*Non, non,* you must not leave yet." Martin's hand snapped out, as though to grip her wrist to stop her. A dominant, forceful move backed by enough strength to break her wrist if he wasn't careful.

Missern was a termite. A shifty little maggot known for manhandling his women.

Before his fingers could wrap around her flesh she had two of his fingers in her hold, pressing back, shocking him into stilling and watching her with narrow-eyed silence.

"You know the rules, Martin," she reminded him softly. "Don't touch me, and I won't touch you." He flinched as she exerted just enough pressure to assure him she could dislocate the digits before he could make a move for her.

"Kira, little love." Josef, Martin's twin, grinned at the exchange. "Release Martin now. He will be a good boy, will you not, Martin?"

Martin's lip curled as she released him, his brow twitching disdainfully as he glared at her.

"Martin's temper is growing more testy Josef," she pointed out. "Are you certain he's had all his shots?"

"Why, you little bitch." Martin wasn't one to take insults lightly from a woman.

Distantly, Kira knew what was coming. She saw the shift of his body, the flash of his hand, and knew there was no way to stop the blow. Even Daniel wasn't that fast.

But someone else was. A breath away from her cheek,

Martin's hand stopped abruptly, and Kira was dragged around the booth, sliding on the smooth leather of the seat as Daniel bounded over the back and landed where she had been sitting.

His weapon was in his hand, his expression furious as he stared at the Misserns. Both men had lifted their hands in a gesture of surrender, though triumph filled their faces.

"Get her the fuck out of here!" Ian's voice snapped at her ear as he pushed her at Daniel. "Now!"

Turning, blazing with fury, she faced a demon she couldn't have expected and a small crowd of bouncers as they moved in to shelter the altercation. Yep, Coronado's at its finest. They didn't care who killed or who died, as long as the customers were shielded from actually witnessing who did the killing.

"Take your hands off me!" She jerked her arm from his grip. "And go to hell. I don't need you or anyone else rescuing me."

Hard hands gripped her upper arms, jerking her close, as his head lowered, his nose nearly touching hers, anger flowing from him like waves of heat.

"Don't push me, Kira," he bit out. "You won't like the consequences."

"Push you, Mr. Fuentes?" she questioned him vehemently. "I have no intention of doing anything so crass. But if you don't let me go you're going to lose a fine set of balls."

"How very interesting," Josef called out gleefully. "Have you met your match, Fuentes? The drug lord and the society princess. Now, who would have guessed at such a match?"

She saw the second Ian realized the mistake he had made in defending her, just as she realized how carefully Martin Missern had played this little debacle. It was well known that Kira did not tolerate men touching her without her permission, and he had deliberately touched her at every chance once he and his brother had joined her in the curved booth.

He had touched and pushed, and taken the opportunity to force Ian to show his hand. Because of something he had heard, something he had been paid to instigate? Or because someone knew something more?

Ian's head lifted, and when he stared back at Martin, his voice was cold, deadly. "We have a meeting tomorrow," he reminded the other man.

"We do," Martin answered smugly.

"Let your brother handle it. If I see you again, I'll put a bullet between your eyes. Do you understand me?"

"You will deal with me or you will not purchase the supplies you need." Martin laughed. "Come now, Ian, why allow a little society tramp such as this one to affect business?"

Pure murder burned in Ian's eyes then. Kira tensed at the icy fire, her heart racing in fear now.

"Consider that meeting canceled," Ian said softly. "You're not the only supplier. And you won't be alive long enough to provide anything I need."

Tightening his hand on her arm, he began dragging Kira through the crowd, ruthlessly ignoring her struggles and her curses.

She glanced over her shoulder at Daniel as he covered the rear, keeping his gaze carefully on the Missern brothers who had stood and now watched their departure, their expressions a mix of anger and concern.

"Hummer's waiting at the door, boss," Deke announced as he and another bodyguard cleared the way through the dance floor.

"Trevor, you and Cristo ride with her bodyguard. We'll meet at the villa."

"Which villa?" one of those other bodyguards called back.

"Mine!"

"Like hell," Kira protested loudly. Not that he seemed to be listening to her. "You can take me to my villa or let go of me now."

He ignored her, of course.

Stumbling, she fought to tear herself out of his grip, only to feel the world tip and sway. A second later she was fighting the knowledge that Ian had thrown her over his shoulder like a sack of damned potatoes. At least he had the presence of mind to wrap his arm around her thighs and hopefully hide the fact that she wasn't wearing panties tonight.

"You bastard!" She tried to ram her elbow into his kidney, only to earn a hard, burning slap to her ass.

Oh no. He hadn't just smacked her butt. He wouldn't dare.

"I'll kill you myself," she screamed, trying to deliver another blow, only to earn another burning caress as they passed the exit.

She hated him. She hated him. She was going to kill him herself. Oh God, just as soon as she fucked him. Just as soon as the burning, tearing arousal echoing from those slaps eased just enough for her to figure out *how* to kill him.

"Get in there." An instant later she was bouncing on another leather seat. That of the extended Hummer, whose posh limolike facing seats, separated from the front driver's area, were a testament to the amount of money the Fuentes cartel had to burn.

Anger and arousal surged through her blood as she jumped for him. A week of aching pain, too many nightmares, and too many fears converged. The vehicle door slammed behind him as her fists struck his chest. His hands gripped her wrists, his larger body slammed her back to the seat, and within a second his lips were on hers, his body covering hers, his hands stroking, his knee parting her thighs, his groan meeting her moans as lust exploded between them.

She wasn't lost any more. It was her first thought as his lips ground into hers and he anchored her body against his. She wasn't lost, she wasn't reaching, she wasn't trying to fill the sudden emptiness inside her any longer. Ian was filling it. He was her match. The one man she couldn't defeat. The other half of her soul.

Her fingers curled as she strained against the grip he had on her. Her hips arched, pressing her sex tighter against the silk slacks he wore, loving the feel of his knee pressing into her.

His lips were devouring hers. Lips, teeth, tongue, he made good use of them all. He nipped and licked, stroked and consumed her. He fired responses in her that she didn't know she possessed, didn't know she could feel.

She was the female equivalent of his dominant force. She should be trying to claw his eyes out, not riding his knee with lusty hunger. And she sure as hell shouldn't be creaming so hard that the bare flesh of her pussy was dampening his slacks.

"Son of a bitch!" His head jerked up. "You're not wearing fucking panties."

He shifted back, his eyes focusing between her thighs, where the hem of her dress had ridden to the top of her legs.

"Panty lines," she mumbled, lifting to him again, arching against the hold he still had on her wrists.

His gaze jerked back to hers, his whisky eyes burning with hidden flames as his hair fell over his face, giving him a sensual, warriorlike appearance.

"Panty lines?" He blinked back at her.

"The dress is tight, Ian," she groaned. "The lines of the panties would have shown through it. Now would you please shut up and just kiss me again?"

Just one more of those openmouthed, "steal her soul" kisses and she might be able to save her sanity at a later date.

"You're not supposed to be here." His free hand followed the deep cut of the bodice of her dress, one finger burrowing beneath the material before dragging it over one hard, spiked nipple.

His nostrils flared. Lust raged in his eyes and in his expression, sparking a burning flame in her womb and whipping it to a conflagration of heat.

She could feel perspiration gathering on her face and beneath her breasts, dampening her but doing nothing to still the heat burning inside her.

"I'm not supposed to be anywhere else," she moaned as his thumb and forefinger gripped the hard point, tugging at it, tightening on it as the pressure of his grip sent wild fingers of sensation tearing across her nerve endings. "Let me go, Ian, let me touch you."

She was desperate to touch him. Had she ever needed to touch a man as desperately as she needed to touch him? She knew she hadn't. Knew that arousal and hunger had never been so fierce, so wicked.

Almost as fierce and wicked as the dark eyes trained on her breasts. They weren't young perky breasts. Not like the women who had surrounded him earlier in the club. Her breasts were full, swollen now with need, her nipples tight and hard, begging for his attention.

"I dream of this." His voice vibrated with dark desires. "Seeing you restrained beneath me, your body begging for my touch. Is that what you really want, Kira? Don't you know what you're risking here?"

She was certain if she stopped to think about it, then she would be terrified.

"What am I risking, Ian?" she whispered instead. "Or are you the one scared of the risk? Afraid that tough, hard heart of yours might be affected this time?"

His pupils dilated, his expression tightening as his brows lowered broodingly.

"I want you." The statement wasn't what she expected. "All of you."

"I need you," he repeated, glaring down at her, his body tense and fierce.

"I'm yours." She was panting? Hell, now she was panting. She wanted him with a hunger and a desperation she knew she had no hope of controlling.

His thumb and forefinger tightened on her nipple, sending

a flash of erotic heat clashing through her system. "I want you beneath me or safely behind me, no matter what. You're driving me crazy putting yourself in danger."

She couldn't help the grin that tugged at her lips.

"No." She couldn't give him that. She wouldn't give him that. "Do you want me, Ian, or one of the mindless little submissives you've been fucking for years? If it's the latter you want, then you'll have to find it somewhere else."

She refused to be less than who she was with him. Not just a lover, but a partner. For so many years she had hidden who she was, always playing a role, always aware of the mission, whichever mission it might be. This time, she couldn't play a role. Not in his arms. Not with her heart.

She watched the gathering ire in his expression, felt the tension that raged in his body. But his touch never crossed the line between pleasure and pain.

"You think this is a game with me," he stated, his rough voice grating now. "Damn you, Kira. I can't think for the need to touch you, to hold you. To protect you." His fingers left her nipple but his head lowered, his tongue swiping over the now tender tip. He nipped the sensitive flesh, causing a shocked moan to leave her throat as pleasure washed through her system.

"I protect myself." Her voice was weak, too weak, as she felt his fingers at her thigh, felt his knee move back only to have his hand cup her sex. Grind against it. The heel of his palm rasping over her clit deliciously. "God, Ian, when will you realize we're together in this?"

Oh God, she could come so easily, from that touch alone. She stared back at him, dazed, on fire for him. All she wanted was the pleasure she had found in his arms before. The erotic high that came from an orgasm she had only found with him.

"You're mine while you're here. Period," he snarled. "I won't tolerate another man touching you or you will disappear, Kira, until this is over. Somewhere where you'll have no chance to escape. No chance to endanger yourself or what I'm doing here. Is this understood?"

The erotic high fizzled just enough for her to stare back at him in shock. He wasn't talking about sex. She would follow behind him in this operation or he would have her kidnapped.

"You wouldn't dare!" she whispered. Though she knew he would. He had hardened that much further, grown that much more determined in only eight months within the cartel.

Fury tightened his expression. "I'm the biggest fucking male chauvinist you'll ever meet in your life. The thought of *my* woman in danger is more than my guts can tolerate. You will do this my way or by God I'll make damned sure you're protected another way."

Dominant. Overbearing. Possessive. But at least he was admitting he was on an operation now.

"Ian, I know what I'm doing." Confusion colored her voice and she knew it. Hell, she was a trained contract agent and had been one for ten years now. She wasn't exactly a new recruit to this world.

Haunting shadows flashed in his gaze before his eyes slid down her body to where his hand cupped her pussy, his fingers caressing it. Her breath rasped from her chest as pleasure threatened to swamp her senses again.

When his eyes came back to hers, they were filled with tormented, raging desire. "I need your promise. You'll be careful. Let me protect you. No matter what."

"That's not an issue, Ian," she said.

"If you were hurt . . ." His throat worked convulsively as he swallowed. "Kira. Don't make me live with that. Don't make me have to live with your death."

What was she seeing in his eyes now? What was that lurking demon of pain that burned like a hidden flame?

"I could make you promise the same thing," she said softly. And she would agree simply because in allowing him to protect her, she could protect his back. And his soul. Because she knew what he intended would destroy a part of him if he were allowed to follow through with it.

For all his crimes, Fuentes was still his father. And for all the horror he had visited on others, he was also still a DHS contact that they didn't want to lose. That they couldn't afford to lose.

His fingers moved between her thighs then, two of them pressing hard and deep, forcefully, inside her weeping pussy. Her hips arched, one heel digging into the leather seat, the other into the floorboard as she worked his fingers deeper and felt the erotic flames licking through her body.

"I find out you arranged that scene with Missern and I'll blister your ass," he said with a groan, coming over her, his fingers fucking into her, stretching her, perspiration beginning to dampen her entire body. "I'll tie you to my bed for a week, Kira. You will never play games with me like that again."

Her head shook. "No game," she gasped, her muscles tightening convulsively on his fingers. "Ian, please."

His lips covered the nipple he had revealed, drawing it into his mouth, suckling with strong, heated hunger as pleasure began to steal her common sense.

She had never known sex could be this good. She had never imagined it. Never thought she could possibly lose her mind in a man's arms.

"Do you belong to me, Kira?" His head rose, his gaze pierced hers as she forced her eyes open. "Seeing you with Missern knowing he was ready to strike you. I wanted him dead."

He was talking to her? Asking her something? Now? While his fingers were filling her, stroking her, the tips rubbing in the most pleasurable spots, areas she never knew could feel so good.

"Belong to you?" she panted.

"Tell me you belong to me, Kira." His fingers moved harder, deeper, plunging into the slick, saturated muscles of her pussy as shudders of response raced through her.

"Always." She screamed the word. She couldn't hold it back, no more than she could hold back the knowledge that she did belong to him in ways that even she couldn't define.

It was a battle she would have to fight with herself later. Not now, because now she was consumed. His lips covered hers in reward, his tongue sinking deep, fucking into her mouth and driving her insane with the need to be closer as he controlled her movements with his hands and his body.

His fingers rasped and filled her pussy, stroked and plunged as the heel of his hand finally gave her the pressure she needed to explode.

She unraveled beneath him. Her breath became trapped in her throat, sensations sizzled across her flesh, and in one blinding second terror washed through her. Because no other man could do this. No other man could bring her to this point. And when the operation was over, if they survived, then Ian would walk away from her forever.

Eleven

IAN COULD FEEL THE NEED, the inferno of lust, tearing through him as Kira exploded around his fingers. It tempted his control, control that had never been tempted, and tore through his mind with the razor-sharp edge of agonized hunger.

And he was running out of time.

Ian blinked the sweat from his eyes as his gaze lifted to the tinted windows that looked out beyond the Hummer. A half hour maybe, before they hit the villa. Not long enough for him to explain what seeing her with Missern, watching the bastard just touch her hair had done to him. It had made him insane with the need to claim her. Kira was a strong woman, an alpha female if he had ever met one. It made it harder for her to understand his need to protect her.

He wanted her fiery, challenging, and defiant, but he also wanted her to recognize the fact that he was in control. She had to. Her life might well depend upon it.

He didn't have the time to reach that inner woman, but he did have the time to let the hunger inside her free. To a point. God help him if he got his dick inside her; he'd be there for the rest of the night. There would be no leaving the vehicle because he'd be inside her for the rest of the night.

As her orgasm eased through her, he released her arms,

slid his fingers from her giving flesh, and tore at the leather belt cinching his hips.

He couldn't take her, but he could have her mouth on him again. He needed that. The sight of her taking him with primitive pleasure, tasting him, working for his pleasure.

He watched her expression shift from satiation to renewed hunger as he pushed his pants to his thighs and drew the hard length of his cock into his hand.

"Do I get to have fun now?" Amusement filled her tone as she came slowly to her knees.

Ian braced his hand on the ceiling of the vehicle and clenched his teeth to hold back a snarl. He tightened his fingers around the shaft and watched as she licked her lips.

Then she slowly bent. Sweet God, which did he want to watch more? Her mouth taking his cock, or her tight ass as it lifted behind her?

He compromised. He watched as her lips sank over the pulsing, dark head of his cock, and he let his hand fall in a light smack to her ass.

She flinched and stilled, her eyes lifting to him. Defiance sparkled in the witchy depths, but so did pleasure and arousal. He tapped the side of her ass once more, smiling at the sharp, involuntary response that had her lifting into the sharp caress.

She didn't know if she should allow herself to enjoy it or not. That bit of feminine confusion had every possessive and dominant instinct inside him howling in pleasure. He gave her rear another light tap.

"Suck my cock, kitten. I'll take care of the rest."

She obviously didn't like the pet name either, but that was what she reminded him of. A brave little cat, hissing and spitting when challenged, even as she ached for a touch she had never had before.

It made his lust burn higher, knowing no man had ever stroked her as he did, had never taken her past her own control as he had. It was addictive, challenging, and made him want her with a desire that frankly scared the shit out of him.

His teeth clenched as the moist heat of her mouth surrounded the head of his cock. She was still watching him, wary, uncertain. He liked her like that. It would make each touch sharper, brighter for her. Keeping Kira off guard might turn into an addictive hobby. If she didn't manage to throw *him* off guard first.

Damn it to hell!

She tucked the throbbing crest of his cock against the roof of her mouth and beneath it, her tongue undulated, rippled over the sensitive underside and sent spears of need slamming into his balls. His scrotum drew up hard and tight as the need for release had his cock swelling further in her mouth.

His hand landed on her rear again, then he cupped the blushing globe, caressed it, stroked it as he watched her eyes. The gray deepened, the bluish rings around it darkened. Witchy eyes. Seductive eyes. Eyes that threatened to trap his soul.

"Have you ever been taken here?" He let his fingers caress the narrow crevice between the taut mounds of her rear. "Have you knelt for a lover, Kira? Let him work that pretty ass open and fill it with his cock?"

She jerked. Her eyes dilated, and he knew she hadn't. No, it would have been giving control rather than taking it.

"Haven't you imagined what it would be like to be taken there?" His body tightened at the knowledge that this was an intimacy she hadn't shared with any other lover. His cock throbbed at the thought, clenching with the warning of impending release.

Insecurity flickered in her gaze.

"I bet you're tight here." He let his finger massage the hidden little entrance as it flexed beneath his touch. "Tight and hot. Would you scream for me? Would you beg me to fuck you harder there?"

Sweat formed on her brow as he pulled her hair back with his other hand and worked his cock against her rippling tongue. He was so close to coming it was all he could do to hold the hard ejaculations back.

As he pulled the long strands over her opposite shoulder, he let his fingers twine in them, tighten.

"Suck my dick. Don't just lick it. You know what I want."

Just as he knew what she was doing. Applying direct pressure to the most sensitive spot on the hard flesh, hoping to break his control. She cupped her fingers around his hard balls, massaged and eased farther back.

The next little slap to her rear was harder, hotter. "Don't fuck with me, baby," he said softly. "Not unless you want to face the consequences."

A frown worked at her brow even as her fingers slid back to his scrotum and her mouth began to work over the head of his cock.

His gaze flickered to her blushing butt as he laid a lighter little slap to it. Pleasure, a slow heated burn that would lead her across the threshold between pleasure and pain. "You're going to lift your sweet ass to me. Just a little higher, baby. Lift to me, so I can make it burn so good."

She moaned around his cock, her suckling mouth drawing on him deeper as her eyes seemed to glaze. But she did it. Pulled her knees in tighter and lifted to him.

Sweat dripped down his back as he fought to hold on to his control just a few more minutes. Just a little longer. He wanted her to come with him. He wanted her to know, in this instance, that he controlled her body, her response, and her orgasms.

He guided her mouth with his hand in her hair, pulling at the thick strands, his cock fucking her mouth as he delivered the little slaps to her ass, drawing closer to the saturated flesh of her bare pussy, making her burn. Inside and out.

She was weaker to this form of pleasure than she knew. He could see it on her expression as she tried to fight it, feel it in the suckling heat of her mouth as she tried to push him over the edge before he managed to push her across the threshold.

His. She belonged to him. He felt it in his soul; she

defied him, challenged him with her eyes, pricked at his control with the fierce, heated draws of her mouth. She licked and consumed him until the need to breathe was pleasure and pain, until sweat coated his body and his lungs labored for oxygen.

Her moans echoed around his erection and filled his head, just as the sound of his hand meeting her ass began to match the moaning breaths.

"That ass is mine. That sweet pussy is mine." He laid his hand to her rear again and again, feeling her burn in the cries that surrounded his cock and seeing it in the darkening of her eyes.

She belonged to him.

Just a little more, he knew. He clenched his teeth, allowed his hand to fall harder, closer to her soaked pussy, brightening her flesh and throwing her past the boundary of pleasure and pain. To a place where the two merged. Where they blended in a chaotic storm of hunger and need.

"You're going to come for me, Kira." Her eyes were nearly black, her mouth tight, hungry, as she drew on him, taking him nearly to her throat now, her ass lifting for him, her moans urging him on.

"Feel it, kitten." He kept his voice low, grating. Working easily toward the blissful zone he knew he had drawn her into. A place where nothing mattered but the sensation, the burn of the pleasure and the coming release. "Feel how hot and wet you are." He laid a gentler though burning caress between her thighs. Once. Twice. Back to her ass. Then to the bare flesh of her pussy.

She was shaking now. Shuddering. And God help him, he couldn't hold back. He could feel the cum boiling in his balls, threatening to overflow.

"Come for me, Kira." He delivered a firmer tap against her pussy, then back to her ass. "Give me what I need, baby."

Back to her pussy. Once. Twice. He moved back to her ass then, the little slaps gaining in speed and strength until he felt her explode, heard her scream on his cock. His head fell back as he forced back a shout of release and filled her mouth with his come.

Each jerking, shuddering ejaculation tore a throttled cry from his lips even as he plunged his fingers into the tight depths of her convulsing pussy to feel the release that flowed over his fingers.

She consumed him. Sucked the seed from his balls, and left him so damned weak he nearly collapsed over her. He caught his weight on the back of the seat, his breathing labored, jerky, as the final spurts of his semen filled her mouth.

As soon as he could think, move, Ian eased back from her, pulled his pants to his hips and found his seat before pulling her into his lap. He couldn't give her time to consider what had happened until he gave her body time to ease into the implications of it. Surrender to a woman like Kira was as much about pleasing the mind and the heart as it was about pleasing her body.

"I didn't like that." Her voice was husky, uncertain, as he tucked her head beneath his chin and let his hands caress the rippling shudders that raced through her body. "Not at all. And you call me kitten again, and I'll kill you in your sleep."

"I could tell you just hated it when you drenched my fingers with your orgasm," he mused with a smile. He kept his voice gentle, allowed her to hear and to feel his complete approval of her response.

She was silent as she lay against him then, her arms looped around his neck and holding tight to him.

"Don't do it again," she finally breathed out weakly.

A smile curled his lips and he bent his head over hers and held her to him. God, he loved holding her. Having her in his arms, soft as a sleepy kitten with its claws still extended.

"Maybe I'll do something different next time," he drawled, finding himself wondering at the amusement and sheer pleasure he felt in just this. Just holding her, teasing her.

"Maybe I will too." She nipped his jaw, but he felt her smile.

"You probably will." He pressed her head against him, his heart finally easing its frantic beat as he stared outside the Hummer.

She was a match for him, he had known that all along. Was that why he had avoided beginning a relationship with her? Kira would never stay home, safe and secure, while he fought, and he knew it now. She would always be at his back whether she was supposed to be or not and that was a frightening realization.

He hadn't been lying when he told her he was the worst chauvinist she would ever meet. He was. Protecting her was a part of who he was, ingrained in him during the years he had fought and nearly failed to protect his delicate mother. Women were to be protected, cherished, not placed in the front lines of a dirty, underground war.

"You have to be careful," he told her quietly, staring outside the Hummer rather than at her. "Diego won't hesitate to kill you if he feels threatened." Or if he felt she threatened Ian. That knowledge sliced at him.

"I'm trained in covert ops, Ian," she reminded him again. "I know what I'm doing."

He nodded slowly. He had to give her that. She had survived in the covert underworld for a decade now. A woman couldn't accomplish that unless she knew exactly what she was doing.

"Mistakes happen when emotions get involved," he told her quietly. And, boy, were his emotions involved. "Stay on guard. We're running out of time here. We are and Sorrell is as well. He needs the Fuentes connections to pull off the strike he has planned effectively. We need his identity to stop it. When things go from sugar to shit, and I know they will, I want you safe."

"As safe as you are?"

And that terrified him.

"Safer," he whispered. "I want you safer."

He tucked her against him once again and stared at the black partition that separated the back from the driver's area. They would be close to the villa now. The villa where Diego had no doubt already heard about the confrontation with the Misserns, as well as Kira.

The bastard had been desperate for Ian to find a woman. Not for any softer reasons such as his son's happiness. No, he needed a weakness he could exploit, and Ian knew it. And now, Ian held that weakness in his arms. One neither Diego nor Sorrell would hesitate to use if he gave them the chance.

K IRA WAS DECENT WHEN THE Hummer drew to a stop in front of the Fuentes villa. Her dress was no longer around her hips, and her hair was hastily smoothed out.

If only Ian's demeanor could be fixed as easily.

Five minutes from the villa and he had grown silent, cold. His clothes were restored and the icy façade was back in place. She was only now realizing how much she hated that façade.

As Deke opened the back door and helped her from the vehicle, the villa's front door opened, and Diego Fuentes leaned lazily against the entrance, his head tilted as he watched her curiously.

For a man in his fifties, nearing sixty, he was in excellent shape. His black hair was mostly gray now, his face lined, but his silk slacks and white shirt covered a body that was well toned. There was no doubt he took excellent care of himself.

And she could easily see now that Ian had taken some of his looks from his biological father. But she had already known that. The heavy brows, the strong slash of cheekbones, the sensual lips.

Ian moved past him, his fingers locked on Kira's arm as he pulled her into the foyer.

Diego's smile faltered. "We need to discuss a few things before you retire, Ian." Diego's voice sharpened as they passed him.

"It can wait—"

"This cannot wait." Diego overrode Ian's objections. "I will meet you in my study in twenty minutes. This will give you time to escort your friend to your room or wherever you intend for her to spend her nights and to meet me in my study. I will be awaiting you there."

Diego turned on his heel and stalked through the foyer to the back hall, leaving Kira and Ian standing just inside, surrounded by the bodyguards.

This was a mess. How in the world did Ian survive the daily tension that she could sense between him and his father?

She looked around the opulent entrance, glimpsing the high-ceilinged main room to the right and the dining area that opened behind it.

"It's a very nice villa." It was one step down from an elaborate mansion. The Fuenteses definitely lived well.

"It's something," Ian muttered. "Come on, I'll show you to my room and then go see what the old man wants."

The shadow of bitterness in his voice wasn't lost on her, though she doubted anyone could have caught it unless they had studied the shades of his voice as she had each time she heard him speak. A mix of regret, sadness, and fury. It gave his voice a grating edge, deepened it. And broke her heart.

He led her across the foyer to the curved wooden staircase. With his hand firmly at her back, his fingers rubbing almost imperceptibly against the silk of her dress, he led her up the stairs.

Along the hall, double doors were opened by a housemaid with a shy smile before she retreated in the opposite direction. Behind them, the three remaining bodyguards trailed like ghosts.

He pushed open the doors into a wide sitting area complete with a wide-screen television, a wet bar, and a wide, comfortable couch. "The bedroom is in here." He led her across the room to another set of doors. Pushing them open, he stood back and allowed her to step into the room. She almost wished she had stayed in the sitting room.

The huge, larger-than-king-sized bed dominated the room. It was surrounded with shimmering panels of netting, and the massive posts and thick mattress were intimidating. But the metal rings set in the corners and the middle of the headboard and footboard had her swallowing tightly. She knew what those rings were for. She had been in the fringe clubs and on the periphery of the BDSM clubs long enough to know how easily those rings would hold the slender chains attached to wrist and ankle cuffs.

Across from the bed was a heavy mirrored chest, a dresser off to another side of the room. There were metal rings set in one wall as well.

"Interesting." She tried for nonchalant as she murmured the word. "Did you decorate it yourself?"

A sharp laugh left his throat. "Not hardly. It came this way. Make yourself at home, I shouldn't be long. One of my men will bring your things when Daniel arrives with them."

"Daniel is staying close by, Ian." She turned as he moved to leave the room. "Make certain he's given a room."

"We'll discuss this when I return." His expression hardened. "And before you argue, hold the thought. We can fight it out after I get finished with Diego. Just try to stay out of trouble until then."

She gave him a brief, quick nod, even as her teeth clenched to hold back the very argument he was talking about. Daniel was nonnegotiable though. He and Jason both would likely have a stroke if he wasn't close enough to keep an eye on her. It had been bad enough when she worked the Atlanta mission and ended up shot. Damn, it had taken her months before she was allowed to go to the bathroom without one of them standing outside the door.

"I'll see you in a bit," he said, and before she could react, he cupped her neck in his hand, jerked her to him for a brief, hard kiss, then turned and left the suite.

Kira lifted her fingers to her lips, an involuntary smile touching them at the tingling feel of that forceful kiss. She wondered if he was aware of the expression on his face when he had delivered it. It wasn't just sexual. Something else had been brewing in his eyes, almost a promise.

She turned, stared at the bed again, and let her eyes drift closed in regret.

Betraying him was going to kill her. Because she knew that once she did, it was going to destroy that fragile hint of emotion she had just glimpsed. And when that happened, she didn't want to think of the well of emptiness she would feel.

In saving him, she just might end up destroying both of them. Because she couldn't allow him to kill his father. That was her mission. If Ian was running an operation here, then her job was to keep Diego Fuentes alive.

Twelve

IAN DIDN'T BOTHER KNOCKING ON Diego's study door. He was tired, pissed, and the adrenaline high had him on edge. He was more than aware of the mistake he had made at Coronado's where Kira was concerned. What he had done had placed her smack in the middle of the war getting ready to be waged between the cartel and Sorrell's terrorist network. As well as brought her to Diego's attention. There wasn't a doubt in Ian's mind just how ugly and how bloody it could become.

"Do not berate me!" Diego was waiting for him. He stood behind his desk, glowering as he stared back at Ian.

Ian paused, lifted his brow mockingly, and pulled back the caustic insults he had been ready to deliver. Daddy dearest was in a mood tonight, it seemed.

"I had no intention of berating you," he lied as he closed the doors behind him, barely glimpsing the surprise that came and went on Diego's face when he turned back to him. "I was curious as to what was so important that you had to call me in here like a child who had missed curfew." Ian forced a vein of teasing mockery into his voice.

Diego softened marginally, the corner of his lips tugging up almost involuntarily.

"Do you think I offended your Miss Porter?" He suddenly frowned.

Ian shrugged. "I doubt it. She's a woman. She's probably used to grown men acting like asses." He barely held back the disgust in his voice.

"Ah. If she has been around you very long, then I have no doubt." Diego snorted.

Ian hid his surprise. Damn, the old man was developing some sharp teeth where he was concerned. It had taken much longer than Ian had expected.

"Don't doubt it." Ian grinned, genuinely amused this time. Kira had quite a bit of experience dealing with some of his less charming traits over the years.

Diego grunted at that before saying, "I had several phone calls before you arrived informing me of the confrontation with the Misserns over Miss Porter. It was reported that Martin Missern attempted to strike her?" Diego's black eyes narrowed in anger.

Ian crossed his arms over his chest. "And what else did your little spies tell you about it?"

"Damn you, Ian!" he burst out. "You live in a fishbowl, and you know this. All watch you. Did you not think before you reacted? Did you not know that there would be eyes watching to report how easily Ian Fuentes came unglued over the very delectable Miss Porter? The heir to the Mc-Clane fortune and the very dear niece of one of the world's most influential men?"

But no mention of Kira as the Chameleon, or her work as an agent.

No one knew of the work she did, and Ian intended to keep it that way.

"You have nothing to say?" Diego growled.

"Are you expecting me to defend my actions?" Ian asked curiously. "I realize you missed a lot of years in my upbringing, but I'm a little old for you to counsel me on how I deal with public threats to a woman I'm sleeping with. Don't you?"

Diego paused, his eyes narrowing further as his nostrils flared in ire.

"Josef Missern called just before your arrival to apologize for his brother's actions and to assure me that he alone will deal with the transaction in the morning."

Hell, he should have expected that.

"Fine." Ian shrugged. All the better. He would get the weapons he needed and Sorrell's spies could attest to the fact that Ian took his protection of Kira very seriously.

"You say fine, as though threatening to kill Martin Missern was of no importance?" He shot Ian a contemptuous look. "They will be watching for you now. They will put a bullet in the back of your head without warning. You should strike first—"

"Whoa! Are you suggesting I send men in to kill the Misserns because they might retaliate for my threats against them?" Ian laughed. "God love your heart, Diego. How have you managed to survive all these years if you're constantly killing people off like diseased animals?"

"Because what I kill *are* diseased animals," he snapped back. "Deny this. I dare you."

His uncles hadn't been diseased. Diego's younger brothers, their wives and children, had been murdered with merciless speed the moment Diego learned they were considering turning over evidence against the Fuentes cartel to the American and Colombian authorities.

Ian kept his mouth shut. He didn't care about Diego's excuses or the poor pitiful story the other man would no doubt relate. He just wanted this meeting finished.

He rubbed at the side of his nose before shoving his hands into his slacks and retaining eye contact with Diego.

"Is there a point to this?"

Diego sneered. "You are like a willful child."

"We established that my first month here. Should I have asked if there was a *new* point to this?"

"Take care of the Misserns," Diego warned him. "Do not

give them the chance to strike out at you when you are not looking."

Ian pursed his lips thoughtfully. "I'll consider it."

Diego's eyes widened in surprise. "You will?"

"Of course." He shrugged. "When I meet with Josef tomorrow if he hasn't followed my security instructions to the letter than I'll blow his nasty little head off just like I do anyone else who pisses me off. Satisfied?"

Ian felt a warning itch just beneath his flesh. How much blood had he shed in the past year? How many animals had he already killed? Terrorist spies and cartel enemies were a dime a dozen, there were so many now.

Suddenly, his skin felt coated, oily with blood and guilt and the slime that came from dealing with slugs. And the head slug stood across from him, watching him as though he were proud of him. As though he had said something to be praised for. For God's sake.

Diego nodded slowly and seemed to release a sigh of relief. "I worry." He swiped his hand through his salt-and-pepper hair. "You are strong and they know this. To kill you would be a great source of pride for them. To succeed where Sorrell's agents have failed."

"Stop worrying." Ian rubbed his hand over the back of his neck to dispel the primal sense of foreboding he could feel gathering inside him. "I'll take care of the Misserns. And Kira."

Diego nodded. "Yes, you must take care of Miss Porter. She is known for her reserve and refusal to take a powerful lover. Many will look at you with awe for succeeding in capturing her interest. You are a son to be proud of." He nodded decisively.

Ian barely contained his disbelief. "For God's sake," he muttered. "This is insane. She's a woman, not a trophy."

"Ah, you defend her honor." He chuckled. "Perhaps she will be around a while, yes? Maybe babies one day?"

Ian blinked back at Diego. The old man was going senile. He shook his head. "I'm going to bed."

Diego chuckled. "I do not doubt there will not be much sleep for you this night. Try to rest a little, ah? The Misserns, they are wily. You will need all your senses in the morning."

"Sure. I'll take care of that," Ian said, shaking his head.

Diego was still chuckling like a rabid clown as Ian left the office and headed toward the stairs. Just in time to watch the entry doors open and Daniel and Cristo step inside. They were carrying Kira's luggage and several carryalls. One rather large duffel bag. He was betting he knew exactly what resided in that duffel bag.

"I only brought her essentials." Daniel Calloway's voice was cool, distant. "I'll take those up to her then you can show me a room close enough to hers to make certain she's not murdered in her sleep." His hazel eyes clashed with Ian's.

Master Warrant Officer Daniel Calloway had been a SEAL himself before his retirement from the navy at age thirty-eight. He had immediately taken the position with McClane as Kira's bodyguard.

He was still in peak fitness five years later, though there was a dusting of gray at his temples. Ian bet Kira had given him each one of those gray hairs.

"Cristo, bunk him in with you," Ian ordered. "We'll go over the rules of this little game in the morning."

"Is his room close to hers?" Daniel appeared unwilling to let that bone go.

Ian shot him a mocking smile. "It's close to my room actually. And since that's where she'll be sleeping, I think it will do."

Daniel's lips thinned in disapproval. "For now. That will do."

Deke cleared his throat. "Let's go, man," he urged Daniel. "The boss is still wearing his piece. I'd hate to see him pull it."

They went, but not before Daniel shot him a quiet, warning glare.

Ian pinched the bridge of his nose and strode quickly

through the foyer to the living room. There, he headed straight to the wet bar and the bottle of Crown Royal he kept for emergencies.

Slamming the glass to the bar, he filled it halfway, brought it to his lips, and swallowed with a desperation born of a hunger he couldn't explain, even to himself.

Ian snarled, held back the curse sizzling at his lips, and stalked from the room. He knew, knew she was going to be trouble. The moment he saw her, five years before, he had known.

And by God, he was right.

Thirteen

IAN HIT THE STAIRS, TAKING the steps two at a time, and passed his bodyguards without so much as a word.

He entered the sitting area of his suite and closed the doors with deliberate restraint.

He wanted Kira out of here. He wanted her safe. And now, it was too fucking late for safe. Whether he wanted her here or not, here she was, and he'd be damned if he would fight to keep his hands off her.

Looking around the silent room, darkened and empty, his gaze was drawn to the open balcony doors. Ian moved to them and stepped out into the darkness that filled the night.

Dark, but never alone. The hairs on the back of his neck lifted in primal warning. Hell, he'd been a SEAL long enough to know what it meant. He'd felt it for more than a week now, known he was being watched, and he knew who was watching him.

He let his gaze travel along the hills across from the balcony, mockery twisting his expression.

Where are you, Macey? He could feel Durango team's tech wizard watching him. One of the few friends Ian had ever allowed himself, a man who now considered Ian a betrayer and the enemy.

He was out there, but so were the others. His former

commander, Reno Chavez. His lieutenant commander, Clint McIntyre. The Cajun, Kell Krieger. He and Ian had made lieutenant at the same time. And Lieutenant Junior Grade Mason "Macey" March. He couldn't keep a rank above junior for the life of him. Macey had problems with authority figures and never failed to lose rank by arguing with superior officers other than his commanders. That and hacking their computers.

They were all out there, and they were all watching him. He could feel the bull's-eye painted on his chest and at times he wished they would go ahead and take the shot. He would never be the same after this mission. Once trust was destroyed within a team, it wasn't regained with an apology once the truth was found out.

"Ian?" Kira spoke from the thickly padded chair she sat in against the outside wall.

He had known she was there. He could feel her. Smell her. Just as he could feel his former team members watching from a distance.

At that thought, a frown pulled at his brow as he braced his hands on the balcony railing.

"Who's your backup team, Kira?" he asked, his voice so soft he knew it went no farther than her ears.

"Daniel." Her answer was quick, questioning.

The shadowed darkness of the land that rose around them held his gaze. Friends that had faced death with him countless times now watched him as the enemy. Was that why the Chameleon was here as well? He hadn't confirmed her suspicions that he was there to take Sorrell or Diego down, but somehow she had known.

He turned back to Kira, feeling the tension rise inside him as she watched him silently. She sat, her legs folded beneath her, his shirt wrapped around her as black, silky hair flowed around her like a short cape.

He felt the anger burning in his gut, and the suspicion rising in his mind. Pacing to her, he gripped her arm and pulled her from the chair.

"No one watches you?" he asked as he jerked her close to his chest, feeling her gasp then soften in his arms as he laid his lips at her ear. "I feel them out there, Kira. Who else did you take your suspicions to? Did you pull the team out here with you?"

"No." She shook her head desperately, but believing her didn't come as easy as her answer had.

"Don't lie to me." He backed her against the wall, feeling the hunger inside him, the arousal and need that clawed at his balls like a trapped animal.

Hunger and anger. Helplessness and rage. Once again he couldn't protect someone he loved. She refused to let him protect her. Refused to hide and let him face the danger and he couldn't bear it.

"Ian." She arched against him. "Would I lie to you?"

"In a fucking heartbeat if you thought you needed to," he snarled, knowing it, feeling it. "I don't need you to protect me."

He clasped her head in his hands, tilted it back and found his gaze focused on her lips. Lips that had been red and swollen in the limo, moist with the essence of his cum and slack with the lust beating inside her.

He dropped his hands to her shoulders and dragged the shirt from her, dropping it to the floor of the balcony.

"I wouldn't dare try to protect you." Her head dropped back as his lips pressed to her neck and then opened, his teeth raking, his tongue licking as he grew intoxicated with the taste of her.

"You're a liar." He nipped her neck in punishment. "Tell me what you've done, Kira. Don't make me force it out of you. Don't betray me. Not like this."

He felt her still in his arms.

"Poor little sailor boy," she whispered mockingly, her fingers working the buttons of his shirt slowly. "God forbid that anyone should care what happens to you. Should we take out an ad? To whom it may concern? Ian Richards Fuentes is an island unto himself?"

He jerked her hips forward, burying the hard ridge of his shaft against the giving mound of soft flesh between her thighs.

"Don't push me!" She was up to something, he knew she was. She and that damned team he once fought with. Nosy bastards. They shouldn't be here. Sorrell had taken out more Special Forces teams than he wanted to think about. They had wives, families. They had no business here.

"I wouldn't dare push the big bad cartel lord," she drawled, that soft Georgia accent stroking over his senses and tightening his balls as the last button gave way beneath her fingers. "Why, Ian, what would make you think I'm that brave?"

"Because you're a hellcat," he accused her roughly.

"Can I be your hellcat?" Something, a softness, a need in her voice, shredded the last threads of control that held his hunger back.

Lust surged through his system. The defiance that poured from her did something to him. He didn't want to make her submit, as he should have. Hell no, he wanted to burn inside her fire. He wanted to feel her come apart in his arms and know he controlled it.

Making her submit wasn't what he needed. Controlling that fire, that burning sexuality and energy, that was the challenge. And the male animal inside him was hard and eager to face her defiance.

"You. Are making a mistake." He jerked the short skirt of her stretchy dress over her thighs, his hand finding sweet, slick flesh ready for his touch.

"What mistake?" He heard the moan in her voice, the whimper of need.

"Where are they, Kira?" He parted the folds of her pussy. "I don't have a damned problem letting them watch me fuck you, but you might not like it."

She arched closer. "Exhibitionism turns me on," she panted, her fingers working on his belt, the clasp of his pants.

Fuck it. He knew they were there. She knew they were there. And her body was covered. His former team might be able to tell what they were doing, but they wouldn't see a damned thing. And that was besides the fact he couldn't have made it back to the room before getting inside her if he had to.

Excitement coursed through Kira as she felt Ian's fingers caressing the swollen, sensitive folds between her thighs. The rasp of his fingertips, the warmth of them, were driving her crazy. His finger swirled around her clit, dipped and pierced her core.

She held on to him because her knees wouldn't hold her steady. Her legs were weak, breathing was almost impossible. All she knew was the heat and pleasure of his touch.

And how much she needed it. Ached for it. She didn't give a damn who was watching, though she knew Durango team, knew there was only one of that crew that she had to worry about actually keeping his eyes on them at the moment.

Right now, nothing mattered but easing the pain she could feel coursing through Ian. She heard it in his voice, felt it in his touch. Something had happened with Diego Fuentes that had torn inside him with the force of a dull knife and left a ragged, aching wound.

"I need you," he bit out as she released the straining length of his erection.

"I'm here," she whispered breathlessly. "Right here."

Two fingers pressed inside her pussy, stretched her, opened her for him, and she couldn't help but tremble, but whimper for his touch.

He was her weakness. She had known it a year ago and she knew it now. His touch made a lie of a decade of sexual certainty. His kiss reminded her that she was a woman, a woman who was created to submit to her man. And Ian was her man.

"Come here, kitten," he groaned, his arm reaching beneath her rear and lifting her close.

He was fierce, uncontrolled. She was shaking and out of

control. Her legs wrapped around his hips and her cry pierced the night as he began working his cock inside her.

"Oh God. Ian." She arched back into the wall, her nails biting into his shoulders as she pressed her hands beneath his shirt.

"You're tight, Kira," he groaned at her ear, his teeth catching the lobe to nibble at it erotically. "Tight and hot and so sweet."

She felt his knees bend, his hold tighten on her. A second later a fractured cry tore from her lips as he thrust farther inside her, deeper, harder.

The impalement stole her breath from the pleasure and the pain. She writhed on his erection, trying to work it deeper, loving the burning pleasure, that edge of pain that she had never imagined could be so damned erotic.

She could feel every bulge of vein, every hard throb of pulsing blood. The way his ass clenched beneath her heels, the way his back tightened as he worked deeper, and it only made her hotter, wetter. It only made her crave him more.

"Are they watching, Kira?" His voice was tormented as he stilled inside her, and buried his face against her neck. "Where are they?"

She heard the torment in his voice. They were his friends. Friends who he believed thought he had betrayed them. Friends he would have willingly given his life for.

"I don't know," she panted out breathlessly. She didn't know, not for sure. She suspected. She assumed. But she didn't know, and it was best that way.

His hold tightened on her as he half-lifted her and stumbled to the door.

"Ian?"

"Goddamn you, you're mine!" His voice raged with possessiveness, the tone, his hold, sending a piercing shaft of aching desperation through her soul. He sounded as though he meant it. "I'll be damned if they need to watch this."

He turned to the wall within the room, pressed her to it, and began to thrust.

His cock pounded inside her, he took her ruthlessly, thrusting, penetrating, groaning her name as she watched the stars explode in front of her vision as she tightened around him.

"Ah God. Yes, baby. Come around me," he groaned. "Let me feel it. Every ripple . . ." His head fell back, his breath heaving through his chest as his hands clenched on her ass.

Kira couldn't think. She couldn't plot a next move. She was lost in the pleasure, coming apart and wondering why the hell he was holding back.

"Easy, kitten," he soothed as she shuddered against him. He was moving again, stumbling, until seconds later her back met the sofa and he was pulling free of her grip with a shattered groan.

It was only then that she realized he hadn't donned a condom. And she hadn't considered it. Hadn't thought about it.

"Ian." She tightened her ankles on his back. "I'm protected."

He stilled, only the thick head of his cock remaining inside her as she watched his jaw bunch.

"Protected?"

"Birth control." She swallowed tightly. "I'm protected, Ian. Don't leave me."

He shook his head, his hands clenching on her hips as she felt his cock throb imperatively.

"I haven't fucked without a condom since I was a kid," he groaned, but she heard the need, the hunger in his voice.

"Neither have I, Ian." She blinked back the sudden moisture that wanted to fill her eyes. "I want to feel you. All of you . . . Ian!" She screamed his name as he plunged inside her again. Sweat dripped from his forehead, perspiration covered her body, soaking them both, as she felt the ecstasy consume her again.

Surely she couldn't orgasm again so soon? Surely he didn't have such a hold on her?

But as she heard his harsh groan, felt the first spurt of

semen fill her, she exploded again. Arching in his arms, shaking, shuddering, she gave what she had never given before, and accepted something she had never accepted before. She gave herself, and she took all of the man in her arms.

It should have been frightening. It should have terrified her, knowing what she had just opened herself to. Instead, it felt right.

When he collapsed over her, the deep shudders racking his body, matching hers, she could do nothing but hold on to him and let her tears mingle with their combined perspiration. What the hell would she do now, if she lost him?

IAN KNEW TEARS WHEN HE saw them. He knew the jerk and shudder of a woman's body when she held back her sobs. He'd known those signs for the better part of his life, but he hadn't thought he would ever see them in Kira.

He carried her to their bed, tucked her in, and got in beside her before pulling her into his arms.

He felt her fingers clench at his arm, felt her slender, lithe body as it tried to sink into his. And he had seen her eyes. In the dim light of the room he had seen the shattered realization in her gaze before she could hide it.

She was a trained operative, but she had never gone into an assignment quite like this one, against a man that her heart was involved with. The Chameleon didn't get involved. That agent couldn't be tempted, couldn't be bribed, and not just because no one knew if it was a he, a she, or a figment of someone's imagination. But because whoever, whatever it was, the Chameleon was ice. Unaffected. Unsympathetic to the enemy.

He smoothed her hair back from her face, realizing he didn't want the truth of why she was here, with him, in his bed. A part of him just didn't want to know if she was there to betray him. But he suspected it. There was guilt in his lover's eyes, and it stabbed at his heart.

"You make me forget," she finally whispered, causing him to still against her.

"Forget what?" he asked

"Who I am."

His lips quirked at her reply. "You're Kira."

"I'm more than just Kira," she whispered.

She was the Chameleon. The woman and the agent were struggling now, he had seen it in her eyes, he felt it in her responses to him. He had avoided it each time he had seen her, each time he had held her since she had come back into his life.

"Right here, there's no room for anyone but Kira," he warned her, careful to keep his voice low, to keep her close. "Don't make that mistake. Don't bring something else into this relationship."

She was silent for long moments.

"It's who I am," she finally whispered.

Ian ran his hands over her hair before pulling her head back and staring into her eyes.

"We both know better than that." He wouldn't let her believe otherwise. He couldn't. Not here. Not now. He was not going to face the Chameleon.

Ian watched as she licked her lips nervously, the way her gaze darkened with feminine uncertainty. At that moment he realized, he knew. Yeah, she had a mission. The Chameleon had been sent to him. But it was the woman he was dealing with. It was his woman.

He couldn't lie to himself any longer. Kira was here for more than a fun time in the sack, or to cover his back. She was a contract agent, the Chameleon, and he could see the battle waging in those beautiful eyes. She was there for much more than the man the woman was claiming. The agent was also there. And it was the agent's agenda he needed to know.

Fourteen

SLENDER TENDRILS OF LIGHT STREAKED across the sky as the sun began to rise over the horizon. The faint light eased the darkness that filled the bedroom and allowed Kira to ease up in the bed and stare into Ian's sleeping face.

She had known the moment he slipped into sleep, just as she knew that the slightest movement by her now would awaken him. And how she longed to move, to touch his face, to ease the lines of strain from his brow.

He had sold his soul to his father for his friends' lives. For Nathan, for Kell's lover, for the men he fought with, for a single chance to break the hold Diego Fuentes seemed to have with anyone he connected himself to, and she knew it. There was no other reason that he would risk his soul this way.

Diego was a master manipulator. She had read the secret file the director of the DHS held on him. The games the bastard had played with the DEA, the ATF, and a dozen other agencies would have been laughable were it not for the fact that he invariably won and the agreement he had with DHS protected him if he didn't. Dirty bastard. Diego knew their weakness just as well as he had known Ian's and he used it. Like a chess player laying out his pawns and moving them with insidious control throughout his little world.

And Ian was his favorite. His knight. His source of pride. His only son. And he was using him with an efficiency that bespoke his joy in this particular game. He was thwarting Sorrell, playing the U.S. law enforcement and drug agencies, and holding his son in front of them all like a dog's favorite bone.

Kira closed her eyes at the thought. He was a stronger man than any she had known. Other men would have broken under the pressure by now, or given in. The fear that Ian would turn rogue kept the Homeland Security director up at night, she knew.

It was a heady drug, the power Ian wielded now. It wouldn't be easy for any man to walk away from. And if he didn't walk away from it, it would destroy a part of her.

She fought the hitch in her breath, the emotions that boiled inside her, seared her soul. She couldn't escape the emotions. They wouldn't let her go. They wouldn't ease. Everything inside her drew her to Ian, and had been doing so for years. But now, there was a part of herself that she didn't recognize anymore. A part of herself she hadn't realized existed until that night in Atlanta. A woman who loved.

"Stop staring at me like that," Ian ordered her, his voice its normal roughness. Sleep hadn't made it huskier or deeper.

"How long have you been awake?" She smiled as his eyes opened, thick dark blond lashes shielding the inner depths as he stared back at her.

"Long enough to figure a few things out." His hand moved beneath the sheet, sliding over her outer thigh to her hip as she felt her heart jump at the suspicion in his voice.

"What did you figure out?"

"That you're not here just for me." His lips twisted mockingly. "What are you here for?"

Kira drew back slowly. Sliding the sheet from her naked body, she started to leave the bed, only to find herself held in place by strong fingers that wrapped around her upper arm.

The problem was, no matter her orders, she was here for him. Nothing else.

She turned back to look at him, wondering if she had really portrayed such a cold, bleak image that he couldn't imagine her caring enough about him to follow him. To help him.

"Maybe I'm here for myself," she retorted, tugging at her arm.

That was the truth. She was here to assure herself he lived, that his soul survived, that he didn't do something he would regret for the rest of his life. Fuck DHS and their objectives and agendas. She wasn't there to keep Diego Fuentes alive, she was there to make certain the wicked amusement that had once gleamed in his eyes returned. She was there to share that amusement. And that was the part of herself she was so unfamiliar with. The part that needed to see more than just the cold, hard drug cartel lord. She needed to see the man again. And she needed to love him, just as she loved him now. All of him.

"I hate a liar." He sighed, his eyes narrowing on her as he tugged at her arm, dragging her back to the middle of the bed with him. "I've been giving this a lot of thought, Kira. You couldn't have had the information you did to be in that warehouse last week without help. Where did you get it?"

She rolled her eyes before leaning toward him, allowing her hair to cascade over the side of her face and enclose them in a partial curtain of darkness. No lies. No games. Just the two of them, the truth, and her silent promise to protect him.

"Martin Missern's soldiers like to party," she whispered suggestively. "Ricardo Desoto likes to talk when he gets drunk. He talked."

Desoto was one of Missern's personal soldiers within his main security force. Tall, suave, a Latin charmer with all the sophistication of an alligator on the prowl.

"And you were there?" Something angry flashed in his

eyes as he tugged her close, his other hand gripping her neck and holding her in place, her breasts pressing into the tense, muscled forearm.

"She was there, Ian." The Chameleon.

Kira let her lashes drift partially closed, her voice lower sensually. "I poured his rum, smiled nice and sweet, and ran my nails down his arm as he told me everything he knew. Everything. Even Martin and Josef Missern's propensity to take Sorrell's rejects as lovers before disposing of them very quietly." Her teeth clenched as she drew in an angry breath. "And Sorrell's suggestion to them that Diego Fuentes would be much easier to handle if you were no longer a part of his little world."

Ian's lips tightened, though he released her, slowly, before rolling to the edge of the bed and sitting up. Her hands gripped his forearm, frustration eating at her that he could contain her so easily. They both knew he could shake her off like an irritating gnat if he chose.

He didn't. He stilled, his back tightening, as she inched closer, pressing her nipples against the smooth flesh and laying her lips at his ear. She could feel the sexual tension rising inside him then, as it always did when they touched, when they challenged each other.

"You want answers, Ian? You want to know why I'm here? Tell me, why did you slip into my bedroom in Atlanta? Why did you hold me down in my bed and let me glimpse heaven without the satisfaction of touching it? Did the big bad SEAL get scared of the little woman?"

She slid her arms over his shoulders and he reached up to grip her wrists.

"You want me," she reminded him. "And you hate it. Don't you, Ian?"

She knew he did. She had glimpsed that in Atlanta. His anger, the irritation and frustration in his expression each time they were around each other. The knowledge of it still held the power to hurt her. It twisted inside her and tugged stingingly at her emotions. Which she thought was totally not fair. After all, if he had to affect her so severely, why couldn't she affect him in the same way?

"You're a complication." He unwrapped her arms and rose to his feet, naked, aroused. "Nothing more."

She sat on her knees on the bed, watching him in the dim light of the rising sun as he turned and glanced at her over his shoulder.

"I'm heading to the shower," he said. "I'll meet with Deke in the sitting room while you get dressed. We need to talk before heading down to breakfast."

"About what?" Rising to her feet, Kira paced over to the robe that a helpful maid must have left lying over the cushioned chair at the bottom of the bed. Shrugging it on, she belted it before glaring back at him.

"Your role in this little debacle of an operation," he grunted in disgust. "I still can't believe I was stupid enough to be played so easily by Missern." His narrow-eyed glance of irritation wasn't lost on her.

"Oh yes, this is going to be such a hardship for you." Her smile was all teeth. He better watch out, because she knew how to bite too. "Why didn't you just ignore him, Ian? Martin may have almost gotten the first hit in, but I promise you, I would have gotten in the last."

She knew how to deal with bastards like Missern. It was men like Ian she had always had problems with.

"I should have ignored it." He shrugged, turning from her again. "As you stated, you know how to take care of yourself. But the damage has already been done."

He gave her his back and strode off, naked and buff and so male she would have creamed her nonexistent panties if she weren't so damned pissed off.

"The damage has already been done?" She rushed for the bathroom door, then turned, mortification flaming across her face as she saw him poised at the toilet. "Jeez, Ian."

She heard his smug chuckle a second before the door slammed at her back. Then the snick of the lock. The son of a bitch.

"You are so wrong!" she gritted out after the sound of the toilet flushing.

Not that he paid any attention to her. The sound of the shower finally came through the doors, causing her to pace away from the bathroom door to the closed balcony doors. She pulled them open, stepped out to the balcony, and proceeded to the doors that led to the room Daniel was staying in.

She paused outside the glass doors, peeked in, and caught Daniel's eye where he was sitting in a chair lacing his boots. Glancing to the door of the bedroom, he rose quickly, jerked his shirt from the back of the chair, and shrugged it over his shoulders before opening the door and going out to the balcony.

As the door closed behind him, Kira was in his face, hissing. "Is Durango team on the island?"

Daniel's eyes narrowed, his hand moving to button his shirt lazily as he stared down at her.

"How would I know?" he asked coolly.

Oh hell yes, he knew. She recognized that look on his face and that tone of voice.

"How long have they been here? And before you step over the line and lie to me, I'd remember who signs your paycheck, Mr. Calloway."

She was furious at the thought that Daniel would go behind her back and contact the team. She was even angrier to realize that he would have had to go behind her back to find out enough about this operation to think they were needed.

He blew out a hard breath. "I don't lie to you, Kira, so can the 'Mr. Calloway' crap and the threats. I suspect they're here, but I don't know where, and I'm not bothering to find out. Extra security wouldn't hurt any of us."

"You suspected and you didn't tell me?" She glanced quickly back to the room she shared with Ian. "He knows they're here, Daniel. And if they're here, there's only one reason for it. To take him out."

"Has he gone rogue?" The question was a legitimate one, she knew.

"Hell no, he hasn't gone rogue, nor is he a traitor. Ian doesn't have a rogue bone in his body and you know it. But that's not the point. The point is, he can't afford even the slightest hint that he isn't rogue. What the hell are they thinking to come in here like this?" She kept her voice low, so low that she knew Daniel was reading lips more than actually hearing the words. "Do you think DHS isn't covering his ass? I knew it when they sent me in to protect Diego. They won't admit it, but trust me, Daniel, Ian is sanctioned."

"Have you seen them?" he asked her carefully.

She shot her bodyguard an irritated glare. "You know better than that."

"Has he?"

She shook her head quickly.

"Then don't worry about them. If they're here, they're here for their own reasons. Let's see what happens."

And he had still kept from saying, one way or the other, if he was in any way involved in their arrival.

"Warn them." Her smile was icy. "To make damned sure they don't put him in harm's way. Damned sure, Daniel. Or a lot of heads are going to roll. Do you understand me?" His would be one of them. "Anything happens to Ian, and I swear to you, as God is my witness, they'll pay for it."

His lips quirked, and in that flash of amusement she could almost see why his wife thought so much of him. Almost. Right now she was too damned mad to make the effort.

"You're like a lioness protecting a cub." He folded his arms over his chest as he leaned against the balustrade of the railing. "He's a fully grown male, Kira, he can take care of himself."

"That's not the point."

"It's very much the point. Keep trying to protect and control him, and he'll turn on you."

She stared back up at him in shock. "I'm doing no such thing."

For a moment, his expression was hesitant, then it smoothed out and became determined, assured.

"Yes, you are. And he won't like it. He's pissed you're in this to begin with. He believes it's his job to protect you. To keep you out of harm's way. This isn't a man who can accept the danger you live with. Remember that. Ian will always believe it's his duty to stand in the line of fire and your duty to patch up the wounds whether you like it or not."

And she didn't like it, not in the least, but she had a feeling Daniel was right. Ian wasn't very accepting at all of the fact that Martin Missern had attempted to do no more than strike her the night before. Hell, she had taken worse than that on a New York City street by a would-be mugger.

Her lips pressed together firmly as she crossed her arms over her breasts and stared at the wooden floor of the balcony before lifting her head and giving him her lips to read as she whispered. "If you know where they are, you better warn them. He knows they're here."

And he knew. He hadn't outright lied to her, but she knew him well enough to know he would continue the evasive double-talk to protect that knowledge.

He nodded slowly before asking in a soft voice, "What are you going to do when he sends me packing, Kira?"

"Accept it." Ian's voice was throttled with fury.

Kira whirled around, staring back at his shirtless body framed in the balcony entrance, his dark eyes lit with burgundy depths, his expression tight, controlled.

"Daniel isn't going anywhere," she informed him as he stepped out, pacing closer to them, dressed in nothing more than white slacks and anger.

Muscle rippled beneath dark flesh, flexing powerfully as he stepped closer to her, his gaze hard.

"He leaves today or you risk his life," he informed her coldly. "There are no neutral parties here, Kira. Do you understand me?"

"Daniel's loyal to me, Ian," she snapped. "This is not negotiable."

"You made it negotiable when you stuck your nose in my

business," he growled, his eyes going to Daniel. "I want you to leave."

"Ian—"

"No, Kira, he's right." Daniel laid his hand on her arm, his expression suddenly somber. "Your loyalty might not be questioned, but mine will be. I won't be accepted here."

It wasn't the first time she had been forced to work without her bodyguard, it wouldn't be the last, but that didn't mean she had to like it.

"He would be an asset here, Ian," she gritted out.

He shook his head slowly, his gaze coming back to hers, his eyes cold. "He would be a witness. Those aren't tolerated. Do you understand me?"

And she did understand. The servant that had been killed in the Fuentes household that week, her body buried, forever out of sight, reminded her of it. Diego Fuentes had killed a child because she had betrayed Ian, and ordered the death of another. One whom Ian had had slipped quietly off the island and to the States. One had betrayed, the other had been a witness and a danger to the Fuentes cartel that Ian knew would never survive on her own.

Tracking the rumor of the death and learning the events behind it hadn't been easy. Ian covered his tracks too damned well. And he was covering Diego's just as well now.

SHE FELT HER HEART RACE in her chest, a chill chasing up her spine as she searched his eyes and fought against the truth of the life he was facing.

"I'll return to the villa," Daniel said softly. "You can reach me at any time on the secure cell if you need me." His hand gripped her shoulder as she stared up at Ian, barely feeling his comforting touch. "I'll let Jase know you're okay."

"Keep him away from here, Daniel." Ian jerked his gaze back to the bodyguards. "Far away from here. And while you're at it, keep any other friends or alliances you might have out of my sight. I don't have time to separate suspected enemies from true enemies. And I have all the friends I need right now."

With that, he reached out, gripped Kira's arm, and jerked her to him, away from Daniel's touch. She bounced against his chest, pressing her hands against the solid wall of muscle as she stared up at him in surprise.

"No other man touches you." The muscle in his jaw flexed in fury. "As long as you sleep in my bed, you belong to me."

Possessiveness sizzled in his voice, shocking her even more than the move to jerk her to him had. Shocked her, and strangely, aroused her.

The research she had on him hadn't indicated a possessive nature with women. He rarely had close relationships, and chose his lovers with finicky precision for their submissiveness and lack of possessive tendencies.

Her head jerked around and she stared back at Daniel. He stood silently, watching them, his gaze narrowed thoughtfully.

"Tell him to leave, Kira." Ian was adamant.

She breathed out heavily. "Go back to the villa," she told Daniel. "I'll be okay."

"Get out of Aruba," Ian ordered.

"Ian, that's not necessary," she hissed.

"Disappear, Daniel." He ignored her protest. "Do you understand me?"

The threat in his tone was clear. Shocking.

"Ian—"

"You chose me." Ice formed in his voice and in his expression. "You chose to side with me. That choice comes with a price, Kira. I won't accept more innocent blood on my hands than I have to. Do you understand me?" His eyes moved back to Daniel.

Daniel nodded slowly as he flashed Kira a warning look. "I understand, Ian."

"This is insane. No one will believe he just deserted me."
She whirled on Ian furiously. "You can't just order him
away like this. What about backup?"

"Do you want him dead?" Ian snarled. "Stop arguing
with me, Kira. Here and now. Because as God is my witness
your life just might well depend on it. There's no backup
here for a reason. Do you understand me? It's too fucking
dangerous."

He didn't give her a chance to protest further. Gripping
her arm tighter he pulled her back into his bedroom, only
releasing her when the door closed behind them so he could
turn back to secure it.

As he turned back to her, her lips opened to argue, to
blast him for the high-handed decisions he was making. Before the sound could emerge he had his hand over her lips
and his head next to hers.

"Listen to me." His voice was a furious hiss at her ear.
"Seven days ago a nineteen-year-old child was murdered in
front of my eyes because she was deemed a threat to me. A
bullet right through her fucking head, Kira." Agonized fury
echoed in the lowered tone. "Do you want him to die? Do
you want to die?"

His fingers curled in her hair, pulling her head back, his
gaze blazing into hers as she stared back at him in bitter
awareness of what his life had become.

"Don't make me force you to disappear." One hand
framed her jaw as his expression twisted in grief. "God,
please, Kira, don't make me do that."

His lips covered hers before she could speak. His hand
tightened on her jaw, holding her in place as his lips forced
hers open, his tongue thrusting into her mouth as his lips
slanted over hers.

Moving his hand from her jaw, his arm wrapped around
her hips and jerked her to him, notching his cloth-covered
erection into the vee of her thighs as her arms wrapped
around his neck, her fingers spearing into his damp hair.

The hell he lived in tormented her. The blood he couldn't

escape filled her nightmares as did the knowledge that it
was his father that had forced him into it.

"Don't think," he bit out, tearing her robe from her
shoulders, pushing it from her arms and cupping the tight,
swollen mounds of her breasts. "Don't think. Don't protest,
Kira. Just let me have you. Right here. Right now."

How could she do anything less? Her head tipped back, a
cry spilling from her lips as his lips descended to a tight
peak and drew it into his mouth.

Instant wet heat spiked around the bunched nerve endings of her nipple. His teeth scraped over them, lighting
fires that flashed to her womb, clenching it and spilling the
silken wetness of her response from her vagina. And she
could do nothing but hold on to him. His touch, the feel of
his lips on her breast, one arm holding her close, his fingers
pulling at her hair, holding her head back. And between her
thighs she could feel his cock throbbing beneath the thin
cotton slacks, ready, engorged.

"Ian, this is crazy." Crazy because she couldn't breathe,
couldn't think in his arms. And she loved it rather than hating it as she should. She ached for more. Ached for the
world to recede, the knowledge of blood and death to be
wiped away by a passion that burned like wildfire between
them.

"No, *this* is crazy." He released her as quickly as he had
dragged her into his arms, his eyes heavy-lidded, lust burning in them as he quickly stepped away from her. "Get your
shower!"

The abrupt order had her staring back at him in confusion. "My shower?"

The look he gave her was filled with irritation and lust.

"Diego is waiting on us downstairs and I have a meeting
on the other side of the island in less than three hours. That
gives you approximately thirty minutes to shower and
dress."

"Plenty of time." She waved the time constraint away with
a smug smile as she lashed out with her other hand, gripped

the band of his pants, and tried to pull him to her. Or rather, pull herself to him, because he wasn't moving. But as she gripped the band, her fingers flicked the button loose and the other hand gripped his zipper and slid it down. "Gotcha, babe." Her hand slid into his pants, her fingers curling around the broad, thick length of an erection so damned hard it could be iron. Living iron. Pulsing in her hand and sending a surge of hunger through her so strong it weakened her knees.

The feel of him in her hands, heavy veins pulsing beneath steel-hard flesh, his whisky eyes darkening, heating, was more powerful than any aphrodisiac.

His hand latched around her wrist, holding her stroking hand still.

"I won't be easy. And I won't be slow." A dark flush mantled his cheekbones as his eyes narrowed.

"Did I ask for easy? Or slow?"

He jerked her around, pulling a gasp from her lips as she found herself bent over the arm of the nearby chair, her arms pressed out in front of her, his hands gripping her wrists as she felt the first press of his cock against the swollen, sensitive tissue of her pussy.

"It's a good thing you don't want easy," he growled.

The first thrust buried him halfway inside her, stretched her, sent waves of burning pleasure racing up her spine.

"Do you want easy now, Kira?" His voice was a harsh, low snarl at her ear as he pulled back.

"No." She shook her head desperately, then cried out, her back arching as he buried in fully, fiery agonizing ecstasy racing through her pussy.

She felt his legs bracketing hers, bending as he pulled his hips back, his hard shaft sliding sensually, slowly, from the desperate grip her pussy had on him.

"You want more, Kira?"

She felt the muscles of his thighs bunch, felt his hands slide from her wrists to her hips.

"More. Always . . ." Her head fell forward as a scream of agonizing pleasure poured from her lips.

He slammed forward. No easy. He plunged inside her in one hard lunge, aided by the incredibly slick juices that poured from her. His thick flesh slid to the very depths of her, but the impalement parted tight muscles, stroked incredibly sensitive nerve endings, and sent fiery strokes of pleasure ripping through her, over her.

"Ian, oh God, what you do to me." She panted for breath as he withdrew once again. She screamed as he slammed forward again.

It was too good. So good. Especially when he paused, his cock throbbing inside her, his thighs holding hers steady, his hands tightening almost bruisingly on her hips.

"Do to you?" He held himself inside her as her muscles rippled around him, throbbing inside her, making her crazy with the flexing, heavy weight. "You destroy my control."

He drew back, his cock dragging through the sensitive tissue as a hard groan echoed behind her.

"What's control?" She shivered, then shuddered as he retreated.

She knew what was coming. She tried to prepare herself for it. Her fingers clenched in the cushion of the chair, tightening as he pressed her into the opposite arm. But it wasn't enough. He drove inside her, and she came within a breath of fracturing.

Because he didn't stop. The hard, furious thrusts stroked and impaled, penetrated and stretched her, in half a dozen hard plunges that sent her screaming into orgasm. She clamped down on his cock, felt her release rush through her, pumping through her veins, through her mind with a detonated force that had to rival a nuclear explosion.

Behind her, Ian snarled, groaned, then jerked from her grip and a second later spilled his release against the small of her back.

He collapsed over her, the hard ridge of his cock trapped between them as his hips jerked, stroking it between their combined flesh as she shuddered in the final throes of pleasure. It was only then she realized that he hadn't used a condom.

It wasn't the first time she had been taken hard, or fast. But God help her if it wasn't the first time it had blown her mind.

Ian's hand, calloused and rough, dragged her hair back over her shoulder as his lips pressed against the curve of her arm. Hard breaths rippled over her flesh as he held her close, the now damp length of his cock still throbbing between them.

"You have twenty minutes to shower." His voice was guttural, almost angry despite his harsh breaths, his caressing lips. "And by God, you better not be late."

He pulled away from her as she straightened, turning and leaning against the chair, and she watched him fix his slacks. Within seconds, other than a sheen of sweat on his broad shoulders, he was perfectly collected, while her legs felt like spaghetti and her mind was mush.

"Eighteen minutes." His voice was hard, his eyes were blazing with emotions. Anger and remnants of arousal.

"Eighteen minutes." She tensed her legs and forced herself to move away from him. "I'll be ready in ten."

Fifteen

S HE WAS READY IN TEN. Ian watched as she strolled out of the bathroom dressed in white figure-skimming casual pants and a creamy sleeveless blouse.

Her long black hair was mostly dry and fell around her shoulders and down her back in a cascade of rough silk. Lightly tanned flesh contrasted with the white fabric, and those sexy-as-hell legs looked longer with the should-be-illegal white fuck-me pumps she wore with the outfit. She paced over to the walk-in closet where the maid had unpacked her luggage, disappeared inside then returned with a small, matching leather clutch.

She looked like a fallen angel.

Even after the rough treatment he had given her minutes before, bending her over the chair, fucking her like the animal he sometimes felt he was, she still managed to flash him a teasing smile.

After choosing her clothes, Ian had changed his own slacks. He wore navy now with a loose gray finely threaded cotton shirt that hung over the casual pants. He wore boots today. Not combat boots—damn, he missed those—but comfortable, well-made leather boots that would be easier to fight in if the meeting he was heading to took a nosedive.

A meeting he was going to have to take Kira to. His gaze

checked out her outfit again as his back teeth clenched in fury. She had to appear harmless, though he knew for a fact she was anything but.

He moved to the locked dresser drawer where he kept a few smaller weapons, pulled free a backup handgun and several fully loaded clips before relocking the drawer and turning to her.

"Pack these." He handed her the weapon and ammo.

Without comment she took them, tucked them into her purse, and stared back at him with a glimmer of amusement in her blue-ringed gray eyes.

"I had my own weapons," she told him. "What did you do with them?"

"Daniel has them." He tucked his hands in his pants and let his gaze skim over her again. "Those heels are going to be a hell of a handicap if one of these meetings goes sour."

"My heels weren't a handicap in Russia," she reminded him softly. "And if anyone is going to believe I'm a helpless little female, then the look has to be right. Dress me any other way, and they'll be on guard."

And she was right. She couldn't be seen as anything less than all woman. A trophy. Nothing more.

He nodded slowly. "I'm meeting with Josef Missern. After the assassin that followed him to the buy and last night's confrontation, he's offered me a hell of a deal to make up for any *misunderstandings*. We'll be meeting with him to iron out the details and see what he has."

"I should follow behind," she told him.

Ian watched the frown that pulled at her brow as she began to consider the drawbacks to the meeting.

He continued, "We're meeting on the southeast coast of the island. The terrain is flatter and easier to do a flyover. We'll come in on the ground after Trevor takes the copter over it. We'll be in two vehicles. You and I will be with Deke, and Mendez and Cristo will be in the other vehicle. Missern will be meeting with us in the limo rather than in the open. I'll see what he has and then we'll leave."

"Why not teleconference? It would be safer."

"But harder for me to detect facial and body language," he told her. "Missern knows I'm pissed and he's trying to smooth things over before I retaliate against him. Let's see how determined he is to stay alive."

He watched her closely, gauging her reaction to the mention of his retaliation against the arms buyers. There was none; she nodded slowly as though considering the options.

"When we leave there, I'll be meeting with the men that transport Fuentes drugs from the Colombian ports to American waters. You'll stay with Trevor and Cristo while I talk to them. You won't be a part of that meeting."

Her head snapped up as her eyes glittered in protest.

"Wouldn't you consider that a mistake?" She questioned him with an undertone of the commanding force he knew she was capable of.

"No, I consider you being at that meeting very ill-advised. As my lover, your influential position in American society as well as your recognizable name would be a hazard."

Her lips tightened.

"Why didn't you come in disguise?" he asked her. "Why risk yourself like this?"

"You're not in disguise," she finally answered, her voice low. "We do this together, as who and what we are, Ian. And I don't ever want to hear another name from your lips while you're taking me. No matter the circumstances."

Damn her. He hadn't expected that, and he hadn't expected the sharp tug of response that pulled at his chest either.

"Not using a disguise was stupid." Anger built inside him. Dammit, he hadn't had a problem with control, with the things he had to do, until her. Now, the anger was rising inside him, making him a danger to her if he didn't find a way to contain and control it. "Do you have any idea the risk to yourself and your reputation?"

"Temporary." She waved it away. "When it's over both our reputations will recover."

Irritation flashed through him, emotion wore at his

control. She was too confident, too certain of her abilities. It terrified him.

It made him hard.

He stared at her for long moments, trying to understand the effect she had on him, the strength he saw in her. What could have produced a woman so incredibly feminine and yet so strong? In all the years he had come into contact with her she had been protecting rather than protected, and despite her uncle's insistence on a bodyguard, she was fully capable of defending herself.

She made him crazy, and he was smart enough to know that part of the craziness was based on the fact that he was at heart as chauvinistic as they came. He wanted to protect her. He wanted to shield her. And she was having nothing to do with it. It was playing hell on his control and drawing him close enough to her that he could feel the risk to his own soul.

If something happened to her— He cut the thought, pushed it away and turned quickly from her.

"Let's go. Diego is waiting downstairs for us and then we have to head for that meeting."

No emotion, he reminded himself. If he kept his emotions buried then he could watch her enter the life he was forced to live and hopefully survive it.

Hell. Who the fuck was he kidding? She was shredding his control to the point that the night before he had allowed himself to be drawn into a confrontation with Diego and now he was bending Kira over a damned chair and taking her like an out-of-control bastard.

Hell, he hadn't even kissed her first.

As he escorted her from the room, something had him allowing her to move abreast of him, his hand lying naturally at the small of her back. Just to touch her. Guilt was eating him alive, curling in his gut and burning in his chest.

The memory of her bent over that chair, taking him, taking the mix of arousal, jealous anger, and furious concern she caused in him, had his teeth clenching again. He was going to end up wearing his molars down within days because gritting his teeth was the only option at this point.

He couldn't have her kidnapped and held for her own safety. He'd already broached that option with his boss at DHS during his latest secured contact. She was there to stay, he had been informed. Whether or not he put her covert talents to work was up to him, but he couldn't have her taken out of the game, and he couldn't force her out of it.

She was determined to be a part of this and he still couldn't figure out why. Unless she was working with Durango team.

They moved down the steps and headed through the foyer to the breakfast room. He was taking his lover to meet the monster he called his father and he was supposed to do it with a measure of control. He wasn't supposed to be gritting his teeth in arousal and irritation and fighting a hard-on he shouldn't have because his lover was the most self-assured, psychologically strong woman he had ever known in his entire misbegotten life.

As they neared the breakfast room, the houseman opened the double doors, standing back expressionlessly as Ian escorted Kira into the room.

He forced himself to relax, though his hand slid caressingly over Kira's hip, clenching on the curve in regret at the necessity of releasing her and a second later praying Diego hadn't noticed.

"Ian! My son." Diego came to his feet as they stepped into the room, a wide smile creasing his swarthy face, his black eyes gleeful as Ian pulled a chair out for Kira at the small glass-topped table before taking his own across from Diego.

"Good morning, Diego," he greeted the other man as he waved the timid maid forward to pour their coffee.

All the household help had been changed, but the rumors about Liss's death had made its rounds. They were all silent, wary.

"You did not properly introduce me to our guest, Ian."

Discomfort colored Diego's voice, and sweet merciful Jesus, hurt feelings. A monster with feelings that could be hurt. That oxymoron was terrifying.

"Excuse me, Diego." He forced a sheepish smile to his face. "I find myself a bit nervous."

"Nervous, Ian?" Diego blinked back at him in surprise, his gaze softening as he swallowed the impression of Ian's discomfort.

Kira sat back in her chair and smirked as though she were enjoying the sight of Ian's discomfort.

"Kira." Ian cleared his throat. "Allow me to introduce my father." The word tore through his soul with a lash of fury so potent it nearly strangled him as Diego's eyes seemed to dampen. "Diego Fuentes. Diego, Miss Kira Porter."

"Ms. Porter." Pleasure transformed Diego's expression, rippling over it with a tight, hard spasm as he reached for Kira's hand. "It is a pleasure to know my son has managed to capture the interest of such a discriminating and beautiful young woman."

"Mr. Fuentes, I can see where Ian has come by his charm." Kira allowed Diego to hold her hand for only the briefest second before sliding it free and tucking it into her lap.

She stared back at the drug lord with a hint of reserve and wariness. There was no open friendliness. She wasn't hiding the fact that she was very well aware of who and what he was.

"Ah, she is a smart one as well, eh, my son?" Diego grinned as though he were a proud parent. It was enough to make a SEAL's spine crawl in horror.

"She is at that, Diego." He nodded to Kira as though in indulged amusement.

Diego took his chair once again, waved the maid to his coffee cup, and waited until she filled his cup.

"What would you like for breakfast, my dear?" Diego asked her. "We have a nice selection of fruits. Though our

Ian does prefer his protein." He waved his hand to the buffet that sat along the wall.

"I like a bit of each." Kira eyed the buffet with hungry longing. "It's a good thing I have a high metabolism." Mocking amusement lit her expression and her eyes as she nodded to the maid who waited patiently. "The eggs, bacon, and one of those luscious-looking biscuits. I'll tackle the fruit after."

Diego's brows lifted at her request, even as she brought the strong, unsweetened coffee to her lips and sipped at it with enjoyment.

"Ah, a woman with an appetite," Diego murmured. "I believe the American magazine *Society* described you as 'today's woman.' One whose appetites clearly express the hungers of the modern woman."

Ian had read that article, and laughed. The society image was definitely not the true Kira Porter.

"*Society* insisted on discussing my eating habits rather than the topic we agreed to discuss: the charity work my uncle and myself were doing at that time."

Diego chuckled. "The editor claimed you were doing more to destroy the image of the glamorous socialite than those who had gone before you had done to uphold it. I thought it was clearly the mark of an intelligent, strong woman." Diego sat back in his chair at that point. "I believe the interview also touched upon drug use. Your stand on drugs was exceptionally strong. Your comments that those who trade in the death and misery of the world should be drawn, quartered, and left for the maggots to feed upon." His voice remained warm, encouraging, his gaze curious.

"Diego," Ian said warningly. "Not exactly appetizing conversation for breakfast."

Diego's nostrils flared at the rebuke. "I would know why a woman with such views would lower herself to sleep with not just a drug cartel leader, but also a deserter. Tell me, Ms. Porter, why would you risk your reputation and your safety by sleeping with my son?"

"Mr. Fuentes, what *Society* didn't mention is that I am a woman. *I* choose who I care for. Not convention." She leaned forward, cutting Ian off before he could tear into his father. He paused, leaned back in his chair, and watched Kira instead.

Her expression was revealing now. This *was* the woman. His woman. That expression caused his erection to jerk in his slacks, the broad head to throb painfully now.

"You do not say?" Diego questioned curiously.

"But I do say." She sat back in her chair once again and flashed Ian a look shimmering with hunger. Damn her. She picked a hell of a time to give him that look. To allow him to glimpse the emotions she kept mostly hidden.

"Finish your breakfast then we're leaving." His voice was harsh. He heard it, and he didn't regret it. He turned to Diego. "Do you understand the concept 'mine'?"

"Ian, this isn't necessary," Kira protested with a hint of amusement. "I'm certain your father understands we all have our little kinks."

His gaze flashed to her, the anger rising, burning, threatening his control. He turned back to Diego.

"Did you understand my question?"

Diego nodded slowly. "Yes, Ian. I understand. I will question her no further." There was a warning in his voice as well. "I understand that we must protect what belongs to us."

Ian rose from his chair, breakfast forgotten, coffee forgotten. His eyes locked with Diego's as he reached out his hand to Kira.

She was there instantly, her fingers twining with his, allowing him to pull her from her chair, to his side.

"We've wasted too much time," he said tightly. "We'll stop on the way and get you a snack."

"Protein?" she asked, her voice lower, hinting toward suggestive.

Ian couldn't damned well help it. His gaze almost jerked from Diego's in surprise and his cock definitely became highly interested.

"Definitely protein." He stared back at Diego, watching the other man's expression, the gleam of amusement in his black eyes, the way he relaxed, the aura of death sliding beneath the charm once again.

"We'll talk later tonight," he warned Diego quietly. "I promise you that."

He drew Kira from the room and met up with Deke and the others in the foyer.

"Deke, we need to swing around Palm Beach for coffee and breakfast to go for Kira. Duetch Veronick should work."

"Duetch Veronick." Deke nodded his dark head. "Gotcha, boss."

Ian looked down at her as he escorted her from the villa. Damn her. Kira had to have known what her little innuendo would do to him. Just as Diego was learning there truly were certain ways to work him. Both of them were going to find out, he knew how to work back.

As they stepped from the wide sheltered porch of the villa Ian handed Kira into the limousine before following her into the cool, leather interior.

She slid into the backward-facing seat, settling into the leather and crossing her legs gracefully as she laid her slender clutch beside her. Taking his seat opposite her, Ian stared back at her silently while Mendez closed the door behind them and the vehicle began to move out.

Ian laid his finger on the window control between the two seats, still staring at Kira as the blackened window glass rose between the two sections.

"That look in your eye could almost be arousing, if it weren't so calculating," she drawled, an accent flavoring her voice with a hint of Georgia nights and Southern Belle charm. "What are you thinking, Ian?" Her hands lay relaxed against her legs and her head was tilted to the side as she watched him thoughtfully.

"Drug deals. Arm deals. Blood and death." He smiled mockingly. "What else does a cartel owner think about?"

She licked her tongue over her already glistening lips and her gaze flickered before coming back to him questioningly.

"The vehicle is secure," he told her. "There are no listening devices. We're safe."

"How can you be sure? You didn't check the car when we got in."

Ian sighed before pushing his hand into his pocket and pulling the slender electronic detector from his pants. He flashed it to her before pushing it back.

It was the size of a cell phone, but the electronics it contained were sensitive to a variety of receivers.

She breathed out in regret. "You're not going to let me see that one either, are you?"

"It's an experimental model." He grinned. "But I'm open to negotiations. Answer some questions for me and I'll let you play with my toys."

He watched realization glimmer in her eyes a second before she shrugged her delicate shoulders. "I'll check it out when this is over. Uncle Jason will likely get me one for Christmas."

Ian nodded slowly. "How long has Jason been covert?"

"I didn't say Jason was covert." Her hands tightened in her lap.

"No more than you told me that Durango team was in Aruba." He leaned forward slowly, his voice turning to ice as he glowered back at her. "You were discussing them with Daniel this morning. You were discussing the fact that he would be sent away and his knowledge that Durango team was here."

Surprise and nervousness flickered over her expression then.

"I have the balcony bugged." He leaned back in his seat. "I checked the recording while you were in the shower."

"Then you know I have no knowledge of the team being here."

"But you know Daniel. And he does know where they are. So the first question is, where would Daniel set them up and how would he help them?"

Silence filled the back of the limo. Their gazes clashed, tension exploding in the back of the limo as they battled in a silent war Ian was determined to win.

"Why does it matter, Ian?" she finally asked him. "*If* they're here, they havent disobeyed direct orders not to strike against you. They haven't struck. Maybe they've figured out you're not the loving son you've tried to appear to be, and they're here to help you."

"And do you think I need their damned help?"

If she had thought about his possible response to knowing his former team lay in wait to help him, then Kira knew she would not have expected the fury that burned in his eyes or the hard hand that wrapped around the back of her neck and pulled her nose to nose with him as he came forward once again.

"You will contact Daniel," he told her icily, his voice harsh, his expression forbidding. "And you will tell him to give Reno a message for me. Reno only. You tell Daniel to tell him, 'Killer Secrets.' He'll know what it means, Kira. And you tell Daniel to warn him, I mean every word of it."

Killer Secrets. There were too many personal threads, too many enemies posing as friends, and no way to sort the differences before striking. It meant he was working alone, period, and the situation was too volatile for interference.

Kira stilled. Nathan Malone had mentioned that codeword the month before when she questioned him in the hospital. The threads leading into and out of this operation could get them all killed, and Ian wasn't sharing information. Whether it was because he couldn't share, or wouldn't, she could only guess.

"Did they tell you what that means?" Ian released her slowly, sitting back in his seat with a deliberate relaxing of his body that didn't fool her in the least.

"What?" she asked though she knew what he meant. What he meant wasn't nearly as important to her as what she was seeing in him right now.

Cold, hard purpose. There was none of the arousal, none of the hunger or the need she had glimpsed in him to this point. This wasn't the playful lieutenant who had identified her during the ops where they had connected. He wasn't the frustrated lover trying to protect her. This was the SEAL. And he was determined that nothing would stand in the way of taking Sorrell's and Diego's heads back to the man he called brother.

"Did the team tell you what that code word means?" He didn't blink, his eyes didn't burn. They chilled her to the bone.

"They told me," she admitted, wondering if she was hurting or harming her cause with the admission.

Emotion flickered in the back of his eyes then.

"And you came anyway?" His lips flattened with the first sign of emotion. Anger sparked in his gaze. "Have you lost your fucking mind, Kira?"

Had she? No, he was just that important to her. And when exactly he had become that important to her she wasn't really certain.

"Would you leave me in this battle alone?" she asked him instead. "If you stumbled into this situation and learned the danger I was in, would you walk away from me, Ian?"

"That's different." More emotion. A tinge of stubborn determination and a flash of latent hunger.

"How's that different?" She leaned forward, her chest tightening with emotions she was still trying to make sense of. "How's it different that you couldn't walk away from me, but you expect me to walk away from you?"

"You're a woman." He cleared his throat then grimaced at the unconscious flash of nervousness he would have known she saw in that action. "You don't desert a woman in trouble."

"But I wouldn't believe I was in trouble," she told him. "I'm a trained agent. I would believe I was handling it fine myself. That I didn't need you to protect me. Why would you want to stick your nose into it?"

And why did she need him to admit that he cared more for her than he would any other female agent that his male chauvinism would insist he help? She was the fool he called her if she needed that. Because Ian Fuentes wasn't a man who let himself get involved emotionally with many people. She knew he loved his mother. He respected his stepfather, and he had sworn his life to Nathan Malone after the preteen Nathan had been instrumental in saving Ian's mother's life.

From what she had learned, Ian had a team bond with the other SEALs of the group he had fought with. He respected them, he would have died for them. And he protected them, as he was protecting them now.

He was an island unto himself, the team had revealed. Friendships were all work related, and female relationships lasted only weeks. Ian scratched an itch, nothing more, when it came to those women that he so easily walked away from.

The only thing that had given her hope was the knowledge that Ian *knew* her. No matter her disguise, no matter her persona, he could see through it. It took more than a good eye to do that. And it took more than a good eye for a man to walk away from scratching his itch as he had the night when he slipped into her condo.

She had made him feel something that night. She knew she had. She had been watching his eyes at the same moment she had realized herself that Ian could touch her as no other man ever had.

"You're not answering me, Ian. Why would you help me even if I felt I didn't need your help?" Strike while they're weak. Jason had drilled that into her since she was ten years old, but somehow, she had a feeling he hadn't envisioned this situation.

She slid from her seat, lowered herself to the soft carpet of the floor between them, and wedged herself between his thighs.

And he hadn't expected that. But she hadn't expected it of herself either. Something softened that she hadn't known was hard inside her. She was a woman rather than an agent. A lover rather than a weapon. And the transition was so natural, so freeing, that for the first time in her life, she was beginning to wonder exactly who she was as well.

Sixteen

"YOU'RE TOO QUIET NOW," SHE murmured, her hands sliding up the insides of his thighs then along his tight abs to his chest.

"I would have still tried to protect you." He swallowed, the movement tight, tense. As tight and tense as the muscles beneath her hand. And his eyes were warming, darkening.

"Why would you have done that, Ian? That's my question. Because you're a chauvinist, or because of something more?"

He surprised her when he reached out, trailing his fingers down her cheek, and said somberly, "I am a chauvinist, Kira. I need to protect you."

"And I need to be here with you, Ian." It was all she could do to keep her voice from shaking, her eyes from filling with tears. "I need to watch your back."

"What the hell am I going to do with you?" He pressed his forehead against hers as he framed her face with his hands and stared down at her as though confused by her. "I know what I'm doing here. I can work this better alone."

"And do without this?" Her lips touched his, smoothed over them before she allowed her tongue to peek between her lips and dampen the male curves. "Why should either of us do without, Ian? I can help you. And I can . . . satisfy you."

Love you. Those words had almost escaped past her lips. They did send a surge of heat and fear rushing through her.

Did she love him? Was that why she couldn't let him go? Good Lord, when could something like that have happened?

"You can only distract me," he growled, but his lips were still whispering over hers. His tongue touched hers. His teeth caught her bottom lip and nipped erotically. She shouldn't have felt such pleasure from a simple caress, yet it streaked through her senses and sent heat curling through her womb.

"Only when you need to be distracted." Her hand curled around his neck, fingers sliding into his hair, holding him to her as her lips parted further beneath his.

Unfortunately, he didn't take the offered kiss or satisfy her need for his taste. One hand gripped her hair and pulled her head back enough for her to glimpse the knowing light in his eyes.

"I'm not such a pervert that you can distract me with sex in the limo, Kira," he assured her, amusement mixing with irritation. "And this was a serious conversation we were attempting to have."

"Since when?" She rolled her eyes in mocking exasperation. "All I'm hearing are warnings and dire threats. Chill out, Ian. I make a damned good partner if I say so myself. You should really consider yourself lucky to have me."

A frown jerked between his brows, but before he could speak the door beside him was pulled open. Before Kira could react herself, Ian pushed her back, jerked his weapon from his side, crouching in front of Kira, the barrel of the gun locked beneath Deke's chin.

"Protein," Deke wheezed, his tanned face paling. "Thought you knew we stopped."

Kira peeked over Ian's shoulder at the small covered silver tray. She could smell coffee and bacon and she was hoping against hope there were fluffy eggs under there as well.

Ian eased the gun back as she pushed past him, took the tray, and flashed Deke a smile.

"He's touchy, huh? I told him to chill out."

Deke cleared his throat. "Brought you breakfast as well, boss." He rubbed his neck as he pulled back, reached behind him, and accepted another tray. Leaning forward, he placed it in the seat across from Ian. After delivering the food he moved back quickly and closed the door. A few seconds later the vehicle restarted and was moving once again.

"She sat back, uncovered her tray, and inhaled in satisfaction when she saw the mound of fluffy scrambled eggs awaiting her. Coffee, no cream or sugar. A pile of bacon, two homemade biscuits, a dish of jam, and silverware.

"Almost like home," she murmured. "Why haven't I found this place during my visits here?"

"Veronick doesn't do breakfast for just anyone," Ian snapped. "Goddamn, Kira, you didn't even realize the fucking car had stopped."

Kira dug her fork into the fluffy eggs. "Of course I did. And so did you."

She watched his expression from the shield of her lashes. God, she was loving this. Loving sparring with him, confronting him, pushing him.

He stared back at her in bemused irritation. "How the hell do you figure that?"

She sighed, swallowed, then pointed her fork at him. "I felt it. You tensed, your eyes dilated, then you slowly relaxed. You knew. Deke just caught you off guard when he opened the door."

He dropped his head back, stared up at the ceiling as though he were praying, and breathed out roughly. "You're going to drive me crazy."

"Of course not." She gave him a rather delicate snort. "But I might be able to teach you to have a little bit of fun. Did I mention you had grown rather prickly over the last eight months? You used to know how to have fun, Ian."

He used to know what fun was, anyway.

"I used to know better than to involve myself in operations with you," he bit out. "You're dangerous, you're reckless, and I swear to God I've never met a woman that needed tying down for her own safety more than you do."

She widened her eyes. "Wow. Been holding that in for a while, Ian?"

She had to suppress a smile. He wasn't angry, at least not at her. She was affecting him, and she knew that affecting Ian wasn't an easy thing to do. She hadn't expected him to handle it nearly this well. He hadn't tied her to his bed while he went about his business; she considered that a major step in the right direction.

"Tonight, you're spanked," he informed her darkly. "Spanked until you scream for more, Kira."

"That's punishment?" she asked with a grin as a shiver of anticipation raced up her spine. She could handle that.

"No." He shook his head slowly. "That's my reward for not strangling you."

JOSEF MISSERN WAS AT HIS most charming. He stepped into the limo, taking the rear-facing seat and staring across the short distance at Ian and Kira. A sly smile curled the Frenchman's lips and lit his light blue eyes.

"Ah, how nice to see you again, Ms. Porter," he greeted her. "As lovely as a sunrise and as deceptive as the oceans." He chuckled. "You are a fitting mate to one such as he." He nodded to Ian with a sharp movement of his white-blond head.

"Let's get down to business, Missern." Ian's voice hardened at the obvious flirtation in the other man's voice. If Ian hadn't wanted to kill him before, he wanted to kill him now. "Would you like to tell me the connection you have to Sorrell?"

The slightest dilation in Josef's eyes assured Ian he wasn't off the mark.

"We are here to discuss weapons, my friend." Josef smiled easily once again. "I am willing to make you a one-time deal at a wholesale price in apology for the assassin that showed up at our meeting, as well as the strike Martin would have taken at our fair Miss Porter. His games are sometimes not always understood by those who do not know him."

"And the assassin? Was he a game as well?" Ian asked coldly.

"He was an unknown variable." Josef sighed as though in regret. "We did not know he was there."

"Let's cut the shit, Missern," Ian snapped. "You knew, because you told Sorrell about the meeting. Just as Martin's attempt to strike Kira was a move designed to draw our relationship out into the open."

Josef's sensual lips pursed in amusement. "The information came to us by an anonymous source that told of your connection in Atlanta, and here as well. It seems you have other eyes watching you, my friend."

"And you report your tips concerning me to your good friend Sorrell," Ian suggested. "It's a very dangerous way to live, Josef."

"I did not relay this tip, Ian." Josef shook his head firmly. "Rather, I received it from a source that paid a hefty amount to have the connection proven." He spread his palms upward. "It was a business transaction. Yes?"

"Or your death warrant." Ian dropped his voice to a guttural suggestion, aware of Kira's subtle tension beside him and Missern's flash of fear before he covered it.

"We are men of business, Ian." Josef shifted uncomfortably in his seat. "This is what I have enjoyed in our dealings together. You understand the value of the dollar over the stains of blood. I am here to make amends for these things. I do not wish to war with the Fuentes cartel."

Ian tilted his head and stared back at Josef mockingly before he turned and stared out the window of the car instead. There, Trevor was landing the specially modified helicopter just as planned.

"Ian?" Josef questioned him curiously. "Is there a problem?"

"Order your men down, Josef," he ordered as the Missern bodyguards turned their weapons on the helicopter. "You're in no danger. You have my word on it."

Josef watched him closely but pulled his cell phone from the pocket of his jacket and hit the keypad.

"Pull back," he said into the receiver as his gaze clashed with Ian's. "We have his word no harm will come."

Ian let a smile tug at his lips at the unspoken trust. He had learned that even here, in this world, a man was judged by his word.

"I've exacted my payment for Martin's attempt to touch what belongs to me," he told Josef as he held Josef's gaze. "I'll also accept a hundred M-16s at wholesale price, three grenade launchers, and an amount of ammo to be determined once I return to the villa and discuss our needs with Diego."

Josef blinked back at him. "Quite a bit of apology, wouldn't you say?"

"Consider yourself lucky." Ian lowered the window beside him and nodded toward the helicopter. A door slid open, and the instantly recognizable form of Martin Missern tumbled from the side. He struggled to his feet, his swollen, bloodied face staring in weak bemusement at the limo as several of the bodyguards rushed for him.

"What the hell is this? *Mon Dieu*, what have you done to him?" Josef's hand went to the door only to have his wrist caught by Ian's, twisted, and his body jerked around until his face was pressed into the leather seat as he bellowed in pain.

"He's alive," Ian snarled, tamping down his regret that Kira was here. That she was seeing him as he was. "I should have killed him, Josef. Next time, I'll kill both of you."

He leaned over the arms dealer's body, his head next to Missern's, his eyes glaring into the light blue pain-ridden gaze of the other man.

"The next time Sorrell wants information, the next time he wants you to strike out at what's mine, remember this.

And remember, next time I'll beat the life out of you my-self. I don't think you want that, do you?"

Josef shook his head desperately, sweat beading his brow as broken gasps left his lips.

"I learned a lot of ways to hurt a man in the American military." He twisted Missern's wrist easily, dragging an-other cry from his lips. "Ways that make a man pray for death. Don't make me watch you pray, Josef. It would just piss me off and bite into my schedule. When you do that, I get mean." Ian pressed his thumb deeper into the other man's wrist, gave it a hard twist, and heard it crack. It didn't break. It didn't dislocate, but the distinctions in pain were so slight as to be negligible.

He released the shuddering man, moved back to his seat, and pushed the door open.

"While you're contemplating betraying me and talking to Sorrell on the phone, inform him that if he wants to end this, then he'll meet with me. The next time he sends one of his fuck buddies to strike out at me, I'll start killing them. That's a promise, Josef, you hear me?"

Josef struggled back to the seat, staring back at Ian fear-fully, his once perfectly combed white-blond hair lying mussed around his face now.

"You are letting us leave alive?" he asked hesitantly.

Ian shook his head and tsked mockingly. "I keep my word, Josef. Unlike Sorrell. I'll give you one last piece of advice. Get the hell out of Aruba until Sorrell and I come to an understanding, because I'd hate to have to kill you. Now get out of my limo. I've had enough of you."

He grabbed the lapels of the arms dealer's jacket, jerked him from the seat, and threw him from the car. Josef strug-gled to his feet, lurched toward his bodyguards, and cast one last wary look back at the limo as Ian slammed the door closed.

The helicopter lifted from the ground as the limo pulled from the meeting area and began to pick up speed along the eastern coast of the island.

"Why did we drive out here rather than flying?"

The question wasn't the one he had expected, nor was her calm demeanor. Though he knew he shouldn't have expected anything less.

"Because I like the drive," he growled.

"Liar."

He breathed out roughly. "The first two months I was here I had two copters brought down and three bodyguards taken out. They have a harder time attacking the limo."

"They?"

He grunted a sharp laugh. "Who the fuck knows. Pissed-off SEALs and SFs, Sorrell's men, DEA, CIA, FBI. Hell, there are agents from a dozen alphabet-soup agencies in the world staked out on this damned island since I came here."

And he didn't blame a damned one of them for trying to take him out. Now, it wasn't just him though. It was Kira as well. Son of a bitch. Suddenly, this mission was beginning to seriously tax his patience. In ways he had never imagined possible.

He pushed his fingers through his hair and checked their location. He pulled the Glock free of his side holster, checked the clip then pulled the extra clips from the pockets of his pants and checked them.

Turning, he stared through the back window at the SUV following them. Mendez and Cristo had the heavier weapons with them, Trevor was watching overhead with the copter.

Hell, he wished he was in that damned copter. Unfortunately they were too easy to track and too easy to take out of the sky. And he had too many enemies now.

"What's happening with this meet we're driving to, Ian?"

He returned his gaze to her as he shoved the Glock back in its holster.

He shook his head firmly. "I told you what the meeting involved."

Her expression was scoffing. "Come on, Ian, don't pull that on me. Tell me what's really going on."

"There's nothing to pull." He shrugged. "I need to meet with some of the men that are transporting loads between Colombia and American waters. I give them their GPS coordinates for the first phase of delivery. After that, they receive transportation routes in phases."

What he wasn't telling her was the fact he suspected at least one of the transporters was going to be mildly upset when they learned that their loads had been shifted to other parties.

The men he was dealing with here weren't regular Fuentes soldiers or cartel members. Diego had been using independent contract workers for the most part until Ian arrived. Ian had slowly been replacing those contractors with cartel members. Efficiency, he had explained to Diego. Efficiency be damned; it would make the cartel that much easier to take down when Diego fell.

In this particular instance though, the men he was getting ready to replace wouldn't exactly take it with a shrug and smile. He wasn't firing a union member, he was firing a cutthroat, murderous drug dealer with delusions of status.

Rodrigo Cruz was on the DEA's and FBI's most wanted lists. When this was over, Ian hoped he would be either dead or maneuvered into a position that would allow capture within a matter of days.

At times like this, he was forcefully reminded that perhaps genetics and DNA were indeed stronger than hatred. Because he had learned he could be just as deceptive, controlling, and manipulating as the man who had donated the sperm in his conception.

"How dangerous do you anticipate this little meeting turning?"

He stared at her, proud of her, terrified of losing her, though a part of him knew she was his greatest strength now.

"Oh, I don't know, Kira," he drawled. "I'm meeting with half a dozen cocaine transporters whose fortunes depend upon securing each successive shipment. What do you think?"

"I think that if you weren't planning something to piss them off then there would be little danger involved. Unless you suspected one of them of conspiring with Sorrell."

"Right now, I suspect everyone in the Fuentes camp of conspiring with Sorrell." He snorted. "I've learned to be careful, that's all."

"If that's all, then I can go in with you," she stated.

"Do you want me to tie you to the bed the next time I have a meeting that I refuse to allow you to attend?" He stared back at her, knowing the look on his face was just short of savage. Hell, he felt savage. He knew each time he walked into one of these meetings that it could be his last. And now it could endanger her as well.

"Chauvinism doesn't become you, Ian." She sighed. "Very well, I'll wait in the limo like a good little girl."

Ian nodded sharply. "This shouldn't take long," he told her as the limo neared the port town Oranjestad. "It's just a meeting. The business Fuentes does here in Aruba is simple. Orders go out from here. Dealers pick up their cargo in Colombia. I don't risk actual shipments onto the island."

"What I'd like to know is how you've managed to keep your head on your shoulders here. Aruba isn't exactly a good hiding place."

"I'm not hiding." He shrugged. "I've not been arrested because I've managed to escape every operation sent out against me. I don't have predictable travel routes and I don't let myself become comfortable. And that's besides the fact that money does talk. Aruba hasn't yet given the U.S. permission to conduct an operation against me on their turf."

"I was under the impression Aruba had a very close relationship with America," Kira pointed out. "You're a deserter . . ."

"You didn't do your homework." That word had the power to clench his guts. "The truth is, I resigned my commission.

The papers were logged in to the system during the Atlanta mission; I was due to step down a week later."

"You did it a week early. Technically, a deserter."

He inclined his head in mocking agreement. "My lawyers are arguing that case in Washington as a matter of fact. The cartel has some excellent lawyers."

And that was the truth. Of course, neither the Navy nor DHS was pushing too hard at this time for charges.

A smile tugged at her lips as her gaze went past him to the vista of perfect blue waters that surrounded the island. Her sharp frown was his first warning.

"Evade! Evade!" Trevor's voice across the receiver located in the radio at the side of the backward-facing seat was his final warning.

He pushed Kira to the floor as the limo swerved and the back window began lowering. His head swung around, a curse leaving his lips, as the front of the limo seemed to explode, the car flying across the road and burying itself in the side of a rocky sand dune.

The force of the landing flung him across the car as he fought to hold Kira in place. Even as the vehicle shuddered he kicked the door open, dragging her out and throwing her toward Mendez and Cristo as they rushed for the limo.

"Get Trevor on the ground," he yelled to Mendez as Cristo caught Kira. "Now."

He gripped the driver's-side door, pulling at it before cursing when it didn't open. Turning, he jumped into the back of the vehicle, climbing through the back partition to check Deke.

"How's Deke?" Mendez yelled.

"Alive." Barely.

Ian gripped the passenger door, forced it open then backed out as he dragged Deke's heavy, unconscious body across the seat. Mendez and Cristo helped lift him as wind from the helicopter's rotors beat around them.

"Boss, two speedboats," Trevor yelled as he rushed toward

them, grabbing Deke's legs as Cristo and Mendez grabbed his upper body.

"Get him in the copter," Ian snapped. "Now. Call the villa and have the doc pulled in. Trevor, did you get any ID marks on those boats?"

"I know them, boss." He was walking backward, rushing Deke's lower body to the copter while the rest of them followed. "Both are rentals out of Oranjestad."

They loaded Deke quickly into the copter as Ian turned for Kira and nearly did a double take.

She was poised, shoeless, her hair whipping around her, an M-16 braced in her arms as she secured the area. Ian knew he had never seen anything so damned hot in his life.

"Let's go." He stepped to her quickly, pulled the weapon from her hands, and tossed it to Mendez. "Mendez, you and Cristo get to the villa double time." He pushed Kira into the front of the copter with Trevor before jumping into the cramped back with a still unconscious Deke.

His gaze stayed on Kira as the helicopter lifted off, banked, and raced across the island. He hated using air power.

"Tracking's on, boss, we're showing no locks. We'll make it."

The advanced radar and weapons detection equipment he'd had installed was his best insurance in case of emergency but it wasn't foolproof.

"Just get us there, Trevor," he called out, his gaze meeting Kira's as she turned her head and stared back at him worriedly.

She was in the middle of a war zone and he couldn't force her out or protect her. The knowledge of that ate at his guts and tightened his chest as anger burned inside him.

He wanted her out of here. He wanted her so far from this situation that there wasn't a chance of it touching her, and he knew it wasn't going to happen. She wasn't just a trained contract agent. She was a woman who had a hold on his balls which he couldn't seem to break.

Chauvinism, his ass. This was more than chauvinism, this was an emotion he couldn't conquer and couldn't force behind him. It was a mix of protectiveness and possessiveness, fury and worry. She was getting to him and he had no idea how to stop it.

Seventeen

THE HELICOPTER LANDED DIRECTLY BEHIND the villa. Men raced from the French doors that led to the pool area, M-16s and Uzis gripped in their hands, to surround the aircraft as Ian jumped from the side and motioned to several of the soldiers to ease the lead bodyguard through the opening and carry him into the house.

Kira accepted Trevor's helping hand from the pilot's door, her eyes on Ian, seeing the lines bracketing his lips and eyes, the barely contained rage that glittered in his gaze.

"The doctor is en route," one of the Fuentes soldiers that had converged on the villa shouted to Ian as the helicopter's rotors slowly eased and stopped. "Ramon called when they left town. Another three minutes at the most."

Ian nodded then turned, his hand latching around Kira's wrist and dragging her to his side before heading for the villa.

"Get him in his room and show the doctor straight to him. Get out to the limo and get it towed and ditch it. I want all evidence of this attempted hit wiped away. Understand that?" he snapped to the soldier.

"Sí." The soldier turned away, called several soldiers to him, and rushed to the attached garage rather than entering the house with the rest of the force.

As they moved through the informal patio room and into

the wide hallway toward the foyer, Kira watched as Diego Fuentes came out from his study. He said nothing, but his expression was heavy, concerned. Black eyes were shielded by dark lashes, his lips tightly compressed. He was worried, and perhaps a bit frightened. Kira would have taken the time to reflect more on that if Ian wasn't pulling her quickly up the stairs in the wake of the soldiers carrying Deke.

"Go to our room," he ordered, his voice flat and hard as he unlocked the door and pushed her inside. "I'll be right back." The door closed in her face.

Kira rolled her eyes. There were some moods that she wouldn't mind opposing, but something in his eyes warned her to steer clear of pushing him much harder right now. Waiting would likely be the smartest decision. And when he came to her— She blew out a hard breath. She had seen that mood before, the racing adrenaline, the need for action. When he began coming down, he was going to be ready for more than tea and cakes.

She rubbed at the chill that raced over her arms and tried to still the excitement that began to claw at her stomach. He was going to be hard, confrontational. Ready to go head-to-head with the first person willing to give him the chance.

She knew. The adrenaline wasn't as all-consuming for her as it was for most men she had worked with. She had seen some of the operatives and SEALs she had worked with fight or fuck for hours after coming down from a dangerous situation.

Fucking just for the sake of the adrenaline had never been her thing, until Ian. She could definitely see the benefits of it now.

She pushed her fingers roughly through her hair at that thought. She could have lost him today. And she knew it wasn't the first time he had been attacked. In the past eight months there had been half a dozen attempts.

Turning away from the door, she walked halfway across the room before she realized she had left her shoes in the damned limo. They were a favorite pair too.

She paced to the couch, pulled the slender strap of her clutch purse from over her head, and lifted the cell phone from it.

She glanced around before moving into the bathroom, standing inside the doorway and reaching in to turn on the water in the porcelain sink before hitting the speed dial.

"Son of a bitch, I knew this was a bad idea." Daniel answered on the first ring. "Are you okay?"

"I'm fine." She kept her voice low and hoped any listening devices Ian might have in the room couldn't pick her voice up over the flow of water beside her. "Who was it?"

"We're working on it."

"We?" She pinched the bridge of her nose. "God, he's going to have a cow if you mean who I think you do."

"Don't look a gift horse in the mouth, dammit," Daniel cursed. "We're tracking down the boats. We've narrowed them to one rental agency but they weren't listed as rented. We should have more info soon."

"Get it fast. He's in a killing mood. This could get ugly."

"Any fatalities?"

"None. His head bodyguard is unconscious though. The wound to his head didn't look pretty. Head to steering wheel, I suspect."

"He needs to accept the hand reaching out to help," Daniel growled. "Broach the subject, Kira. He's going to need it."

Her laughter was low and bitter as she kept her eyes on the door. Ian wouldn't accept the risk to his friends and she knew it. He considered this *his* battle because Diego was *his* father.

"Won't happen. Tell your gift horses he sent them a message though. Killer Secrets. And let me tell you, he was serious."

Daniel's curse sizzled over the secure line.

"My thoughts too . . ." She flipped the phone quickly, disconnecting the call and shoving the phone back into her purse as the doorknob twisted.

Sliding in front of the sink, she bent and splashed water over her face, her heart racing in her chest at the close call. If Ian caught her on the phone he'd likely tie her to his bed for the remainder of this operation, because he would know damned good and well what she was doing on it.

Eyes still closed, she turned off the water, gripped the hand towel on the silver rack and pulled it free. Covering her face with it, she quickly dried off, then opened her eyes and didn't bother restraining her gasp.

Diego stood in the doorway, black rage flickering in his gaze as he stared back at her.

"Does he know who did this?" His voice was low, filled with death.

This was the Diego Fuentes she had investigated, the one she had worked to break, in several different missions, and failed.

She shook her head slowly. She didn't have to fake the flash of fear she felt, especially when she saw the butt of the weapon sticking from above the band of his pants.

"You fear me." There was an edge of satisfaction in his voice and a flash of smug amusement in his gaze. "I think I am too used to dealing with Ian. He knows no such fear."

"You're his father. Why would he fear you?" She cleared her throat, wondering if he was susceptible to a bit of flattery.

"Yes." He looked away for a moment, but when his gaze returned to her it was as flat as it had been before. "I am his father, and I still do not know what happened. You will tell me."

She shook her head, swallowing tightly, as she let in the memory of the limo flying and crashing into the rocky outcropping across the road. Fear had nearly immobilized her, but not fear for herself, fear for Ian.

Diego's lips tightened again at the flash of emotion she allowed him to see.

"I don't know what happened." God help her and Diego both if she told him anything Ian didn't want him to know. "One minute we were driving down the coast, the next we were flying in that limo."

He inhaled slowly, his nostrils widening as his expression turned savage. She could have sworn pain flashed in his eyes.

"That is unfortunate," he finally expressed. "I would know who to kill for this action against my son."

"You and me both." She gave him delicate snort as she moved past him back into the sitting room. The tiny bathroom was much too small for comfort when dealing with Diego. "It wasn't exactly a party out there."

"Do you know he would be angry should I retaliate for his sake?" Diego bit out. "He denies me even the smallest pleasures now. Bah. His arrogance. It will get him killed."

And he was telling her this why? Kira stared back at him hesitantly. Diego wasn't known for his compassion or trusting nature. Quite the opposite. So why was he talking to her?

"Maybe he's trying to protect you?" She put several feet between them, though how that would help if he pulled that gun she didn't know.

At her suggestion, his gaze sharpened.

"Do you think this is true?" He frowned as though he hadn't considered that thought. As though the suggestion suddenly filled him with hope.

"Well." Kira licked her lips nervously. "He doesn't let me have any fun either. He even took my guns. Said it was for my own protection."

God, she was playing games with the master here. Ian was right, she had lost her mind.

Diego lifted his hand and stroked his jaw, his sharp eyes watching her like a cobra watches its prey.

"You like to live on the dark side, do you not, Ms. Porter?"

She wagged her brows. "Darth Vader was my hero."

His lips twitched as he wagged his brow in turn. "You are a very naughty little girl."

"Well, I used to try hard." She rolled her eyes mockingly. "As I said, Ian seems to think I should let him have all the fun. He's protecting me."

"And you do not like protection."

"Not used to it." She shrugged as she took a seat on the couch and curled her legs to the side as though she were talking to a normal lover's father rather than one of the most notorious drug lords in the world. A man that could kill her as easily as he could smile at her.

"Neither am I used to this protection," he said thoughtfully. "It would indicate more than a mere job, am I not correct? Perhaps a bit of feeling?"

Kira frowned as though confused. "You're his father, correct?"

A smile split his face then. "Yes. I am his father. He would try to protect me. I did not consider this."

Kira spread her hands and stared back at him questioningly. "What else could it be?" Besides an attempt to make certain that the man he was there to destroy didn't destroy other lives first.

"My son, he has chosen well for his woman." He nodded sharply, opening his lips to say more only to turn in surprise as the door slammed open.

Ian stood framed in the doorway. His overly long dark blond hair was mussed around his face, his expression cold and stony. Deep lines bracketed his mouth and his eyes glowed with fury.

"Is Deke okay?" Kira came quickly to her feet as she watched him warily.

The look on his face wasn't the least comfortable.

"Deke's awake. The doctor is still with him but he'll be okay."

"Ah, this is very good." Diego smiled. "I was telling your woman, you are a man of loyalty. A man to be proud of."

Kira would have winced if the situation weren't as dangerous as she could sense it becoming.

"At least he isn't lecturing you on your rants in *Society* again," Ian said as he stalked into the room, his eyes never leaving Diego. "Are you finished regaling her with my sterling qualities yet?" Savagery echoed in his voice.

Diego breathed out roughly. "I am finished. I will await your report in my office. Hopefully, you will arrive soon."

"Don't bet on it."

Kira could feel the torment echoing from Ian's pores. It wasn't in his face, it didn't show in his eyes, but she felt it. She knew it. It wrapped around her and had her heart clenching in response.

"Will I get a report, Ian?" Irritation was thick in Diego's voice now.

"When I know, you'll know. Until then, do me a favor and give me a while to get a drink and a shower. Being tossed around in my favorite limo isn't my preferred sport."

She heard the deliberate restraint in Ian's voice then. Violence shimmered in the air around him, glittered in his eyes, and tightened his facial features. His voice was a gritty growl now though, the broken quality to it thicker.

"We will get you another limo. I will make certain it arrives quickly." Diego moved quickly for the door, his expression placating, filled with hope. "Take your time, Ian. Rest. Sleep. I will take care of things. I am rather good at that. And I promise to have no fun in my efforts."

He wouldn't kill, in other words.

Ian's back was turned to Diego; the other man couldn't see the flash of dark rage in his son's face or the gleam of pain in his eyes.

"No bloodshed, pop," Ian ordered roughly.

Diego smiled and nodded toward Ian's back as Kira glanced to him.

"No bloodshed, son. I promise this. Find me when you are finished. I will make certain all is well until then."

Ian nodded.

Diego lifted his hand in farewell to Kira with an almost thankful smile before leaving the room and closing the door behind him. She shuddered once the room was secure again. It was like watching an alligator cuddle a baby. One just knew the child would become a snack within seconds, but the sheer shock of the vision was freezing.

As the door clicked closed Ian turned and stalked to it, securely locked it then moved to the locked bureau drawer. The hardware drawer. God, she would love to get her hands on some of those electronic toys he was holding in that drawer.

"Room is secure," he said, his voice carefully controlled.

His body was carefully controlled. His voice, his actions, everything about him was restrained.

"Is Deke really okay?" Kira asked.

"Deke's fine." His fingers went to the buttons of his shirt. Kira's heart went to her throat.

Oh yeah. Adrenaline. She could see the dominant arousal in the flush beginning to mantle his cheekbones now, in the hard definition of muscles that he revealed as he shed his shirt.

Hard body. That was what he was. Corded muscles gleamed beneath richly tanned flesh. They rippled with power, flexed with force at each movement.

"What were you and Diego discussing?" Predatory awareness filled his voice. He watched her like a wolf watching the poor little rabbit destined to be its next meal.

"You," she answered. "He seemed a bit upset that you wouldn't let him wreak blood and death in retaliation for today."

"And you told him what?" His hands dropped to his belt. Kira's eyes followed. She had to swallow, hard, because her mouth was watering at the sight of that bulge beneath the dark slacks. He was hard. Aroused. Intent.

"Um." She swallowed again, nervously, because she had a feeling he was not going to like this. "I told him you might be trying to protect him too."

His lips flattened. "And you based that on what?"

"Well." She pursed her lips carefully. "I might have told him that you wouldn't let me have any fun either because you wanted to protect me. It seemed to go with the image." She clasped her hands behind her back as she watched him, waiting for the explosion. When none was forthcoming she tried to explain. "You know, that whole SEAL persona thing. You can take the boy out of the military, blah blah—"

"Take your clothes off."

She had known it was coming, but when he delivered the order, the response that fired inside her body took her by surprise. It was hard, a fiery wave of intense heat that rushed through her erogenous zones and cascaded through her womb with white-hot intensity.

"I don't think so." Amusement fired inside her along with the arousal though. "I'm not an outlet for all that adrenaline, Ian. At least not yet. We need to talk."

Talking was the last thing he needed to do. Ian let his gaze rove over her body. The white slacks and cream-colored top were smudged with dirt. Her hair was tangled around her face in sexy disarray and reminded him of the feel of it beneath his hands, the warm rough silky sensation that his palms seemed to itch for.

"I don't want to talk, Kira." He advanced on her instead. Perhaps he shouldn't have ordered her to get undressed. Each time he had taken her, other than that first time, he had been quick and rough. He hadn't taken the time to enjoy the feel of her flesh that morning or the night before. Not really.

He hadn't tasted her. Hadn't listened to her scream in pleasure as she came apart in his arms. That was criminal, he decided. Not giving her the full range of pleasure that she needed. Each caress, each lick and kiss, designed to drive her higher.

"Ian," she protested as he stopped in front of her, the dark ring of blue around her gray eyes darkening as the centers became stormy. "There are things we need to discuss."

"Such as?" He ran his fingers beneath the thin strap of her shirt, feeling the pure silk texture and deciding her hair and her skin were softer.

"Such as Diego." Regret flashed in her eyes.

"Diego is the last thing we need to discuss," he told her, pushing back the bleak anger that threatened to build inside him again. The pain. He didn't understand the pain any more than he understood the hunger and need converging inside him for Kira.

He ran his fingers beneath the strap of her blouse until he came to the rounded scoop of the neckline. Heat flowed from her flesh to his fingers, mesmerizing him with the impact it had on his senses.

He had never experienced anything like Kira before and he wondered if the effect she had on him was weakness or strength?

"You can't hide from it forever," she whispered, her voice strained.

Strained because she was breathing harder, her breasts rising and falling sharply, drawing his gaze to the presence of the tight, hard nipples beneath the silk.

"I'm not trying to hide anything, Kira. I just want to pleasure you. Pleasure both of us."

There was a well of emotion brewing inside him. Ian could feel it. He couldn't make sense of it, and he wanted nothing to do with it. He had forced himself to push back his emotions as a boy. Forced himself not to want or to need, until Kira. Damn her, she made him want and need things he was certain would never be a part of his life.

Hope. Warmth. Real passion. And that real passion was his weakness. The honest, burning flame of desire in her eyes and the strength he glimpsed within her held him as nothing else ever had.

"I wanted you out of this," he told her, his hands falling to the hem of the shirt, gripping it and lifting it. "I wanted you safe. So safe. So that when this was over I could find you and finish what we started in Atlanta."

Her arms lifted, allowing him to draw the blouse from her only to drop it on the floor a second later. Her breasts lifted to him with her hard breaths, her nipples hard and peaked, a light sheen of perspiration beginning to shimmer on her lightly tanned flesh as she stood proudly before him. No hesitancy, no coy shyness or attempts to deny what they both knew was waiting to explode between them.

His cock was so damned hard at this point that it throbbed like an open wound.

"Since when did I seem the type that needs to hide?" Her hands moved to his chest, her fingers working on the buttons of his shirt. "When we met in Russia perhaps?"

His lips quirked at the thought of her Russian persona.

"Not in Russia." His hands framed her face, lips lowering to hers as hunger beat at his brain in a steady rhythm.

"Albania?" she whispered against his lips, her hands pushing the edges of his shirt apart to touch the hard, hair-spattered muscles of his chest.

"Never in Albania." She had been a rebel, a competent warrior when she'd had to be one.

"Then why would I need protecting now?" she asked, pushing at his shoulders until he dropped his hands from her face and allowed her to shove the shirt away from his arms.

Her hands smoothed over the powerful biceps, nails digging in as she curled them into the thickest area and clenched.

"You don't need protecting." Admitting that wasn't easy. "What do you need?"

He watched the shadows that flickered in her eyes, regret and sorrow.

"I need you." Her hands moved to the band of his slacks, parted his belt, then the metal clasp that held it secure, before her fingers lowered the zipper. "Give me what I need, Ian. And, maybe, what you need too?"

God yes, it was what he needed. Needed to the point that he wondered if his soul would fracture without it. Without her. Months of living a lie, sleeping it, eating it, drinking it, fucking breathing it every second of the day, had been eating away at him like acid.

Until Kira had arrived. Until she had blown into his life again like a breath of sunshine.

"Come here." He lifted her into his arms, cradled her against his chest, and moved into the bedroom.

He needed something he couldn't name this time. He needed to touch and be touched in ways he couldn't describe. He had been slowly dying inside until Kira arrived in Aruba and now he was burning, throbbing, all-too-living and desperate for more of her.

"What are you doing, Ian?" A flash of vulnerability, of uncertainty in her expression and in her gaze, almost had him smiling as he laid her on the bed.

She could meet him head-to-head in a confrontation, argumentative or sexual, but for some reason this seemed to throw her off balance. Hell, he'd have to remember to relish her rather than gorge on her more often.

"I need more than a quickie, Kira." He released the button and zipper of her pants. Curling his fingers on the waistband and drawing the the pants over her thighs and down her long, sexy legs. And damn, her legs were pretty.

"Why more than a quickie?" She frowned and he couldn't miss the fact that her fingers curled tightly into the material of the blanket beneath her. "Quickies are pretty good, Ian."

"Quickies aren't nearly enough." He dropped her pants to the floor then disposed of his own just as quickly. "Unless you'd like to tell me why you prefer a quickie?"

Eighteen

WHY DID SHE PREFER A quickie? Kira inhaled tightly and stared up at him with the knowledge that she had made a slight tactical error where Ian was concerned. He saw things no others saw, and he was especially adept at seeing through her.

"We're rather running out of time." She cleared her throat nervously. "I know you have business to take care of, and Deke—"

"I hate it when you lie to me." His lips quirked, a sexy little mocking smile that had her womb flexing and the juices spilling from her vagina as he came to the bed beside her.

"What am I lying to you about?" She turned to him, lying on her side, feeling the slight roughness of his chest hair caressing her nipples.

It was an erotic, exotic sensation. Why had she never noticed that before? The extreme pleasure from something so subtle as the feel of those hairs across the tender tips.

"You've always pushed our encounters," he said, his voice hushed as his hand stroked down her hip to her thigh. "Except for the first time. I stole your control then. Is that what scares you, Kira? No control?"

What was her life without control? Without the ability to maintain herself and her emotions? Her emotions especially.

"Sex isn't about control, Ian." She maintained a confident smile despite the nerves gathering inside her. "It's about pleasure, remember?"

Pleasure. All she had to do was make him feel the right amount of pleasure, get the blood pumping and the lust heating, and it might not be a quickie, but it could leave her a part of her heart intact. If he managed to take all of her, she would never be able to defend herself against the results of her own deception.

One hand slid down his stomach as the other curled around his neck. Her lips lifted to his, touching them, whispering over them.

Heat spiraled through her, wrapped around her as strong as his arms, and when his lips responded, opened and joined the kiss, she felt her breath hitch. Her hand tightened on his neck, the other moved to the hard, engorged length of his cock.

She needed to touch him, feel him. Nothing in her life had ever felt so good as Ian did. His touch, the stroke of his hands down her back, over her thigh. The other hand threaded through the hair at the back of her head. Before she could guess his intention, guess his next move, his fingers clenched and pulled her head back slowly, breaking the kiss, breaking the incredible pleasure weaving through her. It also clued her in to the fact that he wasn't going to be so easy to manipulate.

"Ian, this isn't the place for games," she reminded him, her hand curling around the broad length of his erection and stroking it with a long, slow caress.

"Then you shouldn't play them," he growled.

His hips shifted, thrusting his cock into her grip even as his free hand wrapped around her fingers and forced her to release him.

His eyes burned within the darkened centers, the fiery tobacco-brown depths glowing with lust as he came over her.

"Restraining me won't ease either of us." But she still arched to him, raking her nipples over his chest even as he gripped both her wrists in one hand and secured them over her head.

"I won't have to restrain you for long. Just long enough to get the fires blazing inside that hot little body. Isn't that right, Kira? Just long enough to remind you how hungry you can get."

She bit her lower lip and glared back at him. "And you don't get that hungry?"

"Oh, I get that hungry." Strong white teeth grazed over her lower lip as he controlled the subtle movements of her body while she tried to find a position that would allow her to break the hold he had on her. "I get very hungry."

His lips came back, moved over hers, his tongue pressing past her lips to lick at her tongue as his callused fingers curled around the aching mound of her breast.

Kira jerked, nearly flinching at the pleasure of that touch. His fingertips rasped around the delicate nerve endings of her nipple, yet never quite touched the hardened peak.

Her lips parted further, her tongue reaching out to stroke his as pleasure began to envelop her. Rapid, heated pinpoints of sensation built inside her, swirling through her bloodstream, sensitizing her nerve endings. She could feel the need growing inside her, building with his kiss, with each stroke of his fingers around her nipple and each second he held her restrained.

"Ian." She tore her lips from his even as she arched closer to his hard, warm body. "Don't do it like this. Please."

"Just say no, Kira." His lips slid over her cheek, her jaw. "A single word. All you have to do is use it."

Her lips parted, the word hovered on her lips as she gasped for breath.

"I'll stop," he promised, his voice velvet rough. "I'll let you go. I'll shower and attend to business. You'll be safe from whatever demons chase you then, won't you?"

Her teeth clamped shut as a fractured cry tore from her lips. She could say no and he would just stop? She tightened her thighs, pressing them together, desperate to stop the ache building in her clit. If he stopped, it might kill her.

"You're not playing fair," she breathed out roughly. God, even breathing was an erotic sensation at this point.

"I never promised to play fair." He brought her to her back once again, his head lowering, lips feathering over her collarbone, his tongue tasting her skin.

She didn't know if she could bear this. Heat was spiraling inside her body, attacking erogenous zones and sensitizing the rest of her body to the point that pleasure became near ecstasy.

"You have the prettiest breasts." His free hand cupped a swollen mound, his thumb brushing over her nipple.

Sensation whipped around the hard point then zipped across her nerve endings and clenched the muscles of her womb.

He didn't give her time to process the pleasure from it before his head went lower, his lips and tongue painting a trail of hunger straight to her nipple.

Heated moisture surrounded the engorged flesh as he drew it into his mouth and sucked it deep. Kira flinched, a ragged cry tearing from her lips.

"You want to destroy me," she accused him, her voice rough as she ground her head into the pillow.

The feel of his mouth drawing on her nipple, his tongue lashing it, was making her insane. The peaks were torturously tight, throbbing at the continued friction against them. With each rough lick the flames consuming her body seemed to lick higher, hotter.

"I want to touch you too." Her fingers curled, desperation tightening through her as the need to feel him became imperative.

"Not yet." He lifted his lips only to smooth his jaw over her breast.

The faint bristle of stubble rasped over the soft skin of her breast, sending rapid-fire sensation exploding through her.

"Why not yet?" She tried to twist beneath him, to break the hold he had on her wrists, and on her emotions.

She was weak. His touch was more potent than liquor, and he affected more than just her body. That was the problem. He affected parts of her that she wanted to keep hidden. Parts of her that she had kept hidden for so many years that she had forgotten they existed herself.

"Because I want to touch you." His head lifted, the piercing dark flames in his eyes searing her as he pulled himself up on the bed.

He knelt by her head, which made no sense. He wanted to touch her, yet the hard length of his cock was poised just above her lips as he secured his hold on her wrists.

Rather than trying to pull herself up to reach the engorged crest, she went for the sensitive sac beneath it instead.

Ian froze, his breath wheezing from his lungs as Kira's lips covered the side of his testicles, her tongue laving over it as a whispery moan vibrated into the tight flesh.

God help him.

He leaned his head against the thick wood of the headboard and concentrated on breathing rather than spilling his cum. Her mouth should be licensed. It was wicked, bordering on illegally destructive to the male senses. She mouthed the flesh as it drew tight beneath his cock, cum boiling dangerously close to an explosion.

Gritting his teeth, he dragged the slender chain and wrist restraints from the metal loop secured to the back of the bed. Whoever had owned the house and furnished it had had a definite eye toward hiding the accoutrements of sexual pleasure.

As she busied her lips and tongue with his balls, he quickly slid the velvet-lined cuffs over her wrists and secured them with a snap before moving back.

Her eyes flashed first with confusion, until she tugged at

her wrists, heard the chain rattle and felt the security of the restraints. A shade of fear flashed in her eyes then.

"Just say no," he told her, his hands settling on her shoulder and her stomach as he moved to lie beside her once again.

"I'm not your damned submissive, Ian," she bit out, tugging again on the chain holding her. "Are you insane?"

"Insanity is the least of my problems these days," he assured her, narrowing his gaze as she turned her head and stared back at the dark cuffs. "If you want free, all you have to do is say the word. We'll walk away from this."

"So I'm restrained for the torture or I don't get fucked?" Her gaze sliced back to him, darkening with emotion, almost mesmerizing him with the sharp flashes of intensity in the cloudy color.

"You understand perfectly." He smiled down at her in approval. "I knew you were a smart girl."

"You bastard!" Guttural, agonized, her voice had him gauging her reactions much closer now.

"Should I let you go, Kira?" He gentled his voice, placed a soft kiss on her shoulder and stared back at her. "Are you scared?" he asked, daring her.

Kira swallowed tightly, her breathing rough as she stared back at him, seeing his intent in his gaze. He would have whatever he wanted from her now, or he would walk away and she knew it.

"Should I be scared?" She was terrified.

He wouldn't hurt her, not physically, but what he would do had the potential to break her later.

"You should be very scared," he answered. "You're always holding back. Always keeping a part of yourself safe, aren't you? That's why you like the quickies. Why you want to rush to the climax and forget the buildup. What is it about the buildup that frightens you?"

"Boredom," she snapped in reply. "Who wants to lie restrained while someone else has all the fun?" She rattled the chains again with a furious shake of her wrists.

"You're scared."

The certainty in his voice had her breath catching, her eyes locking with his.

"I'm not scared of you," she denied. She couldn't afford to let him know just how much her emotions, where he was involved, truly terrified her.

"Prove it." The slight tug at the corner of his lips, the smug knowing smirk, assured her she had lost this battle.

"Let me go then."

He shook his head slowly. "You want loose, tell me no . . . This time, you won't rush this. Before the night is over, Kira, I'll have all of you, or I'll have nothing at all."

He was serious. She could see it in his face, feel it in his body as he arched over her, in the touch of his hand as he laid it possessively against her stomach before sliding it between her thighs.

"You're wet, Kira. So wet and hot."

Her eyes closed as his fingers slid through the slick cream that flowed from her, tantalizing her with the heat of his touch and stroking flesh so violently sensitive she could barely hold her cry back.

"My little control freak," he said, chuckling. "I bet it was hard to hold that cry back."

Her eyes flew open, or rather she forced them open as far as possible. She felt drugged, weak, yet the blood was pumping hard and fast through her veins and adrenaline was tightening the breath in her chest.

"Bastard." It was a moan rather than an accusation because even as he pointed out the obvious, his fingers were parting the swollen lips of her pussy and pushing heavily inside. "Damn you, Ian."

His lips came down on hers as the cry left her throat, taking it into himself as he sipped at her lips, placing hard, stinging kisses as two fingers worked inside her, stroking, rubbing, and driving her crazy with the sensations streaking through her.

He wasn't joking when he said slow and easy. When he said he would have all of her. He kissed her like a man starved for a kiss. His fingers delved inside her, retreated and returned in deliberately sensual thrusts.

She was burning from the inside out. Wild, fiery trails of sensation whipped over her, clenching her pussy around his fingers, driving the breath from her lungs and starting an ache in her clit that she was afraid would drive her over the edge to insanity.

"Damn, you're beautiful," his voice whispered across her senses as he broke the kiss, his lips moving from hers to her jaw as he ignored her broken cry.

"Ian, please." Her hips arched as his fingers retreated again; this time though they didn't return. They smoothed over her thighs, pressing her legs farther apart as his lips traveled along her neck.

Kira jerked at the restraints on her wrists, her hands itching to feel his flesh beneath them. She gave a whimpering moan as his lips feathered across her nipples. First one, then the other. A teasing, tantalizing touch before he sucked one into his mouth. He laved the tender peak with his tongue, then suckled at it with voracious hunger before continuing on the downward path to her aching pussy.

He couldn't do this. She couldn't allow it. His lips were like a brand against her flesh, sweeping over it with dampened trails of fiery pleasure. She could feel the perspiration building on her flesh, the slick heat of her juices flowing from her pussy, preparing her, increasing the hunger rising inside her.

God help her, she needed. She needed him with a desperation born of some dark hunger that she couldn't explain even within herself.

"Please, Ian. Don't. Don't tease." Her head twisted against the mattress, aching pain building in her chest. She didn't want to lose this need. This pleasure. She didn't want it to build inside her, becoming so sharp and agonizing that the need for orgasm was like a living entity inside her. Only to have it evaporate, die, because her mind refused to release that last shred of control.

He hadn't been the first lover determined to find that inner core inside her. That part of her feminine soul that, once possessed, would never belong to another. He wasn't the first. He wouldn't be the last. But he was the most important.

"Poor Kira," he whispered as he moved between her thighs, wedging into place as he parted her legs further. "Do you want me to stop?"

"This isn't going to work, Ian," she gasped as his fingers smoothed over the cream-slickened flesh of her pussy. "You'll destroy me, but not in the way you believe."

He would steal her ability to orgasm. It always happened.

"Don't worry, sweetheart, I'll take care of you."

The tone of his voice had her eyes opening, her head tilting to stare down at him in dazed fascination. The savage features of his face were taut, his eyes glowing with heat and his lips swollen with lust. But even more surprising was the understanding and knowledge in his eyes.

"I can't give you what you want, Ian," she moaned. "I don't have it."

"You have it, Kira." He pushed her legs farther apart, his head lowering to place a soft, delicate kiss on her clit. "And soon, I'll have it."

It was more than a promise, it was a statement of intent. Ian meant to take all of her.

Kira breathed in deeply. There wasn't enough oxygen. Heat surrounded her, filled her. She felt like the core of a burning sun, waiting to explode but expecting instead the freezing chill of diluted pleasure.

Ian chuckled again, his fingers parting the swollen folds of her sex, his head lowering.

Kira's cry shook her. It tore from her chest, ripped from her throat as he placed his lips over her throbbing clit and kissed it deeply. A kiss. It wasn't suckling pressure, or the rapid flicks of his tongue. It was a purse-lipped kiss that

shocked the little bundle of nerves and had it rioting in desperation.

She needed to get closer to that kiss. Her hands clenched
around the slender chain of the wrist restraints as her heels
dug into the bed and she tried to lift closer, to drive her clit
deeper between his lips.

She could feel the sweat beading on her skin now, small
rivulets running down her forehead, along her stomach.
She was burning alive, desperate. She jerked at the restraint, whimpering cries pouring from her as Ian's lips,
tongue, and suckling mouth whipped her into a frenzy of
hunger.

It was building. Blazing. She had never needed anything
as desperately as she needed Ian now.

"There you go, baby," he crooned huskily, his breath
feathering over the ultrasensitive flesh between her thighs.
"Just let it feel good."

He kissed again. Firm little kisses. Whispery deeper
kisses. He sucked at the swollen folds, each kiss, each
lick, each rumbled growl against her flesh growing hungrier.

She should have lost the desire to come three screams
ago. Instead, it was building, her cries growing more pathet-
ically pleading. She was begging him for release. She could
hear the words, feel the pleas ripping through her body as
lust, passion, and emotion began to flame higher and hotter
inside her.

"Ian. Now." She arched, fighting the hold he had on her
hips. "It's killing me. Please."

Her pussy clenched, spilled more of her juices as his
tongue suddenly plunged inside it. But it wasn't enough.

She twisted in his grip as his tongue stroked, licked.
Her back arched, her fingers tightened on the chains, and
she fought for climax. It was so close. Right there. Waiting
on her.

"Damn you, Ian." Her head thrashed on the bed. She

tried to trap him in place by tightening her thighs against his head.

Firm hands held her thighs wide, her arching hips angled the entrance to her pussy to his hungry mouth, and he consumed her.

"Fuck!" The rough, snarling groan into the swollen, desperate flesh had her shuddering, struggling. "Sweet Kira. Your pussy is sweet. Hot."

She twisted, fought for a deeper touch.

"What do you want, Kira?"

"Now," she moaned. "I want you now."

"What do you want now, baby?" he crooned, his guttural voice rougher, deeper than ever. "Come on, tell me what you want."

"Take me, Ian." Desperation laced her cry. "Now. Please."

"What am I taking? Tell me what you want me to take." He breathed the words over her clit, striking shards of sensation through it as she fought to breathe through the additional pleasure. Agonizing pleasure. A pleasure so intense, so overwhelming, it unraveled her to her soul.

"Me," she cried out. "Take me."

"All of you, Kira?" He asked the question, his lips formed the words and stroked over her clit, ricocheted through her womb. "Which part of you? Just this sweet pussy? Or is there more of you?"

Was there more of her? Did she need more? Did she want more?

"Don't stop." She forced her eyes open, staring down her body as he rose between her thighs, her hips lifting, her voice beseeching as his lips touched her stomach before he rose to his knees. "Please don't stop."

"What part of you belongs to me, Kira?" He came over her, one hand framing her face as his lips touched hers, his gaze holding hers. "What part of you do I take?"

She needed more. More than she had ever needed before.

"All of me." She felt the first tear fall. "Take all of me."

Kira felt the defenses she had worked all her life to build unravel inside her as Ian took her lips in a kiss that burned through her like white-hot flames.

She was lost in him. Out of control. Undulating beneath his heavier, sweat-dampened body, she fought for skin-on-skin contact. The feel of his chest hair rasping her nipples, his hard abdomen pressing against hers. Powerful thighs holding her legs apart, the broad head of his cock tucked against the swollen folds of her pussy.

So close. She could feel the hard, throbbing crest against her sensitive flesh. The heat of it drove her insane. The sense of thickness, of iron-hard strength, had her pussy clenching in agonizing hunger.

"Don't cry." His eyes burned in his dark face as he leaned to her once again and kissed the tear from her cheek before whispering, "It's okay, baby. You have all of me too."

And the last threads broke free. Something tightened then shifted inside her chest.

"I love you." The words tore from her lips.

She ground her head into the pillow beneath her. Oh God, she hadn't just said that. Those words hadn't passed her lips.

"No." She stared into his surprised gaze, frozen, unable to believe those words, those emotions were tearing from her as she closed her eyes and felt her breath hitch.

Then Ian moved. She felt his erection nudge against her, bury inside her an inch, draw back, then with a hard lunge he was buried full length inside her.

Fear evaporated. There was nothing now but the pleasure and the emotions. They merged, whipped inside her, and drew her to a peak of pleasure she hadn't imagined possible.

"Look at me." He stilled inside her. Buried to the hilt, thick and hard, throbbing inside her. "Look at me, Kira."

"Don't. Don't do this." She shook her head. "Finish it. Finish it, Ian."

She couldn't handle it. Sensation exploded through her.

The ripples of exquisite pleasure were too much. Not quite ecstasy, but so close to ecstasy. And it was only building. Rising and burning.

"Look at me, Kira." He held her hips still as she fought to move. "Look at me, baby."

His voice was tortured, hoarse. Kira forced her eyes open and stared into the dark fire of his eyes.

"Take *me* now," he snarled, his expression hard, savage. "Take all of me now."

He withdrew slowly, his cock pulling free of her as Kira gasped at the loss of sensation.

She watched his face now. She had lost her control, lost the ability to hold any part of herself back. And he was losing his now. She could see it. In the racking shudder that flexed the muscles of his chest, the slight tremor in his hands as he jerked a condom from the nightstand by the bed, tore the foil package open and quickly sheathed himself.

His expression twisted as her hips lifted and she managed to drag the engorged cock head over the folds of her sex. She was dying for it. Dying for him. More of him. Now.

Thick, pulsing, his erection pushed inside her once again.

She could barely hold her eyes open, but she needed to watch him. Watch him because he refused to release her gaze. And she couldn't break it, no more than he could break the hold she had on him.

"I need . . ." She swallowed before biting her lip, her lashes drifting lower as he began to move inside her again. Slow and deep.

"I know what you need." His voice was rougher now. Harder.

Kira stared up at him, dazed, awash in a pleasure so deep, so intense, that she wanted it to last forever. She needed it to last forever. To never end.

Perspiration coated her body, sweat beaded on his forehead, ran in rivulets down the side of his face and the broad planes of his chest. She tracked the trails of moisture. Watched them run down his neck, his chest, to his hard abdomen and below.

Her gaze was caught by the below. The sight of his cock moving out of her, glistening slick and wet with her juices, the heavy veins prominent and throbbing before he pushed inside her again.

"Do you like seeing that, Kira?" His voice was strained. "Watching my dick take you? Do you know what it feels like? Like a white-hot vise wrapped around me, clenched on me."

The muscles of his thighs clenched as he retreated, sweat beading on the dark flesh as more of her cream flooded her pussy. She felt it as he pushed inside her, saw it as he retreated.

She lifted her eyes to his once again. She was lost in him. It was too late to hide, too late to control.

"I love you." The cry tore from her, the emotions taking her as hard, as desperately, as he was suddenly taking her.

His jaw was tight, his teeth gritting. And he was the one holding back. She was a part of him and he was sinking into her soul as surely as he was sinking into her body.

"I love you." Her eyes closed as the words tore from her one last time before the explosions of primal, agonizing pleasure began tearing through her.

She arched, bucked, the ecstasy too much to be borne, the intensity riding so sharply inside her that she felt it cut into her soul.

Ian snarled her name as he came over her, his hips moving hard and fast as he fucked her with maddening hunger. Rapture was a continuous explosion inside her now. Pleasure rode pain and for the first time in her life Kira knew what it meant to be touched to the soul as Ian gave one final, desperate thrust, stilled, his cock throbbing and pulsing, his release shuddering through his body as his arms moved beneath her to hold her to him.

He cradled her as the spasming tissue of her pussy held
him. Tight. Gripping. His arms tightened around her, his
head was buried in the pillow by her head, and he held her
as though he would never let her go.

Nineteen

DAWN WAS EDGING OVER THE horizon as Ian stood on the balcony, coffee in hand, staring out at the land that surrounded the villa.

Unlike the Fuentes estate in Colombia, the villa and its grounds weren't surrounded by mountains and jungles. The terrain was flatter, with only a slight rise of hills around it spotted with massive boulders.

The balcony wasn't the most secure place to take his coffee, or to sit and reflect on things he would have been better prepared to deal with once this mission was over. But those thoughts refused to be extinguished. And they centered on the woman now sleeping the sleep of the exhausted in his bed.

He hadn't expected her to say she loved him. Of all the things he had expected when he broke down Kira's barriers, it hadn't been that commitment.

He ran his hand over his stubbled jaw before sipping at the coffee again and staring at the huge boulders and sheltering trees on the rise across from him.

It wasn't that he couldn't feel the eyes watching him, it was that he was beginning to accept that they were there. And he had bigger problems than the knowledge that Durango team was out there. Kira was a much bigger problem.

She had lost her objectivity, and in a woman, that could be fatal. She wouldn't care about her own life from this point on, he knew that about her. If it came to saving him or watching him die to complete the mission, she would give her life for him.

He should have had her tied, gagged, and shipped to a secure location until this was finished. He could have gone on as he was, risking no life or soul but his own, and finished the mission, one way or the other. His life or Sorrell's and Diego's. He had made that vow to himself when they had rescued Nathan eight months before. When he had seen the shape his friend had been in, and had known his father was responsible.

He had promised Nathan their heads, and he fully intended to carry that promise out, no matter what. Even his life. But not at the cost of Kira's.

He lowered his head and ran his fingers through his hair before staring at the rise once again. She was too important. He had known that the moment he realized she was covering his ass in that warehouse. Hell, he had known it eight months before in Atlanta during the operation to protect Kell Krieger's woman.

He was screwed.

He flipped up the secure sat phone he held in his hand and keyed in Macey's number.

"Fuck-tard." Macey's voice came over the line, savagely quiet. "'Bout time you called."

"I have a shipment that needs to go out," he said firmly, closing his eyes at the thought of sending Kira away. "Are you available?"

"If it's raven-haired with a marksman rating, then you can fuck yourself," Macey growled. "I'm not touching that one."

That wasn't relief he was feeling.

"Why are you here then?" he asked. "Take the shot if that's what this is all about. Save us the trouble later."

Ian leaned back in the chair and opened himself to any shot anyone might want to take. He couldn't be certain why

Durango team was there, but if this was all they wanted, then screw it. He was tired of the blood and the death, and he was tired of regret. SEALs didn't forgive betrayal from one of their own. And Ian didn't blame them.

"Killer Secrets." Macey reminded him of the code word he had given Kira. "And we got your message via Kira. Tell me, Ian, what part of friends don't you understand? Do you think I'm going to snipe your stupid ass while you're sipping your morning coffee and your woman is standing in the door watching you as though her heart were broken?"

Ian turned his head.

Whatever expression Kira may have had on her face cleared instantly, but her eyes were still somber, questioning.

"Hang for the commander," Macey announced.

"Lieutenant Richards, I'm going to kick your ass to hell and back when this is over." Reno came over the line, his quiet voice echoing with anger. "Where do we meet and when?"

"No meet." Ian lowered his voice further, never breaking Kira's gaze. "No chance."

"Unacceptable," Reno informed him coldly. "Take your woman on a ride. You know our location."

The connection broke.

Ian blew out a breath roughly as he shook his head. That was a meet he wasn't about to make. There were too many eyes watching, too many ways he could compromise what he was doing.

He stared out at the rock outcropping once again.

"No chance in getting rid of you, is there?" He sighed.

"Not on a bet." Her voice was somber.

"It would kill me if anything happened to you." He admitted that, and even more privately, he realized it would destroy what was left of his soul. And there wasn't a whole lot of that left.

"I won't walk away, Ian. I won't be forced away. If you wanted to try that, then you should have done it before last night."

Hell yes, he should have.

"Ian, I'm not an innocent bystander here," she continued as she moved to him.

She took the coffee cup from his hand and set it on the small table at his side before sliding onto his lap. She wore one of his silk shirts. The material slid over his flesh, warmed by her skin and carrying her scent now.

He couldn't help but surround her with his arms and hold her close to his chest.

"I'm well trained," she whispered in his ear. "I'm fully qualified to walk by your side, don't pretend otherwise."

He cupped her head and held it to his shoulder, bending his head to her, his lips close to hers, his gaze holding hers as he spoke.

"If I lost you here, it would destroy what's left of my soul."

"And if I walked away from you, it would destroy what was left of me," she answered. "We've been playing a cat-and-mouse game for years now. It's time to stop. Here and now. I'm your equal in everything but physical strength and you know it. Don't push me away because you're too much of a chauvinist to work with me."

It wasn't just chauvinism. It was the certainty that losing her would kill him.

"You'll be crucified in the tabloids," he told her.

"Got the T-shirt." She grinned back at him.

His lips quirked. Yes, she did. She had been in the tabloids for years, either for the scrapes she had purposely managed to get into, or for the charities she and her uncle backed. She was controversial, flamboyant, and one of the government's most covert contract operatives. She was damned scary.

He lifted his head and pressed his lips to her forehead as he let his eyes drift closed, allowing himself to enjoy holding her in his arms, feeling her warm and sweet against him. Just a little while longer.

"We need to shower." He opened his eyes and stared into

the clear, blue sky beyond the balcony. "I have to deal with what happened yesterday."

"You're going after them? Do you know who they are?"

He nodded again. He knew who they were. The information had been waiting in his in-box when he rose that morning.

"Sorrell's men," he answered her. "I received news he was in Aruba this morning. Apparently, he's been here for a while."

She nodded against his shoulder. "Are we going for intel or blood?"

"We're not going for either," he said. "I'm sending in a small team of Fuentes soldiers to capture Sorrell's contact as well as the two men in the boat yesterday. They left an hour ago. I just have to wait on the call now."

It was coming to a head slowly. He had managed to foul every attempt Sorrell had made to kidnap or kill him. All that was left was to draw the terrorist into a meeting. Once he identified him, Ian could take him out.

It was a waiting game, and Ian had once believed he had the patience for it. Patience had never been a problem until now. Until Kira had walked into his life once more.

"Are you going to make contact?" Kira asked then, and Ian knew who she was talking about.

Durango team. He looked up at the rise again and sighed wearily. Reno would be pissed when Ian and Kira didn't show up as he ordered. But hell, what could his former commander expect? Reno had no business here. His wife was just out of the hospital with their newborn child; he should have been in the States attending to his family, not out trying to cover for someone whose main objective had been to keep the team as far from this as possible.

Diego Fuentes loved playing with the men assigned to that team. He considered it his personal duty to see just how far he could push each man until he broke. He had nearly broken Nathan. If Fuentes had succeeded in his past plots he would have killed the commander's sister and a senator's daughter; both women were tied intimately to two of the SEALs on that team.

He shook his head in response to her question. "It's almost over. There's nothing they can do to help at this point."

"They can cover your back."

"They can get in my way." He lifted her from his lap, collected his coffee cup, and drew her back into the bedroom.

Closing the door and locking it, he moved to the bureau, flipped the security protocols to active then turned back to her.

"When this hits, Kira, it's going to hit fast. I have to be certain where your loyalties lie."

"In what regard?" Long black hair flowed over her shoulder as she regarded him warily now.

"Sorrell will die." Nothing else was acceptable. "If you can't handle that, then get out now. Don't come between me and this mission."

"Your mission is to kill him?" she asked soberly, her expression concerned. "I would think DHS would need the intel he could provide?"

"He dies, Kira. I don't give a fuck what DHS needs or what they want. So you decide now exactly who has your loyalty. Me or DHS."

He had her loyalty. He knew it, she knew it, but he wanted to hear it. He wanted her to *feel* it.

She licked her soft pink lips, her blue-ringed gray eyes flickering in acknowledgment of the power play.

"You have my loyalty, Ian," she finally whispered. "But don't make the mistake of abusing it. I'm not your puppet and I won't be used as one."

"I didn't ask for a puppet." He stepped to her, pulling her into his arms as he hid the grimace that contorted his features. "We can't let him live, Kira. Even for the intel. He has too many ties, too many spies. I won't risk his escape. I won't risk Nathan or his wife, even for the information."

The shadows of the past washed over him. For a moment, just a moment, he was a child again, screaming in agony through an empty Texas night as his mother lay in his arms, near death. He had screamed until his voice broke, until he couldn't scream anymore. Until hope had leached from his body with the same burning pain that his mother's blood wept from hers.

Out of the night came a child and his father. The boy who had heard his screams and awakened his family. Nathan had saved his life and the life of his mother. Ian hadn't forgotten that. He wouldn't forget it.

"How's he doing?" The question was dragged from him. "He's holding up?"

"He's holding up." He heard in her voice what she refused to voice. The battle Nathan was waging just to live, to survive the operations he had had no choice but to endure and the effects of the whore's dust that had been pumped into him for so many months.

The synthetic date rape drug in such large amounts should have been fatal. Nathan shouldn't have survived the first month.

He released her slowly. "We need to shower. I have to check on Deke, and I have a few meetings to attend in Palm Beach. You'll be by my side. My trophy. Try not to let everyone see just how dangerous you can be for the time being."

If she was going to work this mission then he was going to use her particular talents effectively. She looked like soft fluff. Delicate. Girly. Femininely arrogant.

"I've got your six, bad boy." Her hands smoothed over the side of his ass and Ian couldn't help the smile that tugged at his lips.

"More than you know." A quick kiss to her lips and he turned and headed to the shower. "I'll get things together while you shower; for now, see if you can contact Daniel. You have a four-minute secure window with the security protocols. Make it fast and tell him to stay the hell out of the way. I'd hate to see him killed because he blindsided me or Deke, Kira. Make sure it doesn't happen."

Later, Ian braced his hands against the shower wall and let the warm water flow over him. Control. That was all he needed, just a little more control and he could get through this. It was moving rapidly. The team he had sent in to take Sorrell's men was one of the best he had brought together from among the cartel soldiers Diego possessed when Ian took over the cartel.

Led by a former Russian militant, the men had training and experience that was on a level with some Special Forces teams Ian knew of. They were quick, effective, and merciless. And Ian had learned that mercy in this world brought nothing but more blood. There was no mercy. There was right of might and nothing more.

He lifted his head to the water, letting it flow over his face as his chest clenched and agony welled inside him. The blood he had shed since coming here would haunt him forever. It didn't matter that the blood was as vicious and evil as the world itself. He hadn't killed innocents. It was war, he tried to tell himself. A diseased world and he was weeding out the infection. But that didn't help anymore. It hadn't helped since the first night Kira had shown up.

It had sliced into him the night before as the words of love burst from her lips. Love for Kira would mean everything. Whoever or whatever she loved would have one hundred percent of who she was, she would give her life for whoever she loved. And he couldn't allow that. He had to keep her safe even while allowing her into the mess his life had become.

As his eyes opened, the shower door slid to the side, and she stepped into the steamy atmosphere with him. Her gray eyes were soft, her expression filled with concern, and with love.

He had to touch her. His arms went around her, his hands flattening against her back as he pulled her against his aroused body and took her lips before she could speak.

Whatever Daniel had reported to her, he didn't want to know. Not yet. First, he had to taste her once more. Fill his senses with her heat and her passion.

One hand slid between her thighs and found her creamy, slick with her own need. That was what he needed. Kira wet and ready for him.

Hands clenching in her buttocks now, he lifted her, feeling slender legs grip his hips as he pressed the painfully thickened flesh of his cock head into the folds of her sex.

No condom. Not this time. She was protected. He knew for damned certain he was safe. And he needed this. Needed to take her naked, with nothing between them, nothing separating their lust.

His head fell back on his shoulders at the intensity of sensation that whipped up his spine. His balls drew tight, his jaw clenched with the need to hold back. He could have spilled himself inside her in that moment as inch by inch she tightened around the impalement, her moans whispering around him as he braced her shoulders against the shower wall.

She was like pure heat. White-hot. Cutting through bitterness and pain to the core of his soul and wrapping around it tighter than her legs were now wrapped around his hips.

Opening his eyes, he tilted his head to lower his lips to hers once again. To sip from the shower-wet curves as he opened her slowly, his cock flexing, throbbing.

"It's like possessing life," he whispered against her lips. "And feeling it envelop me. Do you know that, Kira?"

Shock darkened her eyes.

"Do you know what you do to me?" He groaned roughly as he slid in to the hilt and felt her pussy tightening convulsively, milking his flesh.

"What you do to me?" She gasped, her hands tightening on his shoulders. "Oh God, Ian. You make me come apart."

She was coming apart? He was melting inside. He could feel the heat burning him alive as her head lowered to his chest, her sharp little teeth nipping at his flesh as he began to thrust inside her.

Her pussy was so tight. So hot. It seared his flesh with liquid heat and tightened on it with firm, rhythmic milking motions. The sensations stroked over the sensitive nerve endings of his cock head, rippled through the shaft, and struck his balls with fingers of heat. They drew tight beneath the shaft, ached with the need to come. Her lips scraped over his chest, adding to the pleasure tearing through him. Her hungry moans filled his head, the prick of her nails on his shoulders added to the incredible rapture he could only find in taking her, possessing her.

"Don't leave me." He tightened his teeth as the words slipped past his lips, as the emotions tearing through him found voice.

"Never. Oh God, Ian. Never."

He braced her against the wall, held tight, and pounded inside her. He fucked her like the demon he sometimes felt he had become, starving, demented. And she was his softness. His corner of peace.

His hands tightened on her hips as he felt his release boiling in his balls. Holding on wasn't an option. Not when she was crying in his ear, her orgasm unraveling around him, flexing on his dick and tearing his control from him.

He continued to thrust, feeling his cum spurt from his cock in hard, pulsing streams as he locked his teeth against his own cry.

Shudders of pleasure exploded through nerve endings and muscles, racking his body with an ecstasy that still amazed him. An ecstasy found only with Kira. A pleasure that went beyond the flesh and filled the soul.

If he lost her, it would kill him.

Twenty

WHAT HE WAS AND WHO he had become once he entered Diego Fuentes's world had begun to merge before Kira's arrival. Ian had recognized the signs, the lines that had been blurring between what was just and right, and what was expedient. He had been slowly becoming the same sort of monster he was tracking, and he hadn't realized it until Kira had given him her heart.

What part of him did she hold though?

A week later, he locked himself in his office, pulled up the reports Deke and Trevor had managed to collect, and tried to hide from that question.

Unfortunately, hiding from it changed nothing. She owned him. Heart and soul. The good man, and the man that had become dark, honed by the blood and the evil he had witnessed since accepting the name Fuentes.

He stared at the report and the pictures gained by the interrogation of the two men who had sent the missile exploding into the front of the limo the week before. Tourists, they had at first claimed to be. Nothing more than tourists. They had come in on the yacht *Cantrella,* rumored to be Sorrell's favorite seagoing vessel. Just tourists.

Timothy Vangressi and Adrian Hughes were anything

but tourists. Once Ian's lieutenant, Antoli Kovalyov, began questioning them, they had broken easily enough.

He pulled up the video of the interrogation. He didn't wince at the pain Antoli had dealt out to the two men. The fact that they had held out for over an hour was proof of their training. But Antoli had trained under some of the masterminds of torture. He knew tricks Ian hadn't witnessed, even within the interrogations he had seen as a SEAL.

"Sorrell will kill us," Vangressi had finally sobbed, his face bloodied and swollen, although it was nowhere near as sad a shape as his testicles were in. The drugs Antoli had pumped into the other man, and the pain, were too much. "We were to kill him and the girl. If the McClane girl backs him, he'll have too much power. Too much backing. The girl can't be allowed to influence him until Sorrell has the operation." He was slurring his words, gasping for breath as Antoli slowly eased the pressure of the clamps on his testicles and turned down the power to the electrical lead attached to them.

"Who is Sorrell?" Antoli asked, his voice calm, cold.

Vangressi shook his head. "I haven't seen him. He's here, on the island, but he only calls. The cell phone is just for his calls."

"The cell phone you carried?" Antoli could have been discussing the weather.

Vangressi was sobbing. "The cells we carry. Just for contact and orders. That's all. I swear. We met the *Cantrella* in Paris and loaded on. We disembarked after it anchored here and slipped ashore under nightfall with the missile launcher and the paperwork to rent the boats. He knew about the meeting that day. Knew the route Fuentes was taking after we arrived. We waited."

"Who on the *Cantrella* was your contact?"

"Please," Vangressi sobbed, pain and fear contorting his handsome features. "Please. He'll kill me. He'll kill—" His scream was high-pitched, horrible to hear, as Antoli applied power to the electrical leads, straight to the other man's balls.

He would have come out of his seat if he hadn't been strapped to it.

He slumped back a second later, dry heaves racking his body as the power was once again lowered.

"Who was your contact?" Antoli asked again.

"Ascarti," Vangressi whispered. "Gregor Ascarti. He knows Sorrell. He can identify him."

A gunshot followed the information. Then another. Both men slumped in their restraints, their gazes dimmed, death instantaneous from the single bullet buried in each brain.

Antoli was highly effective.

As he watched the video, it hadn't been Vangressi that had filled his mind though, it had been Nathan. The proof of the horrendous torture he had endured during his stay with Fuentes would always scar his mind and his body. There had been no relief, as Vangressi had found. No peace.

Ian pushed his fingers through his hair before rising from his chair and pacing to the bar across the room. Splashing the smooth, expensive whisky he kept on hand into a glass, he turned as a soft knock sounded on the door.

"Yeah?"

The door opened to reveal Diego. As impeccably dressed as ever. White slacks and a white cotton shirt tucked neatly into the waistband. Leather shoes and a gold watch. His black and silver hair was combed back and his patrician features were inquisitive.

"Have you learned much from the interrogation?" he asked as he stepped into the office and closed the door behind him.

"Not enough." Ian shrugged.

He moved ahead of Diego and casually closed the video before the other man could reach his side.

"If you were not my son, I would have killed you by now." Diego stared back at him ruthlessly.

"You didn't let brotherhood stop you, why let fatherhood?" Ian asked as he closed the folders on his desk before looking up once again.

The pain that flashed in Diego's eyes surprised him. It surprised him even more that he acknowledged it.

"You are amazingly adept at going for the jugular, Ian," he said quietly, his voice bitter as he sat down in one of the leather chairs placed in front of the desk. "Perhaps in that, you are more like me than I would have wished."

"Perhaps," Ian acknowledged, and it didn't sit well with him, seeing parts of Diego in himself, recognizing that heredity played more of a role in what shaped him than he liked.

His gaze locked with Diego's as the other man stared back at him intently. Black eyes, bottomless, deep, merciless. Diego Fuentes wasn't known for his softness or his mercy.

"You do not find pride in being my son, do you, Ian?" he finally asked soberly. "It is a source of disgrace rather than pride. All I have built." He lifted his hands to encompass the study. "It is as nothing to you, is this not true?"

Ian leaned back in the chair slowly and regarded the cartel lord.

"I'm here," he finally answered, his voice firm, cool. "As I promised, doing the job I promised."

"For the lives of your friends who have turned their backs on you and revile you. For women who would spit on you should they have the chance. For this, you are a part of all you have fought against, all your life. With the man whose responsibility it was to protect you and your mother as a child and failed. For this, you reward me by being my son?"

There was sadness in his voice and for a moment, just for a moment, regret flashed through Ian as well. As a child he had dreamed of his father rescuing him and his mother from the hell their lives had become. Always running, always fighting to live, to survive.

Once he had realized who and what his father was, the betrayal he had felt had nearly crushed him.

Diego frowned as he watched him.

"As a young man, I thought I knew all I needed to know of human nature." He broke the stare they had maintained, blinking at a suspicious moisture in his eyes before glancing down at his still hands as they lay on his lap. "I thought I knew the shades of betrayal and a man's honor, and how to categorize each." His gaze lifted then. "I learned I was not nearly so intelligent as I believed. And by the time I learned this lesson, it was too late. Those who could have comforted me, who could have been the family I so long for now, are no more."

Ian crossed his arms over his chest and flattened his lips at the hidden message there. Had Diego figured out the reason he was there? There wasn't a chance. He would have been dead had he figured that out.

"There's a point to all this?" Ian asked him.

Diego shook his head, his eyes drifting closed for a second. "There is a message in all things, Ian. Just remember, the mistakes you make at this moment in time will follow you always. Not just into your nightmares, but into your future, and into your soul. There is no greater pain than the realization that you have destroyed the ties that would maintain you as you age. Those ties are important."

"Diego, you're making about as much sense now as Sorrell's terrorist rhetoric does." It also struck at the heart of this mission. Diego's and Sorrell's heads. He would deliver them personally to Nathan. Payback. Atonement. Monsters didn't deserve to live, did they?

Diego sighed wearily before a bitter smile pulled at his lips. "You handle the business as though I have retired and have no say in it. You ask for no advice, you prefer I know nothing of the plans you implement. You are aware, are you not, that this is not working?"

They had no choice but to make it work. When the mission was over, the cartel would come down. Ian had made that vow to himself and, silently, to the friends who had always backed him. It would come down, no matter the price.

"I know your fingers are still in there." Ian glowered back at him. He didn't need Diego's fingers there.

"You cannot reform an old lion from striking out at those who threaten his territory," Diego pointed out. "Those who have died by my hand, those who have suffered, were there to destroy me. I protect only that which is mine."

An old lion. As though the drugs he sold had no effects, no liabilities. Hell no, he was the candy man selling sweets, that was all, and the big bad SEALs and terrorists just wanted to smack him down.

Son of a bitch, was this how monsters justified their evil? Was this how he had justified the blood he had spilled while he had been here? Defending territory? He could feel the blood staining his hands, hear the wails of the dead in his ears, and fought to remember that they hadn't been innocents. They had been drug dealers, murderers, rapists, and animals. No more than Diego himself was. No more than his father was. His chest clenched at the involuntary thought.

Ian leaned forward, laying his forearms on the desk, and replied coldly, "Good men die to protect the innocent. You deal in death, Diego. Just as I deal in it now. Don't try to spray perfume on shit here to make it more presentable. You're a drug lord. We sell death to children. We prostitute them, we dope them up, and we make a profit from it. Period. We aren't lions protecting our home. We're snakes devouring the eggs of humanity."

Diego blinked back at him as though in surprise. "You have given this much thought, I see. Why then are you here?"

Because he had no choice. Because it was his life or the lives of those who had become his friends, his family. He was one man, alone. They were men with families, with lovers, with something to lose.

"That was the deal, remember?" he reminded Diego mockingly, hiding the fury now. Because now, he did have something to lose. "I save your cartel from Sorrell and you give me what I need to save my friends and take out the spy plaguing us. A simple exchange."

"With no emotion involved?"

"Goddammit, I took your fucking name." Ian came out of his chair in a surge of fury. "What the hell do you want from me, Diego?"

"I want you to call me father!" He was out of his seat as well, his own anger unleashed, twisting his expression into a grimace of emotional rage. "I want to know that when Sorrell dies, I will not then have to worry about your knife at my own throat. That I will not have to die by the hand of my son."

"As your brothers died by your hand?" Ian snarled. "Is that it, *Father*? Want to make sure the past doesn't bite your balls off? Son of a bitch!" Ian raked his fingers through his hair before swinging away from the other man.

Diego had paled at the word "father." Hope had sprung in his eyes like a kid at Christmas, sending an emotional blade ripping through Ian's soul.

He would not feel mercy for this bastard. He would not regret. He would not let himself ache for things that could never be.

"You . . ." Diego cleared his throat as he paused. "You rarely care or allow my opinion to matter."

Ian flexed his shoulders, careful to keep his back to the other man.

"It doesn't matter now." He felt like grinding his teeth in fury before he turned back to Diego. And saw, once again, the familiar features that he saw in the mirror each morning.

The hair and eye color were different. Ian was slightly taller, but the shape of the face, the curve of the lips, the arch of the brow, they were the same. He took many of his looks after his sire, and other things as well. Things he didn't want to admit to, didn't want to face.

Diego's smile was slightly less bitter, perhaps more hopeful, and Ian hated that. He hated that he would feel that twinge of regret even more.

"What the hell did you come in here for?" Ian snapped. "I have work to do and meetings this evening. I don't have time for bullshit."

Diego nodded. "Yes, you are busy building the cartel, its people and its product, as well as protecting it. I am here to tell you that the matter of your micromanagement is not suiting me. You will turn over the new routes to me in the morning and you will begin coordinating with me once again. You are a force to be reckoned with, and I admit this, but I am not so old nor so ineffective that I will allow myself to be pushed out. And there is the small matter of how this will end once Sorrell has been identified. Should you walk away, you will not leave me ignorant of my own world."

Ian nodded easily. "Agreed."

Diego would be as dead as Sorrell when this was over, so what would it matter?

Surprise flickered in the other man's black eyes, surprise, hope, and God help him, a father's love. Ian hated the fucking emotion more than anything else. Son of a bitch. He didn't want this. He didn't want to feel. He didn't want to regret and God only knew that he didn't want to risk more than he had come in risking to begin with.

"We will meet in the morning then." Diego nodded briskly before heading for the door. "Will you and your lovely Miss Porter be taking dinner with me before you leave this evening?" He turned as he gripped the doorknob and faced Ian once again. "I have had the pleasure of speaking to her again this afternoon by the pool. She is an intelligent, beautiful young woman. Not exactly the type of female you have surrounded yourself with on other occasions."

Ian stared back at him silently. He would no more discuss Kira with this man than he would discuss his mother.

Diego nodded easily, apparently accepting his silence. "I would enjoy your company this evening if you have time," he finally said. "We need time to know one another, Ian. Time to let the past heal."

He didn't wait for a response. He opened the door and let himself out before closing it behind him softly, leaving Ian alone.

He turned and faced the wall, his hands propped on his hips as he inhaled slowly, deeply. He didn't have time for this. Sorrell would be moving in soon, as soon as Antoli managed to capture Ascarti from the heavily secured yacht still anchored off Aruba's coast. Even if they couldn't take him, Sorrell would know his identity was threatened more than ever; he would come to Ian.

Nearly a year of waiting, watching, and it was almost over. He would make certain it was over.

Turning back to the desk, he pulled up the file that contained the pictures they had been taking of the yacht that week. Ascarti was there, as well as over two dozen unidentified suspects. Deke was working through the identifications upstairs while Antoli and Trevor worked on shooting more pictures and uploading them to Ian.

Progress could be counted in phases, Ian reminded himself. This was just a phase of it. Securing his position here, within Diego's life, within the cartel and its members. When it was over, the cartel would fall like a house of flimsy cards. It would be gone. Washed away like so much dust in the face of a good cleaning. This was just another phase leading to the end, and the emotion, the surging regret for what would never be, would be over once the mission was over. Idealism was a fool's game here. There was nothing ideal in the world he was fighting within, there was only the end result.

There was only success.

At least, that's what he told himself. What he tried to convince himself of. The mission mattered. Success mattered. Revenge mattered, and nothing else.

So why the hell did his heart feel like a ragged wound and why did he remember so clearly that bleak night that Nathan and his father had rescued him? Why did he remember screaming for a father that didn't exist?

Twenty-one

SHE WAS CALLED THE CHAMELEON in the covert underground she had operated within since her twenties, but that night, Kira had to admit that when it came to hiding who and what they were beneath layers of personality shifts, Ian had her beat.

From the moment he had walked out of the study earlier that day, she had sensed the carefully banked fury just beneath the surface. A fury fueled by the emotions roiling in his liquor-colored eyes. Somehow, Diego had managed to get to him this time in ways he hadn't before.

Throughout the day, Ian had managed to hide it. He was patronizingly patient with Diego, laughing with his bodyguards, and playing the role of the heir to a major drug cartel to the hilt. But Kira could sense the tension rising inside him and it wasn't rising from the mission alone. There was something else, something dark, something angry that she couldn't put her finger on.

His mood continued well into the evening, and as the sun finally began to set, Kira moved to the wide balcony doors that led from the bedroom rather than the sitting room. From here, she could see the upper story of the villa she had leased and the glow of lights in the bedroom Daniel had taken.

This wasn't the first mission she had taken that her

bodyguard wasn't directly involved. Actually, it would have been odd had he been involved rather than watching from the sidelines, ready to lend assistance should the danger become more than she could handle herself.

As she leaned against the heavy roof support and stared out at the villa, a frown worked at her brow. She could have sworn she glimpsed an additional shadow moving in the room.

She blew out a rough breath and pushed her hand into the pocket of the silk capris she wore, her fingers running over the slender cell phone she carried. She knew Durango team was over there, knew something was brewing, and it was driving her crazy.

Ian refused, point-blank, to meet with his former team, determined to handle this mission as he had begun it. Alone. Except for her.

She had to admit she was a bit surprised that he hadn't attempted to have her kidnapped and stashed in a safe location until it was over. Or until he was dead.

Dead would be a possibility if the snatches of information she had overheard were true. Ian's plan was to send a team in to capture Ascarti, the one man suspected of knowing Sorrell's true identity. Even DHS and the various law enforcement agencies around the world had kept their hands off him. They tried to place agents in close to him, tried to trail him, track him, and eavesdrop on him, but they hadn't attempted to take him because the fury Sorrell would unleash was just too dangerous. Whoever held Ascarti would feel the full force of the terrorist's fury. Unless they managed to get Sorrell at the same time.

But who would care if that fury came down on a drug cartel and a deserter from the U.S. Navy? She closed her eyes and swallowed back the nervousness rising inside her. Ian had been steadily pushing Sorrell, challenging him indirectly by the sheer fact that he had managed to derail every attempt the terrorist made against the cartel.

But Ian had gone from defensive to offensive this week

when he snatched the two men responsible for firing the missile at the limo. And he had killed them.

Logically, Kira knew he'd had no other choice. Once he snatched the men, he had to send Sorrell a message. That he wasn't playing. That he meant to protect his own territory. But she had to admit, she hadn't believed he would do it. How she thought he would handle it, she wasn't certain, but she saw he was harder, more determined than she had ever believed possible. Determined enough that the risk to Diego Fuentes's life by his son was greater than she had imagined.

She needed to report that, at least to Daniel. It was her job to ensure that Fuentes lived to fulfill his agreement with the U.S. To send DHS the vital information he obtained regarding terrorists and rumored strikes, while he maintained his hold on the drug business.

DHS wouldn't arrest him, detain him, or otherwise strike directly against his main base of operations, and neither would the Colombian government. The Fuentes cartel was handled with kid gloves until the drugs left the processing labs; after that, it was fair game.

It was a dirty deal. Ian would never forgive her or his own government once he learned the truth.

She crossed her arms protectively over her breasts and lowered her head, trying to hold back her own guilt and feelings of helplessness.

Hell, Ian had a right to his fury, to his need for blood. He'd had no childhood because of Diego's bitch of a wife, Carmelita. And Nathan. God, what Fuentes had done to Nathan was nothing short of evil. An evil the United States government was protecting.

Did the end justify the means? She didn't know anymore. She knew this mission had changed Ian. It had made him harder, made him colder.

"You're thinking too hard."

She swung around at the sound of Ian's quiet voice from the open doorway, her heart tripping in her chest at the softened tone.

She had believed him hard, but she heard something more in his voice now. Almost regret. His expression was in shadow, but she could feel the tension radiating from him.

"Enjoying the night," she countered with a smile as he moved toward her. "It's beautiful here."

"And deadly." His arms came around her, his hands gripping her hips and turning her once again, until she faced the villa. "Daniel hasn't left."

"He won't leave." She leaned into him, almost closing her eyes at the warmth and strength that surrounded her. "You knew he wouldn't."

"Neither will they," he murmured at her ear. "Durango team is over there with him, Kira. You and I both know they are. They're going to get themselves killed if they don't head out."

"And you know they won't," she said just as softly. "No more than you would if it were one of them involved. You have to meet with them. Work with them."

She felt his lips against her neck as one hand pulled her hair back from her shoulder.

"This isn't their fight." There was something akin to pain in his voice. She wanted to see his face, wanted to read the emotions there, but as she tried to turn, he held her in place. "Look on the roof." His hand gripped her chin, turned her head until she was staring at the edge of the slanted tile roof. "See, right there where the balcony roof slants away from the side of the house? The shadows are darker there, but there's the vaguest hint of an even darker shadow. Can you make it out?"

It couldn't be a human form; the slight glint of the moonlight against the black was too dull, too slender.

"I see it."

"It's a special lens Macey has. Sort of like the telescope a sub would use. He's hiding around the corner there, that telescope trained on us, watching us. Macey gets off on watching." There was the barest hint of fondness, of laughter, in his voice.

"He's a pervert," she agreed, a grin tugging at her lips.

"That too." He nipped at her ear. "I'll have to kick his ass for letting you know he's a pervert."

Kira snorted. "All you have to do is say hello to that man and you can tell he's a pervert. He didn't say a word."

Ian chuckled. "He has no shame. No modesty. No humility."

"Sounds like the Macey I know." She kept her voice as soft as his, barely more than a breath.

"Reno and Clint will be in the house with Daniel. Kell is most likely skulking around the grounds, watching and waiting. Hell, that bastard could be hanging from the balcony and you wouldn't know it until it was too late. We didn't call him the Cajun Gator for nothing, you know."

"What are Reno and Clint doing?" she asked, desperate to hear that affection, that loyalty that she was certain he had no idea he was revealing.

"Reno is plotting." His arms tightened around her. "Macey is relaying our location, trying to home in with that special mic he has to hear what we're saying, but the jammer in the bedroom is interfering. I bet he's pissed over that. Reno's trying to figure out how to make contact without compromising the team, or me. Clint is going over the information they have, trying to anticipate my next move, figure out where to waylay me. He was at Coronado's earlier tonight, in disguise, watching for me. He's probably cussing me. Reno is brooding. Reno can be worrisome when he broods." Regret shimmered in his voice. "I've managed to avoid them. It won't be sitting well with them."

She stared at the villa, at the point where Macey was watching with the lens. "You're going to contact them, aren't you?"

He nipped her ear, drawing a soft exclamation from her.

"You know he reads lips, you little minx," he growled before his tongue laved over the little sting.

"Why keep them wondering?"

"Because they're sticking their noses where they don't

belong." Anger thickened his voice now. "Reno's wife, Raven, just had her baby. The boy, Morgan, is no more than a few weeks old. Reno worked his ass off for a three-month leave so he could be there. So he could bond with the boy. Clint's newly married. Just a few months. He came back from his honeymoon early to head out here. Kell postponed his marriage to Emily, did you know that?"

She shook her head. She hadn't known they had set a date.

"I better get my invitation." She frowned. "She promised I could be a bridesmaid."

"If you live long enough?" His lips pressed against her neck for a long, agonized moment before he pulled away from her.

Kira turned and watched as he leaned a hip against the rail, his arms crossing over his chest as he glared down at her. He wasn't angry with her. Concerned. He was irritated and just as aware as she was that things would come to a head soon.

"I had Sorrell's missile boys killed this afternoon." He sighed wearily. "They're going after Ascarti before dawn."

Kira blew out a rough breath. "Ascarti was suspected to know his identity, though there's never been confirmation of it."

"I got my confirmation today. A man doesn't lie when he has a live wire hooked to his balls." His voice wasn't hard enough to hide the self-disgust in his tone. "I told Antoli to kill them after he was certain he had all the information he could get. A single shot between the eyes."

"Did you have any other choice?" He hadn't, but to hear the anger and the pain in his voice at his decision eased something inside her.

"There are always choices, Kira." He shook his head at the question. "It was the simplest way to show Sorrell I meant business. Anything else wouldn't have blipped his little radar."

"Then you couldn't do anything else." She shrugged. "They weren't men, Ian. They were monsters. They dealt in death daily, it just happened to have finally caught up with them."

"There is no guilt, don't fool yourself." He grunted, his expression tightening now. "Anger perhaps. A lot of it directed at myself. I've let this game go on too long. It's time to finish it."

"So you're going to do something that will bring Sorrell out of the woodwork. Ascarti isn't it. If he was, then someone would have tried it before. Think about this, Ian. I know you want to keep them out of it, but hold off taking Ascarti until you talk to the others. Work with them. If they didn't have something of value to add to this, they wouldn't be trying to contact you rather than just watching you. You know this as well as I do."

He blew out a rough breath. "Macey's tried to contact me through the secured sat phone for days."

She could see it in his eyes. He knew they had something, knew they wouldn't be so insistent unless it were of vital importance. They would have merely watched and waited, backed him however they could.

"I didn't want them involved in this," he said then. "I didn't want you in it."

"They're you're friends. Did you really think you could convince them you had gone rogue? They aren't stupid, Ian."

"I wouldn't be the first that's stepped out for a life of crime." He grimaced in disgust. "Happens often."

"Not to you. You don't threaten, you defend. They know that. If you wanted to convince them you were all bad and evil then maybe you should have started before the Atlanta operation."

He grunted at that before he pulled his cell phone from the clip at his waist and hit the programmed button to Antoli's cell.

Ian didn't like admitting she was right, she knew that. And he sure as hell didn't like letting Durango team in on his operation. Not because he was its leader, but because Ian felt the risk was his alone, and no one else's.

"Delay the grab," Ian ordered into the phone, his gaze locked with hers, a brooding frown pulling at his brows. "I'll contact you at dawn with further orders."

Seconds later he disconnected the call and shook his head wearily.

"We'll slip over to the villa in two hours," he told her. "Dress to blend in with the night and I'll let Deke know that we'll be out."

She started to nod. Ian's hand cupped around her neck, as the opposite arm hooked around her waist and dragged her against his body. His lips came down on her with a hunger that seared her. His tongue drove between her lips, tasted her, then a hungry growl rumbled in his throat as he began to gorge himself on the kiss.

All thoughts of meeting with Durango team or even breathing became overwhelmed by the sheer, fiery pleasure of his touch.

It was always like this. He could steal her mind with a single hungry look and sear her senses with the lightest touch. He was her addiction, and she prayed to God she never had to go without a fix.

"When this is over." He drew back just enough to speak, then took another, short hungry kiss. "When it's over, we'll discuss your habit of poking your nose into my business."

"Okay," she agreed readily, as her arms tightened around his neck to bring his lips back to hers.

Another sharp, stinging kiss and he pulled away, staring down at her, his gaze burning into hers, hungry and intense. And angry. She could see the emotions roiling inside him, tearing at him. She could feel them. They whipped in the air around her, burned through her soul.

"What else is going on, Ian?" she asked, lifting her hand to touch his roughened cheek. "What happened with Diego in the study?"

He moved farther away from her, his gaze breaking away as he stared out into the distance, his expression becoming hard, set.

"Nothing happened," he growled. "We head out in two hours. Make certain you're ready or I'll leave you here with Deke."

"No." She caught his arm as he turned to go. "Don't close up on me like this, Ian. Tell me what's going on."

His bicep flexed beneath her hold, tightening dangerously as he stared down at her.

"Nothing that applies to this mission," he informed her, his rough voice bleak, the almost ruined quality of it grating. "Nothing that applies to anything but regret, Kira. And that's something I can't deal with right now. We'll deal with that one when it's over."

He pulled from her grasp and moved back to the bedroom as Kira followed him, her heart aching, her need to alleviate his pain, or at least a part of it, thickening her throat.

"We have two hours," she told him, moving to his back, her hands flattening against it before smoothing around his waist.

She laid her head on his back, feeling the tension growing inside him. "We could spare a few minutes."

"Do you think a few minutes are all I need with you?" He caught her hands as they trailed to the band of his slacks. "Never enough, Kira."

"Then a few dozen minutes." She grinned up at him as he turned, the low lamp on the nightstand shadowing his dark, savagely honed features.

"You don't want this from me right now." His hands gripped her arms, his hold tight as the anger came to the surface and burned in his eyes. "Stand back, Kira."

"Why?" She would be damned if she would stand back. "So you can maintain that cold, hard shield you place so much stock in. Tell me, Ian, doesn't it ever get lonely in there, all by yourself?"

His lips flattened. "You don't know what you're talking about."

"Don't I?" She smiled back at him mockingly. "You have to do everything alone. The team you have with you,

you had no loyalties to before this assignment. They're not important to you. Nothing in this deal is important to you except the end result. No one or nothing can be used against you, can it, Ian. Even me."

His face hardened further. "Unfortunately, you can be," he ground out. "You made certain of it."

Shock resounded through her, parting her lips at the emotion that gathered in his voice, in his expression. Like a veil lifting to reveal the soul of the man that she had only sensed before. She saw him. Tortured, hungry, aching.

"Damn you," he suddenly cursed, jerking her to him, his hands pulling at the elastic waist of the silk capris. Material ripped, shredded, the sound of it an erotic hiss as he growled. "I told you. I warned you. You didn't want me like this."

"I want you any way I can get you," Kira gasped, feeling his hand hook in the neckline of her blouse. Buttons scattered and the cloth tore, the shreds pulled from her and tossed aside. "Ian, you keep tearing my clothes."

"Fuck the clothes." His lips went to her neck as he lifted her into his arms, dragging her breasts over the material of his shirt as he moved to the bed. "I'll buy you more."

He tossed her to the mattress, following quickly, coming over her and stealing her lips in another of those soul-destroying kisses. Hard and deep, his tongue licked through her mouth, his lips moving on hers, slanting over them. The heat of it burned into her brain, the need rose with such violent intensity that she felt buffeted by it.

He didn't bother to undress. One hand locked her wrists together, holding them over her head, as the other tore at his belt and the clasp of his slacks. The zipper slid down as he used his knees to push her thighs apart, and within seconds, the engorged head of his cock was pressing inside her.

He didn't take her easy. He didn't take her slow. With a muttered curse and a desperate growl he forged inside her, pushing through the snug tissue and slick juices until he was seated to the hilt.

Pleasure tore through Kira. Nerve endings fired with

brilliant, intense sensation and throbbed with the need for more. Her clit was swollen and desperate, the muscles of her pussy clenched and tightening on his erection.

"Being inside you is like heaven," he groaned as his head fell to her shoulder, his lips brushing over it in hunger. "Like being surrounded by silken fire."

His hips flexed, stroking his cock inside her, rubbing the thick crest into nerve endings so sensitive that the friction stole her breath.

"Hold me, Kira." His voice was so rough, so low, she barely made out the words. "God help me, hold on to me."

She froze for an instant. Just an instant, long enough to allow the broken emotion in his voice to register in her brain. The need she could feel tightening his body, not just sexual need, something more, something darker and bolder than mere lust. Something he was trying to hide from himself.

Her arms tightened around his neck as one of his hands clasped her hip, the other her wrists. He held his weight from crushing her by one elbow as his hips began to move.

These weren't deliberate, sensual strokes. They were mindless, primal. It wasn't just the climax he was reaching for, and the intensity of that primitive hunger tore through her senses. She could feel him. She had never felt another man clear to her soul this way. Had never felt anything that deep.

But it was where he touched her. He fucked into her with desperation, his cock burying inside her repeatedly, stroking the flames of hunger and need higher, hotter. Pleasure fed emotion. Sensation fed need until Kira exploded in orgasm with a power that sent shards of brilliant light exploding behind her eyelids.

"Damn you," he cursed her, his voice more broken than normal, his body shuddering as he continued to thrust through his own release. A release that spilled inside her rather than a condom, that extended the waves of pleasure racing through her. "Damn you for doing this to me."

She held on to him tighter, feeling more than his words were saying. Yes, he damned her, and sometimes she damned herself for pushing into his operation. They had each managed to protect their hearts until now. The only difference between them was that Kira was tired of fighting. She belonged to him, and she wouldn't deny it.

"I love you, Ian." Gasping, reeling from the pleasure, she made the vow again. "I love you."

"Damn you."

She couldn't help but smile. Sadly. With a sense of hope and an awareness of the danger she had placed them both in. Ian's emotions were involved now, whether he wanted to admit it or not. Now, they both had a weakness.

Twenty-two

SHE WAS UNDER HIS SKIN, in his soul, and there was no way to get her out. Ian covered her as they slipped from the villa and made their way over the stone fence to the villa Kira had leased for the summer. He made certain her back wasn't vulnerable, that no one saw her black-clad shadowy form from the house.

He was more concerned with her protection than he was his own. In keeping her safe rather than in advancing the mission as quickly as possible.

Son of a bitch, he had known this would happen. Known she would become so important to him that he wouldn't see her as an equal, or as a partner. All he saw when he saw her was silken flesh and passionate cries. How she held on to him when he loved her, how she shuddered in release in his arms.

She was breaking his heart and she didn't even know it. Breaking down shields he had begun erecting in that bleak desert landscape more than twenty years ago, and had strengthened throughout the successive years. Shields that protected him against loss, that stilled the hunger inside him for something more, something deeper than any relationship he had ever had before.

They were crumpling now, shattering beneath each touch,

each whispered cry in his ear that she loved him. A part of him gloried in them, the other part fought frantically to rebuild defenses that were already shattered beyond repair. Because all he could think about was life without her. If Sorrell managed to kill her, if he took her, if something happened to take her away from him.

The bleak existence he had known before her would be too dark, too brutal to bear.

After crossing the stone fence they crouched side by side, surveying the darkened landscape carefully. He had ordered the Fuentes guards to stay clear of Kira and her bodyguard, and his orders were normally obeyed to the letter. The blood he had shed in the beginning of his rule of the Fuentes cartel had ensured that.

But every now and then Diego managed to secure a soldier's loyalty to him instead. He couldn't be sure they weren't being watched, but he knew they weren't being followed. Deke would be watching for spies though, and if they were out there, he would have the report when Ian returned.

"It's clear," Kira whispered, turning until her face was directly below his. "He's pulled Macey and Kell back if they were out here."

"They were out here," he murmured. "Kell's still out here, trust me."

He stared at her upturned face, the delicate features, her unusually colored eyes, and felt his heart clench again before he looked around carefully.

Now wasn't the time to become mesmerized by the woman at his side. She was his partner here, she demanded nothing less. He would cover her to the best of his ability, and that meant making certain his senses stayed on alert.

The night vision goggles he wore picked up everything but a sign of human life. Kell was getting better. The last time they had practiced stealth, Ian had been able to track him easily.

"Stay close to the wall," he ordered. "Move around until

we reach the back of the house; there's enough foliage cover there to keep us in shadow and night vision can't see through stone."

She nodded as she bent to a half crouch and began moving carefully along the side of the wall.

Her pert little butt was right below his face and he felt sweat bead his forehead. That particular part of her anatomy had the ability to make his dick swell impossibly hard, despite the release he had experienced less than two hours before.

Shaking his head and turning, he swept the area again, paying particular attention to the top of the wall and the branches of the trees that grew along the side of the estate.

Within minutes they paused directly across from the veranda doors, hidden by the wall at their backs and the staggered landscaping of the yard.

Using hand signals, he directed the route for her, then watched, his weapon held steady in his hand, as she crossed half the distance and ducked behind the huge cement fountain. Pausing, she swept the area before turning back to him and holding her own weapon ready.

Ian moved quickly to her position, then, staying close to her back, pushed her toward the veranda door that had been left open.

Of course the team was expecting them and he had no doubt Kell was covering their back the whole way. He and Macey. Ian could feel it, felt the security and the sense of teamwork that had always followed him on the missions they were assigned to work together.

They moved quickly onto the sheltered veranda, straightened and stepped into the open breakfast room it was attached to.

Handguns held ready at their sides, Ian went in first, moving quickly to the side, bringing up the gun at the sight of the figure standing still, arms held out from his side, as Kira swept in low.

"The house is secure," Clint informed them, his voice

quiet. "Come into the sitting room. Kell and Macey will be in as soon as they sweep for any lagging shadows."

Ian holstered his weapon slowly then pulled the goggles from his eyes and stared at the man he had called friend eight months before.

He came to attention; the former easy familiarity with his lieutenant commander hadn't necessitated military protocol in such settings, but for some reason, the gesture of respect triggered intuitively.

"Bastard," Clint growled. "At fucking ease, Lieutenant. This isn't a goddamned firing squad."

It sure as hell felt like one though.

Clint was quiet then, watching them both with brooding intensity as Kira holstered her own weapon and removed her own goggles.

"How long have you been set up here?" Ian asked as Clint turned to lead the way through the house.

"Since the night you installed Kira at Fuentes villa," Clint answered, his voice biting. "Of course you already know that. You had one of your men watching this place like a gator watches fresh meat."

Ian's lips quirked. He would have expected to hear that from Kell, not Clint.

"I assumed you would take the hint when I left you the message to stay out of this."

"Killer Secrets?" Clint grunted. "Yeah, we were just going to drop off the face of the earth for you, bro. You forget, 'Killer Secrets' was for personal endeavors only, not drug cartels."

"Family ties don't make it personal then?" Ian snapped.

Goddamn, what the hell had they wanted, a blow-by-blow account of exactly how personal this was to him?

"That about sums it up, Richards," Clint snarled, turning back to him, anger tightening his features. "Drug cartels and unidentified terrorists do not fucking apply. Remember that."

Clint was pissed, there was no doubt. Ian pushed his fingers through his hair and shook his head at the thought.

"Son of a bitch, McIntyre," he cursed. "Why didn't I just drag all of you in on it, since Diego knows your faces so fucking well. I could have watched him kill you like I watched him kill that little maid. Her brains splattering across the wall before she had time to realize she was dead. Hell yeah, I wouldn't be dealing with your stubborn ass now if I had."

Clint rounded on him, his lips flattening, the muscle at his jaw twitching dangerously. Clint wasn't a man to cross, but Ian had learned to cross the most dangerous of them all. The fury in the other man's face didn't have the power it once held.

He met Clint's anger head-on. No apology. He'd be damned if he'd apologize for any of it.

Clint's gaze sliced to Kira then. "You're slacking, Agent Porter. I figured you'd have him in line by now. Teach him a few manners."

"He's still a work in progress," she drawled, the hint of a Southern accent causing Ian's balls to twitch in hunger despite the tension in the room.

When her fingers slid over his arm, and she aligned herself at his side, something shifted within him. Others stood either in front of him, or behind him; he'd be damned if anyone, man or woman, had ever stood at his side in such a way.

The feeling that swept over him had him fighting to hold back, to keep his damned hands to himself. Instead, his arm slid around her, pulling her to his side, desperate to feel her against him.

Clint's lips quirked. "Keep working on him, he might have potential. Come on in here, we have some serious shit going down. We were planning a break into Ian's room tonight. Thankfully, you saved us the trouble."

Ian's eyes narrowed as he followed Clint through the villa. If they had been considering a move that potentially dangerous, then the situation had gone beyond serious shit. They knew the operation, that was evident; moving in on him could have fouled the whole thing.

"There were ways to make contact," Ian reminded him.

"Sure there are," Clint growled. "Ways that information can be leaked too. From what I understand you're under a total blackout until this mission is completed. I talked to your stepfather; even he hasn't heard anything. We weren't about to rock this little boat by going through channels that could possibly include another nasty little spy belonging to Sorrell. Coming straight to the source. I like that angle."

Bitterness filled his voice, the same bitterness that had filled all their guts when they realized how effectively the government channels had been infiltrated by Sorrell's spies.

"I need to get this over with," Ian informed him. "I have men waiting to grab Ascarti if need be. The opportunity is now or never."

"Never." Clint led the way into the sitting room off the more formal living room.

"Ascarti isn't what you want." Reno stepped from the shadows of the room, cradling an M-16 as he gazed at Ian quietly. "It's good to see you again, Ian."

"Reno." Ian nodded, then glanced at the weapon in his arms questioningly.

"Security." Reno shrugged. "Macey and Kell are on their way back in; until then, there are things to protect."

"There are?" Besides their own sorry asses? But why the hell they thought he was a risk at this point, he wasn't certain.

"There's a reason we've been busting our asses to contact you for a week, Ian," Clint snarled. "You have your head up your ass? Since when did you think we'd jeopardize an op?"

"Since the general information that went out on it said I was a deserter and traitor," Ian snapped back, feeling Kira's hand rub against his back warningly.

Hell, why did that ease the anger beginning to rise inside him? What the fucking hell kind of hold did she have on him anyway? Whatever it was, it eased the violent tension rising inside him and had the other two men watching him with knowing grins.

"Would you believe I had betrayed my country, Ian?" Reno asked then. "Better yet, would you have believed it of Nathan, no matter the evidence?"

"I built the evidence," Ian reminded them. "It was pretty damning."

"A little too damning," Reno agreed. "I'll kick your ass for taking me away from my wife and son after we're finished here. Until then, we have details to attend to."

Macey and Kell stepped into the room.

"Fucktard," Macey muttered as he passed him. "Dumb shit. The least you could have done was let us have some fun too."

Kell chuckled and moved across the room to plop into the heavily cushioned couch that sat along the wall.

"All clear. We have monitors in place as well as motion sensors. We're safe for the time being."

"Jammers are in place," Macey reported. "The villa seems pretty quiet. Old man Fuentes retired to the basement from what I could see. He likes his solitude?" Macey glanced at Ian.

"He likes his playroom down there," Ian snapped. "And the pretty young woman willing to play with him."

The others grimaced.

"You're all here, now what the hell is going on? I put off a grab against Ascarti for what?"

"For me, Lieutenant Richards."

Ian had his weapon out, swinging around to the shadowed opening that led to another room and the petite young woman that stepped through it.

He recognized her. A regular at some of the clubs in the past few months. Red hair, haunted green eyes, and wariness.

"Tehya?" Surprise colored Kira's voice as she touched Ian's arm, indicating that he could holster his weapon.

The others sat and stood comfortably, obviously well aware of her presence before she stepped into the room.

"You know her?" Ian questioned tightly.

"Tehya Talamosi," she stated. "I'm just not certain why she's here."

"It's good to see you again, Kira." Tehya nodded almost regally in Kira's direction. "It's been a few years."

"Tehya."

Ian could feel the tension in Kira's voice now; she was as off balance as he felt.

"Why is she here?" Ian lowered his weapon carefully. "And it better be good, Reno, because I'm ready to kick all your asses for jeopardizing this mission in this way."

Tehya's lips curved with an edge of bitterness. "It wasn't their fault, Lieutenant Richards. Once they learned why I was here, they really had no other choice. We have a mutual goal, and I can help."

She couldn't be more than twenty-two, twenty-three at the most. She was so damned delicate it was hard to picture her as an adult.

"And how can you help?" Ian growled. "Unless you can identify Sorrell for us."

"I can do better than that. I can bring Sorrell to you. I'm his daughter, you see. There is no better bait on the face of this earth."

Ian couldn't believe it. It couldn't be this simple.

"You can identify him?"

Her lips turned down. "Unfortunately, not his face. If it were that simple I would have made the information available to your terrorist enforcement agencies years ago. I don't know his face, but I know his voice and I know the single identifying mark he carries. I can give you that much, and you can kill him for me."

Anticipation rippled through Ian. He felt Kira tense beside him, saw the satisfaction reflected in the other men's eyes.

This was what they had been waiting for. Years of investigations, of planning. They had heard about the wife and daughter who had escaped Sorrell years before. The wife had turned up dead in Nicaragua, but the daughter was rumored to be a figment of the imagination. An urban legend created by the agents desperate to identify Sorrell.

Sorrell's twenty-year rise within the underground terrorist community had been subtle. The power shifts had been carried by men working directly beneath him, yet never seeing him. Somehow, Sorrell had managed to finance and build an empire within the white slave market before sliding into terrorism, and he had done it all without ever being identified. There hadn't even been a strong suspect in the years since his name had popped up. He was an anomaly, a shadow.

"I know Tehya, Ian," Kira murmured. "I knew she was running from something, I just didn't know what."

Tehya's pert little nose wrinkled as her lips tightened.

"When my mother escaped Sorrell, I was only three. She had me placed in a convent while she continued to run. The good sisters there knew I was in danger. They protected me. It took Sorrell only months to find her and kill her. One of the nuns awakened me one night and we slipped from the convent. It was burned to the ground at dawn that morning with six nuns inside. The coroner's report stated that at least one of the bodies had been tortured before the convent was burned. I've been on the run ever since. Always just a few steps ahead of him, always fighting for survival."

"So why move against him now?" Ian wasn't the trusting sort and he didn't believe in a gift horse.

Teyha sighed before glancing behind her at Reno. "When you deserted and took the reins on the cartel in time to keep Sorrell from taking over I knew it was time. He's been gaining on me, tracking me. He found the nun who raised me about ten years ago. She had known Sorrell was close to finding us. She put me in the care of a priest that she knew well and did the same thing Mother had done. She kept running. I have no doubt she gave them a reliable description of me before his men murdered her because within months the priest and I were on the run as well. We ran for years before he found someone he thought could protect me better than he. My life has been filled with blood, Lieutenant. After the priest was killed, I ran away from the retired marine he had placed me with. Within months the marine was dead, and I was alone. I've been alone since I was seventeen, fighting to stay out of Sorrell's hands, always aware of the future that awaits me if he catches me. The only way I'll be safe is if he's dead."

As she spoke, her voice thickened with unshed tears, with the horror of the life she had lived. Kira moved from his side and walked to her, her arms going around the younger girl as she stood in the center of that room, her head lifted, her lips trembling, taking on her own slender shoulders responsibility for the lives her father had destroyed.

"She came to Aruba to ask for your help." Reno stepped forward then. "Macey saw her at Coronado's several times, watching you, trying to get close to you. Kell caught her trying to slip into the Fuentes estate a week ago. He convinced her to let us cover her until we could form a plan."

"Why not let her come to me?" Ian snapped.

"Because one of Fuentes's most trusted soldiers is reporting to Ascarti, Ian. His cousin Muriel. She would have been walking into an ambush if she had entered Diego's villa."

Ian froze inside. Muriel was one of the few within the Fuentes organization that Ian had handpicked himself to protect the villa and Diego.

"Do we have proof?" He was aware of Kira's gaze jerking to him as she slowly released Teyha.

Reno moved to the small table at the side of the room and picked up a file. He handed it to Ian slowly.

In living color the digitally printed photos showed Muriel and Ascarti meeting. The exchange of an envelope and Muriel handing the other man photos. Photos of the inside of the villa and the grounds as well as photos of Ian with various suppliers and transporters.

"Ian." Kira stepped back to him.

"He'll be at the villa in the morning with Diego," Ian said coldly. "We'll take him then and have Antoli question him."

"Antoli's good at what he does. You know he's a plant from within Russia's Federal Security Service, don't you?"

"I'm aware of that." Ian continued to stare at the photos as he fought against the knowledge that this betrayal by his cousin would be a shock to Diego. Diego discussed everything with Muriel and Saul. And why the fuck he should care, Ian didn't know.

Antoli had been a very low-level soldier within the Fuentes organization when Ian came in. Ian had promoted him to security not long after recognizing him. He had known Antoli was a plant from the start. The man had been quietly putting together his escape when Ian waylaid him late one night in Colombia just after reading the file Diego had on him. Which was a hell of a lot different from the truth. Just as it appeared Muriel was different from what he had been perceived as.

He pushed his fingers through his hair as he focused on Tehya once again.

"How will you recognize his voice? If you've never seen him, if you've been on the run all your life, how could you recognize anything about him?"

A bitter smile twisted her lips. "He left me a phone number once. Unfortunately, it's untraceable. Reno has the number. Sometimes, when I want to remember how much I hate him, I call him. He always answers. And it's him, trust me. As bad as he wants me back he would never let anyone else answer that phone. He's assured me, time and again, that he's my father and he wants only to protect me. It's Sorrell, Mr. Richards. I remember that voice from my nightmares. As a child, I heard him rape my mother, his voice so calm, so reasonable, and demonic. I'm staking my life on the fact that it is him."

She was indeed betting her life if what she was saying was true. Ian let his gaze connect with Kira's, saw the concern in it. She knew Tehya, and evidently, she trusted the other girl.

So young. Twenty-three and yet the haunted pain in her eyes made her appear so much older. He'd lived on gut instinct too long to discount her, but that didn't mean he trusted her.

"And I have an ace, one he's unaware I possess." She stared at him intently then, tears glittering in her wild green eyes.

"What ace would that be?" he asked carefully.

"I carry his birthmark. It resembles a scythe. Sorrell's personal mark, the same birthmark he carries."

She turned then, lifted the thin T-shirt she wore, and revealed the mark low in the center of her back, below her hips. In the exact center, perhaps two inches above the cleft of her rear, was the small birthmark resembling the scythe Sorrell used as his own personal mark.

Kira moved her gaze from the mark low on Tehya's back, to Ian. He hadn't tightened, hadn't moved, his expression hadn't altered in the least, but the tension suddenly emanating from him was electric.

"No one knows about the birthmark," Ian murmured. There had been no rumors, not so much as a whiff of information regarding it, Kira knew.

"No one knew about this except myself and my mother. She warned me, before she left me with the nun, to never reveal it. To never let anyone know of it. And I never have."

"Does Sorrell carry the mark in the same area?" Ian asked, moving closer as she stared over her shoulder at him.

Kira watched Ian. He was no longer suspicious; it was as though something had fallen in to place for him, some source of information that only he knew.

Ian bent to sit on his heels, staring at the mark closely.

"We have a chance to get him here, Ian." Reno spoke

softly from the other side of the girl. "She's willing to help us and we have enough to identify him."

"He dies," Ian said, his eyes locked on the mark. "I don't care how much information he could have." He rose slowly, straightening to stare at Reno over Tehya's shoulder. "He doesn't leave alive."

"You'll have to set up protection for her. Something away from the villa," Kira stated as Tehya pulled the hem of her shirt back into place. "You'll have to give him visual proof that you have her. You'll have to threaten to mark her, scar her. If she's scarred, then her value to him is diminished. Sorrell doesn't deal in damaged goods. And his daughter would be an asset. An extension of his ability to create perfection."

"Antoli." Ian nodded slowly. "We'll set up a vid, an interrogation of her, make it look good. Give her the appearance of bruising . . ."

"It will only work if you actually bruise her." Kira shook her head. "Bruising does more than discolor the flesh. To convince Sorrell, you're going to have to go further."

"She's right." Tehya held Kira's hand as several male heads shook instinctively. "It won't be the first time I've been bruised. And if your Antoli is as good with interrogation techniques as I've heard, then he'll know how to do it right."

Courage. The woman had more courage than she should have at her age. To even consider allowing a man as brutal as Antoli to touch her.

Ian let his gaze drift to Kira then. He saw the pain in her eyes, the shadows, and knew she was reliving the loss of her own family to the murderous bastard. She had been ten, but she had escaped the horror Tehya had lived through. Thank God.

"We don't need to beat her up to convince Sorrell." Ian shook his head as he turned his gaze back to the small redhead with the wild green eyes. Eyes that saw too much, that knew too much. Eyes that broke Kira's heart with the pain and rage inside them. "All we need is the visual proof that we have her. He's chased her this long. Make her accessible and he'll mess up. He won't be able to help it. He'll be desperate to secure her."

Kira was watching Tehya's eyes as he said it, saw the terror that flashed inside them. She had courage, but she was smart enough to know what she was getting herself into.

"I'll do the vid," he continued. "We'll take her to a secured safe house, record it, and send it to Ascarti via Colombia," he mused. "We'll give him a short timeline. Make him react quickly."

"He's not far from Ascarti," Tehya said then. "Wherever Ascarti is, you'll find Sorrell close. But if you snatched Ascarti he wouldn't come running."

Ian nodded slowly as he turned back to Reno, his eyes narrowed, the air around him pulsing with danger. "What kind of probables have you run?"

"We checked out the names she gave us of those who tried to help her. They were dead. Deaths were by torture. They died hard and likely gave Sorrell everything they knew. It fits with his particular MO. Evidence we've gathered about his network suggests it was his personal handiwork. No one knows torture in his organization as well as he does. We know he's indeed French, Tehya's mother was of French descent. Reports on her death suggest that she hadn't been in Nicaragua more than a few weeks when she was snatched from the street. There were a few witness reports, but you know how sketchy local law enforcement is there. It was dropped within hours; only the notification and questioning of witnesses was kept until her body was found."

"Her name was Francine Taite. She was the daughter of a French industrialist driven to bankruptcy after her kidnapping. They died before my birth. She was kidnapped and sold, according to the information she gave the nuns, though she never gave his name. Thirteen years after her disappearance as a child, she was dumped out of a dark sedan on a dirty street in Nicuragua. She had been raped. Her fingers shattered, the soles of her feet had been burned. She died slowly," Tehya recited, a frown marring her brow as she seemed to stare off into nothing. "She was tiny, delicate. I remember her crying. I never remember her laughter."

She seemed to shudder as Kira moved to Ian's side. His arm went around her naturally, pulling her to his side, feeling the pain that worked through her as Tehya turned to Reno. "I'll require a weapon. I won't let him take me, Reno. It stops here. Either he dies, or I do."

Reno nodded slowly.

"We need to get this together and get moving on it, before Sorrell figures out what's going on," Ian said. "If he's never more than a step or two behind her, then he knows she's been here watching me. It could be the reason he fired a missile at me rather than a gun on the last attack. Do you have a safe house in mind?"

"Right here." Reno grinned. "She's been here since the night Kira moved out. All we need to do is get this vid made and shipped out and wait for the response. We have everything set up. We were just waiting for you."

"Fucktard," Macey muttered as an aside.

Kira watched the grin that tugged at Ian's lips. Evidently tonight wasn't the first time Ian had heard that particular insult. He stared around at the other men. "First chance I have, I'm telling your women you left them to play on the beaches in Aruba. Fitting punishment, I think, for driving me crazy with that sniper rifle you've had trained on me for the last two weeks."

"Best telescope I own." Macey snickered. "Felt it, did you?"

"Every time you stroked the trigger, I felt it, Macey," he growled.

"Should have shot you," Macey grumbled. "Dumb fuck. You should have let us in on the fun. You're just plain selfish, Ian. I've always said that about you."

Ian pulled Kira against his side. She felt the warmth of his body, the strength, the steady confidence. "You have no idea. Remember, the next time you train that telescope on Kira, I'll shove it up your ass."

Macey winced, but the tension that had filled the room began to dissipate.

For the first time in eight months, Ian felt the camaraderie, the sense of teamwork that he had relied on for so many years.

And in his arms, close to his side, he felt the center of his soul. He had avoided the acknowledgment, tried to deny it, fought to push it away. But as he stared at Tehya Talamosi, and saw a woman alone, fighting to live in the face of a monster, he realized how very similar he had once been to her.

Kira had filled that part of his soul. The part that had been empty and alone. The part that had fought to live even though the danger of the monster had passed. And he prayed that Tehya would find it as well.

Twenty-three

SHE HAD NEVER IMAGINED WHAT kind of life Tehya had endured.

Kira slipped into Ian's room from the balcony, barely glancing at Deke as he rose from the chair by the bed as she escaped to the bathroom.

She felt sick inside. She knew Tehya, she had met her in France nearly six years before. They had had coffee as Kira watched a French diplomat sell classified documents to a Russian agent. They had spent the weekend shopping, laughing, and being girls. Two strangers in a strange land, and Kira had never guessed the danger Tehya had been in.

She had suspected her to be a rival agent. For a while Kira had wondered if she were an assassin or part of a kidnapping team. But the other girl, though distant, her eyes often shadowed with pain, had never mentioned anything that Kira could have used to fuel her suspicions.

She had met her again in Afghanistan working with the Red Cross. Again in America, once again working with the Red Cross, just after Hurricane Katrina. She'd had no idea the hell the girl was living through. Damn, she'd had no idea how young she was or what she was searching for.

Safety. Protection from a monster. The identity of the monster. Why hadn't she put it together?

Kira slammed the bathroom door closed. Why hadn't she figured out that the kid was in trouble? Hell, she hadn't even known she was a kid. It was those eyes. Those wild, shattered, haunted eyes. She couldn't have been more than seventeen the first time Kira had met with her in France. Kira had assumed she was another agent. She had played the game when the girl had sat down at her table, leaned back and smiled and asked if the chair was taken. A very inexperienced agent. But Kira had played the game because all she was there to do was watch and make certain the exchange of information was completed.

God. Damn. Information targeted to Sorrell.

In Afghanistan, Tehya had worked with the Red Cross. The CIA had suspected the terrorist cells there to have ties to Sorrell.

Hurricane Katrina. Sorrell had used the devastation and chaos there to raid several government offices. Kira had tracked two of his men there and coordinated with the small team she had gone in with as they attempted to apprehend them.

Sorrell's men had not only escaped, but had escaped with classified files regarding several federal investigations into a terrorist network they had uncovered.

Tehya had been there.

The day she was leaving she had spotted the girl outside those offices, staring up at them, her eyes narrowed. As though she had known she was being watched, her gaze had found Kira's, locked with it, those haunted eyes shadowed and desperate.

And Kira had misread the desperation.

She lowered herself to the small cushioned chair in the corner of the opulent bathroom and pressed her fists into her eyes.

She had just watched that same girl endure being chained to the wall, dressed in nothing but her T-shirt and panties . . .

Terror had flashed in her eyes as Antoli Kovalyov

chained her securely before pulling the black mask over his face. He had jerked her head back roughly by her long red hair, cupped her neck in his hands, and stared at the camera.

"We have your daughter, Sorrell." His hand had left her neck, gripped her hips with enough force to redden the skin, and jerked her around just enough for the camera to pan in on the birthmark. "As you can see, she carries your mark. You want her, you will now deal with Fuentes."

The camera had panned back to her face. Defiant, her eyes riotous with fear and fury, Tehya had glared at the lens with murderous rage.

God. She was nothing more than a kid. A kid that should have been in college, laughing with her friends, partying too much maybe. Kira fought the monsters in the world so kids like that would be safe, and she hadn't even noticed a child in danger when she had met her.

The bathroom door opened slowly. She heard it. She knew it was Ian, but she couldn't lift her head, couldn't take her fists from her eyes or, God help her, she would cry. And tears wouldn't help anything. It sure as hell wouldn't relieve the pain and fear Tehya had experienced.

"It will be over soon and she'll be safe." She felt Ian kneel in front of her, one hand pushing her hair over her shoulder as the other cupped her face. "It's not your fault, Kira. You can't save the world."

She sniffed, feeling like a child, like she had felt the morning her uncle had awakened her and told her that her parents were gone. She felt lost. And she felt responsible.

She shook her head.

"When my mother and I were running from Carmelita Fuentes all those years ago, I apologized. I told my mother how sorry I was that she was suffering because of me. That she should contact Diego. Tell him about me, and give me up so she would be free."

Kira lowered her fists, the first tear falling from her eyes as she glared back at him. "That wasn't acceptable."

A small smile tugged at his lips. Lips she loved to kiss, loved to feel on her flesh.

"She said pretty much the same thing. She said we can't save everyone, but we can damned sure as hell fight to save those we love. And she loved me. She would die for me. She nearly died." His tobacco gaze darkened, grew fiery. "But she taught me something, Kira. She taught me that we can only do our best. You've done your best. Tehya survived, and God willing, she'll survive this along with the rest of us. But you can only do your best, not beat yourself up because you missed something or someone. It makes you weak. And you can't afford to be weak right now."

His fingertips stroked down her cheek as he stared back at her, his rough-hewn face creased into lines of concern as his lips drew her gaze again.

"I should have known." She shook her head as another tear fell and pain roughened her voice. "It's in her eyes, it was in her eyes then, and I didn't pay attention. She was right there in my face and I didn't see the child she was, or the desperation in her eyes."

"Did you see it in mine?" he asked her then. "Every time I saw you—"

"You got horny." She smiled at the thought, her voice husky.

"Hornier than hell," he agreed. "And desperate to taste you."

"I saw that." She sniffed. "I felt it."

"I looked forward to seeing you. Every time I knew you were close, I looked for you."

"You're trying to distract me," she said, sighing. "You should let me kick myself a while longer."

"No kicking allowed." He cupped her face in his hands and drew her forward, his lips moving to the tears that streaked her face, kissing them away, filling her with a warmth, a need, she had only found in Ian's arms.

"I was married once," she told him, wondering why the hell that had fallen from her lips.

Ian drew back and stared at her silently for long minutes before nodding slowly. "I know."

"He left me." She fought to still the trembling of her lips. "Did you know he left me?"

She was shaking, which really made no sense. It was so long ago. A lifetime ago.

"I knew he filed for the divorce." He was so tender. He pushed her hair back again, leaned forward and kissed the corner of her trembling lips.

"Because he didn't know me." She could barely force the words out. "Because I didn't let him know me. Didn't let him know that every time I left town on business for Uncle Jason that I was facing more danger than he could imagine. He couldn't have handled it. He would have demanded that I stop, and I couldn't stop."

He tilted his head and stared at her curiously, waiting, watching, his gaze understanding. She wanted to scream at him, wanted him to understand that she was flawed, that she didn't always see the things that she should, that she didn't always do the things she should.

She wanted to warn him that she was betraying him, but if she did, God help her, if she did, he would make certain she didn't have the chance.

"And you couldn't handle telling him the truth." His hands stroked over her shoulders, her upper arms.

"He would have felt betrayed," she whispered.

He nodded again. "You were his wife, it was his job to stand beside you, Kira. It wasn't your job to protect him from the truth."

That was such a male point of view, and one guaranteed to piss her off. She opened her lips to argue when she found his fingers pressed against them.

"It's instinct," he said then. "For centuries, it's been our job to protect our home, our women, and our children. We're emotional cowards. We don't talk about our feelings, we're not comfortable putting our soul into words. So we give of ourselves the only way we know how. We protect. We smother those we love in protection, fight for ways to keep them always safe, even from what we deem as a threat from themselves. It's in our genes, Kira. Right or wrong. Emotions are harder for a man to voice, strength is much easier for us to show. It's not an insult, it's the way men show their emotions for those they love. You can't change it."

"I can protect myself."

"And you shouldn't have to, no more than Tehya should have had to. She should have been protected, cosseted from the evil of the world, and sheltered from a father's madness. Instead, she learned to fight, and she learned to survive. Just as you learned from different circumstances. I don't want to steal your strength. And accepting that you can walk beside me, rather than allowing me to clear your path, isn't always easy. Men don't ask their women to walk behind them because they think they're inferior. They do it because they want to shelter them."

"Because they love," she whispered painfully.

Fear slammed inside her now. She jumped to her feet, stumbling to get around him, staring back at him in overwhelming panic as he slowly straightened.

"You don't love me." He couldn't love her. She couldn't allow it, not yet. It was okay to love him, to know he would walk away from her when this was over because of what she had been sent to do. But not like this. She couldn't betray *his* love. Oh God, don't let him love her.

"I don't?" he questioned her, his raspy voice stroking over her nerve endings, surging through her with equal parts pleasure and fear.

"No. You don't." She pushed her fingers through her hair, clenched the strands at the nape and felt the tension tightening in her body until she wondered if she would break. "You can't love me. Loving me is stupid, Ian. Just ask my ex-husband. Hell, I'll even give you his number."

Because she would have to betray him. Just as she had betrayed her husband by not allowing him to know her alternate life. Now she was betraying Ian by not allowing him to know the agenda DHS had contracted her to see through.

She reached behind her, gripped the doorknob, and pushed the door open as he stepped toward her. "Just ask him. He'll tell you. Loving me is the worst mistake you could make."

She watched his expression, watched the glimmer of amusement that lightened his whisky eyes and the emotions that softened the savage features of his face.

He wasn't drop-dead gorgeous, he was rough, dangerous. The features of his face were too sharp and well defined for handsome. And now, they were even more rugged as he stared back at her, obviously holding back, watching her curiously.

"It's hard to find a woman who can walk beside a man like me," he told her softly, stalking her as she backed out of the bathroom. "I'm a prick on a good day, and I have all those male faults that keep telling me I should push you behind me, cover you, shelter you. We'll never bore each other, Kira."

She shook her head, her heart lodging in her throat as she fought any idea that what he could feel for her went beyond lust and a need to find solace amid the life he had been living.

Love was for later, she told herself. It wasn't for now. Not until he knew the truth of her, the truth of what she had been sent to do, and she couldn't tell him that now.

For the first time in her adult life the woman was overshadowing the Chameleon and she was regretting. Regretting the mission, regretting the woman she had become and the deceit she had learned too well. She was regretting the years she had held back, forcing herself back from Ian, forcing distance between them.

She was learning parts of herself she hadn't imagined existed. The sensual woman. The hunger and the needs Ian called forth from her. The tenderness. The insight the woman had into the man she had claimed for her own.

She could excuse herself by saying that she was protecting him until hell froze over, but in the end, she knew he would never believe it. A man should never have to face killing his own father, no matter what a monster he might be. And the honor that was so much a part of him would never be able to accept that his own government had held information back from him.

She retreated further, aware that she was shaking her head repeatedly, that some part of her brain was rejecting the thing she wanted the most, that she had dreamed about for so damned long.

Ian's love.

"Why are you so scared, baby?" His hands flashed from his sides, locked around her wrists, and held her still as he brought his body to hers.

He didn't drag her into his embrace, he stepped into hers, pressing himself against her as he pulled her arms to the small of her back and surrounded her with his warmth.

She used to hate being restrained. Hated being held, until Ian. Now, it sent a heated response streaking through her as a core of once-unknown femininity came violently to life.

She tugged at his hold, a distant part of her aware of the fact that the struggle wasn't about being set free. She didn't want to be free, she wanted to be held tighter, closer. She wanted the world to retreat until nothing mattered but the reality they created with their passion. Until the danger and the deceit swirling around them disappeared and left her free to reach out to the one man who completed her.

"You haven't answered me, Kira." His lips lowered to the corner of hers as he arched her against him. "What are you scared of? You can love, but no one can love you?"

"That's exactly how it works." She had to force the words past the constriction in her throat.

"Why, Kira?" His lips moved over hers, ignoring them when they parted in hunger, when her tongue stroked across his. "Why can't anyone love you?"

"Because they don't know me." She almost felt lost again, as lost as she had felt when her husband had walked out on her. "I'm the Chameleon. Always changing. How can you love someone like that?"

He lifted his head to stare down at her.

"And yet, always Kira," he guessed.

Always Kira. Always alone. She had never recovered the feeling of security and sense of balance that she had known before her parents' deaths. She had lived with the knowledge that her family had died because they had fought against the specter known as Sorrell. Because her father had taken up one lost child's battle and searched endlessly for her and her abductor.

Her father had been a lawyer, her mother had been a child services representative. When one of her children had gone missing and the trail had led to a white slavery organization, she and her husband had followed that trail.

Sorrell had struck back. He had killed her parents and Jason's fiancée and it probably hadn't even blipped on his radar that he had destroyed two more lives in the process. And made two enemies determined to bring him down.

Until Ian, love hadn't been a part of her life. Neither had true security. She realized, in his arms, she felt safe, she felt warmed. And only now did she realize how frightening that was. Because she could lose him so easily.

"We'll talk about love when this is over," she told him desperately. "You'll see then, you don't love me. It's the situation. It's being in this world, having it wrap around you, smother you. You don't love me, Ian. You love the normalcy you think I represent. That's all."

And she knew better. If any man knew what he was about and who he was, then it was Ian. And he was terrifying her. Shaking her resolve. She couldn't let him do that.

He chuckled. Clear, warming amusement echoed in the sound as he pulled her tighter against him.

"Psychology isn't your strong suit, sweetheart."

"Of course it is. I spent years studying under the best profilers we have on terrorism and their victims. Trust me, I know what I'm talking about."

Her voice was breathless; her body was filling with arousal. She couldn't be this close to Ian and not ache for more.

He simply smiled. A slow curling of his lips that sent her senses spiraling with a hunger to taste them, to feel them against her own. It also sent fear ratcheting up inside her. He was staring at her as though he knew her. Knew parts of her that even she didn't understand.

"I love you, Kira."

Emotion exploded in her head, in her soul. She was only barely aware of the thin cry that left her lips, of the tears that rolled from her eyes and over her cheeks. Tears he caught with his mouth a second before his lips covered hers.

"Belong to me," he whispered against her lips a second later. "Right now. Right here. Belong to me."

Oh God, she would always belong to him.

He released her hands but only an act of God could have pulled her from him then. There was no chance she was going to allow anything else to peel her from his body.

Her arms slid around his neck as his wrapped around her back. His lips were on hers, eatable, so eatable. Like rough velvet, stroking over nerve endings, sending fiery pleasure whipping through her body.

Kira arched in his arms, wishing she could meld a part of him inside her forever. A part she could always hold close to her, some part of him that she would never lose.

"My wild little lover." He eased back, ignoring her cry of protest. "We're not going hard and fast this time. Is that how you protect yourself, Kira? Does it have to be hard and fast so you can hold on to those reserves of control you keep in such supply?"

"My control?" she gasped, forcing her eyes open as she felt his hands move to the hem of her black shirt. "You're the one with too much control."

"Let's see about that," he suggested, his rough voice and confident smile causing her to moan at the implications of his dare.

"That's not fair," she gasped. "We both know you can hold out longer. I want to break. You don't."

He chuckled again. "Is that how you see it, Kira? That hard and fast means you've managed to break my control rather than me breaking yours?"

"Duh!" She gasped as the black stretchy cotton shirt cleared her breasts. "What else could it mean?"

"It could mean the pleasure is too important to lose," he suggested as she lifted her arms, allowing him to pull the shirt free of her body before tossing it aside. "It could mean I want to relish rather than devour. Haven't you ever wanted to relish it, Kira? Savor the pleasure and hold on to it forever?"

He was going to lock her soul to him forever. She could hear it in his voice when he spoke of savoring rather than rushing. He was going to imprint himself not just on her body, but on her very spirit to ensure no part of her ever escaped him.

He thought he loved her, thought he knew her. He thought this pleasure could go beyond deceit.

"No restraints this time," he warned her as he pulled his own T-shirt from his body and dropped it to the floor.

She should be running, finding an excuse not to do this, not to allow him to lock her to him more than she already was.

Naked from the waist up, Kira watched as he sat in a nearby chair and unlaced his combat boots while staring back at her.

"Take your boots off, Kira," he told her softly.

She sat on the edge of the bed and braced her ankle on her knee, working at the laces as she watched him, like a puppet without the sense to think for itself.

She licked her lips nervously as they pulled a boot off simultaneously and then shifted to work on the other. Once they were removed he gathered them, along with their shirts, and walked to the closet where he stored them on a rack before turning back to her.

As he stood in the closet doorway, he lifted his hands to the belt cinching his waist, then the closure of the black mission pants he wore. Kira got to her feet, imitating his actions, removing her pants as he watched her, her breathing escalating, moving hard and fast through her lungs.

She couldn't seem to draw in enough oxygen. Couldn't seem to shake free of the hypnotic arousal tearing through her.

"Maybe we should sleep for a while," she suggested breathlessly, knowing better but helpless against the need to find an escape, any escape, from what she knew was coming.

At least a delay. A delay would be nice.

"If that's what you want, the couch in the sitting room should suit you."

He peeled the pants from his muscular legs and any thought of sleep flew out of her mind. As he straightened, his erection pointed out from his body, wide and hard, the engorged crest dark and throbbing with lust.

She felt her pussy clench at the sight, become slick and hot at the need to be filled, taken. To be possessed as only Ian could possess her. As though he were the other part of her, separate but created to fit her exactly.

As she watched, his fingers curved around the thick stalk, stroking, tightening as he felt her eyes on him.

She became increasingly aware of the juices gathering on her pussy lips, knew that in the low light of the room the moisture would be shimmering on the bare, hairless flesh. And that was where his gaze was directed. She could feel it. It made her wetter, even as she felt her breasts swelling, her nipples becoming impossibly harder.

Licking her lips, she slid one hand over her stomach, her fingers dipping down as it slid lower and her eyes moved to his face.

He was watching, a grimace contorting his face, as she slid her fingers over the sensitive flesh between her thighs. Her breath caught at the pleasure. One fingertip raked over her clit, sending hard, brilliant streaks of fire burning over her nerve endings.

"Beautiful," he groaned. "Part your lips for me. Let me see how hard your clit is. How swollen."

She separated the folds of flesh with two fingers while the middle finger circled the torturously hard nub of nerve endings.

Her juices were flowing from her now. She could feel them trickling between the lips, soaking her pussy with the slick excess.

His hand tightened on his cock before loosening his grip. His nostrils flared with lust, as though drawing the scent of her in across the distance separating them.

As she let her fingers push through the thick juices and caress the humid flesh of her pussy, he moved to her. She knew she should act. She should make the first move and push him to the bed rather than standing here, tempting him, teasing him. Instead, her other hand smoothed up her stomach and cupped the swollen mound of her breast.

She was teasing him and she knew it, hoping to tempt him, to break his control.

Kira felt the breath catch in her throat as Ian grabbed her wrist, dragging her fingers from the slick heat of her pussy and lifting her hand. To his mouth.

Oh Lord, she wasn't going to be able to stand at this rate. He brought her fingers to his mouth and let his tongue lick at one before drawing it in and sucking the moisture from it.

His eyes blazed, his expression tightened, and a groan rumbled in his chest. The feel of his tongue stroking over her fingers was sexier than she could have ever imagined it would be. It shouldn't have been this erotic. Fingertips weren't erogenous zones, were they?

Of course they were, but only when Ian was encouraging them to be such.

Kira tipped her head back, feeling her hair stroke down her spine. Another added sensation to lend to the eroticism of the moment. Another blow to her own control.

"Look at me, Kira." His voice stroked over her nerve endings. Rough, rugged, almost ruined.

She forced her lashes open, feeling the heavy lassitude that pulled at them as arousal grew inside her.

"Do you know how beautiful you are to me? How courageous and strong?" he asked her, his tongue stroking over her fingertips one last time before he placed her hand on his shoulder.

Against her stomach she could feel the hard length and throb of his cock and wanted nothing more than to feel it pounding inside the hungry depths of her pussy.

"I'm just me," she told him breathlessly with a quick shake of her head.

"Just you," he agreed, one hand settling on her hip as the other moved up her side to cup the heavy weight of her breast.

"Ian, I don't know if I can handle this." She was shaking on the outside, on the inside she was melting, weakening.

"Pleasure?" He smiled down at her, his expression sensual, wicked. "Of course you can, baby. You can handle all the pleasure I have to give you."

She could die from it, was what she could do.

A startled gasp left her lips as his head lowered, his lips smoothing over a distended nipple.

"I can't stand up." Her legs were shaking.

"I can help with that," he told her, his voice so very considerate, edged with lust and erotic promise.

Insidious eroticism was what it was, because in the next second his lips covered hers, his arms holding her closer, giving her the support of his stronger body. His aroused body. His cock pressing into her belly, throbbing against her sweat-slicked flesh as her nipples were buried in the thatch of chest hair, raking into it, rasping the tender tips.

It wasn't just a kiss. It was an assault against her control. It was slow and savoring, a melding of lips and tongues, whispered groans and weak cries.

It was her arms wrapping around his neck to hold him

closer, her soul devouring the emotional, sensual trails of pleasure to hold for the future. To remember in the event that he walked away and never returned.

"Better?" Ian crooned, his sandpapery voice sending a surge of sensation to strike at her womb.

"Don't have legs left," she muttered, trying to recapture his lips, to hold his kiss to her.

His chuckle was followed by a caress of those lips against her neck, to her ear, down to her shoulder.

"I'll be your legs." He picked her up and carried her to the bed, laying her along it as he came over her, stealing her lips again, his hands stroking over her breasts, cupping them, his thumbs rasping her nipples as his lips followed.

Kira shook her head desperately. She knew what he meant to do, and she couldn't bear it. He was imprinting her soul with his touch, with the pleasure only he could give her.

"Ian, please," she moaned, not that her plea distracted his lips from their course.

Taking stinging kisses from her neck, her collarbone, they arrowed to the tip of a tight, hard nipple, they destroyed any protest she would have further voiced.

"I want all of you tonight," he told her, staring down at her, his eyes darkening as she bit her lip and shook her head slowly. "All of you, Kira. If I have to let you walk beside me, then I'll know all of you belongs to me. Every inch of this sweet, hot body, every particle of your heart and soul. You'll be mine."

Her fists clenched in the blanket.

"No . . ."

"Fuck you, yes!" Anger flashed in his eyes. "You forced me to accept you being involved in this, now by God, you will accept me."

Twenty-four

SHE DIDN'T WANT HIS LOVE. The thought was ricocheting through Ian's head, burning through his own defenses and plain pissing him off.

She loved him. He knew she loved him. He could feel it, see it in her eyes, feel it in every touch of her body, but she didn't want his love in return.

Why?

He cupped the swollen mound of her breasts, felt the heat of her flesh and saw the flush of arousal that colored it. Her nipple was hard, distended, like a tender pebble against his tongue as she writhed beneath him.

Her eyes were shadowed, riotous with fear and pleasure, and that confused him. She confused him. The mix of vulnerable woman and courageous agent never failed to mesmerize him. She wasn't hard or embittered. She laughed, and she cared, and she loved, even knowing that those she loved could be taken from her in a second.

He licked at the tender hard flesh of her nipple and sucked it tenderly into his mouth at the thought. She loved him, though he had given her no reason to love. He had tried to push her away, even as he pulled her to him, several times. And she was always there, a part of him, sliding into his soul as though she had always been meant to be there.

Now she was denying him the same place within her, that same security. Damn her. She had made herself imperative within his life, so imperative that he had pushed aside his own prejudices about having a woman within one of his missions and let her in. She was part of the danger he was facing and she couldn't even enter the part of his soul that he had opened for her?

The hell she couldn't. She would, one way or the other, give them both what they needed.

"You're mine," he whispered against her sweat-slick flesh as he moved from one breast to the other, licking and nibbling, tasting her skin and becoming drunk on it.

"Please, Ian." Her gasp filled his head, passion and lust, defiance and need, echoing within it.

"Tell me you're mine." He licked over the opposite nipple, drew it into his mouth, and nearly shuddered as the taste of sweet female flesh infused his senses.

"I'm yours. I swear. I'm yours." She arched beneath him, pushing the berry-ripe tip deeper into his mouth.

He gave her what he knew she was aching for. His lips closed snug and tight over the tip of her breast. He sucked it inside, drawing on her, relishing the taste of her as his tongue lashed at her nipple.

Her body drew tight beneath his as she shuddered and trembled in his arms.

"Am I yours too, Kira? Do I belong to you?" He lifted his head, glancing up to see the battle she waged reflected in her sweat-dampened features as her head thrashed back and forth on the bed, denial contorting her features as a cry fell from her lips.

He licked one nipple, then the other. He let his kisses trail from one mound to the valley between her breasts and the journey that led to the sweet, seductive spice of her wet pussy.

He was dying to slide his cock inside the velvet heat of her vagina. To feel her muscles tighten around him, stretching as they took him, accepted him. The way her juices slickened the sweet depths, the way they eased his penetration of her. His possession of her.

Oh yeah, he had her heart, even a part of her soul. But he didn't have all of her. Not yet. Not yet, but he would have it before the night was finished.

"Ian, don't torture me. Don't do this." Vulnerability, fear, arousal. It all clashed in her voice as the plea had him laying his cheek against the soft mound of her belly and forcing him to breathe in deep, to remember what he was fighting for.

He wouldn't take from her. He accepted her. Her need to fight for what she believed was right, her need to be here, to see the man that had destroyed her family fall. He accepted those parts of her that refused to allow him to coddle her, to keep her out of danger. He needed her to accept him in turn. To claim him. To demand him.

He needed it, though it made no sense. He knew he loved her, knew she loved him, what did it matter if she was willing to face it at this moment or not?

It did matter. It mattered that he could lose her, that she could lose him, and that vow wouldn't be between them. That she wouldn't know how much he had loved her, needed her. Because for whatever reason, she didn't want to hear the words.

"Do you know what the taste of you does to me?" He nipped at the flesh of her thigh as he made a place between her legs for his shoulders. His hands clamped on her hips to hold her in place even as he ignored her sharp little nails digging into his scalp or how she tugged at the thick strands of his hair.

"Let me touch you," she cried out. "Let me taste you."

"Let you love me?" He smiled as he laid his cheek against her thigh, the spicy-sweet smell of her infusing his senses as he stared up at her. "Let me love you, Kira."

She shuddered, her gray eyes going stormy as she stared at him, pleaded silently with him.

"Let me show you, since you don't want to hear the words."

One hand left her hip to trail between her legs. He felt the heated juices against his fingertips and felt his mouth watering to taste them. She was sweeter than syrup, hotter than sunlight, and she burned him to the very core of his being with her passion and her love.

"Ian, you don't know . . . Don't know what you're doing to me."

"What you did to me?" He parted the sweet flesh, ran his fingers along the narrow slit. "Showing you how I feel? Making you accept that I need as well? Oh yes, Kira. I do know what I'm doing."

Before she could form an argument or pull harder at his hair, he lowered his head and swirled his tongue around the distended, hardened little clit. Softly pink, throbbing with arousal and glistening with her juices, it drew him like a sensual drug, made him hungry, made him ache to feel it within his mouth.

God, he loved her taste. It exploded against his tongue, filled his mouth with the lightest hint of sugar and fiery spice.

He groaned into her flesh, felt her shudder again and felt an overwhelming pride that he could give her such pleasure. The same pleasure she gave him. The kind that whipped through the soul and bound a man and woman together forever.

That was what it was, chains weaving through silken emotions, ensuring that no matter where they existed, together or apart, that they would always belong.

He had never belonged. Until now.

KIRA THRASHED, JERKED, WRITHED BENEATH him but nothing could break the hold he had on her. She pulled at his hair, begged breathlessly, but nothing stopped the destructive strokes of his lips and his tongue or the explosive pleasure of his suckling mouth.

She arched, fighting to get closer even as she fought to hold back the effects of the pleasure.

Oh God, it was so good. His tongue stroked around her clit as his lips sucked at it. When she was close, so close to release, he moved, licked along the shallow slit, sucked the soft folds into his mouth and groaned as her juices fell from her pussy to the caressing fingertips that stroked over the entrance yet never penetrated.

"Am I yours, Kira?" he whispered again.

Oh God, what did it matter? Why did he fucking care? He knew he owned her. He owned her heart and soul, what did it matter if the thought of his love terrified her? She could love him and deal with the loss. She had done that before. Dealt with losing those she loved. But she had never known love. Not like this. If he loved as she did, then it meant she was betraying not just the man, but his soul. She couldn't handle that. She couldn't handle knowing he was out there, without her, betrayed, hating her. Even her ex-husband hadn't hated her by time he walked away. Of course, she had never allowed him to love her either.

She cried out Ian's name as piercing pinpoints of heated ecstasy exploded around her clit. He pulled the little bud into his mouth once again, stroked it, licked and savored it. He kissed it. Suckling little kisses that were gone before they could push her over the edge.

She tried to tighten her thighs, to hold him in place, but his shoulders were there, stopping her. Each time she tried to distract him, his finger would stroke inside her pussy, just a bit, just enough to force her to still, to ache for more.

"Ian, please. Please." She panted beneath the caress, ready to cry, to beg, ready to die if he didn't do something, anything, to ease the sensual pain building inside her.

His finger stroked inside her again, just enough to have her screaming breathlessly for more.

"So soft and hot. So tight and sweet." He rubbed at the entrance as Kira felt more of her juices coating her flesh.

Kira dug her heels into the bed, her hips arching closer.

"Oh God, Ian." Weak, desperate, her cry tore from her

throat as another finger began to play, lower, along the snug opening to her rear.

"You've never been taken here, have you, Kira?" The tip penetrated, just enough, just enough to tug at the nerve-rich area with brutal sensuality.

Her eyes closed. She knew what was coming. She knew . . .

"Ian!" She screamed as his finger penetrated deeper. Just a little bit deeper, then retreated.

His mouth covered her clit as she felt him moving, reaching, the sound of the drawer at the bedside table slamming shut a second later.

She couldn't place the sounds, only the soul-deep knowledge that if he took her there, he was possessing more than just her body.

She had never been taken anally. Seductive toys during masturbation didn't count. The fact that each time she had done so her fantasies had revolved around Ian, did matter. The fact that she could feel his fingers, now slick with lubrication, caressing her there, that sure as hell mattered.

"You don't know what you're doing," she moaned. "You don't understand."

Pleasure was curling up her spine in frantic fingers of sensation as she felt his finger, slick, warm, ease slowly into the tight entrance of her rear as two fingers eased into the frantic, clenching entrance of her pussy.

Neither penetration was deep, neither should have had the effect it did. Flames burned at her, licking over her flesh, as pleasure streaked through every cell of her body and her breath caught in her throat.

Ian's lips covered her clit as her legs lifted, arching her hips higher, a foot bracing on his shoulder as the other flexed on the back of his shoulders. She was opening herself to him and she knew it, giving him access, giving him permission.

He groaned against her clit as he slid fingers deeper inside her.

Kira slid her fingers from his hair, the pleasure swamping her as she cupped her breasts, her fingers playing with her nipples, pulling at them, increasing the fiery sensations destroying her.

She was lost in him now. She couldn't help it. The pleasure was too much to bear, too much to fight. She tilted her hips higher, moaning in ecstasy as his fingers slid deeper inside her. Not deep enough though, not nearly deep enough.

The two fingers slid from her pussy as her own pinched at her nipples, increasing the sensations. His tongue, wicked and hungry, moved between the folds of flesh to flicker over the clenching entrance to her vagina as the finger slid deeper up her rear.

"Ian. God. Please. I can't stand it. I can't." Her feet were braced on both shoulders now, her hips tilted further, easing the penetration of the two fingers sliding slowly inside her rear.

The stretching burn stole her breath. She could feel the fingers easing inside her by slow degrees, penetrating her, preparing her.

"It's okay, Kira." He kissed at the folds of her pussy gently, sucked at the flesh and laved it with his tongue. "I'll take care of you."

Her head thrashed against the bed. He was killing her.

The fingers in her rear slid deep in the next stroke, his tongue pushed inside the gripping channel of her pussy and Kira knew she was losing the battle.

"Fuck me!" she snarled. "Now!"

"I don't want to fuck you, Kira. Isn't there another option?" His voice was grating, his own hunger, his lust, thickening the tone as she cried out, the sound harsh and desperate.

There was only one other option and it wasn't acceptable. It just wasn't.

"Then I'll fuck you," she groaned. "Please, Ian, I can't stand this."

His fingers shifted inside her, stretching her as they

scissored apart and caused the flames burning across her flesh to intensify. Perspiration ran in rivulets over her body now, soaking her flesh, dampening her hair, as she tried to hold on to her senses.

His tongue stroked inside her pussy again, his fingers pumped slowly inside her rear. The alternating strokes were killing her, holding her just a breath from orgasm and building the heat beneath her flesh higher.

Pleasure this destructive should be outlawed. It was a pleasure that went beyond the physical, a pleasure that sealed a woman to the man giving it.

"Do you know the high a man gets when he takes his woman here?" His fingers slid inside her rear again, pumped with deep strokes as he spoke against her pussy.

Her head shook desperately.

"It's better than drugs, Kira. Knowing she's with him this deep. That more than just her body is involved. Knowing you're giving me something you've never given anyone else. It goes beyond fucking, doesn't it, baby?"

"No . . ." The desperate moan was a cry, a denial bred from the knowledge that it was something more.

He kissed her pussy, a gentle suckling kiss at her clit as his fingers retreated and he moved over her, lifting her legs, holding them up with one hand at her ankles.

The tip of his cock pressed against the forbidden entrance of her ass. Kira forced her eyes open.

"Do you want me to fuck you?" Somber, filled with pain, his gaze locked with hers. "Is that all you want, Kira?"

Her lips parted, the soul-deep knowledge that it stopped here washing over her. If she denied him this, she was denying more than the possibility that he loved her. She was denying the man he was, and everything she could possibly have later.

Would his love gain acceptance, understanding, of what she was there to do? Would he see that she had come not to betray him, but to protect him against a decision that she knew would eventually destroy him?

She licked her lips, feeling the sensitivity of them even as she felt her anal tissue parting for the tip of the crest pressing into it.

"Love me," she whispered, almost choking on the pain now. "Please, Ian, please love me."

Her back bowed, a soundless scream leaving her throat, as she felt the head of his cock lodge inside her ass. Her eyes flared open, locking with his, feeling herself reaching for him, her hands latching onto the thick muscles of his upper arms as she placed her legs on his shoulders and braced his weight on the bed.

"I love you, Kira." His voice was grating as he began to work his cock inside her. "I love you."

The intimacy of the act burned through her mind. With each measured thrust, each inch of possession, he claimed more than the untouched entrance he was taking, gave more than the pleasure that surrounded her.

She stared into his eyes and saw a man who loved, perhaps like her, for the first time. A man as wary, as uncertain, as she herself was, but one unwilling to take the chance that if he lost it all in a second, those feelings would be lost as well.

He wanted her acceptance of those feelings. He wanted her to accept his love, just as she gave hers. To see, to feel, to understand.

As he lodged to the hilt inside her rear, stretching her, the pleasure burning up her spine, she stopped fighting his love, as well as her own. She soaked it in instead, took it into her as she took the impalement that had always been taboo with any other man.

"Perfect." He grimaced as he held still inside her, each throb of his cock echoing through her nerve endings as she felt the waves of undiluted sensation beginning to gather inside her.

She was so aroused, so hot, that the juices falling from her pussy eased along the crease beyond her vagina and coated the area he was penetrating, further slickening it when added to the lubrication he had used.

When his hips began to move, thrusting inside her, it blinded her with the brilliant arcs of light that began to cascade around her.

Sweet Lord, it was so good. She had never known pleasure like this. Had never felt taken so thoroughly. With each plunge of his cock inside her ass, her cries grew more desperate, her need for release more imperative. It was building, stroking inside her, overwhelming her.

"Ian!" She screamed his name, or tried to, fought to.

"Soon," he rasped. "Soon, Kira."

"Now. Oh God, let me come now. Please God, Ian, I can't stand—"

Her pussy spasmed, clenching hungrily as her clit throbbed painfully. Just one stroke, that was all she needed.

Desperately she moved one of his powerful hands, pushing it between her thighs as he levered back on his knees, still buried inside her, still thrusting. As her fingers neared her clit, he beat her to it. His hand turned palm up, two fingers plunged inside her pussy, the edge of his palm rasped her clit.

His hips moved harder, faster. The strokes inside her ass burned with brilliant pleasure. Hard, desperate thrusts that powered inside her, fingers in her vagina, stretching her, his cock buried in her ass, burning her.

The release, when it came, destroyed her, remade her. She screamed his name, vowed her love, her voice torn and nearly as unrecognizable as his. His vows, his love, poured over her with the same fierce, heated power that his release poured into her.

Hard, heated jets of semen filled her ass. Her pussy clamped around his fingers, her clit exploded against the pad of his palm. She was coming, dying around him, crying out his name as her soul opened and accepted his.

"I love you, Kira. God help us both, I love you."

He collapsed over her, sweat coating them both, melding them together as their ragged breaths filled the bedroom.

Kira felt her eyes grow heavy, her body languorous.

Even as he pulled from her and eased his weight from her body, she couldn't seem to move.

She needed to get up, maybe shower. Instead she let her eyes close and felt herself slip into sleep.

IAN CLEANED HER WITH A damp cloth. With another he wiped away the drying sweat. Starting at her forehead and working his way down, a smile tugging at his lips as she shivered softly.

He dried her, pulled back the blankets, and tucked her beneath them as the first full rays of the sun speared through the slats of the shades over the balcony doors.

He'd been up more than twenty-four hours, but hell, so had she. He needed just a few hours' sleep, to recharge before he forced Sorrell into the confrontation that was coming.

He should go downstairs, meet with Diego and fill him in. He wanted him in on this, didn't he? Both of them in the same place. It would be like leading the lamb to the slaughter.

Later, he told himself, ignoring the warning little cringe that tightened his guts at the thought. Diego was no lamb. He had made his own choices and those choices had led him here, to this final confrontation.

He brushed the hair back from Kira's face as he slid beneath the sheets with her. She turned into his arms naturally, for the first time seeking him in her sleep rather than maintaining distance between them.

He kissed her lips softly, because he couldn't help himself. She had given him something he had never known before, the chance to love someone who knew the fires he walked within.

She wouldn't be pacing the floor and crying while he was on a mission. Hell, he'd probably be the one pacing the floor and cursing whenever she wasn't within sight. Because he knew her.

He frowned at that. Something would have to change

after this. Neither of them would be able to go back to their old lives. Their old lives wouldn't exist now. Neither of them were the same people they had been when this operation began.

He smiled though, realizing there was no regret in the thought. There were other ways. There were always other ways, other jobs, and damned if he wouldn't be ready for a change, if they survived this.

If they came out of it alive.

His arms tightened around her as he sent up a prayer. Just protect her, he thought. Nothing more. Nothing for him, because that would be selfish. He never prayed for his own survival, but now he prayed for Kira's.

Twenty-five

H E SLEPT THREE HOURS; HE thought Kira would sleep
longer. Ian slipped from the bed and made his way to the
shower, mentally and emotionally preparing himself for
the next few hours.

He would spill blood today, and he would spill it again
before the night was over. As he stepped beneath the
shower's spray he braced his hands on the wall, leaned his
head into it, and breathed in roughly.

He hadn't lost enough sleep yet to weaken him, and he'd
make certain once this morning was over to find an hour for
a nap. He'd learned to sleep where he could, when he could,
if it meant only a few minutes propped against a wall. Or a
few hours curled around Kira.

His arms ached to return to the position he had awakened in. Clenched to hold her against him.

Hell, he was dangerous to himself in this shape. This was
a mission, not an excuse to screw his head up. Or his soul.
But that was exactly what he had managed to do where Kira
was concerned.

Suddenly, he was questioning plans that had been fact
for two years. Questioning his own motivations and wondering about his reasons for getting involved. Honor, glory,
and the American way were wonderful surface excuses, but

when a man set out to kill his sire, there was more to it. It was personal, it had become personal in a desert twenty years before, and he realized with a vague sense of disgust that it had shaped his life, even after the danger had passed.

She was changing him. Or perhaps that was the wrong word. It wasn't a change, so much as a revelation. She had made him realize why so much of his soul had seemed empty for so long. He hadn't even realized what he was missing, what he was searching for, until Atlanta. And even then he had tried to deny it, tried to push it away.

He was the worst sort of male chauvinist, yet he had allowed her into the mission, he had kept her at his side. The logical part of his brain, which worked only rarely when it came to her, assured him she was a capable agent. The emotions though, those had blindsided him, ambushed him.

And now he was in emotional hell.

More blood would stain his hands this morning, and even more once the meeting with Sorrell commenced. He was sure she was no stranger to bloodshed, hell, he knew she wasn't, but he didn't want to kill in front of her. He wanted her to keep that vision of a white knight that she seemed to have convinced herself he was.

Ian shook his head before lifting his face to the stinging water and mentally kicking himself for the fool he was.

Son of a bitch. She had a way of twisting his guts into knots and he couldn't seem to stop it, no matter what he did or how many times he told himself he was doing the right thing.

As he stood there kicking his own ass for his weakness, he felt her. Hell. He lowered his head to the spray again. He hadn't heard her slip into the bathroom, but he felt her. Not just a presence, her presence. Soft, smelling of his possession, warm and willing.

He turned his head as the shower door opened and she stepped inside the large cubicle.

She didn't speak, and his tongue was paralyzed as her hands slid down his back.

"You should be sleeping." He cleared his throat, certain

his already ruined voice sounded like a monster's growl as a smile flirted at her lips.

"I got cold." She blinked against the drops of water that splattered to her face.

He knew better. The temperature was controlled, she couldn't have gotten cold. Hell no, she was hot, burning inside the same as he was, even after the rapture that had claimed them hours before.

His arms went around her. Trapping her against the side of the shower wall, he stared down at her intently, watching the passion that clouded her eyes and feeling the response clear to the engorged, painfully hard length of his dick.

Hell, he shouldn't be this hard. He shouldn't be bending his knees and rooting it against the slick, hot folds of her pussy.

He had work to do. He had killers to take care of, a drug cartel business to run. He had to play the game until the minute he put a bullet in Sorrell's and Diego's heads. That required planning, not fucking himself blind.

"I need to be downstairs." His head lowered to the ripe, plump bead of her nipple and he heard her gasp as he fought to make sense of the thoughts and emotions jumbled inside him.

"Okay." Her hands tunneled into his hair though and held him to her breast.

Ian surrounded her nipple with his lips, drew it into his mouth and let his tongue play with it. He stroked it, lashed it, sucked at it with firm draws of his mouth.

"You're a wild man." A thread of satisfaction filled her voice as he moved his lips to her neck, licking along the smooth column and taking nips of her with his lips.

God, he loved tasting her flesh, loved immersing himself in her scent.

"Horny man," he muttered.

She laughed, her hands flattening against his shoulders as she pushed him back and went to her knees before he could stop her.

Ian stared down at her, unable to move now, unable to form a coherent thought at the sight of his heavy shaft aimed at her soft, pink lips.

Her tongue peeked from between those perfect lips, curled along the underside of his cock and had him gritting his teeth at the wild pleasure that ricocheted up his spine.

Now, if she had given him a chance to recover his sense, he might have pulled her to feet, lifted her until her legs could circle his hips, and his cock could burrow into the paradise he found between her thighs. But she couldn't keep it that simple.

Her mouth surrounded the crest, took him deep, and began a long slow suction as her hands wrapped around the shaft and a groan tore from his throat.

"Ah yeah." He gave himself over to the most wicked, heated head job a man could ever know.

Sweet lips surrounded him, a tight hot mouth stroked him, and that tongue of hers was a curling, lashing little demon of ecstasy.

"Deeper." His hands slid into her wet hair, his fingers tightening in the strands as he braced his legs firmly beneath him. "Take it deeper, Kira."

Slumberous, erotic sensuality transformed her features. She was beautiful. Exquisite. And she was sucking his dick like a favorite treat. He loved it. Loved her.

God help him, he loved her.

His cock slid farther along her tongue as he felt her moan vibrate along the shaft.

"Deeper," he urged her, his voice so thick, so rough he could barely understand the words himself. "Come on, baby, you know what I want."

Uncertainty flickered in her eyes, causing him to pause. She had never . . . ? At least not like this. Not deep, not to the point that a man knew he would lose his mind buried inside her mouth.

He smiled down at her. "Just relax. Let me show you."

His fingers tightened in her hair, tilted her head back just a bit, aligning the head of his cock with the soft inner depths of her throat.

"Breathe through your nose, relax. It's good, Kira. So good."

He watched her nostrils flare as his eyes narrowed and he began to move again. His hips shifted, nearly pulling his cock free of her mouth before he moved inside again, going deeper, just a little deeper, feeling her tighten on him.

"Relax." Ah God, he was desperate, burning for that final depth where he would feel the exquisite clenching at the back of her mouth, feel her tongue rippling along the undershaft.

He pulled back and filled her mouth again, touching that final portal for the briefest instance before retreating. It was so fucking hot, blistering, destroying him.

"A little more," he panted. "Just a little more."

Ah hell. He was dying, burning alive. His balls were drawn so tight against the base of his cock that they felt constricted to the point of pain. The need to come was like a burning lance shooting straight up his spine and sizzling through his brain.

Her long black hair flowed down her back, her exotic face was filled with hunger, and she sucked his cock like a woman starving for the taste of her man.

Ian clenched his jaw tight with the effort to hold back, pushed through her lips again, and swore he was going to die before he managed to come.

It was perfect. It was a haven in the middle of a storm, the center of the hurricane, the depths of a volcano. It was white-hot heat and a pleasure he knew he couldn't live without now.

He felt the back of her mouth relax, though it rippled against the head of his cock. The muscles of her throat spasmed, tightened, and before he realized he'd lost it, his semen was jetting from the tip of his dick and filling her mouth.

Her throttled cry was another ripple along his cock, her

stroking hands, her rapturous mouth. His head fell back on his shoulders as a harsh, guttural shout filled the steamy shower and he pumped his release down her throat.

Damn her. She was still there, the muscles at the back of her mouth spasming and rippling, extending his pleasure until he forced himself to jerk from between her lips. If he didn't, he wouldn't stop thrusting. As good as the release was, as exquisite, as fucking hot, he needed more now.

Ian pulled her to her feet, clamped his hands beneath her ass, and lifted.

"Wrap around me," he snarled.

Her legs went around his waist, her arms around his shoulders, and his cock nudged into the fierce, honey-slick folds between her thighs.

He didn't ease into her, he couldn't. Bunching his thighs, he held her in place and with a harsh cry pushed into the swollen, slick portal of her clenching pussy.

"Son of a bitch." He locked his teeth together as she cried out against his shoulder, her teeth sinking into his flesh.

He was buried in fire. Lightning clashed and burned through his nervous system as sweet, wicked spasms of hunger rippled over his erection.

He was buried to the hilt, balls deep in rapture and sinking fast.

He pushed her against the shower wall, tightened his grip on the cheeks of her ass, and pulled back before impaling her against it with a deep, desperate lunge. He was groaning, whispering her name, his face buried in her neck as her cries echoed in his ears. And he couldn't stop.

Fucking her was imperative, stripping away reality and filling it with the pleasure, the erotic sense of belonging that only came from possessing her. That need filled every particle of his being.

She was a part of him. He filled her body and she filled his soul, and God help him but the thought of losing her was destroying him.

"Hold me," he whispered, knowing he had whispered those words before, knowing he had needed her like this all his life.

"Always." Her voice shattered his control. "Always."

He plunged inside her, thrusting hard and deep, feeling her explode around him as his semen jetted inside her, filling her, marking her, a part of him held forever inside her.

Even as the last shudders of release rippled down his spine, he couldn't let her go. The water streamed over them now, washing along their bodies, steamy, relaxing, but the thought of easing his flesh from hers had him clenching in denial. He wanted to hold her like this forever. Right here. Hold the world at bay and deny the knowledge that anything existed outside the two of them.

"Water's gonna get cold." That Southern drawl was lazy, relaxed, filled with satiation.

Ian grunted in response, his face still buried at her neck, his tongue stroking across her flesh occasionally just to feel the little ripples of response beneath her skin.

She didn't say anything more, just held on to him, her hands stroking along his neck as he fought to gain the strength to pull away from her.

His head lifted and he stared into her eyes, holding on to her as she found her footing on the shower floor. Deep, dark gray orbs ringed in ocean blue. Like a fairy, or one of those damned pixies his mother had been forever telling him stories about when he was a child.

"You're my weakness." He acknowledged the reality of it with the words.

"You're my strength. And I'm yours, Ian. We'll fight better, stronger, together. Don't try to send me away." Somber determination glittered in her eyes. "I won't leave."

He hadn't even realized what he intended to do until she said the words.

"I'll be distracted."

"You'll be distracted even worse when I take a two-by-four to your head after this is over. I won't be protected. I'm not a hothouse flower and I'm not a weakness. I know how to defend myself and you know it. Start this again and I'll make sure you're limping when you face Diego this morning."

She was a wildcat. Pride swelled within him as she faced him, more determined, willful, and confident than any woman he had ever known.

"Muriel's going to die this morning," he warned her. "I can't risk him informing Sorrell that we know he's a plant. I'm killing him."

He had learned lessons since taking over the reins of the cartel. Never give them time to get a message out. In this world, take an enemy prisoner and it was the same as giving them a knife to cut your throat. He wouldn't risk it. Not with Kira's life on the line as well. And taking out Muriel was one less drug-running, innocents-destroying bastard left to breathe precious air.

He knew Muriel's guilt. Knew the crimes he had committed, just as Ian knew he was taking the task of judge and jury onto his own shoulders.

He nodded. Pulling two washcloths from the small shelf above the shower head he handed her one and kept the other for himself.

"We finished this then. Let's shower and get to it."

Kira dressed for battle. She wore soft figure-hugging tan leggings, a matching cotton tank top, and ankle boots made for comfort as well as endurance. She wore a shoulder holster beneath a matching dark brown blazer, but anyone with eyes, or experience, would realize she was armed.

Diego sure as hell didn't miss it. As they stepped into the small office he used, his head turned from where he sat with his cousin Muriel, the traitorous bastard, his brow lifting as he met Kira's gaze, then Ian's.

"She's armed?" There was an edge of condescension in his voice as he directed the question to Ian.

"She's not the first woman to go to war with her lover." Ian's voice snapped with ire as he strode across the room and, as Diego's expression turned to disbelief, used the butt of his pistol against the back of Muriel's head.

The other man slumped against his chair, his coarse black hair feathering over his swarthy features. He was unconscious before he knew what hit him. Diego was out of his seat, suspicion tightening his features even before he pinned Ian with black, furious eyes.

"What has he done?"

Kira could tell Ian was surprised by the question. It flickered in his gaze for only a second before he motioned Deke over.

"Strip him. Make certain he's not wearing a skin tag then have him bound and held in the basement. I'll deal with him later," Ian ordered Deke.

The bodyguard wrestled the broad Colombian from his chair, hefted him over his shoulder, and left the room. Trevor, Mendez, and Cristo placed themselves in defensive positions around Ian and Kira.

Diego's gaze tracked their movements before he turned back to Ian.

Suave, dressed in dark slacks and a white silk shirt, his black and gray hair still full and pulled back to his neck and bound with black elastic, the father stared back at the son coolly.

"I believe I asked you a question, Ian," he stated. "What has he done?"

Ian lifted the file he carried in the other hand and slapped it down on the table between the two chairs Diego and Muriel had occupied.

"He's been giving Ascarti, and in turn Sorrell, information on the entire network. I told you to keep this son of a bitch out of the loop. Do you remember that, Diego?"

Despair flashed in Diego's black eyes as he sat down slowly and opened the file. In living color, the pictures were displayed before him.

Kira glanced at Ian's face and swore she saw a flash of

regret, but it was gone as quickly as it had come, and had been missed by Diego as his attention centered on the photos.

"There was no need for him to betray us," Diego whispered heavily. "I would have given him whatever he asked for."

"Now you can give him what he deserves," Ian snapped. "Or I will."

Diego's lips twisted bitterly as he lifted his gaze to Ian. Kira saw the pain, a flash of anger, and a soul-deep sadness she knew the other man had no right to feel.

"I cannot kill a maid who would give this information to our enemies, but I may kill my cousin who was like a brother to me since his birth?"

"You demanded the right to seek retribution." Ian shrugged. "You can take it, or as I said, I will. I have no problems killing the bastard. Liss was another story, Diego, and you don't want to remind me of that one."

"Then you may have the pleasure." Diego shook his head wearily.

"Growing soft, pop?" Ian snapped. "Maybe it will help you to know that Muriel was behind the attempt to blow my limo to hell last week. If that doesn't faze you, try the meeting with the Misserns and the fucking assassin waiting for me there. He's going to die, and he's going to die before he can contact his good friend Ascarti again and warn him that we're on to him."

Diego's eyes narrowed. "You have proof of Ascarti's involvement with Sorrell?"

"I have something a hell of a lot better than that," Ian growled. "I need you ready to move at a moment's notice. When the call comes in we'll be meeting with Sorrell himself, and we'll end this war once and for all."

Ian was frighteningly cold. Kira watched him warily, seeing the fury he had kept under control for so long edging to the surface now.

Diego, Jansen Clay, and Sorrell had taken great delight

in torturing Nathan Malone, the SEAL they had held for more than a year and half. Ian knew Diego had been involved in the torture, knew he condoned it and added to it even after Sorrell had believed the SEAL had been killed.

Regret might be a fragile light buried somewhere deep within him, but she knew in that moment that Diego was a dead man walking.

"And you have arranged this how?" Diego moved from his chair to the bar across the room, his hand shaking, Kira noticed, as he poured himself a drink and brought it to his lips.

It was tossed back quickly and another poured before he turned back to Ian, his brow lifting in question. "I believe I asked you for details, son."

Kira saw the slight tension that tightened Ian's shoulders, the natural defensive block against the flinch that nearly betrayed his disgust at that word.

She could feel his pain. She couldn't see it, but she ached for him. Ached because this man was his father, this monster that shed blood, filled children with drugs and destroyed lives without a thought to the tragedies that resulted from his actions.

Ian faced this man daily. Faced the horror and the agonizing realization that he had come from this man's seed. Kira wondered if she could have borne that pressure without breaking, and knew she couldn't have. Something inside her would have died had she been forced to play the game Ian was playing.

"I don't have details for you, pop." Ian's voice was savage. "I have something he wants now, and he'll come for it."

Brutal fire flickered in Ian's gaze then. "I'll take care of your cousin, you get ready to move, we may have to leave at a moment's notice."

"You are allowing me to play now?" Sarcasm filled Diego's voice. "What? Hell has frozen over? To what do I owe this glorious surge of allegiance that you would finally involve me in my own business?"

Pain. Kira watched the pain that burned in Diego's eyes as Ian mentioned killing Muriel.

"Give it up, pop. I promised you, when the time came we'd do this together, and that's what we're doing," Ian snapped, the disrespect in the title nearly causing Kira to flinch now. If she didn't know Ian as well as she did she might believe he was enjoying this. But she saw the subtle shifts of color in his eyes, saw the tension that tightened his body.

Diego stared at him silently, his face creased with sorrow, before he nodded wearily and turned back to the bar. The room was thick with tension, with the powerful opposing force of the two men and the connections that bound them, as well as set them on opposite courses.

For Kira, it was heartbreaking, though she knew to Ian it was finally the beginning of the end of this mission, the end of the lifestyle he had been forced to live and the blood that was shed daily.

Ian fought the knowledge that Diego was hurting, fought the memories, the pain of regret as he relived the times he too had been betrayed by those he had trusted. Not that it had happened often; Ian had never been a particularly trusting sort. But he knew the pain, the shame, he knew how it cringed inside the soul and left a lasting scar.

How Diego Fuentes could feel such shame because of a betrayal, Ian wasn't certain. The man should have burst into flames and died a thousand deaths from the horrors he had perpetuated over the years.

Hope lit a fragile light in Diego's eyes though as Ian told him they would be working together. Like a child that had been kicked one time too many, the older man quickly hid the emotion.

What the fuck was he doing? Ian asked himself. He should have never taken this mission, should have never put it into action in the first place. He should have just put a rifle scope on his ass and pulled the trigger despite orders.

The DEA wanted him alive. DHS wanted him alive.

Everyone wanted him alive and Ian had sworn to kill him. He would kill him. God as his witness; no matter how despicable the action would be, there was no other way. He couldn't allow another SEAL, another friend, to suffer because he had betrayed Diego as well.

"When do you expect this meeting to take place?" Diego's voice was oddly weary, resigned.

"I'm hoping soon." Ian crossed his arms over his chest and stared back at him. "We have something he wants, badly."

"And that is?" He seemed uninterested, more concerned with the amount of liquor he could consume now than he was about the imminent end of his worst enemy.

"We have his daughter."

He stared back at Ian in shock, then in glee.

"I thought she was mere wishful thinking." He blinked back at Ian in disbelief. "You have her? She is here? In the villa?" His eyes widened as satisfaction began to gleam in them. "Is she in the basement?"

Ian felt his teeth snap together in fury.

The son of a bitch, even now, nothing could touch him but the scent of death or the dirty little games he played in that fucking basement. Or the death of a friend who played those games with him as Muriel had done.

"She's not in the basement," he snapped, the anger leaking into his voice. "I have her and she's safe, that's all you need to be concerned with."

Diego grimaced. "You have never understood the value of the little games I play, have you, Ian?"

"No I don't and we're not going to discuss them now." Sometimes he felt as though he were dealing with a particularly willful child when it came to Diego.

He missed Diego's subtle smile, but Kira caught the shift of the other man's lips and the playful curl of fondness in Diego's black eyes.

Twenty-six

H E WAS PUSHING IAN'S BUTTONS. He wasn't serious about taking Tehya to the playroom forcefully, from what she understood, Diego liked his playmates willing. But he was serious gauging Ian's temper or his mood. Like a teenager poking at his father's authority. Kira imagined Diego saw it as a game, a prick against Ian for the autocratic way he had taken over the cartel rather than sharing the business as Diego had dreamed.

Diego had wanted a son to share the finer things in life with, and Ian wasn't sharing. They didn't kill together, because Ian became angry whenever Diego shed blood. They didn't plot together and they didn't plan together, so Diego poked at him, prodded, and found what amusement he could. A small amount of gratitude, a measure of confidence that his son felt some small emotion for him, because Ian didn't slice into him. Because he didn't blow up and he didn't threaten to kill or leave. Diego believed there was hope.

Guilt sliced at Kira once again. How hard would it be to watch him die if she couldn't stop Ian from killing him? To know that, monster though he was, he was a monster who craved his son's attention, and even more, his love.

Kira felt a wave of pity so sharp, so intense, she had to

turn her head away from Diego; unfortunately, she found herself staring straight into Ian's eyes instead. Eyes that saw too much, that arrowed in on that pity and narrowed warningly.

Back off.

He didn't have to say the words, she could feel the demand. He didn't want to see it, he didn't want to hear it. And he didn't want to regret it. But she could see the regret in his eyes, regret and determination.

"Games are the spice of life, Ian." Diego's comment dragged Ian's attention from her and back to him. Where he wanted it. His attention was better off there, off her and the guilt raging through her.

"Games are a pain in the ass." Ian shrugged. "I want you to get your men in place, have them converge on and assume protective parameters around the warehouse we have outside Oranjestad. Sorrell will assume we're hiding her there. We'll see if he intends to attack or negotiate."

"But the girl is not there," Diego murmured as he moved to his desk and the open laptop on it.

As he took his chair, a frown flitted over his brow. His fingers began to move on the keypad quickly.

"The warehouse wasn't purchased under a known cartel enterprise," he informed Ian. "We've actually been using it for a few legal purposes rather than illegal." There was a measure of surprise in his tone as he reached for the phone and pulled the receiver toward him.

Ian caught Diego's hand as he began to dial the numbers. Kira watched, as surprised as Diego was when Ian hung the phone up carefully.

He pulled the small electronic device from a holder on the waistband of his jeans. It had Kira sighing; she still hadn't been allowed to play with the jamming device. Ian flipped it on, set it close to the phone then indicated that Diego could make the call.

Diego sniffed as he punched in the number. "Technology isn't always a good thing."

"It's going end up saving your ass though," Ian grunted as he turned away from him, his gaze once again meeting Kira's.

She pushed her hands into the pockets of her lightweight blazer, and forced back the need to hunch her shoulders defensively.

She listened with half an ear as Diego ordered the men into place. He didn't give them a reason why, of course, he wouldn't have to. He had ruled with blood and death for over thirty years, and his reputation as a killer ensured that his men would follow his word to the letter and beyond.

"That is done." Diego returned the phone to its base before going back to the laptop. "I do still have my fingers in a few little pies." He seemed to roll his eyes from behind the cover of the laptop. "Let's see if I can't get a report should we have any unscheduled flights landing in the near future. He wouldn't come by boat, it would be too slow."

"He's already in Aruba." Ian folded his arms across his chest and glared back at Diego.

Diego cast his son a look of disbelief. "I would know if he were, trust me. Sorrell may be rather good at keeping his identity hidden, but he's not that good at keeping his presence hidden. Where he goes, death and the disappearance of lovely young women follow. We haven't had a disappearance in Aruba in over a year. Trust me, he isn't here yet."

Kira turned her back on the two men, her gaze colliding with Deke's, as Diego and Ian began to argue the points for or against Sorrell being on the island. It seemed a useless, pointless argument, until you paid attention to what wasn't being said and let the undercurrents of the conversation ebb and flow instead.

"You're a drug lord, not a terrorist, Diego," Ian reminded him coolly. "I don't think you're as knowledgeable about that particular species of evil as you believe you are."

"Terrorists are not so different." Diego shrugged as Kira turned back to him.

He leaned back in his chair and stared at his son, a quirk

tugging at his lips. "We both have a vision and we fight for that vision. I say we have the right to choose to enjoy the stimulation of the drugs, the same as we have the right to bear arms or to the freedom of speech that Americans seem to be enjoy with such enthusiasm. Personally, I've always a found a drug addict to be much more literate, easier to get along with, and easier to control than your irate, political mismatch of lawmakers that America seems to find such great pleasure in electing to office."

Ian shook his head quickly as though attempting to shake reality back into his mind.

"Don't fuck with me today, Diego," he bit out. "I'm not in the mood."

"He could have a point, Ian," Kira drawled then. "Just think, if all our politicians were happily running out to the nearest convenience store to buy their next fix, they wouldn't be giving the rest of the nation a headache debating laws and freedoms. Anarchy could reign peacefully then."

Diego's burst of laughter was filled with merriment.

"That is a sharp female you have on your hands, my son, I hope you intend to keep her around for a while."

Ian gaze locked with hers again. It was a brooding, dark look, one that sent a shiver down her spine because she could see the warning in it.

"I need to question, Muriel," Ian stated rather than answering Diego's statement.

It was deliberate. Immediately all humor fled from Diego's gaze and his gaze flickered with pain. But even that seemed to bring Ian no satisfaction. Kira could see the tension gathering in him though, the need to have this finished, to have it over.

"Kira, we need to talk first." She was surprised when Ian walked to her, gripped her upper hand, and led her to the door. "I'll be back in a bit," he tossed over his shoulder. "Deke, stay in contact with the guards outside and let me know if you need me."

"Gotcha, boss."

The door closed behind them as Ian headed quickly for the stairs.

"What the hell is your problem?" she hissed.

He was silent, tense, until they reached the bedroom and he slammed the door behind him. Stalking to the bureau, he checked the security on the room, slammed that drawer closed then turned back to her.

She could see the storm in his eyes then, the anger that bit at the edges of his control.

"Don't you dare feel sorry for him," Ian snarled, his voice low, intent. "I saw your eyes, I saw it in your face. Don't think for a minute that you can save him."

She licked her lips nervously. She didn't have a choice but to save him.

"He's a monster," she began, then inhaled roughly as satisfaction glittered in his eyes. "But he's a monster who loves his son."

"Fuck! I knew it." He swiped his fingers through his hair, pushing back the dark blond strands and revealing the savagely honed perfection of his face. "I knew it the minute I saw you on this damned island. You're letting your emotions cloud this now. How the hell can you say something like that?"

"My emotions aren't clouding anything, Ian," she assured him, her voice low as she watched him compassionately, aching for him. "I see the truth you refuse to see."

His brows lowered over his eyes, brooding anger shaping his face and thinning his lips.

"Don't start the psychobabble," he snapped. "I don't want to hear it. If you can't keep your emotions under control then you can stay with the rest of the group and get the hell out of my way."

Whoa, that one hurt.

"Your way or the highway then?" she asked him with a sharp breath. "Wow, Ian, took you a while, but you just reminded me why the hell I've always steered clear of SEALs for lovers. Your attitude sucks."

"If it took you this long to be reminded then you should be locked up for your own protection," he growled as he turned his back on her and paced the large sitting room before throwing himself on the thickly cushioned sofa and staring at her with blistering anger. "What do you think you can do, save him? Why? It's like trying to save a rabid animal."

He glowered up at her, his brows pulled low over his eyes, his expression a mask of offended male pride and anger.

She pushed her hands back into her jacket and sighed wearily. She couldn't tell him the truth and not because she had been ordered not to. He would lose the tenuous hold on the control that had gotten him this far and she knew it. He had lived within this dirty, corrupt world with only one goal in mind, working methodically toward it. Learning that it could be snatched from him would push him from that edge of being a loyal American agent, and possibly into rogue.

"I agree with you." And she did.

His jaw tightened. "Then what the hell are you doing hurting for that son of a bitch? For God's sake, Kira, don't try to deny it. I saw it in your face, in your eyes down there."

He pushed himself from the sofa and stalked to the balcony doors.

"Do you remember Nathan?" he asked her then. "Do you remember what you saw in that hospital?" He turned back to her, his body thrumming with fury. "I saw him when we took him out of that hellhole in California. Wasted to skin and bones, his eyes crazed, his mind nearly as destroyed as his body was. You didn't see that, I did."

"And he's your friend, so you have to avenge it," she said.

"I want to avenge it. But even more importantly I want to make certain it never fucking happens again. Don't stand in my way on this, don't try to convince me differently. It won't work."

She wanted to touch him, wanted to ease the tortured

fury from his face, his eyes, but she knew better. Touching him would mean giving in, and she couldn't give in. Not just because of her orders, but because of Ian. He would never forgive himself. He would never be able to forget that he had been the one to kill his father, no matter the monster he was.

"Will killing him make the pain go away, Ian? Will it make the memories stop festering inside you? Or will it only make them worse?"

"I don't know," he snarled. "You answer that question first, Kira. Will seeing Sorrell die bring your parents back? Or Jason's lover and his child? What satisfaction will you gain from it?"

She didn't flinch. It hurt. Oh yeah, that hurt, because she knew Sorrell's death would afford her a measure of security. But she had made peace with the fact that she might fail years ago.

"Good strike," she said softly. "Sorrell's death will bring closure to the past, Ian. Not to my hatred. Nothing will ever change that. But he isn't my father either."

"Diego isn't my father. He was a sperm donor," he sneered.

"Your mother loved him once." She was broaching dangerous territory and she knew it. Territory that even Diego Fuentes refused to broach.

Ian almost flinched at the memory, his rugged face tightening once again at the mental slap. She didn't say it to hurt him, she said it to remind him. To make him think.

"She was young," he finally said. "She didn't know what he was."

"And once she learned she didn't hate you. You didn't pay for Diego's crimes," Kira pointed out. "I'm not excusing him, Ian, I don't even blame you. But is this something you really want to remember in the dead of night? The fact that you took his life?"

"I'll remember it with pleasure." His voice was strong,

certain, but she saw the flicker in his gaze, the uncertainty. Unfortunately she knew that uncertainty wasn't strong enough to sway the course he had set for himself.

Men were stubborn, SEALs especially so. They had the supreme confidence that they were right, their decisions logical and without flaws. They were determined, arrogant, and essentially a pain in the ass to deal with. It was just her luck to fall in love with one.

She stared back at him, aching for him, and in some ways aching for Diego as well. They were both strong men, but Ian's strength was based on his honor, and Diego's was based within a world that his son could only see as evil.

"Did you drag me up here to argue over Diego?" Kira asked him when she couldn't come up with a single damned argument to save Diego's life. Not one. The man had built his entire life on watching others suffer, watching and using the suffering for his own ends.

"I dragged you up here to ask you exactly where your loyalties lie. Diego and Sorrell are going to die, Kira. If you have a problem with that, then you better speak up now. You don't want to stand in my way later."

Tension pulled at them both. Kira could feel it, she could almost see it pulsing in the air between them.

"My loyalty is with you, Ian," she told him simply. And it was true.

His gaze locked with hers, his intent, burning with an inner rage as his gaze probed hers, searching for a weakness, or a lie. She wasn't certain which at this point.

Finally, he nodded quickly. "I need to make contact with the team, make certain everything's ready to go."

Kira clenched her hands inside her pockets as she turned away from him and paced into the bedroom while he made his phone call. She needed a few moments to repair her control, to center herself and to grieve.

Ian was never going to forgive her when she was forced to

stand between him and Diego. She was going to lose him, and the thought of that was destroying her from the inside out.

IAN COULDN'T DISPEL THE TENSION growing in his gut as Kira moved from the sitting room and into the bedroom. He pulled the secured cell phone from the clip on his belt and hit the speed dial to Macey's phone while he watched her. Watched her and wondered how the hell she could feel any compassion, any pity, for the bastard that had destroyed so many lives.

"Gotcha," Macey answered, his voice low. "Everything's secured. You?"

"Awaiting contact. Any additional info?" Reno and Clint had still been questioning Tehya when Ian and Kira left just before dawn.

"We have a few suspects based on the deaths of her guardians, locations, and sites where they first disappeared. I've managed to put together some profiles from the information she's given us. She really knew more than she thought she did after we started piecing everything together. I've narrowed it down to about half a dozen men and I'm running some profiles based on lineage, physical characteristics that she might share with him, and various other parameters. I gotta tell you though, if one of these dudes is our guy, then we were right all along. Social and political connections, old money, royal blood, and plenty to protect. He's not going to come in easy."

The battle to identify the terrorist had been ongoing for years. Quantico had come up with a profile two years before, but no suspects. It wasn't a relief to hear that the profilers had been right.

"Have you been able to trace the cell phone hers is programmed to?"

"Nada. Secured. No trace, no how. Maybe we'll get luckier once we put the call through this afternoon but I doubt he'll stay on long enough to get a trace," Macey answered.

"Who are our suspects?" Ian asked then.

His brows lifted at the three names Macey gave him. He hadn't been joking when he said this could turn into a mess. All three men could trace their roots back to French and English aristocracy. All three came from old money that totaled in the millions, perhaps more, and enjoyed worldwide respect. If one of them was Sorrell, then it was no damned wonder he had managed to evade them for so long.

"We've almost managed to tie all three men, in one way or the other, to Ascarti. There's even a bit of rumor that I managed to uncover that Ascarti is one of the men's bastard son. I'd almost bet my money on that," Macey finished.

Hell, it sounded like a good bet to him.

Ian checked his watch for the time. He sure as hell didn't want to give anyone time to trace his own call.

"Good going, Macey. I'll check back later." He disconnected the phone before inhaling roughly and glancing at the door where Kira had disappeared into the bedroom.

He moved to the doorway, an edge of remorse biting into him. He had come down hard on her and he knew it. His fury at the thought of Diego working her emotions, her loyalties, strained his control.

"We have suspects." He stopped and watched her, as she checked her weapon and placed extra ammo in the pockets of her jacket.

Her eyes narrowed at his statement. Moving her jacket aside she shoved the gun back into the holster and moved to her feet.

"Who are they?"

"Erick Randolph, Jordan Lorraine, Marco Alloran. All three men are connected to Ascarti as well."

Her brows lifted. "Old-money names," she murmured. "I've met all three. Jason and I have actually discussed one of those men. Lorraine. He's secretive, sometimes reclusive, and was investigated once regarding a plot uncovered to overthrow Jacques Chirac while he was in office, but they couldn't make it stick. Still, that's a long way from white slavery and terrorism."

"It's the best we have at the moment," he said. "The birthmark will tie it in, but it will sure as hell help to have an idea of what we're looking at here."

"You're looking at a man with a God complex." She shook her head before pushing her fingers through her hair and gathering it quickly into a long ponytail. "A paranoid man. A man who believes the world has been corrupted almost to the point of no repair and that women are chattel rather than deserving of their freedom. That fits all three men, but Lorraine most of all. He's an arrogant son of a bitch. He refused to deal with Jason's law firm on an account several years ago when Jason sent me to oversee some details. He had to send a *man*," she sneered. "Self-righteous prig."

He heard the anger in her voice. Sorrell had been behind the bombing that had killed her parents and Jason's fiancée. Because of one man, she had lost most of her family.

Like him, she had spent her life searching for a way to bring down one man. She knew the pain, the horror, of fear and the knowledge that monsters existed.

"Percentage of Lorraine's involvement versus the other two?" he asked.

She inhaled briefly as she checked the ponytail with a quick swipe of her hands and then lowered them to brace them on her hips. Her brow creased, and Ian was treated to the utter delight of watching the agent work. He could see her mind turning over percentages and possibilities, working to fit what she knew against each man.

"I doubt it's Randolph." She shook her head. "He's a hedonist, doesn't care a bit to show his nudity, and he's in pretty good shape for his age. I saw him on a beach in France one year, he doesn't have a birthmark unless he knows how to cover it up. And he was very hairy. Doing a cosmetic coverup would have been virtually impossible. Besides, Sorrell wouldn't be caught dead naked. That would be a private thing for him."

"You saw Randolph naked?" Something like jealousy clenched inside him. Possessiveness. He did not want her seeing other men naked.

"Several times." She shrugged as though it were of little consequence. "It was a nudist beach."

"And you were nude?" he gritted out.

Her brow lifted. "Pretty much. And you're not going to make any completely irrational remarks either, are you? Because we both know those little submissive lovers you took from the fringe clubs in Atlanta weren't exactly for a platonic relationship."

He felt his lip want to curl on a snarl and barely held it back. He might have to kill Randolph whether he was involved or not if he had seen Kira naked.

"Get over it, Ian." She shook her head impatiently, though a smile tugged at her lips. "I promise, it was before I met you."

That didn't help.

"What about Alloran?" he asked. He had to get his mind off her being on a nudist beach.

"Alloran is old money as well, royal blood on both the French and English sides. Some kind of distant cousin of a cousin to the Queen of England." Her frown deepened. "I would have never considered him. What sort of parameters did Macey base his list on?"

"I didn't have time to find out," he said, grimacing. "The cells are secured but I don't want to take any chances. I disconnected before there was a chance of a trace."

She nodded in understanding before glancing at the balcony door. "I need to go to the villa, talk to him and Tehya as well. I've socialized with these men, known them for most of my life actually. My father was on friendly terms with Lorraine, and had done business with the other two. I may be able to help narrow the search."

It made sense, but he'd be damned if he wanted her out of his sight.

"Have Daniel drive over and pick you up, let's make it

look good." If she were seen slipping to the villa she had
leased, it could be viewed suspiciously, and lead Sorrell
straight to Tehya.

"I'll call him." She nodded, her gaze sharpening. "What
will you be doing?"

"Attempting not to strangle Diego," he grunted. "He's
like a damned spoiled-ass brat. How the hell he managed to
hold a cartel of this size together confounds me at times."

"You demanded control to return, and you're not playing
nice with him as far as he's concerned. He's picking at you,
trying to get your attention." And his affection. Ian heard it
in her voice though she was wise enough not to put it into
words.

He shrugged as though the observation made no difference.

"Get over there and see what else you can figure out," he
told her. "And watch your ass."

He strode over to her then, one hand cupping her face,
lifting her chin as the other wrapped around her waist and
pulled her to his harder, aroused body.

"I'll be careful." That breathless quality in her voice
tightened his balls. Damn her, she affected him like nothing
or no one else ever had.

Her hand slid up his arms, gripped his biceps. Sharp little
nails pricked into his flesh and reminded him of the scratches
on his back that she had placed there the night before.

"Make sure you're more than careful." He lowered his
lips to hers, took a stinging kiss, and pulled back before the
need rocketing his mind could get out of control. "Signal
my cell when you get there."

Then she reached up with one hand, her fingers touching
his cheek, then his lips. "You be careful."

He grinned. She could make him feel lighter, he liked
that. When she looked at him, soft and sensual like that,
something inside him loosened, the tension that had been
destroying him lightened.

"I'll send Deke with you and Daniel," he decided as the

warmth in her gaze sank into his soul, heating him, reminding him of everything he had to lose if he lost Kira. "I want
you protected, Kira, let me do that."

He could see the protest in her expression and he didn't
want to fight her over it. He didn't want to have to force her
to allow him to keep his mind clear right now.

She shook her head, but her smile was accepting. "Fine,
I'll take Deke with me. But we're going to discuss this attitude of yours later."

"You can chew my ass to hell and back later," he promised, stepping back from her. "I'll question Muriel and see
what I can find out there."

He should have just killed him, he had meant to, knew it
was the best route to take. Holding him meant giving him a
chance to escape and possibly learning where Tehya was
hidden.

"Hey." He caught her as she moved to pulled back from
him, his mind and his heart struggling, a part of him aching
to whisper the words, another part holding back.

"I promise to be careful." She lifted to him, touched her
lips to his, and stared into his eyes. "I love you, Ian."

One kiss. Just one kiss, and he could let her go. Deep,
hungry, a kiss that dragged a moan from her throat and had
him fighting to keep from throwing her to the bed and hearing her screams again.

"Go." He pushed her away from him, dragging his hands
through his hair and glaring at her. Damn her, he had no
good sense when she was around. "And hurry back."

That perky little ponytail bobbed as she moved quickly
away from him, the long strands of hair falling from the
crown of her head to the middle of her shoulder blades and
tempting him to tear it down and spear his fingers through
the soft, thick mass.

She glanced back at him as she reached the doorway,
paused, and gave him a saucy wink before light laughter left
her lips when he started for her again.

She escaped. Just in time. One more second and he

would have said to hell with Sorrell and thrown her to the floor to bury the aching length of his cock deep inside that tight, soft velvet pussy. Damn her. Damn him. Because she overrode his control and reminded him, each second, of exactly what he could lose if this op managed to go to hell.

Twenty-seven

THE CALL CAME LATE THAT afternoon.

His voice was heavily accented, that of a man who rarely used English, and it was clipped with anger. He agreed to the meet on the condition that they would see the birthmark only, and not his face. He demanded that Ascarti be allowed to accompany him, as well as one bodyguard, and that his daughter be present during the negotiations.

Ian laughed. "I think not. The point between these negotiations is that we each get what we want, my friend." He leaned back in his chair and narrowed his eyes as Diego smiled in satisfaction at the sound of Sorrell's voice on the conference call. "I'll have your identity and you'll have the girl. An even trade. Negotiations aren't worth shit if both parties aren't required to lay insurance on the table."

The silence that filled the line was telling. Ian hadn't allowed the call to be traced, though Macey had the equipment to do just that within a matter of minutes. But Sorrell could have the equipment to track the trace, and for now, they needed a measure of trust.

"I will show you the birthmark upon arrival. My face will remain shielded until negotiations are completed. And you will give your woman into the keeping of my bodyguard until things have been reasonably settled. My daughter will remain in the keeping of one of your men. We both have much to lose, as well as to gain."

He had known it would come to this. He had felt it crawling in his gut the minute he had known Kira was on Aruba, that when the final game came to be played, she would be used to stay his hand.

What Sorrell didn't know was that Kira was no man's weapon. He had to argue with himself, he had to force himself to be logical rather than to allow emotion to influence his decision. The emotion was winning though.

"Diego will be present. If you need insurance—"

Sorrell's laughter was faintly mocking. "Mr. Fuentes, as you and I both know, I have had my spies within your presence. Your relationship with your father is, how shall we say it, less than loving? He is not acceptable as insurance, though I do expect he will attend this meeting. Your woman will place herself on one side of the room with my man. Your man will hold my daughter similarly on the other side of the room. I and Gregor Ascarti will meet with you and your father after this exchange has been made. This is nonnegotiable."

She could protect herself, the logical part of his brain assured him. No one knew who she was, what she was, or how very capable she was in such situations. Ian knew. He had seen her on several missions, read the reports of the men who worked with the Chameleon. He knew she could do this.

But it was placing her at risk.

"Come, Mr. Fuentes, if I can trust my treasured asset in your protection, then you can trust yours within mine." Sorrell chuckled. "Unless you have plans to do other than negotiate."

"I definitely don't have plans to have my woman stolen and sold to line your coffers," Ian snorted.

Sorrell laughed at this. "She is too old. She would be too hard to train effectively, she is safe from such a fate. Young girls, girls who have not yet known the corruption of your society, are those I seek. And as beautiful as your woman is, she is no longer a virgin, nor does she still retain the flush of her youth. Do you agree to my demands as I have agreed to yours?"

"Agreed." The fact that he had no choice boiled in his gut.

Damn her, he had known better than to let her into this. His weakness. She was a weakness and Sorrell knew it. If she hadn't been here, in his life, in his bed, Sorrell would have accepted Diego as insurance, eliminating the chance that Sorrell would have even a measure of power over the negotiations.

"Ah, I can hear the anger in your tone." Satisfaction filled the Frenchman's voice. "Your woman is important to you. This is good. She is a willful, spoiled female though my friend. I fear you will not have a smooth path with this one. It would have been better had you found a more tractable woman."

"I'll take care of my life, Sorrell, you take care of yours." Ian fought for a measure of distance, a place to push back the rage until this was finished. "We meet at midnight—"

"Your woman will be waiting inside the gates of your villa. We will then exit the vehicle and proceed inside. Once again, nonnegotiable. I do not walk into traps, Mr. Fuentes. She will be alone."

"No deal."

Sorrell was quiet.

"You forget, I have something you want, not the other way around," Ian reminded him. "I can kill your daughter as easily as Liss and Muriel were killed. Without regret. Or, I could contact the DEA. I'm sure they'll be quite forgiving of several of my crimes for a chance at your daughter. Perhaps I could get that nasty little treason charge dropped." He let the suggestion trail off there.

He could hear the tension across the line then. The waves of anger pouring from the Frenchman.

"We will arrive at midnight." Sorrell's voice was clipped, enraged. "I will contact you again before arrival. And Mr.

Fuentes, betray me and more than just your woman will die. The women of your former friends, the newborn son Reno Chavez is so proud of, all of them will die, painfully."

Ian snorted at the threat despite anger pulsing through him. "Just be here on time, if you don't mind. I do have other things to take care of once we complete this."

The call disconnected.

Ian reached over, disconnected the phone on the base, and then stared at Diego.

The other's man face was creased thoughtfully, his black eyes gleaming with challenge. Ian could see the charge Diego was getting from trying to anticipate his adversary's next move. It was the same charge Ian felt, that challenge, that sense of not just a physical, but the mental battle being waged.

"I recognize his voice." Diego tapped at the chair lightly. "There was some quality to it, perhaps to his laughter, so superior and arrogant." His frown deepened. "I have spoken to this man before."

The recording of the conversation would have to be slipped quickly to Reno and Macey. Kira was still at the rented villa questioning Tehya. The other girl needed to hear it as well. Though he knew she knew his voice, perhaps without the patronizing, falsely loving tone that he used with her, she could better pinpoint something about it.

"You had better call your friends and inform them of this new development." Diego leaned back in his chair, crossed an ankle over the opposite knee, and lifted the cup of coffee from the side table that he had set there earlier.

Ian stared back at him silently as Diego sipped at the still warm brew.

"What friends?" he finally asked.

Diego shook his head. "Durango team. I am aware that they have been staying in the villa with Kira's bodyguard, Daniel. You could have told me, Ian. I would not have turned down their help. I would be curious though, what price do you pay for this help?"

Ian reached up and pinched the bridge of his nose. Patience wasn't his strong suit, and the longer this operation played out, the less patience he had.

"There was no price," he finally answered honestly, looking back at Diego. "They had information and the woman and came to me with it. They asked nothing in return."

"And when this is over?" Diego's voice tightened. "Will they return to their lives alone, or do you follow with them?"

He could never return. Ian was smart enough to know that. He shook his head slowly. "I think you know as well as I do that there's no going back for me."

He should regret it. Ian knew he should be furious over the fact that his SEAL career, no matter how this played out, was over. There was no regret though. A sense of sadness, yes, but he had been ready for something else even before coming to Diego.

Diego was nodding slowly, his gaze intent, locked with Ian's, searching. What the hell was he searching for? Ian wondered.

"Perhaps I made a mistake in the way I brought you into my world, into my life," Diego said slowly then. "But I would have you to know, Ian, that plans were already in place to help your friends. I would have let none of them suffer unduly because of our games."

"Except Nathan?" Ian asked softly.

Guilt flickered in Diego's eyes. "I know you are aware of the things I did to your young friend, but I also kept him alive. He was not an innocent bystander, Ian. You know this. He allowed himself to be captured. He made the choice to attempt to deceive not just me but Sorrell and Jansen Clay. Had it been me alone that he attempted to gain his information from, he would have fared much better."

Ian leaned forward, his arms braced on the desk, murder in his soul.

"You tortured him for a year after Sorrell finished with him. You could have made certain he was rescued; instead, you continued to torture him, to drug him, to make him break his vows to his wife."

Diego sighed, but there was no regret, only knowledge and acceptance. "I will say again, Nathan Malone was no innocent bystander. You know this as well as I. He had information I could have used, and he placed himself at my disposal. It is the way of this world, Ian. It is the way of the world, period. He made his choices, and still, I made certain he lived, even knowing this was one thing you may never forgive me for."

"And the senator's daughters you kidnapped and had drugged?" Ian asked him. "Did you know one of them died, Diego, and one of your soldiers raped another? A sixteen-year-old child, a virgin, and that bastard raped her in front of her father."

"At her father's orders," Diego snapped. "The kidnapping of those girls was not my decision, I will take no responsibility for it. This was the doing of Clay and Sorrell. To retain the power I needed to fight the bastards I had no choice but to allow the girls to be brought to my estate to be held. I am guilty of many crimes, but those I will not claim."

It took a special kind of monster to compartmentalize people and torture, Ian figured. The type of man that deserved to die by whatever means possible.

"You have never understood." Diego shook his head then. "You are like the religious fanatics. You have your view, your perception, and you never waver. Those who do not share this view and perception are worthy of nothing, no mercy, no chance at life. Is this not true?"

"You should have been shot like a rabid dog at birth," Ian growled.

Rather than taking offense, Diego smiled in pride. "My word is my bond. I do not break it unless others break theirs. I confine my games to opponents who understand the rules. Both sides know death could result. Tell me, Ian, should your new Department of Homeland Security acquire me, do you believe they would merely put me on trial? Would I not be beaten, tortured for the information I have on rival cartels, on suspects they wish to convict? Do you tell me that these agents do not kill senselessly when they are finished with those they abduct for information?"

"I haven't." It happened though, Ian knew it happened.

Diego leaned forward. "No, but you capture those they torture. You go in the dead of the night with your Durango team, you jerk them from their beds and you give them into the custody of those who do."

"Murders. Rapists. Terrorists. Fucking animals that would turn the world into a sewer where nothing but death reigns. For God's sake, Diego, it's hardly the same."

Ian came out of his chair and paced around the table, the anger surging through him demanding action of some kind, of any kind.

"You sit there and argue for your side like Satan himself, laying out your logic, so certain of your right to torture, maim, and kill. Because it's a fucking game to you."

"Because I know this world," Diego yelled, coming to his feet as his own anger rose to the surface. "Do you think I do not see what you are doing to the cartel? Pulling back on the drug shipments, attempting to legalize our diversified holdings." He snorted in disgust. "You would bleach me like dirty laundry. Why would you do this? What is in your mind?"

What was in his mind?

"Maybe I wanted something to leave to my children that wouldn't get them murdered in their sleep," Ian snarled.

Diego opened his mouth, snapped it closed, then stared at Ian in surprise. "You are considering having children?"

Son of a bitch. Damn the fucking bastard to hell. There was hope in his voice. Hope, fear, and a hunger that sickened Ian to his gut.

"I was being rhetorical," Ian snapped, pushing his fingers through his hair as he glowered at Diego. "Look, I don't have time for this fight. We'll fight over this after I deal with Sorrell. Since you know so fucking much about my business, I'll take this recording next door and see about neutralizing this bastard for you. We'll fight about the rest of it later."

He stalked back to his desk, hit the eject button for the recorder, and collected the tape.

"Ian." Diego stepped in front of him as he turned to leave, his expression tortured. Tortured, as though he had a heart, a fucking soul. "I would be a father if you allowed it. The Fuentes cartel would be as you want it, should you decide this is your way. The name Fuentes will live on, and there would be no need for strife between us. You know business. You have profited these months you have been here. I would give this all to you, if you stayed once Sorrell is taken out of the equation. We could do this, Ian."

No they couldn't, because one of them would be dead.

"We'll talk about this later, Diego." He shook his head as he pushed past him and headed for the door.

He couldn't talk about it now, there were too many plans to make, too much to do. And he couldn't make plans like this, couldn't be a part of this even as he was plotting Diego's death.

As he walked through the foyer, Cristo behind him while Trevor preceded him, he suddenly saw himself, not as he had thought he was, but how he might look through another's eyes. A man cold-bloodedly plotting the death of his father.

Did it matter that the father was a monster? Did it matter that once the Fuentes cartel fell, he intended to leave it and the various businesses resulting from it in the dust for the vultures to pick over?

As he stepped into the Rover, Trevor taking the driver's seat and Cristo moving into the front passenger seat as protection, Ian stared through the tinted glass of the door's window and rubbed his hand over his face in frustration.

He had cold-bloodedly planned this before he ever came

to the cartel. Two years of planning, plotting, inspiring just the right amount of curiosity in the right places to draw Diego in.

A man alone, grieving for the loss of his youngest son, without an heir or a family with the exception of a few cousins. A man rumored to have cherished his wife and son. Diego had cherished his son to the point that he had infected the young man with the same evil that filled himself.

An evil Ian couldn't afford to allow to survive.

As Trevor pulled from the gated villa estate and turned into the driveway to Kira's villa beside it, Ian couldn't help but worry about this thing with Sorrell.

He wasn't known for his predictability, or keeping his word. Not that Ian could expect a terrorist to be known for his word; still, it would have been nice if he were the game player Diego was. With a man like Diego, you knew the rules. Adhere to them, or the game is off and there are no holds barred. In Sorrell's case, it was no holds barred from the beginning. He dealt in terror, in death. It wasn't a business to him, it was a religion.

Stepping from the Rover, he had Trevor and Mendez wait outside the house where Kira had obviously left Deke. Stepping up to the wide sheltered doorway, Ian knocked firmly and waited as Daniel opened the door.

"Come on in." Daniel was back in bodyguard mode as he opened the door and stepped back. The minute Ian entered the house, the door closed and locked solidly behind him, and Daniel's demeanor changed.

"We have them in a small servant's room under the stairs, it seemed the most unlikely place to hide the daughter of an international terrorist." Daniel shook his head at the thought. "That was a good idea sending the Fuentes soldiers to guard the warehouse in town. Kell is reporting some interest there by a few unidentified subjects, but so far, nothing on this end."

They stepped beneath the curving staircase where Daniel pushed open a swinging door. It wasn't exactly hidden, but anyone swarming the house would bypass it on first look and continue on to the back of the villa or upstairs.

They stepped into a long narrow room. Ian pulled the recording from his pocket and tossed it to Macey as he stared around the room.

Reno leaned against the wall watching as Kira and Tehya sat on the half bed and talked. Macey had his laptop set up on a small wooden table and nearby dresser. Jamming equipment and satellite link antennae shared space with additional external hard drives and other paraphernalia that Macey considered his base setup.

Kira watched him silently. He knew the question running through all their minds.

"Sorrell made contact. It's happening at midnight at the villa. What kind of support are we going to have?" He directed that question to Reno, whom he knew always had backup.

Reno's lips quirked into a grin as he leaned lazily against the far wall, his M-16 cradled in his arms. Macey nodded and Tehya paled. The resignation that shadowed Kira's eyes had him watching her harder, more intently. He'd had a feeling she was in Aruba for more than sex or love when she first arrived. He hadn't altered that opinion, though he knew sex and love had definitely added in to the factors that had pulled her here.

That flash of emotion that he saw in her gaze proved it, and he prepared himself to defend against whatever might come from it.

She was a DHS contract operative, she had come there with DHS backing, and he knew it. She wouldn't have come without orders. Orders that she hadn't told him about, and he hadn't pushed to find out.

Pushing meant possibly not liking the truth, and though Ian was the type of man who believed in facing reality at all times, he didn't want to face reality with Kira until he had no other choice.

"We have two SEAL teams off the coast, waiting," Reno

reported as Ian held his hand out to Kira. "They'll move in when we give the word."

"Move Miss Talamosi to the Fuentes villa after dark," he told them as Kira took his hand and he pulled her to his side. "Diego knows you're here. I don't want to take the chance that anyone else does, and she'll be better protected if we don't have to split our forces."

"How did he find out?" Kira bit at her bottom lip as he stared down at her, her expression concerned.

"With Diego, only God knows." Ian shook his head. "He didn't say how he knew, but he knows. We'll pull together tonight and get things in place. Keep Durango team hidden at all costs until the meet; we don't want Sorrell warned ahead of the game."

He outlined the layout for the negotiations, watching as Macey frowned and made notes on a legal pad at his side and Reno nodded thoughtfully. Through it all, Tehya sat stoically on the bed, her head lowered, her hands clenched tightly together.

"He'll have men move into place after he arrives," Tehya said softly, once Ian had finished. "A large contingent of men, highly trained and heavily armed. Once he leaves, all hell will be laid on the villa."

"He won't be leaving alive," Ian reminded her.

Tehya inhaled roughly. "And all hell will be visited the moment they believe there are any problems. Sorrell times everything. He's fanatical about it. It's nearly as important as whatever ideal he fights for. If he doesn't call the attack off, then it will commence at a certain deadline, no matter where he is in the game. You must be prepared for that."

Ian nodded toward Macey. "I recorded our conversation," he said to Tehya. "You can go over it with the team, give him what details you may remember. At ten we'll meet at the villa and prepare for the meeting."

"I want that weapon, Mr. Richards," she told him again, her voice low but throbbing with determination. "I can't be taken alive by him."

Ian glanced at Reno. The other man's gaze was compassionate, and concerned.

"There's always the chance you could be rescued, Tehya. If something like that happened, we wouldn't stop searching for you."

Her lips twisted at his promise. "Perhaps you could, but not before he allows my half brother to breed me. You see, it's not love that drives Sorrell to find me. He chose the woman to breed his child with, hoping it would be a daughter. He chose her specifically for her bloodlines, her character, and her strength. He wanted a daughter, a half sister for the son he bred for the same qualities. I won't be raped by my brother, not even for a chance at escape."

Twenty-eight

IAN GAVE TEHYA A GUN. His backup weapon, small and compact, but it didn't take a large gun to commit suicide.

Ian filled Kira in on the confrontation between himself and Diego as well as the fact that Diego was aware of Durango team's involvement. She learned that Diego was also questioning Ian's plans once Sorrell was taken care of.

When they returned to the villa, Ian cleared the servants from the house, sent them back to Palm Beach, and placed a complete lockdown on any transmissions into or out of the villa that he didn't make or take himself.

Fuentes soldiers were positioned around the grounds, but none were inside the villa. Deke, Trevor, Cristo, and Mendez were busy securing the room to be used for the meeting, and Diego was sitting in the living room alone, a glass of whisky in his hand, the bottle at his side, though it didn't appear he was seriously drinking the liquor.

"Ian." He came to his feet as they entered the foyer, the bodyguards still surrounding them protectively. "Garcia was here moments ago. He asked to speak to you regarding the additional men sent to the warehouse. I was not certain how you wished to handle them."

She felt Ian's hand tense at her back as he sighed roughly.

"I need to take care of this," he told her, brushing her forehead with a light kiss as he stepped away. "I'll leave Deke and Mendez with you. I shouldn't be gone long."

She nodded, watching as he moved toward the back of the villa, his tall, leanly muscled body tense and prepared for battle.

When he disappeared into the back hall, she turned to Deke and Mendez. "Why don't the two of you go on to the kitchen and eat," she told them, aware that they had missed lunch while she met with Tehya.

Deke stared back at her, his gaze flat before glancing back at Diego. It was obvious he didn't trust Ian's father, and she couldn't blame him much.

"If you need us, just yell," he murmured.

"I'll be fine," she assured him.

Deke and Mendez didn't hide their reluctance to leave her, but they did anyway. As they headed into the kitchen Kira stepped slowly into the darkened room.

"Saul isn't with you?" She looked around the room as Diego watched her carefully.

"I sent Saul back to Colombia to oversee the estate there several days ago." He shrugged, his face shadowed as she moved to the chair across from him. "He is old. This is not the place for him."

As he resumed his seat she watched as he gripped the glass of liquor between his hands and stared into it as though he weren't certain if he should drink it or throw it.

"Saul was your father's advisor, wasn't he?" she asked.

She was taking advantage of this chance to talk to him, free of Ian's disapproving gaze or the bodyguards' obvious curiosity.

Diego smiled fondly at the question. "He and my father, they began the cartel. Saul was his most trusted friend. He returned to help me after Carmelita's death."

He hadn't mentioned his youngest son, but then she had heard that he didn't.

"Ian, he has completed this promise he made to me quickly,

has he not?" Diego asked then. "I asked him to return to rid me of this problem that Sorrell represents. I did not expect him to do this so quickly."

Sadness filled the monster's voice.

"He's very competent," she agreed as she leaned forward, gripped the decanter of whisky and one of the extra glasses on the table.

As she poured, she was aware of Diego's eyes on her, his gaze thoughtful.

"You remind me much of his mother, Marika." Diego sighed. "She had spirit as well. But a spirit filled with grace. She was a lady. You too have this."

She looked up as she returned the decanter to the table and leaned back in her chair.

"His mother is a very strong woman, she's had to be. I take that as an incredible compliment."

"As well you should." He nodded. "It was meant as one."

He sipped at his drink then, his expression still though somber, his position relaxed. It wasn't a relaxation that bespoke confidence though, it was more wearied acceptance.

Kira sipped at the smooth, expensive whisky and continued to watch him, wondering what caused the small frown between his brows, and realizing that Ian had much that same look when something was bothering him.

"Ian frowns like that when he's thinking." She shared her thought, offering him a small smile as he lifted his head in surprise.

"He reminds me much of myself, sometimes." He nodded, a small, subdued smile tugging at his lips. "He is a good man. A man to be proud of."

Kira nodded rather than speaking.

"He has no pride in his father," he said, his voice almost a whisper now. "No pride in the world I have built for myself nor what I represent. He calls me 'pop,' thinking I am not aware of the condescending meaning behind it. He believes I do not know that he came to me, not for who I am, but for that which I can give him. Sorrell."

He tossed the drink back then reached for the decanter and poured another.

"What did you expect, Mr. Fuentes?" She was careful to keep her voice gentle, without judgment.

He nodded slowly. "I should be angry." He lifted his eyes to flash a quick look at her, mocking self-disgust lining his expression now. "I should be angry with my father, with Carmelita for the hell she caused him and Marika. I should be angry with my father for the deception that stole Ian's mother from my arms. Why am I not angry, Miss Porter?"

He watched her as though genuinely confused by this.

"Perhaps I have grown weak?" he asked then. "I am growing old, my youth is gone. Perhaps this is what comes of a man realizing his chances are gone. When I was young, there was always next year to fix those things I thought I should fix. Next year to atone for the deaths of my brothers. Next year to rail at Carmelita for more children. Next year. Always next year, until one day I awoke to learn that next year could not fix those mistakes I had made."

Shock held her silent now. This was the monster? This man, not broken, not weak, but realizing the choices and the consequences of his life.

"You killed your brothers," she said quietly. "Their wives, their children, because they wanted out of the cartel."

"Is that what you think? That I took those lives simply because they would betray me to your American government?" He laughed at that, though the sound was bitter. "How I wish it had been so simple. That my treachery and blood thirst was so blackened by evil." He shook his head. "No, Miss Porter, I killed in an act of rage. The explosion that destroyed the home I had given Marika, I learned had been set because my brothers had betrayed her location to my enemies. This I was told, and in my grief, I took all they held dear as well, before killing them." He shook his head then. "I should have known better. I should have seen that the madness that was affecting my father at that time couldn't be trusted."

"Your father told you they were the reason Marika was dead?"

"He told me that my brothers were aligning themselves with our enemies, and it was true that they were. It was only later that I learned that it had not been my brothers who betrayed Marika's home, but Carmelita. She did so after my father went to Ian's mother, told her of the business of the cartel, told her that I was vile, deceitful, and all but wed to another. He told her I would kill her once our child was born."

He moved quickly from his seat, paced to the other side of the room, and tipped the glass to his lips.

"So many mistakes," he whispered once he had consumed the liquid. "So many times I wished I could go back." He shook his head then. "I see my son, grown, a man of honor slowly dying inside as he runs this business." He set the glass on the low marble-topped table beside him and ran his fingers through his unbound hair, keeping his back to her as he stared at the curtained window. "It is almost finished, is it not? He will leave when Sorrell has been dealt with." He turned to her, staring at her questioningly.

"Ian hasn't revealed his plans to me, Mr. Fuentes. He hasn't said one way or the other."

He nodded again. "He will leave."

Kira lowered her head, feeling the pain coming in waves from a man who suddenly seemed the least likely of drug lords.

"Marika, she raised a son to be proud of," he said then, turning to face her once again. "A son to make a man regret, and to make a man wish he were strong enough to give his son the only thing he wants from his father."

"What does Ian want from you?" she asked.

Bitterness tipped his lips. "My death, Miss Porter. Nothing would make Ian happier than to see me leave this world forever."

"Or to see you stop feeling sorry for yourself before this meeting." Ian stepped into the room, his voice low but lashing. He strode to the decanter, poured himself a drink, and tipped it back before speaking again. "Garcia has the soldiers in place and everything's quiet for now. Kira and I are going to rest until dark. Send Deke up to the room if you need me."

Kira rose to her feet, hearing the cool, steady tone of his guttural voice, aware that he must have heard much more than Diego's last statement.

"Of course I will," Diego said, a shade of sarcasm filling his voice now. "I but live to serve you now, do I not."

Ian's jaw clenched as he glanced at Kira, then back to Diego.

"It seems to me that you just live to piss me off at times like this," he growled. "I can't afford to have you drunk, Diego. I need you sober and aware tonight."

"You have never seen me drunken," Diego snapped then. "Do not give your woman the impression that I am worse than what I am, Ian. I am no drunkard."

"I didn't think you were suicidal either," Ian stated mockingly. "I hope you'd at least stick around long enough to see this through."

Kira saw the anger glittering in Diego's eyes then, the dim light from the foyer gleaming on the pitch-black of his eyes.

"I always see it through, Ian," he reminded his son roughly. "If I do nothing else, I see all things through."

With that, he stalked across the room, brushed by his son, and made his way quickly through the foyer.

Kira watched Ian as Diego left, the way his shoulders seemed to tense further, his expression tightening more.

"He's not the only one that wants to get drunk," Ian muttered. "Come on, let's go upstairs."

He didn't touch her. He didn't grip her wrist and drag her into the foyer and up the stairs. Instead, he stepped back to the doorway and watched her broodingly.

Kira moved ahead of him, taking the steps quickly and heading to his bedroom suite. She turned to face him once again as he closed and locked the door, then waited until he stepped to the bureau, set his security, and stood staring at the electronics in the drawer for long seconds before closing it and turning back to face her.

He pushed his fingers through his hair, in the same manner that Diego had done earlier. The dark blond strands framed the heavy expression on his face, brushed his shoulders, and tempted her to run her own fingers through it.

"It's almost over," he said then, staring around the room before returning his gaze to her. "Almost over."

She moved to him then, because he should have sounded triumphant, eager to see the finish, he should have been anticipating the end of this night, but she could feel his regret as well.

Not because he would be leaving the cartel, she thought. Instead, she felt the heavy knowledge inside him that things weren't as he thought they were.

He wouldn't say it, she could only pray he would realize it before the night was over, but she knew he was realizing there was more than the monster inside Diego Fuentes.

"I came here to kill him." His voice was soft as he stared back at her. "He was going to rape those girls he kidnapped. He drugged them, one of them died. He allowed his men to rape another in front of her father. He tortured Nathan. He's killed, destroyed lives. He won't stop. Letting him live won't stop the hell he spreads."

Kira inhaled roughly. What was she supposed to say? How was she supposed to relieve the pain that he wouldn't admit even to himself that he felt?

"Ian—"

"Son of a bitch, Kira." His expression twisted, his eyes burning. "I see what he wants me to believe, but I know what he is. He'll never stop. That fucking whore's dust he created has destroyed women. The videos he made from them. Those were innocent women. Women who had nothing to do with his games or this world. Those girls he kidnapped. The blood he's fucking shed."

He swung away from her as she felt the first tear fall from her own eyes. She saw what Diego wanted to be, and Ian saw what he was. The contradiction would tear Ian apart if he let it.

"It's not your place to kill him," she reminded him. "Arrest him. Take him in, Ian. Let DHS deal with him. Don't place this on your soul."

She moved to him, her arms sliding around him as she laid her head on his back. "Don't do this to yourself. Don't let him destroy you too."

He inhaled sharply, his hands pressing against hers, holding them close to his body before he turned, surrounded her with his hold, and laid his cheek against her head.

"It's my responsibility," he said, his voice heavy.

"No—" she tried to protest, but his finger pressed against her lips, his tortured gaze locked with hers.

"I have to do what I came here to do," he told her. "He's not my father, Kira. A father doesn't murder. He doesn't allow his men to rape sixteen-year-old girls, and he doesn't torture good men. That's not a father, that's a monster."

She laid her head against his chest, because she knew that. She knew what he was, and she knew DHS would allow it to continue in exchange for the information he provided. But it didn't stop her heart from breaking, for Ian, for Diego, for herself. Because she knew if she stood in his way, he would never forgive her. And if she didn't, the ramifications of what DHS could do to retaliate terrified her.

"You terrify me," Ian whispered then, his hand cupping her jaw to raise her face to his. "I knew Sorrell would find a way to use you against me in this. I knew it, and I let you stay anyway."

"Because you know I'm good." She sniffed, trying to smile, to lighten the pain she knew was flowing through both of them.

"You're very good," he agreed, a hungry flame lighting his gaze. "Too damned good."

"I can be better." She needed to touch him, to hold him,

just one more time, she needed to show him how much of her soul he owned.

"Really?" he questioned her suggestively as she drew back from his chest slowly.

Taking his hand she moved for the bedroom. "Shall I show you?"

"I'm all about show-and-tell," he assured her, lust beginning to make his voice huskier, raspier. Sexier.

She cast him a sensual look over her shoulder, her lashes lowered, her tongue peeking out to touch her lips suggestively.

"I can show-and-tell," she promised him, stepping away from him as they went into the bedroom, and turning to face him as she slid her blazer from her shoulders and tossed it to a nearby chair.

The shoulder holster was unclipped and placed on top of the jacket before she sat, unlaced her boots, and pulled them from her feet.

Ian's eyes were burning with hunger now. His tortured emotions were receding beneath the arousal. When she came to her feet, gripped the hem of her shirt, and pulled it from her body, he jerked into action. Clothes were tossed to the side, littering the floor, crumpled and left to wrinkle as he pulled her naked body against his own.

Sensitive nerve endings screamed in sensation as he lifted her to him and his hair-roughened chest rasped against her nipples. The peaks hardened almost painfully as the blood thundered to them and a gasp left her throat as their lips met in hunger and desperate need.

She was only barely aware of falling to the bed, but she was very much aware of Ian's larger body covering hers. That wasn't what she wanted. She wanted him stretched out for her pleasure now, wanted to watch that muscular, hard body tight and straining for release as he had watched her softer one.

With her lips still melded to his, stinging kisses raging between them, she managed to wriggle from beneath him, pushing at his shoulders, nipping at his lips, and silently demanding that he roll to his back.

He pulled her with him as he did, draping her over his chest as one hand slid into the fall of her hair that cascaded over her shoulder, the other playing up and down her back, stroking the fires burning inside her higher, hotter.

She was burning alive for him now. She needed him. Needed him inside her, wrapped around her, needed one last memory of his touch and his love to sustain her in the future.

Just in case. Just in case he walked away once he learned how she had deceived him.

Kira pulled her head back, forcing her eyes open as she stared down at him, seeing the brick-red flush along his dark cheekbones, the glitter of lust in his tobacco eyes, and the need in his expression.

He needed her, needed her touch and her love just as much as she needed his. It wasn't a one-way street; they met, they fit together.

"What are you going to do now?" His lips quirked as he stared back at her, his lashes lowered sensually over his eyes.

"You're mine." Her hands flattened against his chest. "I claim you, Ian. Do you know that?"

Something else flared in his gaze then. Possessiveness, satisfaction, and more. As though the claim were a pleasure itself.

"No less than I claim you, Kira." His voice throbbed with demand. "You're a part of me that I never want to lose."

She knew the emotions she had glimpsed in his eyes then. Her chest clenched with them, her womb flexed, and a sense of belonging swept over her with the power of an orgasm. It lit fires inside her that hadn't been there before. Fires that flamed brighter, hotter than ever before and built the arousal to an almost painful degree.

"I need to touch you." A soft cry filled her words as her head lowered to his neck, her tongue stroking over it as his often did hers. "I need to feel you all the way to my soul, Ian."

He tensed violently beneath her, his eyes dilating in response to her ragged cry as her lips nibbled at his chin, stroked back down his neck. She slid down his body, feeling the sheen of sweat beginning to form on his flesh as the raging length of his cock pressed against her thigh.

"Baby, any time you want it," he groaned. "Any time you want me, I'm yours."

If only that were true.

Her lips moved to the hard, flat disc of a male nipple. Her tongue played with it, the salty taste of his flesh exploding against her taste buds as her nails raked down his arms.

She loved his body. The hardness of it, the way the tough, lean muscles flexed and rippled beneath her touch. The way perspiration gleamed on sun-darkened flesh and the scattering of chest hair rasped over her palms and her nipples.

She loved stroking him. Loved the way his eyes narrowed on her and pleasure gleamed in their fiery brown depths.

Her lips moved from one hard male nipple to the other. Her tongue licked over it before she drew it into her mouth and felt it harden further.

Her pussy was weeping with need. She could feel her juices gathering and falling to slicken the swollen lips. Her clit was engorged, throbbing. So desperate that as Kira played the temptress on Ian's nipples she rubbed the desperate knot of flesh against his thigh where she straddled it.

Hard male hands bunched in her hair as she moaned, rocking against his thigh and nibbling at the tight flesh before licking the hard little point.

Her clit raked over tough, hair-spattered flesh and her juices dampened his thigh. The world began to recede as pleasure began to rock through her.

"You're like silk and satin, Kira." His hard, gravelly voice was a different stroke of pleasure. "Silky mouth, satiny pussy. Wet and sweet for me."

She whispered a cry over his chest as she began to move lower. She had to taste him. Needed to fill her mouth with the male strength and hunger beneath her.

"I love touching you." The breathless words whispered past her lips without thought. "I love feeling you like this. So hard and powerful."

She licked at his hard abdomen, raked her teeth over it, skirting the throbbing head of his cock as his hands pulled at her hair.

Tiny streaks of fiery sensation exploded along her scalp as his hips flexed and the engorged cock head stroked along her cheek.

Oh, she knew what he wanted, what she wanted. All of it. Every sensual touch of pleasure wrung from both their bodies.

Her tongue peeked out, raked along the crest, and a muttered groan left his lips. The hard stalk of flesh throbbed and pounded with need as she moved lower.

She licked over the tight flesh, but didn't linger. As she moved between his thighs, her gaze fastened on the tight, hard spheres that had drawn up tight beneath the hard shaft.

Dark blond male hairs stroked her chin as she placed her tongue at the line that separated his balls from his cock. He jerked beneath her, a low groan vibrating in his chest as she licked sensually, enjoying the male taste against her lips, power and lust and salty spice.

"Kira, baby, you're pushing control here." His voice was so husky, so raspy it was like sandpaper in the sensual silence of the room.

"Should I restrain you?" She smiled as she laid a kiss at the base of his cock, then let her teeth rake the area with the utmost gentleness.

He almost snarled in pleasure. The sound had her womb spasming as her pussy clenched with the need to surround his cock.

"Maybe I should restrain you," he groaned. "You couldn't destroy a man's control then."

"If you restrained me, I couldn't do this." She laid her lips along the side of the tight sac, opened them, and sucked the flesh into her mouth. Her tongue stroked, probed, and her mouth suckled sensually as his thighs tensed beside her face.

He liked it. Hell, he might even love it.

Using her suckling mouth, the gentle rasp of teeth, and her lashing tongue, she explored the violently tense sac, feeling the ripples of response in the hard length of his cock and the muscles of his thighs.

"You're going to mess me up with this," he protested, but the hard hands in her hair held her to him. "Hell, you're going to knock yourself out of getting that sweet pussy ate. Do you want to do that?"

"You can dine later." She smiled against his balls. "This time, it's my turn."

She moved higher, licking along the tight flesh of his erection until she reached the crest. Until she could surround it with her mouth and suck it in. Her tongue played, she sucked, moaned, and felt her pussy gushing with slick dampness.

The taste of precum against her tongue had her moaning in hunger. The feel of his hands pulling at her hair, his muscles tightening further beneath her, warned her that his control would end soon.

She looked up at his face, saw the sweat beaded on his forehead as he stared down at her, small rivulets moving along the side of his face as his jaw clenched, his teeth bared.

She tongued the hard cock head, sucked it deep and felt it throb at the back of her throat before her own body forced the end of her play.

If she didn't have him inside her, she wouldn't survive. If she didn't feel the thick, iron-hard flesh filling her, then she might implode from the pressure.

"Come on, baby," he groaned as she moved up his body, one hand moving from her hair to grip her thigh and move it over his body as she straddled his hips. "Give us both what we need."

She whimpered as the engorged crest tucked between the swollen lips of her pussy. Gazing into his eyes, she felt her juices wash from her body, coating his cock head, preparing it to stretch and possess.

"You know what's going to happen," he warned her tightly. "I can't take you easy."

"If I wanted easy," she panted. "I wouldn't have followed you."

His hands gripped her hips as he suddenly shifted, his hips plunging up, driving his cock halfway inside her as her back bowed and a throttled scream left her throat.

"Fuck, feel how tight you are, Kira," he snarled. "So tight and hot over my cock you're burning me alive."

Her head tossed, her lips parted to draw in air as she locked her eyes with his.

"Not enough." She could barely breathe for the pleasure, the hunger. "Not enough."

She could feel the perspiration running over her breasts, feel her juices flowing through her pussy as it stretched to accommodate the girth filling it.

"I have more, sweetheart," he crooned roughly. "God, do I have more for you."

He retreated, pulled back, his hands tightening at her hips. As she felt him gather to plunge inside her again, she tightened the muscles of her pussy and thrust down.

Their cries mingled, wove together, as the force of each movement plunged his erection to the hilt inside her.

There was no stopping her now, and there was no stopping him. Straining, thrusting upward, he fucked into her with hard, powerful strokes and she moved with him, riding him hard, pushing herself to take all the pleasure she could gather.

His hands bit into her hips. Her clit rasped against his

pelvis as she leaned forward, her hands bracing on his chest, and a second later, everything inside her exploded.

She screamed his name, because she couldn't hold it back. She heard her name echo around her as she disintegrated.

The orgasm was violent, clenching the muscles of her pussy around his suddenly spurting cock as his seed jetted inside her. Her womb spasmed, rippled, and pleasure detonated there as well. Her clit burst with sensation as her orgasm echoed and built throughout her body until it exploded in one last fiery conflagration and flung her into a world of star-studded night and rapturous color.

"I love you," she cried, falling against his chest as involuntary spasms gripped them both. "God help me, Ian. I love you."

"Love you," he groaned, his corded body still tight, his cock jerking inside her. "Ah baby, I love you."

Perspiration melded them together as the tiny aftershocks slowly eased through both their bodies. Exhaustion claimed her, dragging her eyes down, reminding her of the sleep she had lost in the past days.

Just for a minute, she thought, letting it have her as Ian held her safe and warm in his arms. She would give in for just a moment.

Twenty-nine

THEY MANAGED A FEW HOURS' sleep then a quick shower at the edge of darkness.

"I need you to dress soft," he told her as she walked naked to the closet where her clothes had been placed.

"Soft in what manner?" She looked back at him, considering her options.

"Sorrell will check you for weapons." His expression was heavy, tormented. "I want him to think you're helpless, weak. He knows who you are, so he knows you're smart. But he doesn't know you're deadly. Let's keep him in the dark where that's concerned."

Kira nodded and moved into the closet. She chose a butter-soft bronze sundress and creamy ultrahigh heels.

Four-inch heels were sexy as hell, and these added another element. Each heel contained a three-inch razor-sharp dagger imbedded within it.

She couldn't carry a gun but the stretchy silk of the dress would be easy to move in. It was short enough to allow her legs a measure of freedom but long enough to preserve her modesty.

Her panties were a thong, her bra lacy and comfortable. When she finished dressing, she was the epitome of helpless female.

"You're fucking dangerous," Ian growled as she checked the daggers in the heels of the shoes before sliding them on her feet.

"Smart." She grinned. "It wasn't easy figuring out how to insert those daggers."

"Yeah, I can see that." He swallowed tightly.

Kira let her gaze flicker over his jean-clad thighs and held back her smile at the evidence of the arousal that filled his jeans.

"You need to get a handle on that hard-on, Ian," she murmured, sidling up to him, her hand smoothing down his chest to the bulge in his jeans.

Her hand shaped it lovingly as his palm slid up her side and cupped the undercurve of her breast.

"Be careful," he whispered against her lips again. "Be safe."

"You watch my back, I'll watch yours," she promised, returning the stroke of his lips against her own. "We'll be okay, you'll see."

Her hand slid back up his chest until it pressed over his heart. She felt the hard, steady thump and strengthened herself with it. It was almost over. One way or the other, the danger that stalked him, the life that would have destroyed him, was almost over.

"Don't stand in my way," he warned her then.

Kira froze and looked at him, feeling the heaviness clench her chest.

"What do you mean?"

"With Diego. Don't stand in my way, Kira."

She nodded slowly. It was her job to stand in his way, to protect Diego, but as she gazed at Ian, she knew she couldn't, she wouldn't do it.

Lives had been destroyed because of Diego. He saw the life he lived as a game, an amusing pastime where he made the rules and he directed the players; that would never stop.

Teenagers had died because of whore's dust. He had made millions off the underground rape videos his men had made using the drug. Innocent women had committed suicide, or lived with the knowledge that their greatest pain was being salivated over by distant watchers.

He had tortured Nathan, tortured him, found pleasure in the battle the other man had fought to stay true to his marriage vows.

He was a monster. It didn't matter that the monster loved his son, because even that would be twisted, used, and would ultimately destroy Ian.

Walking away wasn't an option for Ian. He would know he'd had the chance to stop the horror and hadn't taken it and it would destroy him in ways that killing Diego never could.

"I have your back." She finally whispered the promise, the vow. "No matter what you do, Ian. I have your back."

The brooding pain in his gaze slowly eased away, his eyes becoming flat, hard. This was the cartel heir, the man who had proved he was strong enough, merciless enough, to hold the reins of the Fuentes cartel. All she could think was that DHS was damned lucky he was on their side, rather than the enemy's.

He finally nodded in turn before walking to the dresser. Drawing the Glock from the upper drawer, he pushed it into the back of his jeans then collected the extra clips of ammo.

"He and his bodyguard will be armed," he told her. "Handguns only. Tehya's weapon will be Velcroed to the small of her back, and Antoli will be carrying several weapons. When things go to hell make certain you're in position to either take the weapon from Sorrell's bodyguard or to collect one from Antoli. His job is to protect Tehya above everything else; that leaves me and you to watch each other's backs.

"Durango team and teams four and eight will converge on the estate after Sorrell is inside. They have to take out any forces that follow behind Sorrell before they can move in to help us. We'll be on our own in that room, Kira, don't kid yourself about that." His gaze bored into hers. "We have to keep Tehya safe, as well as ourselves, until Reno and the team can get to us. Understood?"

She nodded sharply.

"Let's go then." He breathed in roughly. "Reno and Macey will have Tehya here within minutes and we're only hours from Sorrell's arrival. We can expect him—"

"—to be either late or early but never on time," Kira finished for him. "When he shows the birthmark, check it closely, then check his bodyguard for one. He's not above a switch. Make him speak to Tehya to confirm voice identification and pay attention to the bodyguard's body language as well as Sorrell's. Above all things, remember Sorrell has stayed unidentified to this point for a reason. How did I do?" She flashed him a knowing smile.

"Dangerously efficient." The smile he gave in turn was easier, more confident. "Let's get this done. I think I've had enough of Aruba. I'm eager to get home."

"Ian." She caught his arm as he moved to turn toward the door. "There's something you don't know."

His expression closed. As though he did know, as though he had been waiting, watching. She felt her throat tighten, knowing she had to tell him the truth about Diego and DHS. She didn't have a choice. She couldn't let him kill without the facts.

"About Diego?" he asked harshly.

"There's more to this than you know."

"Don't." His voice cut like a knife. "I don't want to know."

She stared at him in surprise. "Ian, you have to hear this."

"Later."

"There won't be time later. It'll be too late," she gritted out.

She could see the suspicion in his eyes, and knew he was aware that things weren't as they seemed. That Diego had escaped justice all these years for a reason.

"You know," she whispered.

"That Diego plays games with DHS?" he asked, a bitter, mocking curve curling his lips. "I know."

"And you didn't say anything to me?"

"You didn't say anything to me either, Kira," he reminded her as she loosened her hold on him. "I've always suspected it. We were pulled out of the game when Nathan went missing, given strict orders not to kill Diego when we went after the senator's girls. Every time we've struck against him, we were hampered, our hands tied. I knew he was in bed with those bastards."

"There's a reason." She licked her lips nervously. "It's not just a game with DHS."

"Of course it is." Bitterness filled his voice. "Doesn't matter the reason for it, it's still a game."

He reached out and touched her cheek, running the backs of his fingers over it. "That's why you came here, wasn't it? To protect Diego."

"No." She shook her head. "It was never about Diego. I came here because of you. I used Diego as the excuse."

He leaned forward and kissed her lips. "Thank you for that, Kira. But this isn't about DHS or what they want. This is about letting a monster roam free because politicians and paper pushers believe the information he gives is more important. The needs of the many outweigh the pain of the few. I can't see it that way. I won't see it that way."

"He's still your father," she whispered. "No one would blame you for walking away."

He inhaled deeply, staring over her shoulder for long seconds before his gaze came back to hers. The sadness, the somber acceptance of responsibility, darkened the fire in his eyes and dug creases of pain into his face.

"Because he is my father, the blame would be more mine than DHS's," he told her. "He's my responsibility, because I'm here, in place, with the means and the chance."

"DHS won't let you forget it."

"I have their agreement signed, sealed, and protected. It releases to the major newspapers across the world the minute Sorrell's death is announced. I'm not stupid. I know how that game works too. Now let's go. We'll argue over it later. Later."

He said it as though he had said it to himself often. Later. Now was the time to face Sorrell, to face the decisions he had made over the course of years. Kira only prayed that both of them could live with those choices.

Thirty

KIRA STOOD CONFIDENTLY, AMUSEMENT GLITTERING deliberately in her eyes, when the limousine entered the gates of the Fuentes estate and pulled up to the sheltered entrance to the house.

She stood at the bottom of the steps, but didn't deign to open the door to the luxury vehicle. The chauffeur moved from the front, irritation lining his face as he glanced at her.

She gave him a jaunty smile and stepped back as he swung the door open.

Sorrell and his associate, she presumed. They stepped from the vehicle, exuding arrogance and superiority despite the black masks that covered their faces.

"Kira Porter." A flash of a smile, familiar and faintly disarming, touched his mouth.

She arched a brow and glanced at his companion, instantly knowing who Sorrell was, and it wasn't the charming, smiling masked man facing her.

She turned back to the charmer though. "Sorrell?" She peered at him as though uncertain, unknowing.

His smile was condescending. "You will take us to Mr Fuentes, I presume?" His hand wrapped around her arm, the thin leather gloves doing nothing to disguise the strength in the grip.

"You presume right." She flipped him another smile. "We'll just go through the door here."

The doors were open wide, showing the deserted foyer that awaited inside. "Ian's waiting in the study, as well as his father and your daughter. She's a beautiful young woman. A shame she was raised without her father."

A blessing was more like it.

The fingers tightened on her arm.

"Let's not bruise the skin." She tapped at his wrist with her opposite hand. "Ian gets upset when I get bruised. Mars the skin. He's funny about that."

As was Sorrell. Rumor was that he would kill if merchandise was bruised or in any way broken. He liked giving pain himself, and he knew how to do it without leaving a mark. She restrained her shiver and moved into the house, very aware of the hand holding on to her.

The grip was strong—the bodyguard, she presumed—and he was heavily armed. Beneath the long jacket he wore was a harnessed automatic weapon, most likely Uzi-type. A backup at his ankle and she was betting on another at his back.

The broader, stouter figure who walked on the other side of her wasn't as heavily armed. He was dressed casually in dark slacks and jacket. A weapon at his back would be expected, most likely another handgun harnessed beneath his arm from what she had glimpsed of his jacket.

To come here unarmed would have been idiocy. But it made the upcoming meeting and the plans that were in place harder to execute. She wasn't armed. Ian would be. Teyha and Antoli would be.

Not for the first time, Kira wondered at the plan they had in place. In theory, she agreed with Ian. If they arrested Sorrell, he would soon escape, one way or the other. The only thing they would gain would be his identity and his wrath, and Nathan Malone would never be same. On the other side of the coin, the imminent bloodshed raked at her conscience.

They were monsters. They were evil. They were killers

of the worst sort. But how did that make her, Ian, and Durango team any better?

"In here, gentlemen." She stopped before the door, well aware that Deke and Trevor were watching from the upper landing, well hidden from the two visitors.

The door opened wide, revealing Tehya, for all intents and purposes bound to the high-backed chair across the room. The chair had been placed in front of the wide windows, the drawn shades lending a creamy backdrop to the brilliant, bloodred waves of hair that flowed around her.

Antoli stood behind her, a Glock held in the hand resting comfortably by his side.

"My daughter." There was a sigh from behind Kira as Tehya's gaze clashed with the men behind her.

That voice was soft, almost reverent.

"What a beauty you have become," Sorrell whispered.

Tehya sneered back at him. "Perfect breeder, am I?"

A long sigh whispered through the silence. "You are my child. You would have been adored. You will be adored. Treasured."

"And bred in an incestuous relationship." Her expression contorted in fury.

"I would have loved you."

"You would have destroyed me as you destroyed my mother and everyone else you've ever touched. You bastard!"

At that moment, Kira felt the barrel that pressed against her forehead and the tightening of the fingers on her arm.

"Mr. Fuentes." The stouter, barrel-chested man at her side snapped at Ian and Diego as angry tension filled the room then. "There will be no negotiations. Release my daughter and send her this way, and the lovely Miss Porter might live to see another day."

She hated it when men went back on their word. It just pissed her off.

Her gaze sliced to Ian as he leaned back comfortably in his chair, his legs lifted and resting on the corner of his desk as he watched Sorrell with no small amount of amusement.

Antoli's gun lifted to Tehya's forehead and Diego sipped at his whisky from where he sat beside Ian's desk in a comfortable leather chair.

"You know, we can do this the easy way, or the hard way," Ian said.

The gun at her head said.

"Perhaps the easy way then." He muttered his cue to Kira.

Kira dropped. She simply bent her legs, pulling them up, and let herself fall and roll as Ian's bodyguards swarmed around the two men.

There was a curse, a grunt, and as she rolled to her feet in a crouch, it was to see the two men unmasked. And she couldn't believe what she was seeing. There had to be a mistake.

She had known there was something familiar about the two men, known that she should have recognized something about them, but the French accents had thrown her off. The supposedly natural accents, the arrogance in the tone that she hadn't heard before.

It wasn't any of the men they had suspected. The associate he had brought with him wasn't Gregor Ascarti as they had assumed it would be.

The men, unmasked, were friends, associates of hers and Jason's, European but not French, and so well respected that she knew the knowledge of this would rock the world.

"Kenneth," she whispered, staring at the younger man, seeing the familiar brown eyes, the thinning brown hair.

He inclined his head regally as she turned her gaze to his father.

"You killed my parents," she whispered. "Then cried at their funeral."

Joseph Fitzhugh, distantly related to royalty, and friends with the current president of the United States. Good friends. Hunting-and-fishing-type friends.

"The loss of your parents was regrettable, but necessary," Joseph informed her in frosty tones. "That was a nice move you performed in breaking Kenneth's hold," he complimented her. "I will assume you have had more training than I suspected?"

"Much more," she whispered faintly, coming to her feet as Ian stood at his desk.

Tehya was free, now placed behind Antoli who stood ready, arms outstretched and braced, as he covered the bodyguards. Tehya held the backup weapon Ian had given her, covering the two men as well.

"Quite interesting." Joseph's lips twisted in disgust. "I must admit, Mr. Fuentes, I expected you to keep your word. One man apiece, was that not the agreement?"

"I lied." Ian shrugged easily. "As, it appears, you did as well."

Joseph frowned. "My profile for you did not take into account the influence of your father, perhaps. The conclusions I drew suggested you would keep to your bargain, as your word has always held true. Until now."

"Extreme situations, extreme measures." Ian smiled. "Some things are just worth lying for. Check his back, Deke, let's make sure we have Sorrell before this goes any further."

Trevor jerked the terrorist's arms behind his back, flattening him against the wall beside them as Deke jerked his jacket up. They relieved him of his weapons first, then tugged the edge of his belted slacks down just enough to glimpse the incriminating birthmark. The form of a crude scythe could be seen, perhaps two inches tall, from across the room.

"It's natural," Deke snapped. "We have him."

At that moment the lights snapped off, gunfire erupted outside, and all hell broke loose inside.

Kira scrambled across the room, kicking her shoes off and going low to reach Tehya.

"Weapon," she snapped, reaching for Antoli as gunfire blazed in the room.

A handgun slapped into her hand as Antoli threw Tehya her way.

"Get her the hell out of here," he snarled.

"Kira." Ian's voice yelled through the chaos.

"Clear," she yelled back, pulling Tehya across the floor as bullets ripped into the area they had just been in.

"Stay put!" Ian reached Kira, jerking Kira behind the heavy desk that had been reinforced along the insides with thick metal that evening. Once securing her, Ian crouched and made his way through the darkened room.

The war zone outside and inside blasted through Kira's head as she reached out to grab Tehya and shoved her beneath the desk.

"Listen to me." Kira turned to Tehya, grabbing her shoulder with her free hand and shaking it as Tehya tried to crawl from beneath the desk. "Every Sorrell soldier out there is looking for you, and they will take you. Stay here. Don't fucking move. It's the only way you'll be safe."

"I'll only be safe if he's dead," Tehya snarled back, fury tearing at her voice. "He knew what he was doing here. He meant to kill all of you."

"And he still might if you mess this up," Kira snapped back. "We suspected this. Stay in place. Don't move, Tehya. Swear it to me or I swear to God I'll knock you out myself."

The darkness of the room was almost absolute, the sound of gunfire inside the house and outside a shock to the senses.

Kira nodded shortly before crouching and making her way to the edge of the desk to peer around it.

There was a body stretched out by the door. For a moment, Kira's heart leapt in her chest in fear before she realized it was an unfamiliar form, likely one of Sorrell's soldiers that had moved in close. Blood flowed from beneath him, puddling on the expensive marble of the foyer, and onto the hardwood just inside the office.

A minute amount of moonlight came from the living room and solarium across the foyer as rapid bursts of gunfire continued outside.

Kira glanced back at where Tehya sat, her wild green eyes gleaming with murderous rage. Controlling her wasn't going to be easy, and the danger had just intensified. Kira couldn't move into the fight and she couldn't afford to attempt to get Tehya to a more secure location.

She ducked back behind the desk and scooted in beside the other girl. They both stared straight ahead, weapons held ready.

"Are we pussies or what?" Tehya suddenly hissed.

Kira glanced over at her. "Last time I looked I had one," she informed her, then cursed as bullets ripped through the window across the room and shattered through the wood of the desk.

The heavy steel encasing three sides of the desk pinged and shuddered.

"Fuck!" Tehya breathed roughly. "Do you really want to play the helpless female like this?"

Kira grunted. If she moved, Ian was going to kill her, there was no doubt in her mind—if Sorrell or one of his men didn't do it for him.

"Some fucking Homeland Security agent you are," Tehya griped.

"Homeland isn't my boss." Contract agent, she told herself. There *was* a difference.

"You're an agent of someone's," the other girl argued, ducking instinctively as more pings hit the steel around them. "We're dead here. Is that what we want?"

Unfortunately, Tehya was right.

"Ian's going to rip me a new one," Kira said.

"Sucks to be you," Teyha agreed. "Do we go?"

Bullets rained around them, and Kira swore one of those pings nearly ripped through the steel into her kidney.

Kira bit her lip in indecision. Sitting here like a sacrificial lamb didn't seem like the best idea in the world, that was for damned sure.

"Sorrell's going to try to move through the house and circle back here. He'll suspect we stayed in place." Kira flinched as more bullets ripped into the room. "We'll hit the foyer and make our way to the back of the house."

Damn, she wished she had one of those handy receivers the rest of the teams were wearing. At least she would be able to contact Daniel. He would be looking for her exclusively, she knew that. All she had to do was find him. One thing was for damned sure, he would never expect her to stay put.

More bullets pinged into the steel.

"Fuck, let's go. Stay at my back and keep up, and for God's sake, if you see Sorrell, then we fucking run."

Crouching, Kira eased from under the desk, staying low before checking the darkness for any movement. Tehya followed behind her. Kira's night vision was a little better now, giving her a measure of confidence as she looked back at Tehya and gave her a quick hand signal to hold in place until she secured the path to the door.

Crouching by the side of the desk she waited, knowing that once she moved past it she would be undefended until she reached the foyer.

She pulled her shoes off, slid the daggers free, gripped the small blocks that doubled as the bottom of the shoes' heels between her fingers, and moved forward.

As she cleared the desk, something hit her in the side, the gun went flying from her hand, and the breath whooshed out of her lungs as she landed on the floor.

A fist rammed into her side again before she could gather herself, before she could evade it, then hard hands circled her neck, cutting off her air.

She caught the glitter of enraged eyes and Kenneth's shadowed expression before she rammed the daggers into his side and bucked against his hold.

"Bitch!" he snarled, but his grip loosened, just enough, the pressure of his knees on her arms shifted as she bucked, and the next second a gunshot filled the air before he was kicked off her.

Tehya gripped Kira's arm, jerking her from the floor and back to the desk as gunfire filled the room again.

Kira shook her head, staring at Kenneth's fallen form in shock for long seconds.

"Here." Teyha shoved the gun that had been knocked from her back into her hands. "Are you okay?"

"Fuck! Didn't see that coming." Kira was still trying to breathe, to process the quickness of the attack and the death.

"Let's get the hell out of here," Tehya hissed. "Those bastards out there know we're in here."

She was right. They had to get out of here now.

Staying low, Kira covered the short distance to the doorway first, weapon held ready, scanning the darkness quickly before sliding to the side of the wall and covering the other girl's route.

As Tehya slid in beside her, bullets cut through the room, almost as though someone knew they were there, knew where to strike hardest.

She could hear men screaming outside, shouted orders and foreign curses. The front door was still wide open, leaving them defenseless.

Moving quickly, Kira pulled Tehya after her, dragging her beneath the staircase and peering out wearily toward the open door before motioning Tehya to the back hallway that led to the servants' stairs on one side and the kitchen on the other.

Damn Ian. He had run off to play the hero and have all the fun by himself, again. Diego was nowhere to be found, and Ian's bodyguards were likely the buffoons yelling from upstairs.

Sorrell was still in the house, she knew he was, she could feel it. Her and Tehya's best bet would be to get outside, sheltered by the heavy gardens, and find a nice place to lie low.

Directing Tehya's gaze to the back hall, Kira motioned to the kitchen and out the back door with hand signals, watching the other girl's face as her eyes narrowed and she nodded in understanding.

Holding up three fingers, Kira counted down the seconds.

One.

Two.

Three.

She ran quickly around the corner beneath the staircase and ducked into the hallway, weapon drawn and scanning the darkness, before throwing herself across the open doorway.

She could see Tehya from where she stood now, watching her closely. No gunfire had ripped through the foyer, though there was plenty of it outside and the voices were coming closer.

Holding up three fingers she counted again, watching Tehya's shadowed face. One. Two. Three.

The other girl followed her movements exactly and within seconds they were both flattened against the wall, Kira covering the servants' stairs and Tehya watching the hallway that led to the kitchen and pantry.

Touching Tehya on the shoulder, Kira indicated herself then pointed to the doorway. When Tehya nodded Kira pointed to her, then pointed two fingers toward her own eyes before holding up three fingers. Wait until Kira looked back through the door, then give three seconds and follow.

Tehya nodded, holding her weapon in a two-handed grip to the side of her thigh as they both quickly checked back toward the stairs and then the pantry.

Holding the Glock likewise, Kira eased to the kitchen doorway. The gunfire was much lighter outside now, the American voices yelling orders, assuring Kira that the SEAL teams were on top. Out back, the action was even lighter. With any luck she and Tehya could slip into the heavy foliage of the gardens at the side of the house and remain hidden to avoid stray bullets or overzealous soldiers.

She paused at the side of the doorway, crouched nearly to her knees, and peeked in before diving into the room and rolling to the side of the wall.

She swept the room with her eyes and her weapon, her heartbeat tripping in her chest at the flashes of light outside the shattered windows.

Her back to the refrigerator, she turned, peeked around it quickly, and pulled back. Waiting a second, she peeked around again before sliding around to the front of it. If she remembered correctly there was a doorway leading to the pantry right beside it. She needed to check.

She was going to check when a shadow flashed and agony snapped her wrist.

IAN HAD SUSPECTED SORRELL WOULD pull something but he hadn't expected the extent of the chaos he could cause. Staying on Sorrell's ass after Kenneth fell and tracking him through the villa wasn't easy.

He wouldn't leave the house, Ian thought as he made his way along the back hall that led to the servants' stairs. He would stay in place, wait for his forces to overtake the villa then collect his daughter. He hadn't expected the trained Navy SEALs that converged on his soldiers and he sure as hell wouldn't be expecting the fact that Macey's listening device had recorded every second of the meeting. The SEALs knew who they were looking for and what his capture would mean.

"Ian report," Reno's voice snapped into the receiver at his ear.

Ian paused on the upper landing, looking into the long hallway with narrowed eyes through the night-vision goggles he had grabbed from a drawer in his desk after the lights had gone out.

"He's still in the house. I saw him hit the servants' stairs but I haven't found him yet," Ian reported.

"Teams two and four have taken a few hits," Reno said. "We're still clearing out Fitzhugh's forces with your soldiers' help. We're making progress. What about the girl?"

"Get me some help in here if you want her," Ian snapped. "Antoli was down last time I checked and he was her protection. Deke is at my back and the others are checking the house."

He glanced back at Deke before giving him a signal to proceed.

Ian ducked across the hallway, flattening himself in the

doorway of the linen closet there as Deke crouched and aimed his weapon into the hallway.

Nothing stirred.

Sorrell was hiding, waiting.

As Ian prepared to move again a shattered feminine cry drifted up the stairs. Kira's cry, rife with pain, fear. Ian knew that Sorrell had her.

Thirty-one

HER WRIST WAS BROKEN, KIRA knew that the moment the gun dropped from her hand and Joseph Fitzhugh jerked her back into his barrel chest.

"You fucking bitch," he snarled in her ear. "I should have killed you along with your parents. This is what I get for having mercy on you."

"You were going to kidnap me." She knew that the moment his identity was revealed. "That's why Jase hid me all those years. Why he surrounded me with bodyguards."

She fought to breathe through the pain.

"Jason was an idiot. A very lucky idiot," he snarled at her ear. "He was supposed to be with them. Everyone but poor little Kira, who would have made me so much money."

His hand tightened on her wrist, bringing a ragged cry from her throat as the pain threatened to steal her consciousness. Bastard. Son of a bitch. Did he think a broken wrist was going to disable her?

"Poor little Kira is going to kick your ass," she hissed, then screamed again as he applied pressure to her wrist once more.

"Where is my daughter?" His voice was low, evil, the smooth French accent almost natural, definitely worthy of an Academy Award.

"We were separated." She breathed through the pain, fighting to keep her head clear. God, she was going to fucking kill him.

"You're lying to me."

She shook her head desperately, praying Tehya stayed hidden.

"It was too dark. I couldn't find her. I was looking . . ."

He twisted her wrist and she lost it. Her stomach roiled, pitching with the pain as darkness threatened her vision.

Gagging, she leaned over, fighting to hold on to consciousness.

"Don't you puke on me, you stupid whore." He jerked her back from him, using his hold on her wrist.

Agony blazed through her mind, exploded in her head as she went to her knees. And it kept exploding.

He jerked her again, nearly ripping her wrist off as he fell. Kira's free hand clawed at his, breaking his hold, only distantly aware of the explosions that didn't seem to stop as she pitched to the floor, rolled, and cradled her wrist to her chest while the pain continued to resound in her head.

She heard someone screaming her name. Screaming hoarsely. Ian. That was Ian's voice. Ian's hands lifting her as she fought to hold on to consciousness through the agony resounding through her arm.

Oh hell, she was a pussy, she thought, just as Tehya had accused.

IAN HELD KIRA AS SHE passed out. Mercifully. He cradled her in his arms as Daniel rushed to her, his hands moving to the broken wrist, hurriedly splinting it as Ian stared at Sorrell, otherwise known as Joseph Fitzhugh.

Lights had swept into the kitchen the minute Kira's screams had sounded. And Tehya had rushed in, firing every round the Glock held straight into her father's chest.

She stood over him, staring down at his body, her face bloodless, her green eyes wilder than before as Antoli stood

behind her, watching her like a man tormented, the gash in
his head bleeding profusely.

Deke, Trevor, Mendez, and Cristo were all in good shape,
all armed and standing around Ian and the two women protectively as the gunfire outside finally leveled off.

"Where's Diego?" He finally realized the other man
hadn't been seen since the lights went off.

Deke looked around the room then back at Ian in confusion.

"Reno, Diego's missing, do you have a fix?" Ian
snapped. He had attached a transmitter to Diego as well as
the two women without their knowledge well before Sorrell
had shown up.

"Tracker shows he's with the women." Macey's voice
came through the line.

"He's not here."

"His signal is right there beside the two women," Macey
repeated patiently.

Ian looked around. Kira was in his arms, Tehya beside her.

"Deke, check me for the transmitter." Resignation filled
his voice.

Deke moved to him quickly, running his hands over the
collar of Ian's shirt as Ian continued to hold Kira to his
chest.

"Here it is."

Diego had slapped his shoulder before Sorrell had arrived. He had known about the tracker.

"He's flown," Ian snapped into the link. "Find the bastard. Son of a bitch. He got away."

DIEGO STARED AT THE LIGHTS blazing in the villa an hour
later, surrounded by his personal team of soldiers and
sailing for home.

He gripped the rail of the borrowed yacht, grief lying
tight in his chest, clenching his stomach. Tears would have
fallen had he been alone.

A boy should not be forced to kill his father, he thought to himself, continuing to stare at the receding lights of the estate Ian had moved them into. At his side, laughably enough, was his DHS handler. It was amazing really how his deal with DHS had worked out through the years. Such as now.

"My dear Mr. McClane, how do you think Ian is going to feel once he learns how easily you managed to slip me from the island and also that you warned me of what may well happen?"

McClane sighed at that. "It would be nice if he didn't find out, Fuentes. You know what they say about burning bridges. As your legal counsel in this matter, I can assure you, it could be a deal breaker with DHS."

Diego chuckled, but the sound was rusty, bitter.

He hadn't had his son long enough, hadn't had a chance to pull free those more calculating tendencies he knew Ian must surely possess. He hadn't had enough time to gain his loyalty, and he had known it. Just as he had known it was Ian's intention all along to kill him when this was finished.

"A man shouldn't have to murder his own father," he whispered then, aware that the agent was listening.

"If I didn't agree, I wouldn't have had the yacht waiting for you."

Diego nodded and sighed again. Wearily.

"Marika raised a fine man," he told Jason then.

"Yes, she did, despite Carmelita's attempts to have him killed."

He was always being reminded of this. As though there were a way he could go back in time to change the past. If only he could. He would have given his own soul to do just that.

"Did you know about him when I made my deal with DHS?" Diego wondered aloud.

"None of us knew about him until he and his stepfather approached the director," Jason assured him, his voice as cold and unemotional as ever.

Yes, that sounded like Ian, and Marika. They wouldn't have wanted anyone to know the shameful secret of who Ian's father was.

He couldn't find it in himself to blame the boy; as Jason said, Carmelita had made his life hell. She had helped mold the man Ian had become, and Diego cursed her to hell for it.

"The estate is secured?" he asked then.

"Secured. Ian will receive his orders tonight that you're protected by DHS. And in return you sign the papers I brought that you'll refrain from taking any U.S. government personnel hostage. Should you learn they are agents of the U.S. you will contact me and I'll take care of them."

Diego nodded. Yes, it had been a mistake to allow Clay and Sorrell to hold Nathan Malone. The testing of the whore's dust on the SEAL had been amusing, and it had taught him something about the depth of a man's soul. Malone had never broken. He had always known that the women brought to him were not his wife.

"Perhaps I will concentrate on some of the plans Ian placed into motion while he was with me," he mused. "Several of those business look very lucrative."

"Going legit, Fuentes?" McClane's voice was mocking.

"Legit?" Diego frowned. "The time has passed for that, my friend. Very much so. But perhaps it is time to face the future. No children, no grandchildren, no time to teach a child about the legacy being passed to him. Perhaps it is time to just let it go."

He didn't give McClane time to answer. He turned, pushed his hands into his pockets, and entered the lavish interior of the yacht before continuing to his room. It wouldn't take long to reach Colombia. A plane would be awaiting him and he would fly home where Saul waited for him.

To an empty, lonely estate.

Could anything be worse?

Thirty-two

KIRA OPENED HER EYES, GROANED, and closed them again. She remembered. Oh hell yes, she remembered passing out like a wimp. And that was it.

She stared around the bedroom, the same bedroom she and Ian shared at the Fuentes villa. There was no broken glass here, no shattered windows or bullet-riddled furniture. Just her.

"You're awake."

Her eyes jerked to the doorway, to Ian as he stepped into the bedroom, then to Daniel and Durango team as they entered behind him.

She glanced at the cast on her wrist and the sunlight outside the room.

"How long was I out?" She hated passing out. Tehya was right, she was a pussy. It was the whole pain thing. She hated it, it just pissed her off, and if it was strong enough, caused her to pass out. It was pathetic.

"Close to ten hours." Ian sat on the bed beside her, reaching out to smooth her hair back from her cheek as she looked at the cast on her wrist once again.

Anything to keep from looking at Ian.

"Teyha's safe," Daniel told her from the bottom of the bed. "She's on her way to Fitzhugh's estate in France to allow the authorities, both French and American, into his private computers. With him and his legal son dead, she'll have to have a few DNA tests, but it will be relatively easy for her to claim his estate. And we need his files."

"He's dead?" She looked up at Ian in surprise.

"Tehya," he said simply. "He was distracted with you, he didn't see her step into the kitchen. She emptied the Glock in his chest."

A daughter had killed her father.

Had Ian killed his? She continued to stare up at him, the question in her eyes.

"It would appear DHS warned Diego months ago that he could end up tasting one of my bullets," he said coolly. "He escaped during the chaos. The last word we had on him was that his DHS handler was escorting him back to Colombia. They're revising his agreement with them. With any luck, he'll never torture another SEAL."

It didn't sit easy with him, she could see that, but she could also see the acceptance in his eyes.

"We're heading back downstairs," Reno announced then. "We have a carrier headed this way and a copter ready to escort us home. I should be home in time to wake my wife and newborn son with the news that Ian's home and all's well." He nodded to both of them. "Be ready to roll."

Durango team strolled from the bedroom, leaving her alone with Ian and Daniel.

"Jason's called me back, he even promised me a vacation." Daniel grimaced. "Can you hide the wrist until I collect my bonus? It's really not my fault you were hurt this time, Kira. And I'm telling you, Caroline is going to make me quit if Jason decides to bruise my face again."

She rolled her eyes at his pitiful, hangdog expression.

"Jason won't know about the wrist until you get your bonus," she promised, almost shaking her head at him. "But you really need to have a talk with Caroline, Daniel. Bodyguards get bruised sometimes."

"By the bad guys," he growled, disgust suddenly weighing heavily in his voice. "Not by the damned boss because the charge doesn't know how to keep her butt out of trouble."

She grinned at that, then glanced at Ian. He was no more amused than Daniel was. She cleared her throat, wrinkled her nose, then picked at the tattered, bloodstained material of her dress. Damn, it was ruined.

"Get on out of here, Daniel," Ian ordered him then. "You should have a few days before Jason gets a look at her. By then the bruises should be . . . Well, worse anyway."

Yeah, she was bruised. She could feel a nice one forming beneath her eye and had already glimpsed the ones on her arms. No doubt about it, Jason was going to have a healthy little meltdown over this one.

She was quiet as Daniel made his way out of the room, the door closing behind him, leaving her and Ian alone, the silence in the room weighing heavily between them.

She lifted her eyes to meet his, saw the edge of sadness and pain and wanted to weep.

"I talked to DHS while you were out," he told her softly. "Diego was warned months ago about what could have happened tonight. I'm amazed he didn't murder both of us before Sorrell arrived."

She shook her head. "He loves you."

Ian shook his head at that. "I don't know if that knowledge should terrify me or reassure me. One thing's for certain, he's out of my reach. His new agreement with DHS will curtail many of his games with government agents, according to the director. I have to content myself with that."

"And will you?" She ached for him, ached for the loyalties that tore him in two and the knowledge that the man who sired him was more a monster than a father.

"I won't go gunning for him." He shrugged. "He stays away from us, I'll stay away from him."

"Us?" she whispered. Until that moment she hadn't realized how terrified she had been that Diego would separate them, that her disagreement over Ian's decisions would drive him away.

"I wasn't going to kill him." He gave his head a brief, hard shake. "I wanted to, Kira. I wanted to so bad sometimes it boiled in my gut like acid. But you were right, killing him wasn't my responsibility. The agreement I suspected he made with DHS tied my hands and I knew it."

She breathed in slowly, deeply. "None of this is your fault, Ian," she told him softly. "Fuentes, Sorrell, Nathan. You couldn't have prevented it."

"I would have, if I had known Nathan was alive before I did. I would have gotten him out of there, no matter what it took." No matter how many times he had to sell his soul to Diego. Kira understood that; she would do the same thing if it were Jason or Daniel.

"So. What do we do now?" she asked almost fearfully.

He stared down at her silently. "What do you want to do?"

"Love you forever," she whispered.

Some of the tension seemed to ease from him then. "It won't be easy for a while, you know. The press is already converging on the island. The papers in the States were carrying pictures of us together a week ago. We've already caused a sensation. 'The deserter drug lord and the society princess.'" He sneered at the caption description.

She eased up in the bed, her breath hitching as he immediately eased her into his arms.

"The press will love us once they learn the truth."

He grunted at that. "I'm not reenlisting. There's no way I'd be effective now and I'll be damned if you're going to be off causing trouble somewhere without me keeping an eye on you. I'd go insane."

"My job is done, Ian." She stared up at him then, knowing in her heart it was over now. "I wanted Sorrell, and now he's eliminated."

His eyes narrowed. "Home and hearth and white picket fences?"

She would have been angry at the disbelief in his tone if she hadn't glimpsed the hunger in his eyes as well.

"I like white picket fences." Hope bloomed in her heart, the dream she had pushed aside, a home to share with someone who knew her, body and soul. A life that didn't involve bloodshed and disguises, and maybe, just maybe, a baby. She would like to have a family with this man, a man who understood her, who loved her.

"I like white picket fences too." A grin tugged at his lips. "I have a place, in Texas."

"I know," she drawled. "And I love it. There's even a white picket fence."

He chuckled, the sound rough, almost tentative, as he laid his forehead against hers, his tobacco-brown eyes, edged with hidden flames that had nothing to do with rage, warming her from the inside out. "Go home with me?"

"You couldn't chase me off with a stick."

"No sticks," he promised, lowering his lips to hers. "But don't discount a spanking, I told you to stay put under that desk."

"I like it when you spank." Her laughter dissolved a second later beneath his kiss, beneath the passion and the love that suddenly filled her soul and burned through her mind. "I love you, Ian, desperately."

"I love you," he breathed against her lips. "Forever, Kira. With all my soul, I love you."

He had thought he had secrets from her. A man alone, fighting alone. He realized in that moment that from the first, this woman had seen past those secrets, seen into his soul, even when he couldn't see it himself.

He cradled her to him as the painkiller Daniel had injected her with earlier drew her eyes closed again. Held her as she slept, and for the first time in his life, he realized how empty his life had been before her. He had had secrets that could have killed her, that could have killed him. And now, he had someone who could share the secrets, fight by his side, and love in return.

For the first time in his life, Ian no longer felt alone. And he realized that as long as he held Kira in his arms, he would never be alone. He was home.

Read on for an excerpt from

Heat Seeker

by Lora Leigh

Available in September 2009

from St. Martin's Paperbacks

"**W**HAT ARE YOU DOING HERE?" She kept her lips against his shoulder to hide the words, her voice low enough that only he could hear her.

"We need to talk." He didn't answer her question, but she hadn't really expected him to.

"Too bad." She luxuriated in the feel of his body against hers, even with the clothing that separated them. There was something about him that she couldn't ignore, couldn't forget. Something that drew her like a moth to a flame. It was a very dangerous position to be in.

"Come on, Bailey." His lips brushed against her ear. "Just a few minutes of your time. I promise, you won't regret it." His hand stroked from her hip up, along her back, then back again.

"I regret meeting you to begin with," she told him softly, noting the tension that tightened his body. "Why would tonight be any different?"

His hand tightened at her hip. "You never know, I could surprise you."

She almost laughed at that statement. There was no surprise in store for her. The best he could do was manage to amaze her with the delivery of whatever he wanted from her. She had no doubt why he was here.

"You're on my turf now," she warned him. "I doubt there's anything that you could do here that would surprise me, John."

She surprised herself sometimes though. Now was one of those times. She was amazed at her reaction to him, at the excitement that filled her. He had taken the prize from her hands last time, and he was no doubt determined to do the same thing this time.

"It's important," he told her. "We need to talk, after the party."

"After the party I'm going to be incredibly tired." The song drew to a close as she stepped back from his hold. "Maybe later. Leave your number with the doorman. I'm sure he'll make certain I get it."

He didn't let her go. Catching her arm, he drew her from the dance floor and to the wide double doors leading from the ballroom.

She had a feeling he wouldn't let this go so easily.

"Mr. Vincent, I can't leave my own party," she protested with feigned lightness, her temper beginning to burn though.

"Just for a moment, Miss Serborne," he promised as they passed the wide doors and he headed unerringly to the back of the house.

Their progress was being noted. The tingling at the base of her spine was building, assuring her that whoever had been watching her for most of the night still had their eyes on her. She'd tried to pinpoint the sensation all evening and had yet to assign it to one particular guest.

Whoever it was, they were good. Better than she would have expected considering the people she knew she was dealing with. Of course, they had been skating by for years now, they would have grown adept at hiding, she assured herself as John drew her straight to her personal office.

The door had been locked earlier. It wasn't locked now. Her brows arched as he opened the door and drew her inside before closing and locking it.

"Thank you for making such a spectacle of me." She

rounded on him furiously. "You dragged me through my own party like a disobedient pet."

"And you were growling at me every step of the way." He glowered at her. "What part of, 'We need to talk,' didn't you understand?"

She crossed her arms over her breasts as she lifted her brow in curiosity. "You don't take 'no' for an answer at all well, do you, Mr. Vincent?"

His lips twitched in amusement. Now, didn't it just make her day to know she amused him in some small part?

"I must admit, I have problems with that word," he finally admitted. "Perhaps my mother said it too often when I was a child."

She gave a little snort at that. She doubted any woman had ever told him no.

"So what was so important that you felt the need to make a spectacle of me at my own party?" she questioned him coldly. "I hope it's a matter of life or death, because really, there could be no other excuse for it."

His brow lifted. The dark blond color against his sun-bronzed flesh was incredibly alluring. He could have been a fallen angel, too ruggedly handsome for words, and too charming for his own good.

"You play the part of the society princess very well," he mused. "I wouldn't have expected it of you."

She gave a little shrug of her bare shoulders. "You could say it's in the blood," she said mockingly.

At least, that was what her mother had always told her. That she had the blood of American royalty running through her veins and she should always remember it. There hadn't been a single member of her mother or her father's family who hadn't married well, who hadn't married into true blood, if not blue blood.

"It was easy to forget when you were trussed up, blindfolded, and gagged," he murmured with a wealth of amusement now. "The society princess got replaced by the gutter fighter then." He rubbed at his jaw where she had managed to head-butt him all those months ago.

"Back any animal into a corner and it's going to come out biting," she promised him. "Now, are you going to tell me what the hell you want or do I have to start guessing? I really don't have time to guess, John."

His lips pursed thoughtfully. "You're still pissed over Atlanta, aren't you?"

"Now why would I be pissed over Atlanta?" she asked him. "You just kidnapped me and nearly drugged me. You were directly responsible for my release from the agency, and you refused to help me in any way while I was there. So what reason would I have to be pissed?"

John nodded. "As I assumed, you really have no reason not to help me then." His grin was confident and way too arrogant.

"And you live in a dream world that I can only envy, big boy. Someone should be kind and awaken you."

His eyes narrowed. "We have a situation, Bailey, a very delicate one."

"Sucks to be you." She wasn't about to admit that she was blazingly curious about his "situation." No doubt, knowing him, the men he worked with wanted nothing more than to use her.

"You like pushing, don't you?" he asked softly, dangerously.

"I like wasting my time as well," she informed him haughtily. "Now why don't you get the hell out of my way and let me get back to my party? I was rather enjoying it before you decided to intrude."

She moved to grip the doorknob and slide the lock open when he shifted, and before she knew it, Bailey found herself pushed up against the door, John's large body pressing against hers, heating it further.

She exhaled sharply at the sensation of his body suddenly flush against hers, of being surrounded by him. It had obviously been too long since a man—no, not just any man, since Trent—had touched her. It had been too long since she had felt the warmth and hard thickness of an erection pressing against her, and now she was stunned with how her senses were rioting with it.

Bailey felt her knees weakening, she felt her heart racing, her breath coming hard and fast.

God, she wanted him. She wanted this man like she hadn't wanted in so very long. And it had almost destroyed her the last time.

"Don't," she whispered, her hands pressing against his chest as his head lowered, his lips coming much too close to hers.

"Don't what? Don't kiss you?" His lips quirked with sexy humor and dangerous intent. "Afraid you might change your mind, Bailey?"

"You like messing with my head," she said, her voice shaky. "If you think you can use my body against me, John, then you'd better think again. It's not going to happen."

"Bet me."

The hard growl that left his lips was the only warning she had before his lips were covering hers and reality began to recede. Wicked, driving hunger rose to the forefront of her senses, a starving need for touch that she couldn't fight against, that her body had no desire to fight against.

Need and knowledge warred inside her mind now. The need for this kiss that she couldn't seem to get enough of, and the knowledge that he was going to do exactly what she had sworn she wasn't going to allow him to do. He was going to use her body against her. He was going to make her hungrier, he was going to fill her senses with him and sap the strength to fight from her.

She'd known in that warehouse two months ago that he was dangerous for her. She had known that her best course of action for her sanity and her heart was to stay as far away from him as possible.

She'd run as far as she could run, and here he was, exactly where he shouldn't be.

Her arms twined around his neck as his hand gripped her hips, then slowly slid to her thighs as he pressed a knee between them. The hard muscle of his upper leg rode against the mound of her pussy, stroking the swollen bud of her clit as she fought for breath. Her hands speared into the overly long strands of dark blond hair and she held on for dear life as her hips writhed against his leg.

The friction against that most sensitive part of her body was overwhelming. Lust clamored inside her brain, the need for sex drove sharpened spikes of sensation racing over her nerve endings straight to her sex.

Her tongue rubbed against his, fought for dominancy in the kiss, and finally conceded as he wrapped his fingers around the mound of a breast.

Bailey froze, her breath stilling in her throat as his thumb stroked over her nipple. She could feel the rioting pleasure rising inside her. She wanted to tear the material of her dress out of the way, she wanted bare flesh to meet bare flesh.

In the arms of a stranger.

God, she had lost her mind. She had lost what little control she still had of herself and finding it again seemed a hopeless cause.

She was so desperate for the past that she was creating her own fantasy, and she knew just how dangerous that was.

"No."

She tore herself from his arms, stumbling away from him as she covered her lips with the back of her hand and stared at him in horror.

For a moment she had thought that he even kissed like Trent. Just like Trent. With the same voracious hunger, the same lustful intent.

"Get out!" she panted desperately. "Get out of my home before I have you thrown out."

He looked as shell-shocked as she felt. Staring back at

her, his gray eyes thunderous, his lips swollen from her kiss, he looked as though the pleasure had punched him just as hard as it had her.

"This isn't over," he warned her. "We will talk, Bailey."

"When hell freezes over," she snapped, furious with herself as well as him.

His lips thinned. "Invest in plenty of heat then," he warned her. "Because it's coming. And it's coming fast baby."

He jerked the door open and stalked out. Every line of his body was tense and hard, projecting the furious lust that practically sizzled off his body as he stalked down the hall and back to the front of the house.

Bailey followed behind him, her heels snapping against the marble floor as she silently cursed him, as well as herself.

She'd be damned if she was going to allow him to manipulate her or to destroy what she was working on here. She knew his kind. He would take over, he would insist on dominance, and she had no intention of allowing anyone to dominate her at this point.

Stepping into the foyer, she watched as he stalked past the open doors the doormen pulled open for him. One hand pressed to her stomach, the other hanging at her side, she fought to find her equilibrium once again.

Breathing in deeply, she licked her lips, then looked around, only to find her gaze caught and held by Raymond Greer's. Her head lifted as her lips tightened. Just what she needed, for the bastard to see a weakness in her.

He was watching her like a beady-eyed cobra waiting to strike. Calculating, manipulating.

She nodded toward him sharply before moving quickly back to the ballroom and the party she had organized so painstakingly. She was on a deadline. She didn't have time to be drawn into John Vincent's games. She didn't have time to allow her heart to be broken again.